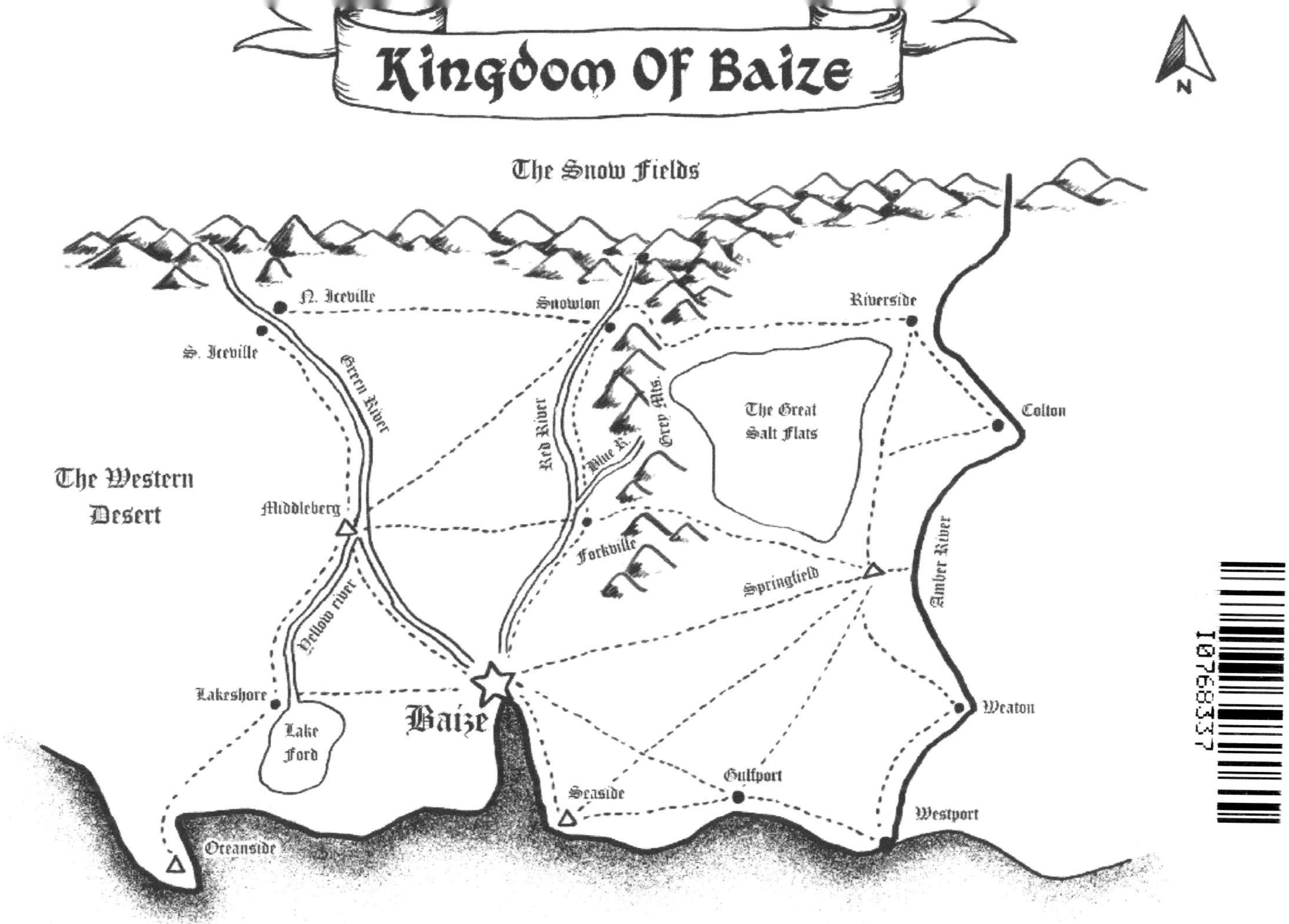

I0768337

Kingdom Of Baize
N
The Snow Fields
The Great Salt Flats
The Western Desert
Grey Hills
Amber River
Red River
Blue River
Green River
Yellow river
Colton
Weston
Westport
Riverside
Springfield
Gulfport
Seaside
Snowton
Fortville
Baize
N. Ireville
S. Ireville
Middleberg
Lakeshore
Lake ford
Oceanside

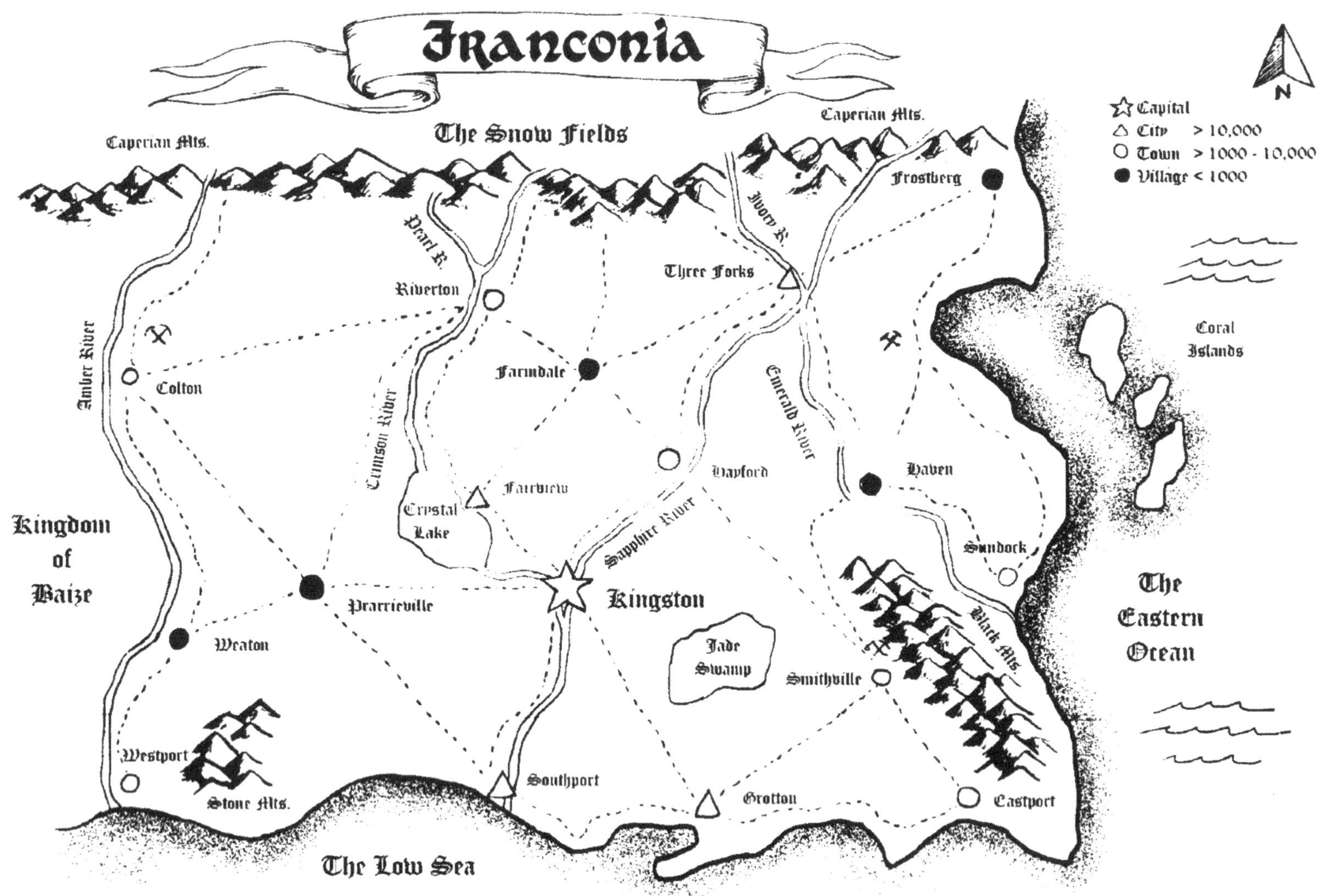
Franconia
N
Capital
City   > 10,000
Town   > 1000 - 10,000
Village < 1000
The Snow Fields
Caperian Mts.
Caperian Mts.
Caperian Mts.
Frostberg
Pearl R.
Ivory R.
Three Forks
Riverton
Coral Islands
Amber River
Colton
Crimson River
Farmdale
Emerald River
Fairview
Crystal Lake
Hayford
Sapphire River
Haven
Sundock
Kingdom
of
Baize
Prarrieville
Weaton
Kingston
Jade Swamp
Black Mts.
The Eastern Ocean
Westport
Stone Mts.
Southport
Smithville
Grotton
Eastport
The Low Sea

The Peace of Minds

Robert Jones

Other Books by Robert Jones

The Honor of Dragons

The Valor of Sorcerers

The Compassion of Enemies

The Conflict of Interests

The Peace of Minds

The Resumption of Hostilities (Forthcoming)

Table of Contents

Dedication

For Linda, with love

Acknowledgment

The acknowledgments go to the designers at Author Book Publications (www.authorbook publications.com) for the cover design and portraits, and Rizky Nugraha for the maps and the illustration of the villa.

About the Author

Robert Jones served in the United States Army for 23 years before retiring. He currently works for the Federal Government. This is his third novel in the Honor of Dragons series, and is the sequel to The Valor of Sorcerers. He lives in Northern Virginia with his wife and two children.

Foreword

Sorcerer Donovan and his new wife, Sorceress Rachel, have been assigned as magical support to the Royal Expeditionary Force. The Expeditionary Force is currently conducting a sweeping tour of all of the towns and cities in Franconia, looking for dragon 'Changed Ones,' and auditing Treasury vaults. Apparently, there is a lot of gold missing from the King's accounts.

Wizard Edward and his new wife, Mage Kathy, have returned to Franconia after completing construction of the Great Salt Lake in Baize. Edward has been appointed as the Chief of Military Wizardry in Franconia, so it's his job to come up with a plan to deal with the dragon threat.

The Great Dragon, Gek, has been injured and can no longer cast the spell of Change, which means that he is 'stuck' in dragon form, much to the disappointment of his human son, Richard. The dragons need a new strategy for dealing with the human magic-users, who seem to be thwarting them at every turn. However, they have learned about the humans' ability to change into dragons, so they'll be better prepared in the future.

With the collapse of the Peace Treaty with the Sea Dragons, Mage Andrew and the sailors of the Royal Franconian Navy are preparing for more attacks from the Sea Dragons, who have been dropping heavy stones on their ships from high in the sky, out of crossbow range.

The Peace of Minds brings this episode of the wars between dragons and humans to an imperfect end. The question is: How long will this truce last?

JASPER, THE STONE DRAGON

Chapter One:
A TON OF BRICKS

onovan frowned as the flames slowly covered his shield. He and his wife, Sorceress Rachel, were trapped under tons of bricks and timbers. The Great Dragon had collapsed the building next to them while they were busy suffocating the two Stone Dragons with protective shields. The Stone Dragon that Donovan had encased had died first, and Donovan had seen the building coming down on top of them just in time to erect a shield around both of them. The problem was, they were now trapped underneath tons of rubble, and the dragon had apparently spewed burning inferno on top of the debris, just for good measure.

"Donovan?" "Yes, my love?" "Where are we?" asked Rachel, regaining consciousness. "Well, it seems that we're trapped under several tons of bricks and timber. That Great Dragon pushed over the building we were standing next to and collapsed it on top of us. I barely managed to get a shield around us in time," said Donovan tiredly. "OK, but why is there fire outside the shield?" asked Rachel. "Either the dragon flamed the debris as he left, or the structure caught fire as it fell. I'm not sure which."

"Are you going to do something about it?" "I was planning to. Do you want me to put the fire out?" asked Donovan. "Yes, please." *"AQUARITOUS,"* said Donovan, cupping his right hand and turning it over. Several hundred gallons of water rained down on the debris over their heads, completely extinguishing the fire, but leaving them in total darkness.

"Well, that's not optimal," observed Rachel. "Are you injured?" asked Donovan. "I hit my head, but I'm alright, other than being trapped under a ton of bricks," replied Rachel. They lay in silence for a moment. "Are you planning to get us out of here?" asked Rachel. "I'm working on it. I'm just not sure which spell to use. Any suggestions, Mentor?" "Wind, maybe," suggested Rachel. "Can you try a strong Wind spell?" asked Donovan. Rachel nodded and said, *"GUSTO,"* with a backhand wave of her left hand. Nothing happened.

"How about Blast?" asked Rachel. "I'm not sure that will work," said Donovan, "have you ever fired a Blast spell *through* a shield before?" "No." "Neither have I. I keep thinking back to my first shields class as a Level One; you know, when you throw rocks at each other." "What about it?" "Well, Level One Kelly kept angling her shield, sending the rocks I threw back at me, so I tried erecting a shield, then throwing the rock. The rock bounced off the inside of my shield and hit me in the leg. I don't fancy trying that with a Blast spell," said Donovan.

"Hmm," said Rachel, "there's also the chance that the Blast spell would shatter the shield. I kind of like that shield right where it is right now." "There's another problem, even if I could fire a Blast spell outside the shield, I might hit one of the rescuers who, I assume, are trying to dig us out as we speak. That wouldn't be very appreciative," said Donovan.

"No, it wouldn't. OK, not the Blast spell. What else have we got?" asked Rachel. "Well, the Remove spell might work, assuming it doesn't just remove my shield, but then we have the same problem about rescue personnel."

"Can you conjure a Hearing Enhancement to determine if there's anyone digging through the rubble around us?" asked Donovan. "Why can't you do it?" "You always ask me how I can hold two spells at once, and I always tell you that I don't. I hold one spell, then *cast* the other. Right now, I'm *holding* this shield. If you want me to try *holding* a Hearing Enhancement, I'll try, but it might not last very long," explained Donovan. Rachel grinned and said, *"AUDIO,"* while putting her left hand behind her left ear, palm forward. She listened for several long minutes. "I hear someone," said Rachel, " maybe quite a few people, digging, but I can't tell how close they are. It could be that we're under several feet of bricks."

"So, I guess we can't use the Remove spell. It would probably vanish the shield, anyway," said Donovan. *It was maddening! They taught me 38 spells at the Wizards Academy, and now that I need one to save our lives, I can't think of a useful one,* thought Donovan. "I don't mean to be a nagging wife," said Rachel, "but we're going to run short of air if we don't think of something soon."

Suddenly, Donovan smiled, "You're a genius!" He craned his neck and gave Rachel a kiss on the cheek, then lay flat on his back and said, *"REDUCTO,"* while pinching his right thumb and forefinger together. The layer of bricks and timber next to the shield shrank to red brick dust and sawdust. Three more attempts, and it seemed like the shield was only covered with dust. "Try that Wind spell again." This time, the dust was blown high into the air, and sunlight streamed down through the shield.

"OK, I'm going to release the shield. We need to stand up and get out of here before the bricks on the sides cave in. Ready? *CODA!*" Donovan's shield vanished, and the two magicians stood quickly. The bricks on Rachel's side began to collapse into the hole, and several bricks struck her on the left ankle. Donovan grabbed her, conjured a Strength Enhancement, and jumped clear of the debris field.

Donovan and Rachel landed, somewhat unsteadily, and looked around. They were surprised to find themselves standing next to Mage Gregory, the 6th Regiment's Battle Mage. Gregory recoiled in shock at Donovan and Rachel's sudden emergence from the rock pile. "Thank goodness! Everyone in the city has been digging through the rubble looking for you two! We thought you were goners! How did you survive?"

"I put a shield over Rachel and myself just as the building started coming down. The problem was the fire and all the bricks," said Donovan. "Yes, we figured that at least one of you was alive when it started raining without a cloud in the sky." "The problem with putting out the fire, was that it left us in complete darkness," said Rachel. "Hmm," said Mage Roark, as he walked up. "What spell did you use to get out from under all that, Dig?" "No," said Donovan, "I didn't think Dig would work through my shield."

"Blast? Remove?" asked Mage Gregory curiously. "Same problem," said Rachel, "Can you fire a Blast spell through a shield? We were afraid that it would either rebound or crack the shield and let the bricks fall on us. Remove might have just vanished the shield. Besides, even if it worked, we didn't want to risk hitting someone on top of the rubble." The two mages stood there, stumped. Finally, Mage Gregory said, "Off the top of my head, I can't think of another spell that would have freed you from that pile. How did you do it?"

"Reduce." said Donovan with a smile. "Reduce?" "Yes, Donovan shrunk the bricks outside the shield to dust-size, then I blew the dust away with a Wind spell." "That's brilliant!" said the two mages. "Yes, it was. Now, can someone heal my ankle, please? Some of the bricks toppled in from the side as we made our way out of the hole." Donovan knelt down, put his left hand on Rachel's ankle, palm down, fingers closed, and said *"SANA,"* before collapsing on the road.

Gek tried again, *"MORPHIUS,"* he said, clapping his hands together. Still nothing. He tried again, and again, and again without result. *It must be my missing fingers*, he thought dejectedly. Awakened by the clapping, Annalise came out of the hut. "Daddy!" she shouted enthusiastically, "You are home! I missed you!" Setting his concern and disappointment aside, Gek wrapped his daughter up with his tail and said, "I missed you too. What have you been doing while I was gone?"

"Richard and I helped Bruce gather some driftwood. Then we helped mommy make a back door to the hut, so we can get in and out without breaking things," said Anna. "That is good. We do not want to break any more of Bruce's things." "Mommy says that it is so that when I get bigger, I will be able to go outside without going through the living room. Do you want to see it?" "Of course I want to see it. Is it finished?" asked Gek.

"Almost. Mommy says that it might not be big enough for you to fit through," said Anna. They walked around to the rear of the hut to find a single-hinge door opening off the back room. "We might need two doors," said Anna. "Mommy said that once you got home and changed into a human, you could help Bruce saw the wood." "That might be a problem," said Gek.

"Why is that?" asked Azure, coming around the hut. Gek held up his disfigured left hand. "What happened?" asked Azure. "I knocked over a building on top of two human magic-users who were trying to kill two of our Stone Dragon cousins. After the building fell on them, I paused to admire my handywork, and another magic-user fired a spell at me. His spell missed my body, but hit my hand, lopping off two fingers."

"Oh, Gek! Does it hurt?" "No, but I cannot conjure the Change spell anymore. I think I am stuck in dragon-form from now on." Annalise cheered. "Stop that, Anna! This could be a serious problem for us. Gek, are you sure?" "I have tried the Change spell several times, but nothing happens," said Gek.

"I am sure that Richard will be disappointed, but we will get by. I suppose that *I* will have to help Bruce with the back door now," said Azure. "Anna, please go check on your brother. I need to talk with daddy for a minute." Anna nodded her head and walked off unenthusiastically. "So, how did the attack go?" asked Azure. "It was a disaster. It was going well until two Great Dragons appeared and killed Chrystal and Cyan, the two Sea Dragons, and the two Fire Dragons, Ember and Spark. One Snow Dragon was killed by a crossbow bolt, and then two human magic-users killed the two Stone Dragons. Only one Snow Dragon and I survived. While we killed a lot of humans and destroyed many buildings, I would not call the attack a success," said Gek.

"You were attacked by two Changed Ones?" asked Azure. "No. It seems that the human magic-users have learned how to change into dragons, and one of them was Donovan. This was probably what happened during the previous attacks on the Snow Dragons," said Gek. "Humans changing into dragons? Are you sure?" "Yes. A Fire Dragon Changed One from Three Forks flew to the quarry after the attack and told me about how the humans have learned how to change into dragons, and informed me that *Sorcerer* Donovan has left the Wizard's Academy and is in Three Forks. This is a *big* problem."

"So, what can we do?" asked Azure. "Well, for one thing, not attack a human town that has a lot of magic-users in it. There must have been at least six magic-users in Three Forks! We should have attacked a town with fewer magic-users. One or two could not have stopped us, plus, I do not think *all* of the magic-users have learned the Change yet. Otherwise, we would have been attacked by more than two Great Dragons. We also need to find a way to track Donovan," said Gek. "One of us will need to inform the Dragon Council about this at the next meeting," said Azure.

"Yes, and it will probably have to be me, since I can no longer transform into a human," said Gek. "Do not give up hope. We may be able to figure something out," said Azure. "How could a human transform into a Great Dragon?" wondered Azure. "There are not that many humans who have seen you." "You are right. Let me think, the only human magic-users who have seen me are Andrew, Anne, and Celeste. But Donovan may have seen my mother," said Gek.

"Plus, anyone who has seen them transform. Your likeness may be spreading throughout the human magic-user community," said Azure. "Should we kill them before they spread the knowledge any further?" asked Gek. "That depends. Do you think Ard's Binding spell died with him?" asked Azure.

Andrew reported back on board the HMS VALOR just after sunrise. Maria walked him as far as the gangplank, then kissed him goodbye. "When will you be back?" she asked. "I'm not sure. We're going to relieve 3rd Squadron and send them here from their patrol route around Eastport. They should be here in about two weeks. When they arrive, install the new Compound Seabows. There are four ships in 3rd Squadron, with six Seabows each. Make sure the ship's magician stays with you as you install the modifications. I wouldn't put it past the Sea Dragons to attack Sundock again," said Andrew.

"That will give me time to bury my father," said Maria sadly. Andrew wiped a tear from her eye and said, "I'm so sorry I can't stay to help with that. If you need any assistance, ask Mage Lisa, the Sundock Regional Mage. Tell her I asked for her help. I'm sure she'll be of assistance," said Andrew. "ALL ABOARD!" the Bos'n cried. "I've got to go," said Andrew. He gave Maria another kiss, then hurried up the gangplank as it was being withdrawn.

"MARRIED BATTLE MAGE ON DECK!" shouted the Bos'n, grinning. "ALL HANDS, MAKE SAIL!" commanded the Commodore. The HMS VALOR slowly eased away from the dock. As she left the harbor, the crew trimmed the sails, picking up speed, and heading south, toward Eastport, and 3rd Squadron.

Maria remained on the pier until the HMS VALOR vanished over the horizon, then headed to the town mortuary, where her father's remains were being kept temporarily. She arranged for a burial plot, coffin, and gravestone. When the undertaker, Mr. Stone, asked her if she wanted a viewing or any sort of funeral service, Maria answered that neither she nor her father knew anyone in Sundock, and so there was no need for any type of memorial service. Maria cried briefly and the mortician handed her a handkerchief.

Maria wiped her eyes and dabbed the handkerchief under her runny nose. The cloth smelled faintly *reptilian*. Maria pocketed the handkerchief, thanked the mortician, and left the mortuary, headed to the Regional Mage's Office.

"...and here is your new office!" said Wizard Noland. Edward looked around the dusty, elaborately decorated corner office on the third floor of the palace. "This place looks like it hasn't been used in a decade," groused Edward. "Well, it hasn't. Not since Wizard Raymond died anyway. You know that King Henry X wasn't overly fond of magicians and didn't see the need for a Chief of Military Wizardry. His son apparently shared the same views until recently. With the threat from the dragons, things are changing in Franconia."

"So I noticed," said Edward. "I think you two had this all arranged before I even set foot back in Franconia." "I must admit, I may have had a conversation with the King about your next assignment after you returned from Baize. After all, you now have a unique insight into the Baizian military and their magical capabilities," said Noland. Edward grunted.

"I suppose there's no arguing that point, although, I only saw one battalion of their soldiers, but my observations were that they are not particularly well trained or led," observed Edward. "Perhaps Mage Kathy could also lend her insights?" Noland asked Kathy.

"I'm afraid that I know only slightly more about the Baizian military than Edward," said Kathy, as she surveyed the dusty office. "My duties as the Assistant Court Wizard were confined to checking the accounts of the kingdom, conducting audits, and handling administrative paperwork for Court Wizard Louis."

"Well, I'll leave you two to it," said Noland. "Kathy, as soon as Edward thinks you're ready, I will happily schedule you for the Wizard's Test. That is, assuming that administrative magic isn't all you practiced in Baize." Noland closed the door quietly, leaving Edward and Kathy alone in the office.

"Where should we start?" asked Kathy. "How about a kiss?" asked Edward. Kathy kissed her new husband, then said, "OK, save the rest of that for later, we need to get this place cleaned up." Edward shrugged and asked, "So, what do you think? Wind or Remove?" Kathy considered the question, "Can you confine the 'Remove' to just the dust, without losing anything else, like the curtains?" "I'm not sure," confessed Edward, "I've never had an office before, and I never let my house get this dusty."

Just then there was a knock on the door, and six palace servants entered carrying brooms, mops, dust rags, and an assortment of cleaning supplies. "Good morning, sir," said the head of the cleaning crew. "Wizard Noland sent us up to clean your office. It hasn't been used in years, you know. Anyway, you two run along! We'll have it spic and span by tomorrow morning."

Edward and Kathy were unceremoniously ushered out of the office by the cleaning crew, and found themselves standing in the hallway, wondering what had happened. "So, Mrs. Francis, how about I give you a tour of Kingston? We appear to have some time on our hands." Mage Kathy readily agreed, and Edward escorted her out of the palace and they spent the rest of the day walking around the city. Edward pointed out the various military barracks and the quarters for the King's Personal Guard. Then they moved into the town and toured the various merchants that provided supplies to the palace and the military.

Last on the tour was Edward's house. After Replicating a key for her, Edward ushered Kathy inside. The house was simple, but was well apportioned and surprisingly clean. "You've been in Baize for most of the last year! How come this house isn't covered in dust like the office was?" asked Kathy. Edward winked and said, "We have a maid that comes in once a week, on Foursday, just to keep the dust down. As a Battle Mage, then a Battle Wizard, I was seldom home. I decided early on that I didn't want to come home to a dusty house after every deployment, and I knew that I couldn't count on Donovan to do any cleaning," said Edward.

"I'm sure this maid is young and comely," teased Kathy. "Mrs. Haywood is neither young nor comely," said Edward. "Those were neither of the qualities I looked for in a housekeeper," said Edward. "I'll need to introduce you this Foursday. I selected Foursday because I knew that Donovan would be in school then, and I wanted the house clean when he visited on Endday afternoons. I'm surprised he never noticed it."

As they walked around the house, Edward discretely plucked the portrait of Joyce, his first wife, off the mantelpiece and put it in the pocket of his robes. "So, will this do, Mrs. Francis, or would you like to go shopping for another house?" asked Edward. "This will do, *for now*," said Kathy, "but eventually, we'll need to find something more befitting your new station."

"Hmm," said Edward, "I'll make you a deal, as soon as you pass the Wizard's Test, we'll buy a new house." "You have a deal," said Kathy excitedly, "now, is the bedroom that way?"

"Are they gone?" asked King Donald. "Yes," replied Wizard James, the Court Wizard of Baize. "They transformed into dragons and left the evening after you inspected the reservoir." "I hope they weren't offended by the abruptness of our request that they return to Franconia," said the King. "King Henry is probably eager to have Edward back in Franconia, instead of helping a neighboring King with civic improvements. Besides, their work here is done. We can certainly handle the return of the apprentice magicians to their towns, and the improvement and staffing of the recreation area on the north end of the lake."

"I hope you're right. As you said, Edward would make a bad enemy." "I doubt he feels slighted much," said James. "Besides, I understand that Wizard Timothy married Edward and Kathy before they departed. If she remembers her ties to Baize, she may be a valuable source of information and influence in the years to come." "Yes, she did grow up in Baize, after all. So, what is there for us to do now?"

"I've already administered the Sorcerer's Test to the ten apprentices that Edward, Kathy, and Mage Elianna thought were ready. Nine of the ten passed, so you now have nine new sorcerers, and one more who will be ready to test again soon," said Wizard James. "What are your thoughts on where we should assign them?" asked the King. "I think two of them, Sorcerer Ronald and Sorceress China, should remain here in Springfield to assist Wizard Timothy. I also think that Mage Elianna should remain in Springfield and establish a Springfield School of Magic, akin to what Edward described as a 'Regional Mage's Office,' which every city and town in Franconia has. Elianna is originally from Springfield, and she might welcome such a posting."

"Then who would take over her position in Middleberg?" asked the King. "Newly promoted Sorcerer Stephen was a student under Mage Elianna in Middleberg. He would be an ideal candidate, even though he is not yet a mage," replied James. "Do you think he's ready for such an assignment?" asked Donald. "My assessment is that Stephen was almost ready for promotion to sorcerer before he left Middleberg to come here. All that was lacking was some skill with serums. Apparently, Mage Elianna had her students making Healing Serums only, and while Middleberg now has an impressive stockpile of Healing Serum, her students did not learn any of the other serums that sorcerers need to be able to produce. If Stephen had not spent most of the last year digging in the dirt, he might already be a mage."

"Why did Mage Elianna focus exclusively on making Healing Serum?" asked the King. "She felt it was the serum most likely to be needed in the event of a dragon attack, and I agree with her assessment. Truth, Love, Sleep, and Death Serums will be useless in this conflict. Still, sorcerers and mages need to know how to produce them. According to Stephen, Edward recognized this shortcoming and actually set up some sort of serum laboratory here in the garrison, and they have been teaching the most advanced apprentices serum-making for the last few months. The lone apprentice who failed his Sorcerer's Test did so because he was unable to produce an effective Truth Serum."

"Very well, what about the other six sorcerers?" "Once we return to Baize, I will consult with Admiral Vandall and General Diaz to find military units that need magical support," said James. "So, what's left for us to do here?" "I recommend that we bring in each apprentice magician, award them the one-gold bonus you promised, then place them under a Secrecy spell, not to reveal the extent of Wizard Edward's involvement in the project. All of the credit for this achievement should go to you, Wizard Timothy, and Mage Elianna. We don't need a hundred young magicians in the kingdom, extolling the virtues and prowess of a foreign Wizard," said James.

"I had the same thought. It's a shame, though, to deny Wizard Edward and Mage Kathy their due," said the King. "Sire, in a few years, all anyone will remember is that *you* were the driving force behind the King Donald III Reservoir and Recreation Center," said James. "I like the sound of that," said the King. "Still, if you have to spell people to secrecy, it seems like you're doing something wrong."

Chapter Two:
CLEAN-UP ON AISLE NINE

"Has this happened before?" "Yes. Once at the Academy, when he overdid it while using a Seeing spell to find his father, Wizard Edward, who was in Baize," said Rachel. "That's a long way off for a Seeing spell," said Mage Roark. "I know. Wizard Noland should have warned him. He was unconscious for three days at that time." "So, what do you think caused it this time?" "Probably using a Seeing spell from Hayford to find the dragons in the quarry north of here; then changing into a dragon and flying here; then spelling that garrison guard to sleep; then Changing back into a dragon and killing a Sea Dragon; and two Fire Dragons; then Changing back into a human and killing a Stone Dragon before erecting a shield to protect us both from a building falling on us; then putting out the fire with a Water spell; then Reducing the bricks and rubble to dust; then using a Strength Enhancement to jump clear of the debris while carrying me; then healing my ankle without drinking anything in between," said Rachel.

"Yes, that would certainly do it," said Mage Roark. "In my defense," said Donovan, waking up, "I lost my water bag once I transformed into a dragon, so I couldn't drink anything during the fight with the dragons, or while we were trapped under the bricks." Mage Roark laughed. "Even so, you should have taken some water before you transformed to go fight the dragons." "And you certainly didn't need to conjure the Healing for Major Wounds spell to heal my ankle," said Rachel. "It wasn't that bad, and there were plenty of other magicians around who could have done it."

"As far as I knew, the other magicians were as tired as I was from the fight, and I will always over-Heal you," said Donovan reasonably. "Now, what's going on? How long have I been out, and what were the losses from the attack?" "You've been asleep for two days, and the fires are all out in the city," said Battle Mage Gregory as he entered the room. "What were our casualties?" repeated Donovan. Mage Gregory sighed, "We have about 300 dead and another 600 or so wounded. Between the fires and the ice, there are at least fifty buildings in the city with some sort of damage. Still, it would have been much worse if not for you two." "I guess it's fortunate that the dragons made a mistake then," said Donovan.

"A mistake? What are you talking about?" asked Mage Gregory. "They attacked a city with a Regiment stationed in it, plus a fairly large Regional Mage's Office. That's seven magicians. What if they had attacked Frostberg instead? As I recall, there are no troops stationed in Frostberg, and only a single sorcerer in the Regional Office." "He's right," said Mage Roark, "it would have been a massacre."

"Do you need any help with the wounded?" asked Donovan, as he started to get out of bed. "Not from you. At least, not yet. You need to rest for at least a day. I'm amazed that you're awake already. You need to eat something to get your strength back, but no magic for today. Understood?" "But there are hurt people out there!" said Donovan. "Yes, and you could probably heal about two of them before you fell unconscious again. Rest. We'll handle the wounded. Three Forks has a lot of Healers, and many of the wounded only have minor injuries," said Mage Roark.

"Has the Royal Expeditionary Force arrived yet?" asked Rachel. "My Seeing spell indicates that the ship they're on should arrive today," said Mage Roark. "They have two Healers who are excellent," said Rachel. "We'll need them, and you, Sorceress, but Donovan needs to rest today," said the Battle Mage.

"OK," said Donovan. "One last question, what was the building that fell on us?" Mage Roark grimaced, "That was the Three Forks Treasury building, the tallest building in the city except for the City Hall and the Garrison." "Then you have another problem," said Donovan. "What's that?" asked the Regional Mage. "All that fell on us was bricks and timbers. I didn't see any gold or silver coins in the wreckage." The mage looked shocked. "Are you sure?" "Trust me, we got a good close look at the debris," said Donovan.

"But, there should have been thousands of golds in that building!" said Mage Roark. "That's one of the things that the Royal Expeditionary Force is inspecting during our tour of Franconia. The Treasury in Kingston was plundered by the former Minister of Internal Security, who was a dragon Changed One. The King is concerned that Minister Jasmine may have had accomplices in other towns and cities in the realm," said Rachel.

"How many treasuries have come up short?" asked Mage Roark. "So far, Prarrieville, Colton, and Haven have all come up short, and we still have Three Forks, Frostberg, Sundock, Eastport and Grotton to check." Mage Roark whistled. "What are you doing about it?" "We're rooting out the people, or dragons responsible; the entire Colton Regional Mage's Office, for instance, and," Rachel looked around, then whispered, "and replicating coins to replace most of what we think is missing."

"That could be quite a lot here," said Mage Gregory. "I'd suggest you round up the Treasurer and anyone else who had access to the vault. Make sure they're not dragon Changed Ones, then determine how much may be missing," said Donovan. "How do we identify Changed Ones?" Donovan and Rachel explained how to go about identifying dragon Changed Ones, and the Binding spell or hand removal required if the Changed One was hostile.

"If it's been two days, the culprit may have already fled," said Donovan, "but also check the Blacksmith shops in town. That seems to be the preferred occupation for Fire Dragon Changed Ones." The two mages hurried out of the room, headed for the now-demolished Treasury building. Rachel sat on Donovan's bedside and asked, "So, how do you feel?" "Hungry," replied Donovan, "Are you all right?" Rachel nodded sadly, "Yes, but I've never seen so much pain and suffering before. There are so many injured people, or those who have lost loved ones or businesses. It's heartbreaking."

Donovan took her hand. "I know it's hard," he said. "Now you know why I have so little tolerance for hostile dragons. They would have razed the whole city if we hadn't stopped them."

"So, why the Major-Wounds spell on my ankle?" asked Rachel. "I was standing right next to you. Plus, I knew you had a prior injury to that ankle that didn't quite heal right. I thought I'd try to fix it while I was at it," said Donovan. "How did you know about my ankle? I broke it as a child when a horse stepped on it!" "I've known since we began dating, you limp, just slightly. I have often thought about offering healing, but didn't quite know how to broach the subject. I just took advantage of the situation," said Donovan, grinning. "Well, it worked. My ankle feels so much better now. I guess I'd just gotten used to the discomfort. Thank you."

"Any time. Do you have any other childhood injuries you would like me to look at?" asked Donovan as he tried to look down her shirt. "Not at this time," said Rachel, blushing. "Now, you get out of that bed and go to the kitchen and find some food. I'll be back later." Rachel gave him a kiss, then headed out to the city to help the injured citizens.

The HMS VALOR sailed south, towards Eastport and 3rd Squadron. The problem was, 3rd Squadron was likely at sea, and it was a big ocean. There was a good chance that the two groups of ships would sail right past each other. Andrew was up in the Crow's Nest again, using a Sight Enhancement. About mid-day, a blue Sea Dragon descended from the clouds and headed for the aft deck of the VALOR. An excited crewman let fly a crossbow bolt, which passed clean through the dragon's left wing.

"HOLD YOUR FIRE!" screamed the dragon, "IT'S ME, ANNE!" "STAND DOWN!" yelled Andrew from the Crow's Nest, "DRAGON MESSENGER ARRIVING!" Andrew scurried down from the top of the mast and rushed to the aft deck, where Anne (in dragon form) was examining the hole in her left wing. Andrew erected a Seeming of a curtain across the deck and Anne changed back into her human form and put on the clothes she was carrying in a canvas bag.

"What was all that about?" asked Anne. "I thought we had a truce with the Sea Dragons." "We did," said Andrew sadly, "but the King's ministers made a mess of the proposed Peace Treaty, and the dragons refused to sign it. Apparently, dragons can't read. So, not only did they not agree to the 37-page Peace Treaty the King sent back, but they also canceled the temporary truce we had. They attacked Sundock three days ago. That's why the crew is a little jumpy. Are you injured?"

"No, not really. I think my arm might be bruised from the shot through the wing, but I'll be fine. That's terrible about the Treaty. Is everyone in Sundock OK?" "No," said Andrew. "While the casualties were minimal, James, the arms merchant who invented the crossbow, was killed. He was one of the only people on board our ships during the attack. Everyone else was in town on shore leave. The Sea Dragons cast Concealment spells on themselves and dropped big rocks and stones on the ships from high in the sky. We never saw it coming," said Andrew.

"Oh, my. I may have inadvertently given them the idea for that," said Anne. "What?" "Yes, you see, when they returned me to the ship after I healed their injured on Acropo, I cast a Concealment shield around Gek as he carried me close enough to the ship to be spotted after he dropped me in the water. Then he cast his own Concealment shield as he flew away. It's very hard to fly and hold a Concealment shield because of the power drain. I never dreamed that they would use it as a way to attack us. I'm so sorry," said Anne.

"It's not your fault, Anne. No one can think of every contingency. If the King hadn't mucked up the Treaty, it never would have happened. You should have a talk with your sister and get her to talk some sense into the King," said Andrew. "However, would Celeste be able to talk sense to the King?" asked Anne, confused.

"Haven't you heard? Celeste is the new dragon messenger to the King. I've heard that they're even dating. Celeste might end up as the next Queen of Franconia," said Andrew. "I can't believe it! My sister, the fainter, is dating King Henry?" asked Anne. "Just so. I understand that when she delivered the draft Peace Treaty to the King in Southport, he became attracted to her and they have been an item ever since. Wizard Noland had to appoint Sorcerer Phillip as a replacement dragon messenger to the Navy," explained Andrew.

"Will wonders never cease! I hope the relationship is consensual. I would hate to think that Celeste is being coerced somehow." "I asked her the same thing," said Andrew, "and she assured me that the feelings are mutual. Anyway, what brings you to 1st Squadron this fine day at sea?" "I was on my way to Frostberg with the Concealment cloaks for the magicians in 2nd Squadron, when I saw you sailing by, so I thought I'd drop in and see what's happening," said Anne.

Just then, Commodore Matthews walked up. "Sorceress Anne! So good to see you again. I suppose that Andrew has caught you up on current events?" "Yes, Commodore. He was just about to tell me why you're heading south." "We're looking for 3rd Squadron to tell them that the truce is off, and the Sea Dragons are on the attack again. Also, if they can make it to Sundock, there's a new modification to the Seabows that will allow them to be drawn by a single sailor. Mage Andrew's wife is standing by to install them on each ship," said Commodore Matthews.

"Andrew's WIFE?" asked Anne, looking at Andrew. "I was getting to that," said Andrew, displaying his ring-adorned finger. "I got married to Maria, the arms merchant's daughter." "The one who was killed in the attack?" asked Anne. "The very same," said Andrew. "Anyway, where's 3rd Squadron?" "They're about three leagues east, and ten leagues south of your current position," said Anne. "Would you like me to deliver a message to them?"

"Yes," said the Commodore. "Tell them that the truce with the Sea Dragons is over, and that I recommend that they make best possible speed to Sundock to get the modifications for their Seabows. Also, their magicians need to be on the lookout for Concealed Dragons, carrying heavy stones."

The back door to the hut was finished. Now the dragons could enter and leave without tromping through Bruce's living room, usually knocking over or breaking something in the process. Gek was still down because he was unable to change back into a human, but not as disappointed as Richard. As Bruce had observed, the human baby born to dragon parents was growing at an amazing rate compared to human children. Richard was already walking (and running) and was beginning to speak in complete sentences. Unfortunately, his favorite sentence currently was, "Why, Daddy, why?" Seemingly, a request for Gek to change back into human form.

"Someone needs to go warn the Sea Dragon Clan about the human magic-users being able to change into dragons," said Gek. "And I suppose that by someone you mean me?" asked Azure. "It would probably be better coming from you, rather than me," said Gek. "You should also tell them about Ard and Donovan." "I agree that they need to be told," said Azure, "but I am not sure it is a priority right now. I mean, it is unlikely that a bunch of human magic-users are going to attack the colony disguised as dragons. Only Anne knows where the colony is, after all."

"I am sure that by now, Anne has told the other magic-users where the Sea Dragon colony is. If not the precise cavern, at least on Acropo," said Gek. "I still say it is unlikely that the humans would try to attack the colony," argued Azure. "You may be right," conceded Gek. "So, what do we do now?" "Maybe we should start gathering up some rocks," said Azure.

The Royal Expeditionary Force disembarked from the FS SWIFT at the pier in Three Forks, and found a city in turmoil. Many of the residents of the city were busy repairing their homes and businesses, while others were gathering their things to flee. Major Gerald moved the Expeditionary Force through the city to the garrison and was surprised by the amount of destruction. Some buildings still smoked and smoldered, while others were coated in a thin layer of slowly melting ice. Soldiers of the 6th Regiment were posted on most of the street corners, maintaining law and order, and preventing looting of the damaged or abandoned homes and businesses.

Once the Royal Expeditionary Force arrived at the garrison, the soldiers moved to the stables and began caring for their mounts, while Major Gerald and the two Company commanders went in search of the Regimental Commander. They found Major Franklin in his office. "Gerald! Come in! It's good to see you again! How was the trip?" asked Major Franklin. "Taking a ship beats riding all the way here from Hayford, but it took longer than usual to get offloaded. Why are so many people leaving Three Forks?" asked Major Gerald.

"The dragon attack has everyone spooked. About ten percent of the citizens were either killed or wounded, and almost everyone suffered some kind of loss. Some of the people just don't feel safe here anymore, and you know, I can't really blame them." "But where will they go? I'm not really sure that many other cities in Franconia are all that much safer." "I've tried to explain that to them, but some of them just won't listen to reason," said Major Franklin.

"I hate to say it, but there's not as much damage as I expected…" said Major Gerald. "Yes, and we have your two magicians to thank for that." Major Franklin laughed, "They came barging in here, spelled one of my guards to sleep, and vanished the lock on my gate. Mage Gregory grabbed them both in Tether spells, and Donovan started shouting about an imminent dragon attack."

Major Gerald smiled, "Yep. That sounds like Donovan. So, how did he convince you?" "He practically ordered Mage Gregory to give him a dose of Truth Serum! According to Gregory, he drank the whole vial, then, calm as you please said, 'I'm Sorcerer Donovan from the Royal Expeditionary Force, and you're about to be attacked by nine dragons. Well, that got the mage's attention. He released them and rushed them right in here. We barely had time to discuss the matter before those damn dragons attacked!"

"So, what happened?" "Well, I sent the soldiers to the armory to get their crossbows. We don't have enough of them, by the way, and the magicians all headed down to the city center to face the dragons, except for Donovan and Rachel," said Major Franklin. "What did they do?" asked Gerald. "Believe it or not, they changed into Gold Dragons and flew off to fight the attacking dragons." "Yes, that sounds like something Donovan and Rachel would do." "So, the two of them flew up behind the two Sea Dragons that were spraying water everywhere, which the Snow Dragons were freezing to ice. Then they bit off their heads! If you can believe that! I wouldn't have, except that I have two headless blue Dragons in the courtyard. One of the Snow Dragons turned around to find out why the water stopped, and one of my soldiers made the best shot of his life, and put a crossbow bolt through his head. The other Snow Dragon took off for the Snow Fields as fast as his wings could carry him," said Major Franklin excitedly.

"Next, one of the Gold Dragons, I assume it was Donovan, swooped down on top of one of the Fire Dragons, grabbed him by the back and shredded his wings with his hind feet. Then he carried the Fire Dragon high into the sky, and dropped him on the road outside of town!" "Did it survive?" asked Major Gerald. "No way! That Fire Dragon fell like a stone. Meanwhile, Rachel was wrestling with the other Fire Dragon, trying to flame it, but I guess dragons are fire-proof, because it wasn't working. Then Donovan comes circling around them and blows fire right down the Fire Dragon's throat! Well, that killed him."

"Then all that was left were the two Stone Dragons and the enemy Great Dragon," said Gerald. "Right. The two Stone Dragons were walking down Main Street like they were taking an Endday stroll, burning or smashing everything in their path. Donovan and Rachel landed in front of them, changed back into humans, and put shields around them, trying to suffocate them." "Did it work?" "Well, it was kind of chaotic, but the report I got indicates that the Stone Dragon Donovan had shielded died first, but then the Great Dragon entered the fray by knocking the Treasury building down on top of Donovan and Rachel."

"No! Did they survive?" asked a concerned Major Gerald. Major Franklin smiled, "Yes. It seems that Donovan got a shield over himself and Rachel just in time. Sorcerer Walt from the Regional Mage's Office wasn't quick enough, though, and he was killed by the falling stones. Anyway, the Gold Dragon flamed the debris for good measure and flew off to the north, but Mage Roark thinks he winged him with a Blast spell." said Major Franklin.

"How did Donovan and Rachel get out from under all the rubble?" asked Gerald. "Well, first, Donovan conjured a Water spell that put out the fire, then it seems he used a Reduce spell to turn the bricks and timber that were on top of them to dust. My mage was very impressed by his creative thinking. Anyway, once the bricks were dust-sized, Rachel used a Wind spell to blow the dust away, then the two of them jumped out of the hole in the rubble. Some of the bricks from the pile fell on Rachel's ankle as they made their way out, but Donovan healed her. Right before he passed out."

"Is he all right?" "Fine, he just slept for two days. He woke up this morning. I have to tell you, that is one very impressive magician you have." "I know," said Gerald, "I just hope he doesn't kill himself by overdoing it. I understand that this is the second time he's ended up unconscious." "According to Mage Gregory, magicians get stronger by pressing their limits," said Major Franklin. "Then Donovan may end up being the strongest magician in Franconia someday. I'm not surprised he didn't give it a thought before he Healed Rachel though. She is his wife, after all."

"So I heard. How did you go from no magical support to those two?" Major Gerald smiled, "Timing is everything. I had just asked Wizard Noland about getting some magical support for the Royal Expeditionary Force, when Donovan passed his Sorcerer's Test. Rachel was already a Mentor." "How has it worked out? I mean, having a woman in your command?"

"Sorceress Rachel is a big asset. She's helpful, and the men all respect her. Even the ones she had to put in their place," said Major Gerald. "How did she do that?" "Usually with a rock to the back of the head. It's been quite effective." Major Franklin laughed.

"So, what can we do to help?" asked Major Gerald. "I hate to admit it, but there's been some looting in town. Even with a Regiment of soldiers, I can't protect every business and home all day and all night. Regional Mage Roark is doing what he can, but even with his fifteen Enforcers, it's just too much. There are too many businesses that were damaged and we can't protect them all." "I might be able to help with that," said Major Gerald. "You see, all of my troops have Concealment cloaks, so we can provide invisible assistance. Once the criminals figure out that we could be anywhere, that should cut down on the looting."

"And just how did you come by these exorbitantly expensive cloaks?" asked Major Franklin. "Wizard Edward and Mage Curtis figured out how to make them. They made one for all of my soldiers. We asked the King for permission to issue one to everyone in the Royal Guard, but he refused after a dragon Changed One, who had infiltrated my command, tried to assassinate Marshall Guzman at the Royal Ball while wearing his Concealment cloak. After that, the King balked at the idea. Still, we have a cloak for all of your magicians in one of our wagons."

"Why would a magician need a Concealment cloak?" asked Major Franklin. "So they can save one of their spells for something besides Concealment," said Gerald. "Ingenious. And these cloaks are just like the one my Specialist has?" "Close enough," said Major Gerald. "If you like, I'll send my men out to meet the men you have on patrol, then have them don their cloaks and poke around. I'll bet we can nip this looting in the bud." Major Franklin looked relieved. "That sounds like a great idea." Major Gerald looked at his company commanders, "Captains, you know what to do." Both Captains nodded and moved quickly to round up their men.

"Where's Donovan?" asked Gerald. "I'd like to see him." Major Franklin led the way to the room where Donovan was staying, and they found him pacing the floor. "Major Gerald! Finally! Can you get me out of here? I'm going stir-crazy!" said Donovan. "Slow down, now! I heard that you overdid it again and passed out," said Gerald reasonably. "I know," said Donovan, "but I feel much better now that I've had something to eat and drink. I feel fine, and they need my help out there!" "Including Rachel, there are nine magicians out there, plus all the Healers! What more do you think you can do?" asked Major Gerald.

"Sir," said Donovan, trying to calm himself, "as I told Major Franklin, I think someone robbed the Treasury. And you know what that probably means. We need to investigate quickly before the culprit gets away." "The Treasury was robbed?" asked Major Gerald. "Maybe," replied Major Franklin. "That's the building that the Great Dragon knocked over on them, and Donovan assures me that he didn't see any gold coins in the rubble, which he got a good look at, so it's possible. It's also possible that the gold was stored in vaults in the basement. With all the looting and healing going on, I haven't had time to check on it yet."

Major Gerald thought for a moment, then said, "All right, Donovan, you take Lance and go check out the Treasury, but if there are Changed Ones involved, you do not try to handle the problem yourself. Understand? I don't want to have to fine you another week's pay." Donovan nodded and, as he left the room, said, "Coming Lance?" The Specialist lowered his hood and smiled. Major Gerald gave Lance a keep an eye on him look. Lance nodded and followed Donovan out of the garrison, out into the street.

"You fined your sorcerer a week's pay?" asked Major Franklin. "Yes," replied Gerald, "We were interrogating a dragon Changed One in Prarrieville, who confessed to killing Donovan's mother a few years ago. Before we could learn much more from her, Donovan froze her to death. It was understandable, but hasty." "Why kill her that way?" asked Major Franklin. "Because that's the way she killed Mrs. Francis. You've got to admire that boy's sense of justice," chuckled Gerald. Major Franklin just shook his head.

Once on the street, Donovan could see the destruction that had been done to the city of Three Forks. There were damaged and charred shopfronts, destroyed vending carts, and several roofs still had icicles dangling from their eaves. The sky was overcast and the temperature was considerably colder than it had been in the southern cities of Smithville and Hayford. Donovan and Lance walked carefully along the busy streets, headed for the site where the Treasury building once stood.

Soldiers patrolled the streets, helping residents where they could, but always on the lookout for unscrupulous characters, looking for a quick score. When they reached the enormous pile of bricks and timbers laying in the middle of Main Street, Donovan said, "There it is." "You mean that you were trapped under all that?" asked Lance. "Well, maybe not all of it," said Donovan slyly. "Let's go around and see if there is anything left of the foundation."

The sorcerer and the specialist took a side street and came around the collapsed building from the opposite side. Stepping carefully, they surveyed the damage. "There might be a basement under all that," said Donovan, "I'll just need to use a Remove spell to clear away these bricks and timbers." "Just don't overdo it," cautioned Lance, "I don't want to have to explain your passing out to the commander."

"DELERE," said Donovan with a flick of his wrist towards the pile of bricks and broken beams. They vanished at once, leaving a smooth, flat surface. There was no indication of a stairwell leading down to a lower level. "Humph," said Donovan. "No basement that I can see. You?" Lance walked around what had been the ground floor of the Treasury, looking for a hidden trap door or other secret passageway to a lower level where the vaults might be concealed, but he found nothing.

"I didn't really expect to find a basement," said Donovan. "Why is that?" asked Lance. "It's the rivers," explained Donovan, "I doubt that very many of the homes or businesses in Three Forks have basements, the water level is too high because of the rivers. You start to dig a basement, and before you get ten feet down, water seeps in and collapses your hole. It's the same thing in Kingston. My house had a cellar, but I think my father sealed it with magic." "I had no idea," said Lance.

"Do you see any gold coins in the debris field?" asked Donovan. Lance looked over the giant pile of bricks and timbers, and shook his head. "No, I do not. I don't see so much as a copper." Donovan sighed, "We better find the Majors and the Treasurer, but I suspect that the Treasurer is long gone by now."

Chapter Three:
HIDE-AND-SEEK

Maria hurried across town from the funeral home to the Regional Mage's Office. As she entered, a young man rose from the receptionist's desk. "Can I help you?" he asked. "Yes, my name is Maria Perrucci, and I need to speak with Mage Lisa if she's available. It's a matter of some urgency," said Maria. "Just a moment, and I'll see if Mage Lisa has time to speak with you," said the receptionist. He quickly walked through the door behind his desk, closing it firmly behind him.

A few minutes later, a middle-aged woman with black, curly hair and dark skin emerged from the back office. "I am Mage Lisa. How can I help you?" she asked. "My name is Maria Perrucci," Maria began— "That is funny," said Lisa, interrupting, "there was a Battle Mage from the HMS VALOR, who had the same unusual last name, who came by last week." "My husband," said Maria. "He sailed with the morning tide. Anyway, my father was the arms merchant who was killed on the HMS VICEROY a few days ago," said Maria.

"I am so sorry," said Lisa, "I did not know that Mage Andrew was married." "Commodore Matthews married us last night before the VALOR sailed this morning," confirmed Maria. "I had no idea," said Mage Lisa. "So, what can I do for you, Mrs. Perrucci?" "Well, I went by the funeral home this morning to arrange for my father's burial, and…

well, I think there's something off about Mr. Stone, the mortician." "Off how?" asked Mage Lisa. "Here," said Maria, handing Lisa the handkerchief that Mr. Stone had given her earlier in the day.

"What am I supposed to do with this?" asked Lisa. "Smell it," said Maria. Mage Lisa took a tentative sniff of the handkerchief, then started to hand it back to Maria. "I do not understand," she said. "My husband told me that Dragon Changed Ones smelled *reptilian*, and that Stone Dragon Changed Ones usually had names that were types of rocks. I find it suspicious that Mr. *Stone* handed me a handkerchief that smells like a lizard." Mage Lisa looked shocked and gave the handkerchief another sniff. "You may be right," she said, "but I cannot barge into the mortuary and kill Mr. Stone on the basis of a stinky handkerchief."

Maria sighed, "I didn't suggest that. I *do* strongly suggest that you pay Mr. Stone a visit and see if you can get him to use a contraction. You *do* know that Dragon Changed Ones can't use contractions, don't you?" "Yes, I know that Changed Ones do not use contractions, and Mage Andrew informed me that, if you have to kill a Stone Dragon, you need to enclose it in a protective shield. I also know that all Dragon Changed Ones are not hostile, that some prefer to remain in human form."

Mage Lisa looked decidedly uncomfortable and hesitant to go confront a potential Stone Dragon Changed One alone. "I will certainly take your concerns under consideration, Mrs. Perrucci. Thank you for stopping by this morning," said Mage Lisa. Sensing that the conversation was going nowhere, and doubting that the Regional Mage was going to do anything at all, Maria left the office and returned home, wondering what to do next. She finally decided that she would speak to the magicians in 3rd Squadron when they put into port in a few days. She just hoped that she had that much time before something terrible happened.

When Edward and Kathy returned to the Chief of Military Wizardry's office, it was as clean as the day the last occupant left it. The desk, bookshelves, chairs, and filing cabinets gleamed like new wood, even the empty cage for the Messenger Hawk was spotless, and the food bin was full, just in case someone wanted to send him a message. "This is fantastic!" said Kathy. Edward nodded his agreement at the wonderful job the cleaning crew had done in such a short time. Edward walked over to the wall-sized map and said, "I think I'll find out where Donovan and Andrew are."

Taking his truncheon out of the holster on his waist, he held it before the wall map and concentrated on locating his son and his nephew. After a few moments, a diamond shape with an "S" in it appeared in Three Forks, and another diamond, this one with an "M" inside, appeared in the ocean, halfway between the towns of Sundock and Eastport. "Hmm," said Edward, "Donovan is in Three Forks, presumably with the Royal Expeditionary Force, and

Andrew and the HMS VALOR are patrolling the sea between Sundock and Eastport. I wonder what the Expeditionary Force is doing in Three Forks, and why the VALOR is so far south. I expected them to be somewhere around the Coral Islands."

"They must have gotten new orders from Admiral Cross," said Kathy. Just then, Wizard Noland knocked on the door. "Come in," said Edward. Wizard Noland, the headmaster of the Franconian Wizards Academy, entered the office and said, "This place certainly looks cleaner. Have you settled in yet?" "Hardly," replied Edward. "The cleaning crew you sent did an amazing job, but we only got here a few minutes ago. Can you tell me why Donovan is in Three Forks, and Andrew and the HMS VALOR are between Sundock and Eastport?"

Wizard Noland took a seat in one of the dark leather chairs and said, "That's why I came over this morning, to catch you up on recent events. A lot's been happening in Franconia while you two were off galivanting in Baize." Edward refused to rise to the bait and merely said, "Go on." Wizard Noland smiled and said, "A few months ago, Leonard, the Minister of Finance, reported to me that a significant sum of gold was missing from the treasury in Kingston." "How much?" asked Edward. "About ten thousand golds. As near as I can determine, Jasmine simply vanished them with a Remove spell. She had no need of gold." "TEN THOUSAND! That would bankrupt the kingdom!" exclaimed Edward.

"Yes. So, over the course of a couple of weeks, the faculty and I replicated almost all of the missing gold, then I told Minister Leonard that we found it in a hidden room in Jasmine's apartment," said Noland. "He believed you?" "I think he was so desperate that he would have believed anything. He was afraid that if he reported the theft to the King, it would mean his head." "He may have been right. King Henry would not have taken kindly to the loss of ten thousand golds," said Edward.

"Certainly not," said Noland, "but Wizard Daniel had a disturbing thought: What if Jasmine had accomplices in other cities in Franconia? There could be a sizable amount missing. So, when I reported the theft and recovery to the King, I suggested that he send the Royal Expeditionary Force on a tour of all the towns and cities in Franconia to inventory their Treasuries. While they are out, they are distributing the Concealment cloaks to the magicians who don't have theirs yet. Donovan and Rachel are also visiting all of the Regional Mages' Offices to check for Dragon Changed Ones."

"That could take months!" said Edward. "Yes, but I still think it's worth doing. This way, we get the cloaks distributed, do the inventories and replace any missing gold, and continue the hunt for Changed Ones," said Wizard Noland. "Well, Donovan is in Three Forks, so how much longer do you think this mission will take?" "The Expeditionary Force left on a ship, headed for Southport, a little over four months ago. As I understand it, the plan was for them to proceed from Southport to Westport, then to

Weaton, making a loop from west to east. If they're already in Three Forks, I would say that they're about two-thirds of the way to being finished. I imagine that they'll head to Frostberg next, then travel by sea to Sundock, Eastport, and then Grotton before returning to Kingston. They should be back in a couple of months."

Edward nodded his understanding. "I hope they don't run into too much trouble. OK, that explains Donovan—why is the HMS VALOR so far south?" "Remember the peace treaty that the Sea Dragons proposed? Well, King Henry and his ministers kept adding things to it, so it ended up being a 37-page document, which the dragons refused to sign. It seems that dragons can't read. So now, not only do we *not* have a peace treaty, but the dragons have cancelled the temporary truce they had agreed to. I'm not sure why the VALOR is moving south, maybe to inform Vice-Admiral Jordan about the treaty."

"Is that all?" asked Edward. "We put Stone Dragon scales on the roofs of all the palace buildings, and construction crews are busy installing them on most of the other buildings in Kingston. The scales are strong, hard, and fireproof, and they replicate easily, but we haven't been able to come up with any other use for them. We also installed large, pedestal-mounted crossbows, we call them Guardbows, on the battlements and watchtowers of the palace," said Wizard Noland.

"When Kathy and I got to my house yesterday, we noticed that Donovan and Rachel are *not* living there. Do you know where their house is?" "They bought a cottage, down along the river on the west end of town. You can't miss it. It's the only one with Stone Dragon scale shingles."

"Well, I guess you should get back to the Academy. I'm going to look around the office and see if I can find anything useful." Wizard Noland rose and headed out of the office. He paused at the door and said, "I expect to see you soon, *Mage* Kathy."

The rest of the morning was spent looking through the desk drawers, bookshelves, and filing cabinets in the large office. Since the office had been unoccupied for almost three decades, Edward did not expect to find anything that would help them with their current difficulties with the dragons. Before leaving the office for lunch, Edward conjured a large, two-pedestal desk for Kathy and placed it a short distance from his desk.

"Wouldn't it be better if I had an outer office?" asked Kathy. "Absolutely not," said Edward. "You are the Assistant Chief of Military Wizardry, not my receptionist. I want you to know everything I know, and I don't want anyone thinking you're less than you are. After lunch, we'll start getting you ready for your Wizard's Test."

"The gold is gone, I tell you," said Donovan. "If there was any in the rubble, the people would be climbing all over it looking for it." "You're probably right," said Mage Roark,

"But *some* of it might still be in there." "Who had access to the treasury?" asked Rachel. Mage Roark thought, "The treasurer and his assistant, the mayor, and maybe some of the accountants that worked in the building. Why?"

"Because we need to round all of them up and try to find out what happened to all the gold. Do you have any idea how much was in the treasury?" asked Donovan. "No. I would assume there were a couple thousand golds, but as to the exact amount, I have no idea." "How do you propose we sift through the rubble?" asked Mage Gregory. "Normally, I would just suggest using a Remove spell, but that would remove any gold along with the bricks," said Mage Roark.

"You're going to need those bricks to rebuild the building," said Donovan. "It would be a shame to just vanish them all. Plus, it would be costly to buy replacement bricks." "What do you suggest?" asked Mage Gregory. "We could use a Reduce spell to shrink the bricks down and make them easier to gather and store, then you could enlarge them again when you're ready to rebuild." "I like it," said Mage Roark, "that way, we don't destroy the bricks, and we might find any gold that's trapped under the rubble."

"In the meantime, we need to find the mayor, the treasurer, and his employees. One of them is undoubtedly a magician," said Rachel. The four magicians left the garrison and headed over to the still-standing City Hall. Entering the mayor's office, Gregory said, "Good morning, Mayor Tine, how are you doing today?" "Hello, Mage Roark," said the mayor, "It's another difficult day, I'm afraid. Too many tasks and not enough hands. What brings you in this morning?"

"I was wondering if you knew where the city treasurer, or one of his assistants, was. We haven't been able to locate him since the dragon attack." "Who, Burns? Now that you mention it, I haven't seen him either, or that worthless assistant of his, Mr. Sanders. Why are you looking for them?" Donovan held up a finger, then cast a Silence spell around the group. "The reason that the Royal Expeditionary Force came to Three Forks was to audit the treasury. Some of the other cities in the kingdom have come up short lately, so the King sent us out on an inspection."

"The treasury building was destroyed by that dragon," said the mayor. "I know," said Donovan, "My wife and I were under it." "Mayor, may I introduce Sorcerer Donovan and his wife, Sorceress Rachel? They were the magicians who transformed into dragons and killed or drove off the Sea, Snow, and Fire Dragons, and also killed the two Stone Dragons," said Mage Gregory. The mayor brightened considerably and moved to shake hands with Donovan and Rachel. "A real pleasure to meet you both! I can't tell you how much we appreciate your actions!"

"We were glad to help mayor. The treasurer?" asked Donovan. The mayor thought for a moment, then said, "Now that you mention it, I haven't seen either of them since the attack…" "Do you happen to know how much gold was in the treasury?" asked Mage Roark. "Not off the top of my head, but I could check the ledger," said the mayor. "Please do," said Mage Roark. The mayor opened his roll-top desk and opened a green leather-bound book. "Let's see… according to this, there were three thousand, two hundred and fifty-six golds, five hundred and sixty-nine silvers, and seventy-one coppers in the treasury during the inventory last week. What's the problem?"

"We haven't found any coins in the rubble," said Mage Roark quietly. "Well, of course not!" said Mayor Tine, "The treasury building is where the accounting took place. The coins are in the vault in this building! Come, let me show you." The mayor led the four magicians down the hall to a large steel door, which he opened with a large key that he produced from his waistcoat. "See? Everything's in order here," said the mayor. Donovan walked forward, looking at the sacks of coins, arrayed on heavy-duty metal shelves. "Do you mind?" he asked. The mayor nodded. When Donovan touched a bag of coins, it vanished in a flash of light, a Seeming. *All* of the coins were Seemings, which vanished when touched. The treasury was completely empty. The mayor fainted.

"Well, now we know why we didn't see any coins in the rubble," said Donovan. "We need to go find the treasurer and his assistant and see what we can recover." After reviving the mayor and assuring him that they would go and immediately attempt to locate the missing gold, they jotted down the treasurer's home address and that of his assistant.

As they left the City Hall, Donovan suggested that some of the other sorcerers in the city could begin reducing the bricks of the collapsed treasury building, now that they didn't need to worry about destroying any gold. The magicians found Mr. Burns' home empty, and with no signs of hidden rooms or compartments. The gold wasn't there. Proceeding to Mr. Sanders' home, they were immediately struck by the opulence of the residence. Mr. Sanders was clearly living well beyond his means.

When they entered the door, they were greeted by a liveried butler who asked, "Who may I say is calling?" "I am Mage Roark from the Three Forks Regional Mage's Office. This is Mage Gregory, Sorcerer Donovan, and Sorceress Rachel. We would like to speak to Mr. Sanders, if he is available," said Mage Roark tactfully. The butler went off to an upstairs room to find the master of the house. The four magicians looked around, admiring the smooth marble floor and the sculptures and pieces of art that adorned the walls. "The assistant treasurer certainly does well for himself," murmured Donovan.

"Maybe he came from money," speculated Mage Gregory. The butler returned and said, "Unfortunately, Mr. Sanders has a very full schedule today, what with the city's destruction and all. I'm sure you understand. He asked me to schedule some time next week for—" *"INCOGITA,"* said Donovan, and the butler slumped to the polished floor. "Check upstairs, I'll check the back," said Donovan, rushing down the hallway. As Donovan exited the rear portico, he spied a well-heeled gentleman racing for the detached carriage house. *"NERVO,"* said Donovan, making a grabbing motion with his right hand, tethering the very well-dressed Mr. Sanders in his tracks.

Rachel and the two mages came out of the door and joined Donovan as he approached the tethered man. "For someone too busy to speak with us, you seem to be abandoning your duties, sir," said Mage Roark. "Unhand me, you villains! Do you know who I am? I will see you all in chains!" said Mr. Sanders. "I sincerely doubt it," said Mage Gregory. "Mr. Sanders, can you please explain to me how an assistant treasurer can afford such a luxurious home?"

"My father was Colonel Sanders, if it is any business of yours! He was the commander of the entire Franconian National Militia! This was his house!" "I see," said Mage Gregory, "where is your father? We'd like a word with him." "Father died two years ago. He left me the house. Now unhand me!" "First, say 'can't,'" said Donovan.

"Who are you to be giving me orders?" sneered the man. "I am the one who is about to end your life if you can't convince me that you're not a Stone Dragon Changed One," said Donovan coldly. Mr. Sanders slumped, "I cannot," he said. "Please do not kill me, I meant no harm to anyone. I just could not go on as I was." Mages Gregory and Roark were stunned by the admission. "Where is the gold that was in the Three Forks Treasury?" asked Rachel.

"It is in the strong-room in the house. If you promise not to kill me, I will show it to you." "First, you must promise not to change back into a dragon, and to never harm a human," said Donovan. "I, Harold Sanders, promise never to change back into a dragon, and to never harm a human," he said, as Donovan drew his finger along the ground, saying *"PROMISA."* Sparkling points of light descended and alit on Mr. Sanders, completing the Binding spell. "You are now under a Binding spell," said Donovan, "if you ever break your word, you will die, immediately." "I understand," said Mr. Sanders.

He led them back into the house and took them to the strong room on the second floor. Inside, there was more gold than was missing from the Three Forks Treasury. "How can you have so much wealth?" asked Mage Roark suspiciously. "As I said, my father, who was also a Changed One, was a Colonel in the Royal Militia. The job paid well, and father and mother spent frugally, except for the purchase of this house, which was in a state of disrepair when they purchased it. Both of them knew enough magic to restore the house to this regal state, then, when I was able to secure a job at the treasury, there was income to sustain it."

"What happened to the treasurer?" asked Donovan. "I have no idea. I have not left the house since the day of the Dragon Attack, except to secure the gold that was stored in the vault in City Hall. I never suspected you would discover the theft so quickly. I had planned to leave tomorrow, but abandoning my childhood home was difficult."

"Have your coach brought around, and we will return the gold to the vault. As long as we do not discover that you had anything to do with the disappearance of the treasurer, you may go back to your life. However, I must warn you, stealing from the treasury again will be considered doing harm to humans and invoke the Binding spell." "Thank you!" said Mr. Sanders.

"One last question," said Donovan, "why didn't you help the dragons when they attacked Three Forks?" Mr. Sanders looked down, "Unlike my father, I am a coward. I feared to fight. Besides, I have many friends in Three Forks and, all things considered, I probably have the best life of any Dragon Changed One in the land."

After returning the gold to the extremely grateful mayor, the four magicians returned to the garrison. "*Mr.* Sanders was certainly not what I expected," said Mage Roark. "Indeed," said Mage Gregory, "and to think, he and his parents lived right under our noses for decades, and we never suspected a thing. It's a bit unnerving."

When they gave their report to Major Franklin, he was very relieved. "We just have one other immediate problem right now." "What's that?" asked Rachel. "We need to report this attack to the King, and our Messenger Hawk Center was destroyed in the attack. Going by boat, it will take weeks to get the news to Kingston." "I don't know about weeks," said Donovan, with a smile. "Rachel, would you like to go visit your parents for a couple of days?"

After receiving permission from Major Gerald, Rachel prepared to depart for Kingston to report the attack on Three Forks to the King and Wizard Noland. Mage Gregory gave her a message pouch with messages inside for both the King and the Headmaster of the Wizards Academy. "Just don't do anything stupid while I'm gone," Rachel told Donovan, before she transformed. "I *never* intentionally do anything stupid," replied Donovan reasonably. "Say hello to your father for me, and hurry back."

Donovan erected a Seeming of a curtain while Rachel disrobed and put her clothes into a heavy canvas bag along with the message pouch. Once transformed, she extended her wings and took off into the overcast, early morning sky, hoping not to frighten the people of Three Forks. It was a long flight to Kingston, but Rachel figured that by leaving early in the morning, she could reach the Wizards Academy boat dock before it got too late that night. She navigated by following the Sapphire River and arrived in Kingston a little before midnight.

Rachel landed at the Academy marina and changed back into her human form. She dressed quickly. There was little chance of anyone being around at this time of night, but you never knew. She opened the portal and entered the Academy, feeling sorry that she probably just woke Wizard Faith, the Academy Gatekeeper, from her sleep. An alarm sounded in the Gatehouse whenever the portal to the boat dock was opened, and Wizard Faith had to investigate if she was not expecting anyone to be opening the portal.

As Rachel walked from the boat dock to the Academy Courtyard, she spied Wizard Faith, and Mage Curtis, both hurrying toward the portal. They were both a bit disheveled, and Faith's shirt was buttoned incorrectly. "What are you doing here at this time of night?" asked Faith. "I just flew down from Three Forks with an important message for Wizard Noland and the King," said Rachel. Faith grumbled about Rachel's bad timing, but escorted her to the Headmaster's cottage. Mage Curtis retreated to the Gatehouse.

"You might want to straighten your shirt before we knock," whispered Rachel. Faith blushed and straightened her attire, then knocked on the door to Wizard Noland's cottage. After a few minutes, a bleary-eyed Jerry, Wizard Noland's door warden, opened the door. "Hello, Wizard Faith, what brings you by this late at night?" asked Jerry. "Sorceress Rachel has just arrived from Three Forks, and she says that she has an urgent message for Wizard Noland," said Faith. "One moment," said Jerry.

A few minutes later, Jerry opened the door and invited Faith and Rachel into the parlor. Wizard Noland joined them a few minutes later and asked Jerry to make a pot of tea for the group. "It's not that I'm not glad to see you, Rachel, but it *is* kind of late," said Noland. "Yes, sir. I'm sorry. In the future, I'll try to time my visits better. I left Three Forks early this morning, and it took me this long to get here."

"I understand," said Noland. "So, what's happening in Three Forks?" "Sir, four days ago, Three Forks was attacked by nine dragons; two Sea Dragons, two Snow Dragons, two Fire Dragons, two Stone Dragons, and one Great Dragon. The Three Forks Messenger Hawk Center was destroyed in the attack, so the 6th Regimental Commander asked me to fly here and report the attack to the King," said Rachel.

Wizard Noland sat up straighter in his chair. "Nine dragons? Of mixed clans? That's never happened before! How bad is the damage?" "There were about 300 killed and 600 wounded, and about fifty or so buildings damaged or destroyed," said Rachel. Wizard Noland looked relieved. "That's tragic, but less bad than I would have expected after an attack by nine dragons."

"Yes. You see, Donovan told Major Gerald that he had a 'bad feeling' about Three Forks while we were just wrapping up our inspection in Hayford. Major Gerald asked Donovan to use a Seeing spell to try and determine what could be wrong in Three Forks. The Seeing spell revealed the dragons together in the abandoned rock quarry just north of the city. So, Donovan and I changed into Great Dragons and flew to Three Forks to warn the garrison," explained Rachel.

"Then what happened?" asked Faith. "The dragons attacked. The soldiers were still retrieving their crossbows from the armory, and the magicians rushed to the city center to confront the dragons. Donovan and I changed back into Great Dragons. We snuck up behind the two Sea Dragons who were spraying water, which the Snow Dragons were freezing into ice. We… well, we bit the heads off the Sea Dragons. They taste *terrible* by the way, then a soldier killed one of the Snow Dragons with a crossbow. The other Snow Dragon fled."

"That left five," said Noland. "Yes, the two Fire Dragons were too busy flaming everything in their path to look behind them and see what had happened to the Sea and Snow Dragons, so Donovan grabbed one of them by the back and shredded his wings with his hind legs. Then he carried the dragon high into the sky and dropped him outside the city." Faith whistled. "Meanwhile, I was fighting with the other Fire Dragon, but it just wouldn't burn! I practically coated him in burning inferno, but he seemed unaffected. Then Donovan flew around in front of the dragon I was wrestling with, and blew inferno right into his mouth and throat. That did the trick."

"What were the Stone Dragons doing while all this was going on?" asked Noland. "I guess they ran out of inferno, because they were walking down Main Street, side by side, smashing everything in their path. So, Donovan and I landed in front of them, changed back into humans, and enclosed them in protective shields." "I assume it worked?" asked Wizard Faith. "Yes, but after the dragon Donovan had shielded died, the Great Dragon pushed a four-story building over on top of us. Donovan got a shield over us, but we ended up trapped under tons of bricks and timbers, which the dragon flamed just for good measure, before he flew off," said Rachel.

"Let me get this straight," said Noland, "You and Donovan were trapped under tons of bricks and debris, protected only by his shield?" "Yes," said Rachel. "Donovan conjured a Water spell to put out the flames, but then we were left in darkness." "How did you get out?" asked Faith. "First, let me ask you a question. Can you fire a Blast spell through a shield?" The two Wizards looked at each other and thought for a moment. "I'm not sure," said Noland finally,

"I've never tried. It might rebound and hit you." "Or crack the shield," said Wizard Faith.

"That's what we were afraid of. It's also why we were reluctant to use the Remove spell. I don't know if it would have removed the bricks or the shield. We were also concerned about harming any of the rescuers, who we assumed were digging through the rubble to find us." The two senior Wizards sat in thought for several minutes before asking how Donovan and Rachel finally resolved their dilemma.

"Reduce," said Rachel, smiling. "Donovan reduced the bricks and timbers to dust, and then I blew the dust away with a strong Wind spell." "Reduce, I'm not sure I would have thought of that," said Faith. "Anyway, once the bricks were gone, Donovan released the shield, and we used a Strength Enhancement to jump clear of the wreckage, but some of the bricks fell into the hole and hit my ankle. Donovan healed me, then promptly passed out. He woke up yesterday," concluded Rachel.

"Incredible!" said Wizard Noland. "You two have done very, very well!" Rachel blushed at the rare praise from Wizard Noland. "Anyway, here is the message from Mage Gregory for you," said Rachel, handing over the message pouch. Noland opened the message and read it quickly. It said:

Wizard Noland,

I am sure that by now Sorceress Rachel has informed you of the heroic actions of herself and Sorcerer Donovan in the defense of Three Forks. Those two are truly outstanding magicians. I recommend, and Mage Roark concurs, that Sorcerer Donovan Francis and Sorceress Rachel Francis, be immediately promoted to the rank of mage. We can think of no one more deserving.

Mage Ronald Gregory and Mage Jarvis Roark

Chapter Four:
PROMOTIONS

Mage Lisa entered the mortuary swiftly, looking for that idiot who called himself Mr. Stone. "Lisa! What brings you here this early in the morning?" asked the mortician. "You, you idiot. Did you speak with Mrs. Maria Perrucci yesterday?" "The arms merchant's daughter? Yes, of course. She came by to see to her father's internment. Why do you ask?"

"Because she has identified you as a potential Dragon Changed One! She came to see me yesterday to report you, and she asked me to conduct an investigation!" "Oh, my. I wonder how she detected me." "You gave her a handkerchief that smelled like a dragon! She brought it to me as proof," said Lisa. "One of my handkerchiefs? But I give them out to everyone! Almost all of my customers are saddened by the loss of their loved ones, and begin crying at some point during our discussions. Maria must be very perceptive," said Mr. Stone.

"Or be married to a Battle Mage," said Lisa. "The question is what to do about her." "Perhaps you could convince her that the scent that she detected was merely from the embalming chemicals we use here. They are quite strong and could easily be mistaken for a dragon scent," proposed Mr. Stone. "Hmm, that might work," said Lisa. "I will tell her that I came by to investigate, determined that you could, in fact, use contractions, and that the odor on the handkerchief was merely embalming fluid. In the meantime, you need to leave town for a few days. Tell your assistant that you had a death in the family and that you need to go to Haven for the funeral. Your assistant is a human, right?"

"Yes. Miss Franks is a human, and she will certainly not arouse any suspicion," said Mr. Stone. "I hope not. The last thing we need is a Battle Mage nosing around. Very well, you need to leave town tomorrow," said Mage Lisa as she walked out the door.

After Wizard Noland read the message from Mage Gregory, he rolled it up and put it in the pocket of his dressing gown, and said, "In the morning, we need to go deliver your report to the new Chief of Military Wizardry. It's much too late tonight, and the King is at his Winter Palace in Southport for the next few months. We'll send a Messenger Hawk to him tomorrow. For the moment, why don't you go and find an empty room in the Mentor's quarters for the night? I think your old room is still unoccupied. I'll see you in the morning, and after breakfast, we'll go over to the palace."

Rachel left the Headmaster's cottage and walked across the courtyard to the Mentor's quarters. She thought that she saw Mage Curtis peeking out through the curtains of the Gatehouse as she went. *None of my business,* she thought.

The next morning after breakfast, Wizard Noland met Rachel, and they headed out toward the palace. They went up to the third floor and down the hall to a corner office. The nameplate on the door read, CHIEF OF MILITARY WIZARDRY. Wizard Noland shocked Rachel by knocking on the door. "Come," said a familiar voice.

Rachel entered the room to find her father-in-law, Wizard Edward, and Mage Kathy sitting in the office. "This impetuous in-law of yours came knocking on my door at midnight last night. You're fortunate I didn't send her to your house straight away," said Wizard Noland with a smile. "Rachel!" said Edward as he came around his desk and gave her a familiar hug. "How nice to see you! But I thought you and Donovan were in Three Forks! What brings you here?" Rachel was surprised to see Donovan's father in Kingston. The last she had heard, he was in Baize, near Springfield, helping construct a giant reservoir of some type.

"Wizard Edward! I thought you were still in Baize! Hello, Mage Kathy, it's nice to see you again," said Rachel, recovering from her shock. "Is Donovan here?" asked Edward. "No, he's still in Three Forks, recovering. He overdid it again and passed out. He just woke up the day before yesterday." "That boy! He better watch himself, or one of these days he's going to sleep for a month! So, Rachel, what brings you back to Kingston?"

"Sir—" began Rachel, "Edward, when we're alone, my dear." "Edward, I came to report to the King and Wizard Noland that a week ago, the city of Three Forks was attacked by nine dragons, from all five clans. We managed to repel the attack, but there were almost a thousand casualties, and the Three Forks Messenger Hawk Center was destroyed. With no Hawks to send, I volunteered to deliver the news while Donovan recuperates."

"Hmm. The King is in his Winter Palace in Southport for the next few months. Is there any immediate threat?" asked Edward. "No, S—Edward," said Rachel. "Good. Then I want you to give me a report on what the Royal Expeditionary Force has done since leaving Kingston three months ago, ending with the current situation in Three Forks."

Rachel sat down and explained about the trip by ship to Southport; how the Treasury was in order, but how they found that Sorcerer White in the 4th Regiment was a Changed One. "He accepted the Binding spell, and Donovan recommended that he be transferred to the Regional Mage's Office, in exchange for one of their Sorcerers," said Rachel. "Why?" asked Edward. "Donovan said that a Battalion Sorcerer who was under a Binding spell not to harm a human was useless, but that in the Regional Mage's Office, he could still hunt down rogue magicians and help the Enforcers maintain law and order."

Edward thought for a moment. "That's a good point. But why were you looking for Changed Ones in the Royal Guard? I thought you were just checking the Regional Mage's Offices." "We took all of the Concealment cloaks from the Academy in our wagon. We figured that this was an opportunity to get them all distributed quickly." Edward smiled. "That was an excellent idea! Where did you go after Southport?"

Rachel told Edward and Noland about the visits to Westport and Weaton, how Westport was in order, and that while the Weaton Treasury was a little short, it was because the town council was spending freely to help get the town back on its feet after the recent dragon attack. "Then we went to Prarrieville. The two sorcerers in town are human, but the treasury was almost empty. We interviewed the treasurer, Luke, but determined that it was his assistant, Miss Blaze, who was the culprit. We offered her some Truth Serum-laced tea, and she confessed that she was a Fire Dragon Changed One. We tethered her and continued the interrogation. She confessed to stealing the gold from the treasury and being involved in the weapons theft that you investigated years ago, Edward. She said that the Company Commander, Lieutenant Gravel, sold the missing weapons to a traveling peddler that visited Prarrieville about once a month, but that the Lieutenant had died of a heart attack some time back, and that that source of income had dried up." Edward nodded but remained calm. "Then what?"

"Then Donovan asked who had killed his mother, and Miss Blaze admitted that she did it. I'm so sorry, Edward. Donovan asked two more questions, and Miss Blaze admitted that the three blacksmiths in town were also Fire Dragon Changed Ones. Then, without another word, Donovan froze her to death." "He what?" asked Mage Kathy. "He used the Temperature Reduction spell and froze her to death, right in her chair." "But why?" asked Kathy.

"Because that's how my first wife, Joyce, was killed. She froze to death in mid-summer. Please continue, Rachel." "Major Gerald was very upset. He was angry with Donovan for not continuing the interrogation. He fined him one week's pay of five silvers." Edward reached into his pocket and extracted a gold. He slid it across his desk to Rachel. "This one's on me." "Sir, I mean, Edward, that's not necessary. We do not want for coin." "Nevertheless, five years ago I offered a one-gold reward for any information about who killed my wife. You two have earned it. Take it. I insist." Rachel reluctantly pocketed the coin.

"Wait," said Rachel, her mind catching something, "Your *first* wife?" she asked. Edward smiled and held up his left hand, displaying a wedding ring. "Yes, Kathy and I got married just before we left Baize. We would have invited you, but it was a very rushed event," said Edward. "Congratulations!" said Rachel. "At least you didn't have any *uninvited* guests," said Rachel, referring to the Stone Dragon Changed One that had transformed during her wedding to Donovan and wreaked havoc on the proceedings. Kathy laughed.

"Getting back to Prarrieville; what happened next?" asked Wizard Noland. "Donovan, Major Gerald, the two specialists, and I went to the blacksmith shop to find and detain the three Fire Dragon Changed Ones, but they were already gone. We searched Miss Blaze's house and found all but forty-five of the missing golds and returned the rest to the Prarrieville Treasury, with the recommendation that, in the future, two people conduct the monthly inventories." Mage Kathy nodded, "That's always been my policy."

"Later that night, Donovan apologized to Major Gerald and promised to do better in the future. They discussed where the Expeditionary Force should go next," said Rachel. "And what did they decide?" asked Edward. "Well, Donovan pointed out that the Treasury in Fairview was probably the biggest outside of Kingston and Southport, and posed the most risk." "That's undoubtedly true," said Edward. "So, you went to Fairview next?" "Well, Major Gerald took me and 2nd Company cross-country to Fairview, while 1st Company and Donovan went to Colton. We traveled under concealment." "Why?" asked Edward.

"Donovan said that he had a 'bad feeling' about Colton. He couldn't say why, just that he felt something was wrong there." Edward and Noland exchanged glances, but neither said anything. "So, what did you find in Fairview?" asked Kathy. "A well-run treasury, with an uncooperative treasurer. That idiot absolutely refused us entry into the vault, despite the written order signed by the King. I eventually had to spell him to sleep to gain entry," exclaimed Rachel. "And what did you find?" asked Edward. "That everything was perfectly in order. Not a copper missing." Kathy laughed again.

"What did Donovan find in Colton?" asked Wizard Noland. "Well, about a mile outside of town, Donovan got a very bad feeling again. He asked Captain Fletcher to take the company off the road into a grove of trees while he got out his map. When he used a Seeing spell, he found the 9th

Battalion arrayed in an "L-shaped" ambush with two companies dug in across the road and the other two in the woods between the road and the Amber River." Wizard Noland whistled. "What did the Expeditionary Force do?" asked Edward.

"Donovan, Healer Bone, and Specialist Lance went out ahead and circled around the 'open' (east) side of the ambush. They got around behind the two dug-in companies. Specialist Lance took out their rear sentry with his blowgun, then Donovan put a Silence spell around the Battalion Commander, and Mage Arnold, who was with him." "Why would the Regional Mage be with the Battalion Commander?" asked Wizard Noland.

"Because he had him under a Compulsion spell," said Rachel. "Donovan paralyzed Mage Arnold, then they all uncloaked and asked Captain Bond what he was doing, setting an ambush for the Royal Expeditionary Force." "What did he say?" asked Kathy. "According to Donovan, he yelled for his troops and magicians. Fortunately, the Silence spell prevented anyone from hearing him," said Rachel. "Wait, you're saying that Donovan paralyzed the mage, while holding a Silence spell on the two of them?" "Yes," replied Rachel. "He shouldn't be able to do that," said Edward quietly.

"As Donovan has explained it to me, he wasn't *holding* two spells, he was only holding the Silence spell, then he *cast* the Paralyze spell," said Rachel. "That's not really how it works," said Edward. "Anyway," Rachel continued, "Donovan realized that the Commander was under a

Compulsion spell by Mage Arnold, so he dissolved that spell," said Rachel. "That's three," murmured Edward. Noland nodded slightly. "Once the Compulsion spell was lifted, Captain Bond said that the battalion was awaiting a large gang of criminals who had been terrorizing travelers on the road. He insisted that he had orders that there be 'No survivors.' Sorcerer Scott, the Battalion Sorcerer, confirmed the order."

"Interesting," said Edward. "Then what happened?" "Well, Sorceress Janice, Mage Arnold's assistant came up and tried to kill Donovan with the Kill spell. He removed her right hand. Then she tried to change into a dragon, but without her hand, the Change spell wouldn't work. Donovan asked Lance to put her to sleep with his blowgun, since he couldn't hold the Paralyze spell, and still conjure the Sleep spell. When the two Changed Ones woke up in the city jail, neither had hands. Sorceress Janice drank copious amounts of Truth Serum-laced water and spilled her guts over the next several hours. She was a Snow Dragon Changed One, and she said that Mage Arnold was a Fire Dragon. Mage Arnold was in the next cell, but Donovan cast a Silence spell on him so Janice couldn't hear him shouting for her to stop talking."

"Eventually, Janice ran out of information and fell asleep. Donovan told Mage Arnold that he only wanted one thing from him: the location of the Fire Dragon colony. Arnold refused and died of thirst four days later." "That was a good try, but I've already located the Fire Dragon colony in the Grey Mountains in Baize," said Edward. "What happened to Sorceress Janice?" asked Kathy. "Donovan slipped some Death Serum into her water. She died peacefully," said Rachel.

"What about the Treasury?" asked Edward. "It was empty," replied Rachel, "but with the information we got from Janice, we recovered all but fifty of the 500 missing golds." "That means that the Colton Regional Mage's Office is currently unmanned," said Noland. "You're going to have to assign some magicians to them, Edward." "Me? I thought that assignment of magicians in Franconia was your job," Edward said to Noland. "Only because the Chief of Military Wizardry post was vacant. It's your responsibility now. I'm responsible for training the sorcerers, then you assign and promote them," said Wizard Noland with a grin. "Then we need to talk once we're through here," grumbled Edward.

"Anyway," Rachel continued, "the Expeditionary Force met up in Riverton, which, happily, had no Changed Ones, and all the coin that they were supposed to have. From there we went to Farmdale, where the Royal Expeditionary Force were treated like conquering heroes by the citizens." "As well they should be," said Edward. "The Farmdale Treasury was intact, but nearly empty, on account of there being no crops harvested last year. Mayor Norville sends his regards and insists that they will do better this year," said Rachel.

Edward smiled, "I'm glad to hear that." "Their sorcerer gave us pause though," said Rachel. "How so?" asked Edward. "Well, he was six feet seven with red hair. Fortunately, he could use contractions. He got quite a laugh when we told him we thought he might be a dragon." Noland laughed, "It's good to know that not every magician with red hair is a Changed One." "So, from Farmdale, you went to Three Forks?" asked Edward.

"No, Hayford," replied Rachel. "Which was in order, except that the mayor might have been skimming a little off the top of the tax payments. Not much, maybe four or five golds, we told him we would check again next year. That should keep him in line. From there, Specialist Dirk and I flew to Haven, while Donovan and Lance went to Smithville." "Alone?" asked Kathy. "Yes, they're both small towns. We didn't expect any trouble." "Was there trouble?" asked Noland. "The Haven Treasury was empty, and the treasurer, the village Sorceress, Cindy, escaped. Haven is a small village, so only about forty golds were missing. I easily replicated them and pretended to find them in a bag in Cindy's closet. I think Specialist Dirk is suspicious, though." Edward laughed, "Dirk is no fool. I'm sure he knows that you replicated the coins. Don't worry about it."

"What did Donovan find in Smithville?" asked Edward. "That dragons have been using the old mines to hide in during the day. The local sorcerer saw a large dragon carrying a baby dragon, fly out of the mouth of the mine while he was looking for two human children who had gone 'exploring.' The mine was empty, but the children had been spelled to sleep. Donovan and the local sorcerer sealed up the mine entrances so that at least children and vagrants wouldn't be able to get in. He doubts that their efforts will stop a dragon though."

"Yes. I imagine a dragon could break through almost any barrier erected across the mine entrance," said Edward.

"What happened next?" "Well, we flew back to Hayford, and Donovan said he had a bad feeling about Three Forks," said Rachel. "Did he say why?" asked Edward. "No. Again, it was just a feeling. So Major Gerald asked him to use the Seeing spell again. That's when he found the nine dragons in the old rock quarry just north of Three Forks."

Edward steepled his fingers and looked at Wizard Noland, "AUGURIM?" he asked. Noland nodded and said, "It sounds like it. We need to verify it though." "What's 'AUGURIM?" asked Rachel, concerned. "It's the spell of Foresight," replied Wizard Noland. "We teach you 38 spells at the Academy, including the Seeing spell, which you know, is a rare ability. No one has been able to cast the spell of Foresight in almost a century, so we stopped trying to teach it to students at the Academy. It sounds like Donovan might have that ability."

"But he used no incantation!" said Rachel. "I understand, but we know so little about that spell, we may have it wrong. The gesture is placing the palm of your left hand on your forehead. Have you ever seen him do that?" asked Noland. "Many times," said Rachel. "When you return, you need to tell him about this spell. It could be invaluable in this conflict," said Edward. Rachel nodded.

"So, what happened after Donovan found the dragons in the rock quarry?" Rachel related the events of the trip to Three Forks, the entry to the garrison, the dragon attack, and how they had changed into Great Dragons and killed five of the attacking dragons. Then she told them about killing the

Stone Dragons, and how the remaining Great Dragon had collapsed a four-story building on top of them.

"Wait, you're saying that you and Donovan were trapped under tons of bricks and flaming timbers?" Rachel nodded, shivering at the memory. "How did you get out?" asked Kathy. "Well, first, Donovan conjured the Water spell to put out the flames," said Rachel, "but that left us in total darkness. We must have been buried under several feet of bricks, stone, and wood." "Which spell did you use to get out?" asked Edward.

"Let me ask you something," said Rachel. "Can you conjure a Blast spell while holding a shield?" "NO!" said Kathy forcefully. Edward and Noland looked at her in surprise. "A friend of mine tried that when we were apprentices together. She kept getting pelted by fragments of rock while we were practicing the Blast spell, so she conjured a protective shield and tried to fire through it." "What happened?" asked Noland. "The Blast rebounded off the shield and struck her. If I hadn't been there to heal her, she might have died," said Kathy.

"That's exactly what we were afraid of," said Rachel, "well, that and the chance that the Blast spell would crack the shield. We had the same concern about using the Remove spell—that it would just vanish Donovan's shield. We also didn't want to hit anyone digging through the rubble looking for us. I tried to use a strong Wind spell, but the bricks were too heavy." The three senior magicians sat in thought, considering which spell they would employ in a similar situation. "Edward, I understand that you've had to dig yourself out of graves a couple of times. Which spell did you use?" asked Rachel.

"I used the Dig spell. Of course, I wasn't holding a shield at the time. The top of the coffin kept the dirt off me, and there wasn't a ton of dirt above me," said Edward. "How did you get out?" "Well, I was getting a little panicked by then," said Rachel, "and I told Donovan that we needed to think of something soon before we ran short of air. That gave him the idea to use the Reduce spell." "Reduce?" asked Edward. "Yes, Donovan reduced the bricks and timbers above us to dust-size. He had to cast the spell three times, then I used another Wind spell to blow the dust off the top of the shield." "That's brilliant!" said Edward.

"Once the way was clear, Donovan released his shield and conjured a Strength Enhancement. He grabbed me and jumped clear of the debris field. Unfortunately, some of the bricks on the side of the hole fell in and hit my ankle before we jumped clear. As soon as Donovan healed me, he passed out," said Rachel.

"No wonder. It's a miracle he didn't pass out sooner. He's gotten strong," said Noland. Edward nodded. "We were discussing his not drinking anything between spells when he woke up in the garrison infirmary," said Rachel. "He said that after changing into a dragon, he no longer had a water bottle, so it really wasn't his fault that he passed out," said Rachel. The group laughed at the truth of the predicament.

"So, Donovan is still in Three Forks recovering. Did you have an opportunity to inventory the Treasury?" asked

Edward. "The Treasury building is the one the dragon toppled over on us, and I can tell you, there were no coins in the rubble," said Rachel. "Fortunately, the Treasury was just an office building, the coins were in a vault in City Hall, which was undamaged. Unfortunately, all three thousand gold coins in the vault were Seemings."

"Did you recover any of them?" asked Kathy. "Yes, the assistant treasurer was a Changed One, as were his now-deceased parents. He willingly submitted to the Binding spell, and all of the missing funds were recovered. We still haven't located the treasurer yet though," finished Rachel.

"What an extraordinary adventure you've had so far," said Edward. "Do you know what Major Gerald plans to do next?" "I believe the plan is to head for Frostberg, inspect the city, then secure water transport to go to Sundock, Eastport, Grotton, then back to Kingston," replied Rachel. "That sounds like a good plan. I would advise not remaining in Three Forks any longer than necessary. With winter approaching, you'll have a miserable time on the road if it starts snowing," advised Edward.

Rachel shivered at the thought. "Anyway, with the Messenger Hawk Center destroyed, I came to bring the news. By the way, Donovan says that the dragons made a mistake." "How's that?" asked Edward. "They attacked a city with seven magicians in it; nine after he and I arrived. If they had attacked, say Hayford, they probably could have razed the entire town and killed everyone." Edward and Noland considered this disturbing thought. "Donovan's right, and the dragons will probably come to the same conclusion eventually," said Edward. "So, what do we do?" asked Kathy.

"We should probably take the fight to them. We know where the Sea and Fire Dragon colonies are, and, as I understand it, there aren't many Great Dragons left. The Snow Dragons live in the Snow Fields and are probably dispersed, and not in a single colony. That just leaves the Stone Dragons, and we know how to deal with them."

"You're suggesting that we attack?" asked Noland. Edward nodded, "We can't just wait for the dragons to start picking off our smaller towns, one by one. We need to hurt them and bring them to the negotiating table." "Another peace treaty?" asked Noland. "It may be our best course of action. I need to speak with the King."

"Before you go rushing off to Southport, you need to see the message that Mage Gregory sent," said Wizard Noland, handing over the rolled-up parchment. Edward read the message, then handed it to Kathy. "What do you think, Michael?" asked Edward.

Wizard Noland smiled, "Have I told you about the end of Donovan's Sorcerer's Test? Well, as you know, we test the applicant's shields last. While Wizard Mira, Dylan, and I were striking Donovan's shield with every object in the Forces Training Area, Wizard Dylan conjured a cloud of sawdust, which he ignited and blew at your son with a Wind spell. Do you know what Donovan did? He extinguished the fireball with a Water spell before it even reached him."

Edward looked shocked and said, "He shouldn't have been able to do that!" "I know," said Wizard Noland, "Wizard Mira was most shocked." "Why? What's wrong with that?" asked Rachel.

Edward looked at Noland, who nodded. "Rachel, a sorcerer should only be able to cast one spell at a time. Donovan is mistaken that holding one spell while casting another is somehow different. It's the power drain from the spells that matters. When we conduct the Mage's Test, we ask sorcerers to cast and hold two spells simultaneously for three hours. Most sorcerer's conjure Hearing and Sight Enhancements, which are the least taxing. Wizard Noland could have promoted Donovan to mage when he cast the Water spell while holding a shield, especially considering how exhausting the rest of the Sorcerer's Test is."

Edward retrieved the parchment from Kathy, opened his desk drawer, and extracted a rubber stamp and ink pad. He stamped "APPROVED" on the parchment, quickly replicated the message, and handed a copy to Wizard Noland. "This is for the Academy records," said Edward. Noland smiled and put the parchment in his pocket. "Rachel, if you would please rise," said Edward.

Rachel stood up, uncertain of what was happening. Edward rose and said, *Sorceress Rachel Francis, you and Sorcerer Donovan Francis are both hereby promoted to the rank of Battle Mage, for the heroic defense of the city of Three Forks, and on the recommendations of Mages Gregory and Roark of that city. It will be so recorded in the records of the Wizards Academy. Congratulations.*

Chapter Five:

SUSPICIONS

Mage Lisa knocked on the door to Maria's cottage, and Maria answered quickly. "Hello, Mrs. Perrucci, I just came by to inform you that I visited Mr. Stone this morning and I determined that he can, in fact, use contractions. Also, the scent you detected on his handkerchief was embalming fluid. Mr. Stone apparently keeps a supply of handkerchiefs in his work area, and he did not realize that the odor had seeped into the cloth of the handkerchiefs. He said that, since he works with the embalming fluid and other chemicals all day, he has become desensitized to the smell," said Lisa.

"Well, that's a relief," said Maria. "Did he happen to say when my father's body would be ready for burial?" "No, I am sorry, but I did not ask about that. I had other things on my mind. It usually only takes a couple of days. I suggest you go by tomorrow and ask. By the way, Mr. Stone's brother died unexpectedly in Haven last week, and he just received the message today. So, the final arrangements for your father will be made by his assistant, Miss Franks," said Mage Lisa.

"Then I will visit tomorrow," said Maria. "Thank you for investigating my concern. I know that you have a lot of other things to occupy your time." "It was no trouble at all," said Lisa. "I am sure that I will see you around town. Good day." Mage Lisa left the cottage and walked briskly down the street, headed back to her office. Maria watched her go. She'd noticed that the mage didn't use a single contraction during their conversation, and her suspicions were now greater than ever that there was something wrong in the town of Sundock.

"Are you serious?" asked Rachel. "Completely serious," said Edward, smiling. "Now, why don't you go see your parents and tell them the good news, then meet us later at the King's Table Tavern for a celebratory lunch at midday? I'll get us some reservations. Michael, you are, of course, invited." "I would be honored," said Wizard Noland.

Rachel rushed out of Wizard Edward's office and into town. When she arrived at her father's tailor shop, there was a line of customers extending out the front door. Rachel pushed her way past them, receiving scowling looks from the customers. Her father was in the process of taking the measurements of a rather large woman, and Rachel's mother was translating her father's sign language for the customer. "You said you wanted this dress in green velvet, correct?" "Yes," said the rotund customer, "with gold trim." "Of course," said Rachel's mother.

Looking up, Rachel's father saw her and quickly placed the last pin in the paper mock-up of the dress he was designing and rose to his feet. Startled by his abrupt movement, Rachel's mother looked around to see what had caused her husband's quick actions. "Rachel! Welcome back, dear! We thought that you'd be away for some months yet!" said her mother excitedly.

"I just came back to deliver a letter to the King and Wizard Noland," said Rachel. "I can't stay long, but while I was in town, I couldn't resist coming to see you." Her father gave her an enthusiastic hug, then signed, *Where's Donovan?* Rachel signed back, *He's in Three Forks. What's with all the customers?*

Mr. Turner grinned and signed, *I have become the preferred tailor of the nobility here in Kingston. Everyone was so impressed by your dress at the Royal Ball that I can barely keep up with all of the new orders. Being the 'Official Tailor of the Wizards Academy' has not hurt either. That's wonderful,* signed Rachel. *Can you two break away long enough to join me for lunch at the King's Table Tavern at midday? Donovan's father, his new wife, Mage Kathy, and Wizard Noland will be joining us.*

"We wouldn't miss it for the world, darling. We'll just have our new assistant, Jośe, take care of the shop for a couple of hours," said Rachel's mother. Mr. Turner nodded enthusiastically. *Then I'll leave you to your work. I'll see you at noon,* signed Rachel. She made her way out of the shop, past the glares of the waiting customers, and headed toward her house.

The cottage was just as they left it. Rachel opened the front door and was relieved to see that their house cleaner had been keeping the dust down and that everything was in order. She settled into one of the armchairs in the living room and drifted off to sleep, despite the excitement of the day.

She was awakened a couple of hours later when their housekeeper, Ahmanda, opened the front door and was startled by her unexpected presence. "It's OK, Ahmanda, I got into town late last night and will be leaving later this evening. I didn't mean to startle you, I just drifted off to sleep in this chair. I have a meeting at noon with Wizard Noland at the King's Table Tavern," said Rachel.

"Then you better get going," said Ahmanda, "It's almost noon now." Rachel rose quickly and headed out the door. She was embarrassed at having slept so long, and it wouldn't do to keep Wizard Noland, Wizard Edward, Mage Kathy, and her parents waiting. She arrived at the tavern just after the noon bell rang and found the others already at the table. She noticed that both Edward and Noland knew sign language, and were having a conversation with her father, while Mage Kathy spoke with her mother.

"Ah, there's the guest of honor!" said Edward. Rachel blushed and began to apologize for being late, but Edward brushed her off. "No need for apologies, my dear. After all you've been through lately, I'm surprised you can keep your eyes open. I was just telling your father and mother about yours and Donovan's promotions."

The meal was one of the best Rachel could remember, and she was sorry that Donovan was not there with them. As the dessert (blueberry cobbler) was being served, her father stiffened, and after the waiter left, signed to Wizard Noland, *That waiter smells like a lizard.*

Donovan wandered the streets of Three Forks looking for ways to help the people. The rubble from the Treasury building was almost cleared away. The Sorcerers from the Regional Mage's Office had been reducing the size of the bricks and moving them to an adjacent lot, where they returned them to normal size for when the reconstruction effort began.

The body of the Three Forks Treasurer had been found among the rubble. He had apparently been seeking shelter inside the building when the dragon pushed it over. Fortunately, there had only been two fatalities when the treasury collapsed, the treasurer and Sorcerer Walt from the Three Forks Regional Mage's Office. All the other citizens had fled the area when the two Stone Dragons began smashing everything in their path as they walked down Main Street.

Donovan nodded to the soldiers who were stationed on almost every street corner, keeping the peace and preventing any more looting. He noted the presence of the Royal Expeditionary Force soldiers under their Concealment cloaks, and whispered to them as he passed, asking if they needed anything.

Finding little else to do, Donovan returned to the garrison and volunteered to brew some Healing Serum for the local healers, figuring that this was probably the best use of his time. Major Franklin agreed enthusiastically and asked Mage Gregory to show Donovan where the serums laboratory was.

The first order of business for Donovan was to replicate the ingredients used to make Healing Serum. Most of the stocks of supplies had been depleted due to the demand for Serum. After several hours of replicating Eucalyptus leaves, bone marrow, yarrow root, and the other herbs required to make Healing Serum, Donovan rested a bit and had something to eat and drink.

After his respite, Donovan began making Healing Serum in earnest. He used every cauldron in the laboratory and had a dozen bubbling serums in progress simultaneously when Mage Roark stopped by to check on his progress.

The Regional Mage was stunned to see so much serum being produced at once. "How can you make so much at one time?" he asked. "I could make more, but I only found twelve cauldrons," replied Donovan. "If you could find or replicate more cauldrons, I could make more." "Where did you find all the ingredients? I thought our stocks were running low," said Mage Roark. "I replicated more supplies before I started. This batch should be ready in less than a glass," said Donovan, pointing to the half-empty hourglass on the table.

"Could you use some help?" asked Mage Roark. Donovan smiled, "No one *ever* declines help." "Then I'll send over the two surviving magicians from my office. They could both use some practice making Serums," said Mage Roark. "What are the most common injuries?" asked Donovan. The Mage thought for a moment, then said, "Most of the injuries are burns or broken bones. Why do you ask?"

"Because my father taught me that you can make Healing Serum for specific types of injuries," replied Donovan. "For burns, you add a half-measure more agave, and for broken bones, a quarter measure more bone marrow to the Serum." Mage Roark was surprised by this news. "I had no idea that you could tailor a Healing Serum to a specific type of injury. How did your father discover this?" "He had lots of practice as a Battle Mage," explained Donovan, "and I believe that he experimented on wounded horses and other animals. He told me that the magician that invented Healing Serums never claimed that they couldn't be improved. It's just that once they found a formula that worked, he or she stopped experimenting."

"Well, I'm glad Edward survived the fight with the dragon; we were all saddened to hear about his supposed demise. I'll go find my magicians and send them over right away. Just don't overdo it. I don't want to have to explain it to your wife if you pass out again." Donovan nodded his understanding and took a drink from a flagon of water. "Not to worry, sir, making Serums is easy."

A glass later, Sorceress Janet and Sorcerer Trevor appeared to help. Donovan asked Janet to cool the finished

Serums and pour the contents into vials and label them with the date. While Trevor cleaned the used cauldrons and then replicated them, in order to double the number of Serums they could make at a time. While they were doing that, Donovan worked to replicate the ingredients required to make Healing Serum. Once all of the cauldrons were clean and ready, the three magicians resumed making Healing Serum. Donovan gave Sorceress Janet and Sorcerer Trevor instructions on how to tailor the serums to be more effective for burns or broken bones, and half of the serums were made for each ailment. Donovan felt a little uneasy giving orders to the older, more experienced magicians, but they didn't seem to mind.

By the end of the evening, Donovan, Trevor, and Janet had produced 84 vials of Healing Serum, and Donovan had refilled the Serum supply stocks twice. "I don't think anyone has ever made so much serum in one day before," said Sorceress Janet. "I just hope we have enough," said Donovan. "Let's get this to the garrison infirmary, so they can start administering it." The three magicians carried the chests of Healing Serum to the infirmary, which was overflowing with injured citizens of Three Forks.

There were beds in the hallways and in the infirmary cafeteria. Donovan immediately ordered the three beds in the dining area moved to another location, chastising the infirmary personnel for putting the injured people so close to where food was being prepared. "How could you allow patients to be put in the dining area?" Donovan asked the healer in charge of the infirmary. "I had no idea that my staff put them there," said Ashleigh. "I've been working almost non-stop since the dragon attack. Thank you for correcting that oversight."

Donovan informed the Healer about the new supplies of Healing Serum and how some of it was constructed to be more effective against certain injuries. Ashleigh was very grateful for the new supply of Healing Serum. "Our stocks ran short almost immediately," she said, "so we've had to limit Healing Serum to only the most severely injured. With this much, we should be able to release many of the patients, and get the beds out of the hallways and supply rooms."

"Are there any injured soldiers still here?" asked Donovan. "I'd like to get them healed and back to duty." Healer Ashleigh said that there were maybe twenty soldiers in the infirmary as well as Sorcerer Cliff, from the 6th Regiment, who was being treated for burns.

Donovan plucked one of the Serums made for burns out of the chest and said, "Take me to Sorcerer Cliff. We should heal him first so that he can get back to duty." They proceeded to the second floor of the infirmary, where they found Sorcerer Cliff with heavy bandages on both of his arms. He sat up (painfully) as Donovan approached.

Healer Ashleigh said, "Sorcerer Cliff, this is Sorcerer Donovan. He's been making Healing Serum all day, and he has some Serum tailored for burn victims, for you." "Thank you, Donovan," said Sorcerer Cliff, "I am eager to get out of here and resume my duties."

Donovan noted the lack of a contraction, and, as he leaned over the cot, he detected a 'dragony' smell coming from Sorcerer Cliff. "Ashleigh, would you get Sorcerer Cliff a glass of water?" Ashleigh looked confused, but went to the washroom to fill a mug of water for the patient. When she returned, Donovan said quietly, "Ashleigh, please go and find either Mage Roark or Mage Gregory and bring them here. I'll take care of Sorcerer Cliff." Ashleigh was alarmed by the request, but hurried to comply with Donovan's instructions. Donovan took a vial of Truth Serum from his robe and added it to the mug of water before presenting it to Sorcerer Cliff.

Sorcerer Cliff emptied the cup eagerly, believing it to contain the Healing Serum. He sighed with relief as he mistakenly perceived the Serum to be healing his self-inflicted burns. Donovan remained at his bedside and was relieved when Mage Gregory arrived quickly.

"How are you feeling, Cliff?" asked Mage Gregory. "Much better now," replied the Changed One. Donovan placed a Tether spell on Cliff, constricting his arms and hands and binding them to the cot. "What are you doing?" asked Mage Gregory. "I'm confining a Dragon Changed One," replied Donovan. "Cliff, what dragon clan do you belong to?" Sorcerer Cliff struggled against the Truth Serum, but eventually said, "I am a Fire Dragon." Mage Gregory immediately cast a Silence spell around the three of them, and the interrogation began.

Cliff eventually admitted to having abandoned the city during the dragon attack and flying to the rock quarry to inform any surviving dragons about the humans' ability to change into dragons. Donovan cursed, knowing that their carefully guarded secret was out and that it would soon be common knowledge among the dragons. He wondered how that would affect the dragon's actions in the future.

Cliff grudgingly accepted the Binding spell and the transfer to the Regional Mage's Office. "We need to let Wizard Noland know that our secret is out," said Donovan. "The next Dragon Council meets in less than a month, and I'm sure that the news of our ability will spread."

"But, we still don't have any Messenger Hawks," said Mage Gregory. "Well then, after I show you and the other Sorcerers how to change into a dragon, I guess I need to get Major Gerald's permission to head back to Kingston myself."

"Are you certain"? signed Edward. *"Yes,"* replied Brian. Quickly casting a Silence spell around the table, Noland asked, "What do you suggest we do?" "Well, we certainly don't want to confront him with all of these people in here," said Edward. "Let's wait until closing time."

The four magicians finished their meal and paid the bill. The celebratory mood had evaporated with the discovery of the Changed One. Mr. and Mrs. Turner returned home while Edward, Noland, Kathy, and Rachel remained near the

King's Table Tavern, ensuring that the Changed One did not slip away unnoticed.

As the last drunken customer staggered out just after midnight, Noland said, "Rachel, you wait out here while Edward, Kathy, and I go in. Make sure he doesn't slip out a back door." Rachel nodded her understanding as Edward and the others quietly vanished the door lock and entered the tavern. Almost as soon as they entered, a side door opened, and the Changed One waiter emerged. He looked around cautiously, then proceeded rapidly down the street.

After Rachel seized him with a strong Tether spell, the alarmed waiter began screaming for help. "HELP! THIEVES!" he shouted. Rachel cursed and quickly conjured a Silence spell, which prevented any further cries from being heard. Holding two spells at once, Rachel felt the power drain immediately and took a drink from her water bottle.

Edward, Noland, and Kathy emerged from the side door and moved quickly to the Tethered Changed One. "That was quick thinking with the Silence spell," said Kathy. "How are you holding up?" Rachel said, "The power drain is noticeable but manageable." Wizard Noland smiled. "Spoken like a Mage."

"So, let's get this fellow back inside where we can have a conversation in private, shall we?" asked Edward. The four magicians escorted the bound and silenced waiter back inside the tavern and seated him at the closest table. "I'll just go inform the owner that we need to use this area for a while, and that he'll be compensated for the trouble," said Wizard Noland.

Once Noland had returned, Rachel released the Silence spell, and Edward asked, "What is your name?" The frantic waiter said, "I am Alfred, sir, and I assure you that I have done nothing wrong!" Edward stared at Alfred for long seconds before the waiter confessed, "All right! Maybe I took the three silvers that the drunken deputy minister forgot he left on the table! But that is no reason for four wizards to detain me!" Edward laughed, "Is that why you think we've secured you? No, sir. It's because you are a Dragon Changed One. What clan are you?"

"Sir, I do not know what you are talking about. My name is Alfred Perch, and I live on Prince Street. I have worked here for five years, and the owner, Taylor, can vouch for me!" said Alfred desperately. "So, a Sea Dragon, eh?" asked Noland. "We don't see too many of your kind around Kingston. I'll tell you what, you have a drink with us and we'll give you a chance to convince us that you are who you say you are, and not what we suspect."

Kathy walked behind the bar and poured five mugs of ale from the tapped keg, covertly slipping a vial of Truth Serum into one of the mugs. Placing the drugged ale before Alfred, and instructing Rachel to remove the Tether spell from Alfred's right arm, she said, "Now Alfred, I advise you to make no sudden movements. Just sit there and drink your ale while we talk."

Needing the liquid courage, Alfred slowly picked up and drained the mug of ale (and Truth Serum) in one pull, then he wiped his lips on his sleeve. The four magicians sat silently sipping their drinks, giving the Truth Serum a minute to take effect. Then Edward said, "So, Alfred, you are a Sea Dragon Changed One who has been working here as a waiter for five years. Once the dragon attacks began, why did you remain?"

Alfred struggled against the Truth Serum briefly, but then confessed, "I bear humans no ill will. While my life here has not been especially prosperous, I have enough. Believe it or not, life as a Sea Dragon can get very boring after a few decades." "How have you evaded detection by the Kingston Regional Mages for all this time?" asked Noland. "Magic-users seldom come here. It is too expensive for them. In the last five years, I have only seen magic-users in the King's Table Tavern maybe a dozen or so times. It is the same story for all of the Changed Ones in the city."

This news shocked the magicians, and Noland asked, "You mean that there are more Changed Ones in Kingston? How many?" Alfred smiled, "Perhaps a dozen or more," he said, "all in occupations that go unnoticed by you magic-users. Some of us have positions in high-end shops, which offer goods and services which are too costly for magicians. Others are tanners, refuse-haulers, or undertakers, positions that you all consider 'low-class' and beneath your notice."

"Astounding," said Edward. "Undertakers? I would never have guessed it." "Yes," said Alfred, "also, many of the blacksmiths in Franconia are Fire Dragon Changed Ones.

It is an occupation that suits their nature, and they enjoy the heat, the fire, and the red-hot steel. Stone Dragon Changed Ones find work as masons or morticians, while Sea Dragons prefer work near the water."

"And you say that there are 'dozens' in the city?" asked Rachel. "Maybe several dozen," said Alfred smugly. "Will you help us find them?" asked Kathy. Alfred shook his head, "No. There is little trust between our races, whatever you do to me, I will not betray my clan or my dragon cousins in the city. We have done you no wrong."

"Very well," said Edward. "I will offer you the same choice we have given to the other Changed Ones we have discovered. Will you submit to a Binding spell, never to harm a human? If so, we will leave you as you are: a waiter at the King's Table Tavern. If you do not agree, then we will have to resort to more drastic measures."

Alfred nodded in understanding. "What happens if I violate this Binding spell?" "You will die. Instantly," said Noland. The Changed One thought for several minutes, and eventually decided that there really was no choice. The Binding spell was cast, and Wizard Edward said, "Just to be clear, I would consider warning the other Changed Ones in the city as 'doing harm to humans,' so I suggest that you just confine yourself to your job here." Alfred nodded in understanding.

After confiscating the three silvers that Alfred had unlawfully taken from the inebriated deputy minister, Noland gave them to the tavern owner as compensation for the inconvenience. The four magicians left the tavern, after replacing the vanished lock on the door. They observed Alfred moving up the street, slowly, towards his apartment.

"We need to discuss this development in the morning," said Edward. "Rachel, can you bring your father to my office around ten tomorrow morning? Michael, we will also need Mage Curtis." Rachel said, "I had hoped to return to Three Forks tonight, but I guess it's too late for that now. What do you want my father for?" "He seems to have an ability to detect Changed Ones, probably because of his hearing impairment. I would like him to consider searching the city for us, with magical support, of course. While my signing ability is good, I use it mostly for military conversations, which is why I would like you to be present tomorrow. I'm sure the Royal Expeditionary Force can do without you for one more day, Mage Rachel."

While the request was made in a kindly tone, Rachel understood that it was not really a suggestion, but an order from the Franconian Chief of Military Wizardry. "We'll be there, sir," said Rachel. She proceeded to her parents' house above the tailor shop to let them know that she was OK, and to inform her father about the meeting with Wizard Edward the next morning. Then she went home and tried to sleep. By the time she got there, it was almost three in the morning.

WIZARD DANIEL

Chapter Six:
VISIONS

Donovan landed at the Wizards Academy's boat dock just after nine in the morning. As he opened the portal, he met Wizard Daniel and a dozen Level Three students who were headed out for a 'Magic on Water' lesson.

"Donovan! What brings you back so soon? Are you looking for Rachel?" asked Wizard Daniel. "No, sir. I have an urgent message for Wizard Noland," said Donovan. "There's been a lot of those lately," said Daniel, "well, you'd better hurry. I think he has a meeting in the palace in less than an hour."

Donovan nodded his thanks and rushed across the Academy to the Headmaster's cottage. He arrived just as Noland was walking out the door. "Donovan! What are you doing here? I thought you were in Three Forks, recovering."

"I'm completely recovered, sir, but while interrogating a Changed One that we captured in Three Forks, we learned something that you need to know about. Since Three Forks still doesn't have any Messenger Hawks, I came myself," said Donovan. "Well, I'm on my way to the palace for a meeting with the new Franconian Chief of Military Wizardry. You might as well come along," said Noland. "Has Rachel headed back to Three Forks yet?" asked Donovan. "I hope not," said Wizard Noland with a smile. "Since she is supposed to attend this meeting."

While Donovan was curious about who the new Chief of Military Wizardry was, he decided to hold his questions. He knew that if Wizard Noland wanted him to know who it was, he would have told him. They walked up to the third floor of the palace and proceeded to the corner office. Noland knocked on the door, then entered saying, "I found another stray Sorcerer wandering around my Academy this morning, and decided to bring him with me. He claims to have an urgent message for you."

Donovan entered the impressive office and found his father standing behind the desk. "Dad! When did you get back? Wait, 'Chief of Military Wizardry'? When did that happen?" Edward smiled as he came around the desk and gave Donovan a hug. "So many questions," he quipped.

"I returned about two weeks ago and was appointed to this prestigious post just before the King left for Southport for the winter. Once we finished the reservoir, King Donald wanted us out of Baize as soon as possible," said Edward. "US?" asked Donovan. "You mean the King allowed Mage Kathy to leave with you?" "Yes. King Donald released Kathy from all obligations to the Kingdom of Baize and allowed her to return to Franconia with me," said Edward.

"That's good," said Donovan, "I really like her." "Why, thank you, Donovan. I really like you too," said Kathy as she entered the office pushing a tea cart. Donovan blushed. "I seem to be short one teacup," said Kathy, "I was only expecting six." "Allow me," said Donovan, as he quickly replicated another teacup.

As they waited for Rachel and her father to arrive, Edward filled Donovan in on the events of the previous evening. "Dozens!" exclaimed Donovan. "How could we have missed that many?" "Apparently, we were looking in the wrong places," said Noland. He related Alfred's description of the occupations normally sought after by Changed Ones.

"Well, the Regional Mage is really going to have his hands full," said Donovan. As he spoke, there was a knock on the door and Mage Curtis entered. "Did I hear something about having my hands full?" he asked. Wizard Noland laughed and said, "Yes, and we'll get to that problem in a minute. Mage Curtis, you remember my son, Sorcerer Donovan." "It's nice to see you again Donovan. I've heard good things about you." said Curtis. "I've heard the same about you, sir," replied Donovan.

As Curtis and Donovan shook hands, there was another knock on the door. Donovan slipped behind the door as it opened, and Rachel and her father entered. "Good morning, Wizard Edward," said Rachel, as the door closed behind her. "Tag, you're it," said Donovan touching her on the shoulder. Rachel smiled at the familiar voice and touch. "I was still 'it' from the last time," she said turning and giving Donovan a kiss.

"What are you doing here?" Rachel asked. "I caught a Changed One, disguised as one of the Sorcerers in the 6th Regiment, and we learned something that I needed to inform Wizard Noland about. I was afraid that I was going to pass you on your way back to Three Forks," said Donovan. "I hear you had an adventure last night."

"Yes, and we'll get to that in a moment," said Edward, "but there's something we need to take care of first. Donovan, would you come stand over here please?" Donovan looked confused, but moved to stand beside his father. Edward took out a roll of parchment and read, formally:

"Sorcerer Donovan Francis, for your heroic defense of the city of Three Forks, and on the recommendations of Battle Mage Gregory and Regional Mage Roark, you are hereby promoted to the rank of Battle Mage. This advancement has already been recorded in the Archives of the Franconian Wizards Academy. Congratulations."

Donovan stood, stunned, "But, I've only been a Sorcerer for…" "It doesn't matter how long you've been anything, son. We promote based on ability, not longevity," said Edward. "In that case," said Donovan, "you need to promote Rachel too!" Edward smiled, "I did that yesterday, and once is enough. Now, let's discuss the events of last night, and what brought you to Kingston."

The assembled magicians discussed what they learned from the Changed One, Alfred, the night before, and Mage Curtis was disturbed by the news that there were potentially dozens of Dragon Changed Ones in Kingston. "Finding them all is going to be quite a challenge," said Curtis. "Especially since I only have one Sorcerer on my staff."

"I've considered this, and until I identify additional Sorcerers to fill out your office, I'm authorizing you to use the eight Sorcerers currently assigned to the 1st and 2nd Regiments here in Kingston, for the express purpose of discovering and dealing with all of the Changed Ones in the city. The Regimental Battle Mages will remain with their commands, but the Battalion Sorcerers will report to you beginning tomorrow." Mage Curtis looked relieved.

Edward then turned to Mr. Turner and began signing. After last night, I would ask that you help us in this search. I believe that you have mentioned that you have noticed that some of your customers smell odd, and that you have noticed the scent in other places in the city. If I provide a magician to escort you, would you be willing to help us find and identify these Changed Ones?

I would be happy to help, but my shop is currently overwhelmed with orders. If you left a Sorcerer in my shop with me, I could point out any of these 'Changed Ones' who come in, but I can't just leave my shop unattended at this time, signed Mr. Turner.

What about on Endday afternoons? asked Rachel. Aren't you normally closed then? *Yes,* signed Mr. Turner, *My shop closes at noon on Enddays. We could search the city then. Excellent!* signed Edward. *Mage Curtis here will come by your shop on Endday and walk around the city with you after you close.*

That part of the meeting concluded, Mr. Turner was excused to return to his tailor shop. Once he was gone, Edward turned to Donovan and said, "So, Mage Donovan, what was so urgent that you flew here from Three Forks to tell us?"

Donovan grinned at being addressed as 'Mage,' then said, "The cat is out of the bag. The dragons know that humans have learned how to change into dragons."

"One of us needs to go tell Cobalt and Sky about how the human magic-users can change themselves into dragons," said Gek. "Can we just wait for the next meeting of the Dragon Council?" asked Azure. "I do not think so," replied Gek. "We are incurring great losses to these human 'Changed Ones.' I think we should pause our attacks until we devise a strategy for dealing with this unexpected threat."

"Do you think that a human in dragon form could infiltrate the colony?" asked Azure. "I deem that unlikely," said Gek. "If an unknown dragon suddenly appeared on Acropo, it would arouse suspicion, and only Sorceress Anne knows the way into the caverns," said Gek. "She may have told another magic-user," worried Gek.

"It would take a very brave human to enter into the caverns alone…" said Azure. "I agree, but what if a dozen magic-users gained entrance? Could the clan fight off that many?" "You ask disturbing questions," said Azure. "Very well, I will leave tonight." "At least Anna is eating solid food now," said Gek.

"Yes, but Richard is growing much faster than I expected. Very soon, he will grow tired of this place, and our re-location options are very limited, unless you can find a way to change back into a human," said Azure. "Maybe Cobalt will have a useful suggestion," said Gek. "I miss Ard," said Azure, sadly. "So do I. I wonder, do you think his Binding spell is still active?"

Azure thought for a moment, then said, "There is really no way to tell. If we kill either Donovan or Andrew, we might still die. There is really no way to test the Binding spell." "How many of us are still bound to the spell?" wondered Gek. Ard, Gek's ancient grandfather, had cast a Binding spell on the members of the Dragon Council, requiring them to abide by their ancient agreement not to eat people, and he added an additional requirement that the dragons must protect any offspring of Wizard Amanda, who was a dragon-friend of old. The dragons had determined that there were only two surviving members of Amanda's line: Sorcerer Donovan and Mage Andrew.

"I think there are only five of us left: you, me, Cobalt, the Snow Dragon, Bliz, and the Stone Dragon, Jasper," said Gek. "The two Fire Dragons, Victor and Lumen, the Stone Dragon, Amber, and the Snow Dragon, Frost have all perished in battle, along with your father, Teal, of course," said Gek. "We know that Andrew is still aboard the HMS VALOR, somewhere in the Eastern Ocean. Do you know where Donovan is?" asked Azure.

"I thought he was still at the Wizards Academy, being guarded by a Changed One. But the Fire Dragon Changed

One in Three Forks told me that a Sorcerer named Donovan arrived at the garrison just before our attack, and that he was married to another magician named Rachel," said Gek. "That could be a big problem!" said Azure.

"I know," replied Gek. "If the magic-user who arrived in Three Forks and foiled our attack is indeed the man that we are bound to protect, then we need to kill his wife before they have any children."

Donovan's pronouncement left the assembled magicians stunned. "Why do you believe that, son?" asked Wizard Edward. "After I recovered from my overexertion," said Donovan, "I wandered around Three Forks, looking for ways to make myself useful. I ended up in the garrison Serums Laboratory, making Healing Serum. Between myself and the two Sorcerers from Mage Roark's office, we made about 84 vials of Healing Serum in one day."

Wizard Noland whistled, "That's quite an accomplishment. Even for three of you working together." "I suppose," said Donovan, "but I had to replicate serum ingredients three times in order to have enough. Anyway, when we were done, we took the serums to the garrison infirmary to give to the injured. One of the casualties was Sorcerer Cliff from the 6th Regiment. He had burns on both his arms. While I was talking to him, I noticed that he didn't use contractions, and when I leaned in close to examine his burns, I detected the faint scent of dragon."

"So, what did you do?" asked Mage Kathy. "I gave him Truth Serum instead of Healing Serum and had the Chief Healer summon Mage Gregory. Once he arrived, I tethered Sorcerer Cliff to his cot and questioned him. He admitted to being a Fire Dragon Changed One, and actually boasted about fleeing the battle and flying to the rock quarry where he told the surviving Great and Snow dragons about how humans have learned how to change into dragons."

"But, how would he know that?" asked Mage Curtis. Donovan reddened, "Because I told all of the magicians in the garrison all about it just before the dragons attacked! I was so stupid! I never stopped to consider that one of them might be a Changed One. This is my fault." Edward put a comforting hand on Donovan's shoulder, "You can't blame yourself, son. You were in a hurry to save the garrison and the city. No one can think of everything." Donovan nodded sadly.

"The question is, What will the dragons do with this information?" pondered Wizard Noland. "Will it make them more cautious, or more aggressive? I wonder." "I think it will encourage these multi-clan attacks," said Rachel. "I would think that the Snow and Sea Dragons will be very unlikely to attack alone, when it seems that a single Great Dragon can rout them." "I think Rachel's right," said Donovan. "Although it seems they decided on the combined dragon attacks without the knowledge of our ability."

"So, what's our next move?" asked Wizard Noland. Everyone looked at Edward. "First, I think I need to go see the King and get his permission to resume the attack on the Coral Islands. Maybe we can bring the Sea Dragons back to the bargaining table, if we don't try to add anything ridiculous like 'fishing rights' to the agreement. I had Wizard Cassandra bring me a copy of the treaty the Sea Dragons rejected, and it's actually a good thing that we did not agree to that treaty." "Why is that?" asked Wizard Noland.

"Because, while the treaty required the dragons not to attack our sailors or port facilities, it didn't say anything about them not attacking humans who were not sailors. I suspect that the attack on Three Forks may have been planned even before they rejected the treaty, and they were planning to attack our land forces. I've always said that these creatures are cunning. Our next agreement has to be that they will not attack humans." The other magicians nodded their understanding and agreement.

"Next, after my wife passes the Wizard's Test tomorrow, she needs to return to Baize and encourage King Donald to attack the Fire Dragon colony," said Edward. "Wait, I'm taking the Wizard's Test tomorrow?" asked Kathy. "Wait, your wife?" asked Donovan almost simultaneously with Kathy's question. Edward smiled, "YES, to both of you. Kathy, you need to be on equal footing with Wizard James and the Baizian Chief of Military Wizardry, or whatever they call the position, and, Donovan, meet your new step-mother."

Surprisingly, Donovan smiled and said, "Good luck on the test tomorrow, Mom." Everyone laughed.

"Now, Donovan, you and Rachel need to get back to Three Forks immediately. I want the Royal Expeditionary Force moving to Frostberg by the end of the week. Tell Major Gerald to make all possible speed to Frostberg, then find a ship heading to Sundock, Eastport, Grotton, then back here. We need to finish rooting out the Changed Ones disguised as magicians and get those Concealment cloaks distributed as soon as possible." Donovan and Rachel nodded, both dreading the flight back to Three Forks with no sleep.

"Mage Curtis, you need to begin searching for these Changed Ones in Kingston immediately. We can't risk them attacking or, worse yet, fleeing to join forces with the other hostile dragon clans. Michael, how is the accelerated training coming? When will I have additional Sorcerers I can deploy?" Wizard Noland scratched his bald head and said, "I need another month, Edward. Some of the provisional Mentors are just not ready yet."

"Focus on shields, Blast spells, Tethers, Healing and Sensing Enhancements, and the Kill spell, of course. We may have to send them out before they are fully ready." Noland nodded. "Mage Curtis, you are dismissed. The rest of you stay for a moment," ordered Edward.

Mage Curtis left quickly, headed for his office to plan how they would conduct the search of Kingston. After he closed the door, Donovan asked, "What else?" Edward smiled, "We need to explore something, son. Rachel told us that on your way north, you said that you 'had a bad feeling' about first Colton, and then Three Forks. Can you describe this feeling?"

Donovan thought hard, "I really can't describe it. It was just a gut feeling that something was wrong as we approached each of those two towns." Edward nodded, "Now, I want you to look at this wall map, and examine the position of the four towns the Royal Expeditionary Force has left to visit: Frostberg, Sundock, Eastport, and Grotton. Take your time and tell me if you have that same feeling about any of those towns."

Donovan walked over to the map of Franconia that took up the entire wall of his father's new office. He looked at the map, searching his feelings. Finally, he said, "Sundock and Grotton. Something doesn't feel right about them." Edward frowned, "Are you sure? Mage Charles, the Grotton Regional Mage, has an excellent reputation and is a very competent magician." "I can't explain it," said Donovan, "It's just a feeling." "Come over here and sit down, son. I want you to try something."

Donovan moved behind the desk and sat down. "Now, there is a spell that has not been taught at the Wizards Academy in almost a century, because no student had the ability to conjure it. It's called the spell of Foresight. Using it, a magician can see into the future. It has been described as "Just having a bad feeling" about something, someone, or somewhere. Wizard Noland and I believe that you may possess this ability. The incantation is "AUGURIM," and the gesture is placing your left palm against your forehead. Repeat the incantation, please, without the gesture.”

“AUGURIM,” said Donovan. “But I’ve never said that before! How could I conjure a spell without an incantation? Wizard Loren said that having to say the incantation was one of the Safeguards of Magic!” Edward smiled, “Remember what I told you on our trip to Farmdale? About how you were able to hit a bird with a stone, just by willing it? Well, it’s rare, but sometimes it happens. It may be the same with this spell. We know so little about it. But the fact remains that you had a ‘bad feeling’ about Colton and Three Forks several days before you arrived, and there was certainly something very wrong in both cases.”

“That’s true,” confessed Donovan. “So, after the incantation, what do I do?” Edward looked at Wizard Noland, and they both shrugged. “We have no idea. Try this, just think about Sundock first, and maybe dragons, and see what happens,” suggested Noland. Donovan sat in his father’s chair, tried to remember the city of Sundock, which he had only visited once, many years ago. He placed his left hand on his forehead and murmured, “AUGURIM.”

Donovan sat still for a moment, unsure of what to expect, then a vision of the city of Sundock appeared in his mind. He saw the docks, the ships moored to the piers, the cobblestone streets, and the weathered buildings of the town. He remembered to think about dragons, and through a fog of mist, a dragon appeared in the town. Donovan tried to determine its location, but what he saw just didn’t make any sense. The dragon appeared to be in the Regional Mage's Office.

Donovan tried to hold the image, but his hand slipped, and his head fell forward, striking the desk. "ENOUGH!" said Edward forcefully. Donovan shook his head to clear it, a lump growing on his forehead from where he had hit his head on the desk. Kathy handed him a glass of water, and Donovan drank eagerly.

"What did you see?" asked Wizard Noland. "A Sea Dragon in Sundock," replied Donovan shakily. "Just one?" asked Edward. "Yes, but it looked like it was in the Regional Mage's Office!" said Donovan. "That probably means that Regional Mage Lisa is a Sea Dragon Changed One. You two will need to be cautious when you arrive in Sundock. You're tired, Donovan. I forgot that you just flew here from Three Forks," said Edward. "Why don't you and Rachel go home and get some sleep? Come back tomorrow morning and we'll have you take a look at Grotton. You're clearly too exhausted to try it now, and I won't have you passing out again. One day's delay shouldn't matter."

Donovan agreed, and he staggered out of the office, his arm around Rachel for support. "Michael, could you make sure they get home all right? Then come back. We have much to discuss." Wizard Noland nodded and rose from his chair. "That's quite an extraordinary son you have, my friend." Edward smiled, "And he didn't think he had the spark." Noland laughed as he eased out of the office.

Once they were alone, Kathy said, "So, what do I need to know about the Wizard's Test?"

Chapter Seven:

CONSEQUENCES

Sorcerer Cliff walked casually along the street in Three Forks. The rebuilding effort was still underway, and many of the shops were still closed or had very limited hours, as the owners had to balance income against repairs. Cliff assumed that he was being followed; he was still very much under suspicion as a Dragon Changed One, and he knew that he needed to lose whoever was following him. As he neared his destination, he ducked around a blind corner quickly and cast a Concealment spell over himself. He was standing in a recess in the outer wall when Sorceress Janet hurried past him, searching both sides of the street. After Janet turned the corner at the next block, Cliff released his Concealment shield and doubled back, heading for the empty schoolhouse two blocks away.

All lessons had been canceled until further notice, so the school was dark and empty. The lone teacher, Miss Woods, had a room in the back of the facility. Sorcerer Cliff had left a coded message for Miss Woods the day before. It was a simple blue rag, left on a fence post near the school, but the meaning was clear: *I need to speak with you.* As Cliff entered the unlocked door, Miss Woods was waiting for him, seated at the front of the classroom.

"What is so urgent?" she asked. "I need you to deliver a message to the Sea Dragon Clan on Acropo," said Cliff. "You want me to transform and fly to Acropo?" asked the

Sea Dragon Changed One, "Why?" "The Great Dragon, Gek, son of Cobalt, the Sea Dragon Clan chief, asked me to find out if Sorcerer Donovan and his wife, Sorceress Rachel, survived the battle last week. He indicated that it was of vital importance to the Dragon Council, although I do not know why," replied Cliff.

"And now, you expect me to simply up and go, without a moment's notice?" asked Miss Woods. "Yes. The school is closed for the time being and will likely not reopen for at least a month. With so much turmoil in the city, your absence will not be missed. You can go and return without compromising yourself," said Cliff. Miss Woods hesitated, but finally agreed. "When should I leave?" "There is no time like the present," said Cliff smugly. "Your message is simple, "Sorcerer Donovan and his wife, Sorceress Rachel, both survived the dragon attack on Three Forks last week. Repeat it to me, please."

"Sorcerer Donovan and his wife, Sorceress Rachel, both survived the dragon attack on Three Forks last week," repeated Miss Woods. "Is that all?" "Yes. That will be quite sufficient," replied Cliff. "Wait," said the Dragon Changed One, "I thought that you were under a Binding spell, to never injure a human. Will this violate the spell?" Cliff scoffed, "I hardly think so. It is just a simple message. Now, you should go, while it is still dark."

Miss Woods and Sorcerer Cliff left the school by the back door and entered the children's play area. Miss Woods quickly disrobed and changed into a Sea Dragon. She noticed Cliff's lingering gaze. "We will speak when I return," she said. "Of course," replied Cliff.

As the Sea Dragon lifted off into the air, Cliff's breath caught in his throat, his muscles contracted and spasmed, and then his heart stopped. As his body fell into the sawdust that covered the playground, Cliff realized that sending a simple message did, in fact, violate the Binding spell.

As Wizard Kathy left the Forces Training Area, Edward appeared at her side, handing her a water bottle. "Congratulations, dear. I never doubted you for a minute." Kathy drank the water gratefully. "For a test that only took an hour, that was very difficult!" she gasped. "Of course it was. Did you expect it to be easy?" asked Edward. Kathy had passed the Wizard's Test by placing a Silence spell on Wizard Noland, a tether on Wizard Mira, and Paralyzing Wizard Daniel. She also realized that if Edward had not warned her about the Seeming cast over the hourglass, she might have fallen for the trick.

"Anyway, you did well, and, after you return from Baize, we can start looking for the new house I promised you," said Edward. "When should I leave for Baize?" asked Kathy. "Tomorrow morning will be soon enough. We still have to find out what Donovan sees in Grotton later this morning. Are you quite recovered?" Kathy nodded, somewhat weakly, and Edward quickly cast a Healing spell for minor injuries. "That feels wonderful," said Kathy. "I should have let you do that in the Salt Flats."

Edward and Kathy had recently returned to Franconia after spending almost a year in Baize, constructing a giant reservoir in the middle of the Great Salt Flats. The Salt Flats had been expanding for decades and were close to entering and contaminating the Amber River, which was the border between Franconia and Baize. Once the reservoir was complete, Donald, the King of Baize, had thanked Edward for his help, released Mage Kathy from her obligations to Baize, and asked them how soon they could leave.

They walked slowly through the city on their way from the Wizards Academy to their office in the palace. When they arrived, Kathy noticed that her desk was now the same size as her husband's (it had been slightly smaller earlier). "Nice desk," she commented. "It's no more than you deserve. So, how does it feel to be one of only four female Wizards in Franconia?" asked Edward.

"Let's just say that I'm glad to be in Franconia. I doubt that I would ever have had the opportunity to take the Wizard's Test if I had remained in Baize," replied Kathy. "That's their loss," said Edward. "So, Wizard Kathy, what do you think we should do about the Sea Dragon Changed One in the Sundock Regional Mage's Office?"

Kathy thought for a moment, then said, "Well, we can either wait for the Royal Expeditionary Force to get there in a couple of weeks, or we can send a dragon messenger to

Andrew and have the 1st Squadron return to Sundock. Where is Sorcerer Phillip now?" Sorcerer Phillip, a former classmate of Donovan's, was one of two magicians who were designated as dragon messengers for the Royal Navy. Their job was to transform into Sea Dragons and deliver messages from Naval Headquarters to ships at sea (or between different squadrons). The other dragon messenger was Sorceress Anne, who was the driving force behind the initial truce with the Sea Dragons, and later, the formal peace treaty (which the dragons had rejected).

"As far as I know, both Anne and Phillip are at Fleet Headquarters in Grotton. That is, unless the admiral has sent them out with new orders for the fleet," said Edward. "It will probably be faster just to wait for the Expeditionary Force to get to Sundock, that is, if the weather holds." "What about the weather?" asked Donovan, as he and Rachel entered the office.

"I was just telling Wizard Kathy here that you two and the Expeditionary Force will probably be able to get to Sundock faster than if I ordered 1st Squadron and Mage Andrew to redeploy back there from their current position near Eastport. That is, if you can beat the snow." "Snow?" asked Rachel. "Yes, as Donovan can tell you, very soon winter is going to settle on Frostberg, and the snow will severely impact travel to and from the city. That's one reason I'm anxious for you two to return and get the Royal Expeditionary Force moving."

Donovan nodded, remembering the bitter cold and heavy snowfall he encountered the last time he was in Frostberg in winter. "Wait, did you just say, 'Wizard Kathy?'" Edward smiled, "Yes, I did. Kathy passed her Wizard's Test this morning." "Congratulations!" said Donovan as he and Rachel moved to give Kathy a hug. "Was it hard?" asked Donovan. "Exhausting," replied Kathy. "Well, they never make anything easy over there," said Donovan with a grin.

"Nor are we supposed to," said Wizard Noland, entering the office. The five magicians laughed. "So, are we ready? I know these two need to be on their way if they're going to beat the snow," said Wizard Noland. With that, Donovan sat back down at the desk and prepared to conjure the spell of Foresight. "Now Donovan, Grotton is closer to us than Sundock, but I'm not sure that has any bearing on how taxing the spell will be. DO NOT push yourself too far. You already have one lump on your forehead."

Donovan nodded and cast the spell. For long minutes, nothing happened, then a vision of Grotton became visible in his mind. The town was in flames, with people running for cover as dragons circled overhead. The ships in port were all ablaze, as if they had been the primary target of the attack. Donovan tried to discern the types of dragons that were attacking, but there were too many, and they were moving too fast.

"That's enough," said Edward. "What did you see?" "Grotton was under attack," said Donovan wearily, "dozens of dragons, circling overhead, most of the ships in port were on fire and the attack was moving toward the city proper." "Do you have any idea when this attack might occur?" asked Edward. "No. It could be happening now, or a month from now," said Donovan. "Well, now that we know that an attack is coming, we can move magical support to Grotton and be ready for it when it happens," said Edward.

"Rachel and I could go now—," started Donovan. "No," interrupted Edward. "I need you two to get back to Three Forks and get the Royal Expeditionary Force moving. I know they won't leave without you. There are a lot of moving pieces on this chessboard, and you are only two of them. Now, I want you two to go home and get some sleep. I'll meet you on the Academy boat dock at sunset." "But—" "That's an order, son. I'll get some help moving toward Grotton. You worry about Sundock."

Donovan nodded, and he and Rachel headed for the door and home. "Do you want to stop by and see your parents?" asked Donovan. Rachel shook her head, "Maybe on our way to the boat dock this evening. I need to get you into bed." "My thoughts exactly," said Donovan with a leer.

Azure landed on Acropo. She had been pleasantly surprised to find no human ships between the eastern coast and the islands that the Sea Dragons called home. She dove underwater and entered the submerged cave that was the entrance to the Sea Dragon's lair. When she emerged into the grotto, she found Cobalt, Gek's Sea Dragon father, pacing around the pool. "Cobalt! It is good to see you again,"

said Azure. "It is good to see you too," replied Cobalt. "Where are Gek and Annalise?"

"They are at Bruce's house. You look troubled, what is wrong?" asked Azure. "I do not suppose you saw two Sea Dragons while you were on your way here, did you?" asked Cobalt. "Cyan and Chrystal left to take part in the attack on Three Forks over a week ago, and they have not returned yet." Azure lowered her head. "I am sorry, Cobalt, Gek says that they were both killed by a Great Dragon during the attack."

"A Great Dragon? How can that be? I thought that, other than Gek and Ard, the only other Great Dragons were Ig and his family, and they live across the river near Lake Ford!" exclaimed Cobalt. "It was not a dragon that killed them, or even a Changed One. The humans have learned how to change into dragons." "Are you sure?" asked Cobalt, worriedly. "Yes. Gek met a Changed One from Three Forks, who slipped away from the humans to inform any dragons who survived the battle. This is a very troubling development."

"Indeed," said Cobalt. "Does Gek know how many of the humans can affect the change?" "Not exactly. It could only be done by a magic-user that has seen a dragon before, so the number is limited, but growing as the humans spread this knowledge amongst themselves." "That means that we need to attack quickly, before this knowledge becomes commonplace among the magic-users," said Cobalt.

"There is another potential problem," said Azure, "the Changed One that Gek met said that a sorcerer named Donovan arrived in Three Forks just before the dragons attacked." "DONOVAN? The descendant of Wizard Amanda? I thought he was still in the wizard's school!" "As did we," said Azure. "It may be another magic-user named Donovan. Gek is unsure. However, this Donovan has a wife, who is also a magic-user. If it is the same Donovan, Gek says we need to kill his wife before she has any children," said Azure darkly.

Cobalt thought, "More likely before she becomes pregnant. Harming even an unborn child might trigger the Binding spell!"

"How can we discover if Ard's Binding spell is still active?" asked Azure. "Well, I suppose one of us could break our promise and see what happens," said Cobalt, "but those of us bound to the spell might die as a result. That is the only way I can think of to test the spell, and I, for one, do not think it wise to attempt it." Azure shuddered.

"So, tell me, how are your children?" asked Cobalt, changing the subject to something more pleasant. "Anna is growing fast. She can already fly, swim, and eat solid foods, and she has finally accepted her human brother," said Azure. "Really? That is good news!" said Cobalt. "How did that happen?" "Gek and I were both planning on attending the last meeting of the Dragon Council, but Richard would not go to sleep. In desperation, Gek tried the Sleeping spell on him. It did not work, which proves that he has the spark of magic. Unfortunately, Richard began repeating the word and motion, which kept putting Bruce to sleep. It became a game for Richard. Bruce was not pleased, and we could not leave Richard alone with Bruce, so Gek had to stay behind. That is why I came to the council meeting alone," explained Azure.

"Anyway, while I was away, Anna was prowling around on the beach, probably looking for Ard, when a cougar pounced on her. Fortunately, Richard was nearby and he put the cougar to sleep with the spell. After that, Anna decided that he was not useless after all." Cobalt laughed. "We may have to leave our current residence soon," said Azure. Bruce's hut is really not big enough for three dragons. Do you have any idea where we might settle?"

Cobalt considered the question. "My cave on Perfo is unoccupied; that might be the best place for the four of you, at least for the time being," said Cobalt. "There may be some Sea Dragon Changed Ones on the mainland who have human children that could be of assistance. I will make inquiries. Is that the only reason you came?"

"No. Sadly, Gek lost two fingers from his left foreclaw during the battle in Three Forks. Without those fingers, he is unable to change back into a human. Do you know of a Healing spell that could restore his fingers?" asked Azure. Cobalt thought, "No. I am unaware of any spell that can restore that which has been lost. I guess he will just have to remain a dragon. That is not such a bad thing, Azure." "I know, it was more for Richard that I was hoping. He is sad that his father can no longer change into a human," said Azure. "Is Aqua here?"

"Yes. She is staying in Teal's old chamber," said Cobalt. "I will go and see her, and get some rest. I need to return to Gek tomorrow." Azure walked down the passageway and found her mother, Aqua, in the chamber that used to belong to her father, Teal. Teal had been killed in a battle with the humans a few months ago. He had been protecting the human magic-user, Andrew, who had been targeted by another member of the clan who had not recognized him.

"Hello, mother," said Azure. "Azure! Welcome home, child! It is good to see you again. Where is Annalise?" asked Aqua. "She is on the mainland with Gek. I just came to deliver news to Cobalt about the battle of Three Forks." "Indeed? How did the first-ever combined dragon clan attack fare?" asked Aqua. "We lost seven of the nine dragons that attacked, including both Sea Dragons, and Gek was injured. There were too many human magic-users in Three Forks. Gek says that we should have attacked a smaller human town that had fewer magic-users in it. While they killed many humans and destroyed many of their buildings, it was not a victory."

"How is Gek?" asked Aqua. "His injury was minor. He lost two talons on his left foreleg, but because of that, he cannot change back into a human again. Richard is most upset." "I can imagine," said Aqua diplomatically. It was no secret that she did not approve of Azure's human child. "So, what will you do now?" "We need to find a place where we can raise a young dragon and a human child. While both are growing at an astonishing rate, it will be years before

Richard can perform the spell of change and transform into a dragon," said Azure.

"If he even has the spark of magic in him," said Aqua dismissively. "Oh, he has the spark. We tried to spell him to sleep one night with the Sleep spell, but it would not work. Instead, he learned the word and began tormenting Bruce by spelling him to sleep repeatedly. Bruce was not amused." Aqua laughed so hard that salt water came out of her nose. "How wonderful! This boy may prove to be an asset to the family after all!" Azure smiled, "I am glad you approve. Richard also saved Anna by spelling a cougar to sleep when it attacked her. We had no idea that the Sleep spell would work on animals. Do you have any suggestions about where we might be able to raise the children?"

"I will give it some serious thought, my dear. Something must be arranged for such a talented child!" "I agree. Is it all right if I sleep in here today? I have to leave at sunset to return." "Of course, Azure. Please, make yourself comfortable. I will just wander around the cavern and see if anyone has a solution for your dilemma. Sleep well. I will return at sundown."

Aqua left the chamber, still chuckling about Richard. Azure hoped that between her and Cobalt, they could come up with a solution to the situation. They just could not stay in Bruce's hut for much longer. Cobalt's cave on Perfo was certainly a possibility, but most of the vegetation was still charred and blackened after the attack by the humans. It would not be a very nice place to live. If anything, moving to Perfo would only be a short-term solution. Azure laid her head on the cool, damp rock and was asleep in minutes.

When Azure awoke that evening, Cobalt had troubling news. "A Sea Dragon Changed One arrived from Three Forks last night. It appears that Sorcerer Donovan and his wife, Sorceress Rachel, both survived the dragon attack on Three Forks last week." "Do we know if this magic-user is the same 'Donovan' that we must protect?" asked Azure. "We must assume so," said Cobalt. "It seems that Donovan has been assigned to something called the 'Royal Expeditionary Force.' It is a small company of highly trained soldiers that travels around Franconia at the direction of the King. It is undoubtedly the same force that attacked and killed Gek's mother, Liza."

"What are we going to do about it?" asked Azure. "I instructed the Changed One, Wood, to kill this Sorceress Rachel as soon as she returns to Three Forks. We need to stop this family tree from spreading."

The HMS VALOR and 1st Squadron sailed into the port of Eastport at dawn. It had been a relatively pleasant trip south; no icebergs or angry Sea Dragons, just fair skies and a following sea. "I hope 3rd Squadron made it to Sundock without incident," said Andrew. The Commodore merely grunted. "So, what's the procedure here, sir?"

"We take on foodstuffs and fresh water, give the crew two days' shore leave, then head back out. I suppose we should keep at least two magicians on board at all times, just in case an invisible dragon decides to drop a stone on the ship," said Commodore Matthews. "I think that's a wise precaution, sir," said Andrew. "We should also leave a couple of Seabow crews aboard, just in case." "You really think they would attack this far south?" asked the Commodore.

"I wouldn't put it past them," replied Andrew. "Well, I'm going ashore now to arrange for our resupply. You and Sorcerer Marvin from the VICEROY stay aboard today, and you can go ashore tomorrow. I'll leave one Seabow crew aboard each ship. Tomorrow, Sorcerer Roger from the VICTORY will stay on board." Andrew nodded his understanding of his orders.

"Sir, while you're in town, could you take care of that tax issue for Maria? Even though her father was killed, I think she still plans to continue running the business, and wants to ship that Smithville steel from here to Fairview to make crossbows for the crown. In fact, she's more determined than ever," said Andrew. "I'll take care of it," said Commodore Matthews gruffly. "What's the name of the company?" "Prestige Arms, based in Fairview, sir," replied Andrew. "Consider it done. Keep a sharp lookout, Andrew. I hope you're wrong, but I don't trust those dragons."

As the afternoon wore on, Andrew grew bored. Stevedores arrived and removed empty crates, barrels, and casks from the holds of the three ships, and returned with full containers of supplies and casks of water. To keep himself busy, Andrew began replicating Seabow bolts. You could never have enough of those. As evening fell, Andrew walked down the gangplank and over to the HMS VICEROY where he found Sorcerer Marvin dozing in a chair on the deck.

Shaking him awake, Andrew said, "One of us needs to be awake at all times. Why don't you go below and get some sleep? I'll take first watch. I'll wake you a little after midnight." Sorcerer Marvin nodded his head groggily and headed below to his cabin. Andrew took the opportunity to walk around the HMS VICEROY, having never been aboard her before.

After walking the ship from stem to stern and speaking with the Seabow crew on duty, Andrew walked over to the HMS VICTORY and performed the same inspection. Walking around helped keep him awake and familiarized him with the slight differences between the ships. It also kept the Seabow crews on their toes. Andrew surprised them by telling the crews that he didn't mind if they played dice games while they were on duty, as long as they stayed awake and alert.

Returning to the VALOR, Andrew went below deck briefly and brought up a teapot. He magically (and carefully) heated the water and brewed a strong pot of tea. Just before midnight, he heard someone quietly sneaking up the gangplank.

"Quiet, you idiot! Or you'll wake the guard!" whispered a voice. Andrew conjured a Hearing Enhancement, which enabled him to detect at least three men creeping up the steep boarding ramp. When they reached the top, Andrew stepped forward and said, "Can I help you, gentlemen?" The three sneak thieves started. One jumped overboard, one tripped and slid back down the ramp (painfully), and the third leapt towards Andrew, brandishing a cutlass.

The short naval sword bounced harmlessly off Andrew's shield, and the brigand immediately realized his mistake. "Please, sir Wizard, we meant no harm! We're just poor wharf-rats, trying to eke out a living! Have mercy!" Unwilling to listen to any further protests of poverty or innocence, Andrew paralyzed the scraggly-looking man, while he considered what to do with him. This seemed to be a matter for the Eastport Enforcers, although, since he was captured on board a Royal Navy ship, there was precedent for the Commodore to impose sentence (normally keelhauling). While Andrew considered his options, he glanced up at the bright half-moon and noticed a distortion pass across it, high in the night sky.

"DRAGON ATTACK!" Andrew shouted, his Voice Enhancement carrying the warning to the other two ships. "GET SORCERER MARVIN! PREPARE THE SEABOWS! ALL HANDS ON DECK!" he shouted, as he scanned the sky for the Concealed Dragons. A large stone crashed down on the stern of the VICEROY, narrowly missing the ship's wheel and rudder assembly. Andrew fired a Blast spell in the direction of the distortion, but couldn't be sure if he hit anything.

More stones and tree trunks began falling from the sky. Abandoning the Blast spell, Andrew instead conjured angled shields to deflect the unidentified falling objects (UFOs). Several rocks and stones, and even an iron anvil that a dragon had picked up somewhere, bounced off Andrew's shields before he detected a large distortion, flying in lower than the others. "CONCUSIO," Andrew muttered, while making a throwing motion with his right hand. This time, the Blast spell hit the distortion dead center, and a blue-green Sea Dragon fell into the sea behind the VALOR, a smoking hole in its forehead.

While Andrew was searching for additional dragons, a large log fell from the sky, smashing the paralyzed brigand where he stood. Andrew cursed himself for leaving the man helplessly immobile, but he had other things on his mind. With the Paralyze spell broken, the power drain on Andrew lessened slightly, and he resumed his search for any more Concealed Dragons. Several more stones fell towards the ships, with two of them striking the HMS VICTORY, which was too far away from the VALOR for Andrew or Sorcerer Marvin to effectively shield.

Nearing exhaustion, Andrew hoped that the attack was nearly over. Suddenly, a large Sea Dragon appeared off the stern of the ship. This one had apparently already dropped its load of rocks and was instead spraying a thin, razor-sharp jet of water at the deck of the VALOR. In desperation, Andrew conjured Seemings of several large hawks and sent them directly at the dragon's eyes. The dragon was not afraid of the birds and refused to alter its course. When the dragon's nose touched the Seemings, the Seemings vanished in a flash of light, temporarily blinding the dragon, who promptly smashed head-on into the mizzen mast.

The collision cracked the mast and knocked the dragon unconscious. The Sea Dragon fell to the deck and lay motionless. Andrew ran forward and said "DELERE," while flicking his right wrist towards the dragon's neck. The Remove spell worked perfectly, and the dragon's head was cleanly severed from its body. However, Andrew wasn't able to admire the results of his effort, as he crashed to the deck unconscious, the power drain overwhelming him.

Chapter Eight:
PREPARATIONS

Donovan and Rachel arrived at the Wizards Academy marina shortly before sunset to find Edward, Kathy, and Noland waiting. They looked worried. "What's wrong?" asked Donovan. "The Sea Dragons attacked our ships in the port of Eastport last night. While Andrew and Sorcerer Marvin from the HMS VICEROY prevented any serious damage to the squadron, it's a disturbing development." "Is Andrew OK?" asked Donovan.

"Your cousin is fine," said Edward. "But, like you, he overtaxed himself and was still unconscious when the Messenger Hawk was dispatched. They did report that he used a unique technique to kill one of the Sea Dragons though." "Really? What did he do?" asked Donovan. "The sailors on board reported that he cast several Seemings of birds at the dragon's face, and while temporarily blinded by the flash, the dragon ran into the mizzen mast and knocked itself out. Andrew then used the Remove spell to decapitate it as it lay on the deck. Then he passed out," said Edward.

Donovan grinned, "Well, I guess that's one way to do it, but there's seldom a ship's mast around when you need one." Wizard Noland laughed, "That's true. Still, we didn't expect an attack so far south. The report states that we only killed two or three dragons, and had one sailor and one civilian killed, plus the damage to the ships." "So, what's 1st Squadron doing now?" asked Rachel.

"The report didn't say. I suspect there just wasn't enough room on the message parchment. I cast a Seeing spell after receiving the message, and the squadron has put back out to sea, probably headed back to Sundock," said Edward. "Then maybe we'll meet up with them there," said Donovan.

"I hope so," said Edward. "Once you get back to Three Forks, you need to tell Major Gerald that the Expeditionary Force needs to get moving to Frostberg immediately. Here is an order from Marshall Guzman. I really shouldn't be giving orders to military units. Unless there is an urgent need for them to remain in Three Forks, I want them on the road tomorrow. Before you go, here is a new Messenger Hawk for Three Forks," said Wizard Noland, as he handed over a bird cage covered with a black cloth cover. Please don't frighten the Hawk, he's already a bit skittish."

With nothing further to discuss, Donovan and Rachel each gave Edward and Kathy a good-bye hug and shook hands with Wizard Noland. The three Wizards turned their backs as the two mages disrobed, placed their garments in a heavy canvas bag, and transformed into Great Dragons. Rachel grabbed the canvas bag while Donovan secured the Messenger Hawk's cage in his talons. The two Gold Dragons lifted off and quickly vanished out of sight, heading northeast, following the Sapphire River.

"So, they're off," said Edward. "In the morning, Kathy will transform and head into Baize. While I was looking for the VALOR this morning, I also noted that King Donald has returned to the capital, so it will take Kathy at least two days to get to him. Once she's on her way, I'll transform and head to Southport to convince the King that we need to attack the Coral Islands again to try and back the Sea Dragons off. I'll also inform him of Kathy's mission to try and convince King Donald to attack the Fire Dragon colony in the Grey Mountains."

"Other than intensifying the battle training for my students, what else can I be doing?" asked Noland. "We need to get a message to Mage Charles in Grotton, informing him of the impending attack by the dragons. It seems strange that the dragons would attack there, though. I mean, Grotton has even more magicians than Three Forks, especially with the Royal Navy Headquarters and Wizard Lake and his staff in the city."

"Could Donovan have been wrong?" asked Edward. "I just don't know. We know so little about that spell. He's been right so far, so I'm inclined to give him the benefit of the doubt, but you're right, it would be a foolish move on the part of the dragons," said Noland. "Maybe they don't realize how many magicians we have in Grotton," speculated Kathy. "Or maybe the Changed Ones we haven't detected are going to add their numbers to the attacking force," said Edward.

"That's a troubling thought," said Wizard Noland. "But you're right. There may be dozens of undetected Changed Ones in Grotton too!" "Which means that Mage Charles needs to increase his efforts to find and bind them before it's too late," said Edward. "I may need two Messenger Hawks for that long a message," said Noland.

"After I speak with the King, I'll head over there myself," said Edward. "Are you sure that's wise?" asked Noland. "With Wizard Kathy in Baize, we need someone in your office to coordinate our efforts." Edward sighed. "I know. I guess that task will fall to Wizard Cassandra. She's not doing much now with the King in Southport. Why didn't she accompany him?" Noland grimaced, "The King informed her that he was confident with the protection of Sorceress Celeste, and that he felt that Wizard Cassandra would be of more use here."

"That's shortsighted," said Edward. "Cassandra is a Wizard and Celeste is only a Sorceress, and not one of our strongest either. Except maybe as a healer." "I made that very argument, but the King was adamant. He also pointed out that Southport has a Regiment stationed there and a sizable Regional Mage's Office," said Wizard Noland. Edward thought, "He's not wrong about that. Well, at least we can make good use of Wizard Cassandra while I'm away."

As they left the boat dock, Wizard Faith approached, looking worried. "What's wrong, Faith?" asked Wizard Noland. "Sir, the cobbler who owns the shop next to the Gatehouse is here, asking for you. He says he's a Sea Dragon Changed One, and would like to submit to a Binding spell before he's discovered by Mage Curtis."

Edward landed in the dragon-receiving atrium of the King's Winter Palace in Southport two hours after dawn. He and Kathy had both departed the Wizards Academy while it was still dark to avoid alarming the citizens of Kingston. Edward transformed quickly and donned his Wizard's robes. As he left the open courtyard, a slightly disheveled Sorceress Celeste arrived.

"Wizard Edward! What brings you to Southport?" she asked. "I have an urgent message for the King," replied Edward. "How are things going here, Sorceress Celeste?" Celeste blushed and said, "Everything is fine. The renovations to the palace are complete, and to Henry's satisfaction. He's having those Stone Dragon scales put on the roof, and I'm helping the construction workers install the Guardbows on the battlements and guard towers. Those modifications should be completed within the week."

"That's good," said Edward. "We may need those upgrades sooner rather than later." "Why? What's happened?" asked Celeste. Edward looked slightly uncomfortable, but said gently, "That news should be given to the King first. I'm sure he'll want you there, but I don't want to compromise your position by giving you information before I tell the King." "Of course, I understand completely," said Celeste. "Henry should be just getting up now. I'll go and let him know you've arrived with news. I'm sure he'll want to speak to you first thing. Why don't you just have a seat in the receiving room? I'll have a servant bring you some tea while you wait."

Edward grudgingly followed Celeste to the overly ornate receiving room outside the formal audience chamber. The room was designed to impress and intimidate visitors, with lots of gold leaf, heavy crimson tapestries, and paintings of battle scenes, most of which were pure folklore. The tea arrived quickly, and Edward waited patiently. Almost a glass later, a Page entered and told him that the King was ready to receive him.

Edward placed his teacup back on the tray and entered the enormous audience chamber. Looking around, Edward was astounded by the size and décor of the room. It could easily hold a hundred people with room to spare. The deep red curtains were partially opened, letting in the morning light, and the white marble floor glistened. The King's throne was at the opposite end of the room from the door, and it took a couple of minutes for Edward to cross the room. He had no intention of rushing across the floor. Edward noted that a smaller throne-like chair was positioned on Henry's right hand, and Sorceress Celeste was comfortably seated in it. The meaning was clear: Celeste was not the Queen yet, but it would not be long before their marriage and her coronation.

"Wizard Edward, it's good to see you again. I understand you have news?" asked Henry. "Yes, sire. In the few short weeks since you departed Kingston, there have been a number of developments concerning the dragons. First, the city of Three Forks was attacked a little over a week ago by no fewer than nine dragons, two from each clan except the Great Dragons, who only had a single dragon in the attacking force."

"What were the damages?" asked the King. "Your Majesty, the report I received indicates that there were about 300 killed and twice that number injured. There was also considerable damage to the city proper. It was fortunate that your Royal Expeditionary Force, with their magical support, arrived just before the attack. They were able to kill seven of the nine dragons that attacked, but two Sorcerers were killed while defending the city."

The King looked concerned, "Have the dragons ever attacked together like that before?" "No, sire. They have not. It seems that they have realized the advantages of combined attacks. My report is that the Sea Dragons sprayed water on the people and structures of the city, which the Snow Dragons then froze into ice. Fortunately, Sorcerer Donovan and his wife, Sorceress Rachel were able to eliminate both the Sea and Snow Dragons before they could cause too much damage," said Edward.

"How did they do that?" asked Henry. "They both transformed into Great Dragons and flew up behind the Sea Dragons and took them by surprise. One Snow Dragon was felled by a well-placed crossbow bolt, and the other fled. Donovan and Rachel then attacked the two Fire Dragons and killed them," said Edward. "Incredible!" exclaimed the King, "But, what about the Stone Dragons?" "Two of your magicians enclosed them in protective shields and suffocated them, sire," said Edward. "Wonderful!" said the King.

"The attack was repelled, and the dragons suffered significant losses, sire, but, as I said, there was considerable damage to the city," said Edward. "Why did it take so long for this news to reach me?" asked the King. "The Three Forks Message Center was destroyed in the attack, as well as all of their Messenger Hawks. In order to get the news to you, Major Gerald sent Sorceress Rachel, in dragon form, to Kingston with the news," replied Edward.

"Where is Sorceress Rachel? I would like to thank her personally," said the King. "I sent her back to Three Forks yesterday, Your Highness. With orders that the Royal Expeditionary Force continue its mission and depart for Frostberg in haste, before the snow comes. I also promoted both Donovan and Rachel to the rank of Battle Mage for their efforts in the defense of Three Forks. Wizard Noland agreed with my decision."

"I think that sounds fair. Can you tell me what the Expeditionary Force has discovered so far?" asked the King eagerly. "Yes, sire. The Expeditionary Force has uncovered numerous Dragon Changed Ones during their visits and killed or bound all of them. As Wizard Noland feared, there were a few of the towns and cities whose treasuries did not contain all that they should, but I believe that all but 95 golds have been recovered to date." "Ninety-five golds!" exclaimed the King. "That is all that was *not* recovered, sire, out of several thousand that were missing," said Edward reassuringly.

The King muttered under his breath that 95 golds was still a considerable sum, but Celeste whispered something in his ear and he regained his composure. "So, you said the Expeditionary Force is headed to Frostberg?" "Yes, sire. They may be on their way already. Once there, they will commandeer a ship and travel to Sundock, Eastport, Grotton, and then return to Kingston. They should be back in about two months if they do not run into any trouble."

"Thank you for coming, Edward. While the news is not all good, things could be much worse." The King rose as if to indicate that the meeting was over, but Edward said, "Excuse me, sire, but that is not all of my news." "Indeed?" asked the King, sitting back down slowly.

"Two days ago, Sea Dragons attacked the city of Eastport. While the dragons were driven off with minimal damage and we only suffered one casualty, the attack was similar to one Wizard Kathy and I experienced in Baize," said Edward hastily, realizing that he was losing the King's interest. "How so?" asked Henry. "In both cases, the dragons cast Concealment shields around themselves and dropped heavy stones or logs onto the people below. While Mage Andrew aboard the HMS VALOR was able to deflect many of the projectiles, it is most fortunate that he was awake and alert, since the attack took place at midnight. I should also mention that a similar attack happened to the port of Sundock a week ago."

"What is your point, Wizard Edward?" "Sire, I would like your permission to send the 1st Fleet to blockade and attack the Coral Islands. We need to take the fight to the dragons rather than just waiting for them to attack us." The King brightened at this suggestion, "Do you think it would be successful?" "Sire, the last time we attacked the Coral Islands, a single squadron of four ships inflicted so many casualties on the Sea Dragons that they sued for peace. I think a more forceful attack might be able to take them out of the conflict altogether."

"I like it! You have my approval! Is there anything else?" "Just one last thing, Your Majesty, I sent my wife, Wizard Kathy, to speak with King Donald of Baize in order to encourage him to mount an attack on the Fire Dragon colony, which I discovered while I was in Baize. If the Baizians can inflict substantial harm on the Fire Dragons, maybe we can end this conflict."

"Do you think King Donald will authorize such an attack?" asked the King. "I have not known King Donald long, sire. I only met with him a few times while I was in Baize, but he does seem to care about his people, and the Fire Dragons are more of a threat to Baize than they are to us. I hope Kathy can convince him to take some action. His new Court Wizard, James, seems to be a reasonable man." "Let us hope so. Well, thank you for coming, Wizard Edward. Now, if you'll excuse me, I have some matters of state to conduct this morning," said the King dismissively.

"Of course, sire. Thank you for seeing me," said Edward, as he turned and headed out of the audience chamber.

Edward closed the door to the receiving room and headed back down the hall toward the courtyard, intent on leaving the palace immediately. "Wizard Edward, wait!" said Celeste as she ran down the hall after him. "Is there something else, Celeste?" asked Edward.

"I'm sorry that Henry was so abrupt with you. He doesn't take bad news well," said Celeste. "Few men do, Celeste, but the King needs to hear truth spoken, and I will not sugar-coat bad news," said Edward. "I know. Please excuse him. For some reason, he has been preoccupied with money lately. The loss of 95 golds is disturbing to him," explained Celeste. Edward humphed, "The loss of 95 golds would be ruinous to a merchant. But the curtains in that room undoubtedly cost more than that. If the king is worried about coins, he should spend less on decorations," said Edward.

"I know, and I've tried to rein in his more extravagant spending. I'm really afraid that he's going to go overboard on our wedding," said Celeste. "Then you need to remind him what happened at my son's wedding. Even with a limited guest list and a venue *inside* the Wizards Academy, a Stone Dragon Changed One got in, disguised as a caterer, and injured fifty people. I know a royal wedding is a big deal, and there will be much pomp and ceremony, but he needs to consider security, and with the war with the dragons, I do not have an abundance of magicians to spare, even for a day, for a spectacle."

"We had not considered that," said Celeste. "I know," said Edward, "but I have. Try to impress upon him that a small, private ceremony is much more secure and much less *costly*. That should impress him. One more thing that I didn't have the opportunity to mention in there, the dragons have learned that humans can transform into dragons. This puts our Dragon Messengers at greater risk, both from the dragons and our own troops. You need to be cautious if King Henry sends you out with a message."

"How did the dragons learn of this?" asked Celeste. "That's not important. What *is* important is that they know, and we know that they know," said Edward. "Also, there may be a lot more Changed Ones in Franconia than we ever suspected. It seems that some of the merchants that cater to wealthy clients are Changed Ones. We missed them in our initial search because magicians do not move in those circles. We are conducting a more thorough search in Kingston, but you should be on the lookout here in Southport as well. I will go and speak to Regional Mage Jordan before I depart today, and inform him of this development."

"Thank you, Wizard Edward. I'm glad that you're back," said Celeste.

Kathy landed outside of the city of Baize at nightfall, two days after departing Kingston. She spent the first night in Weaton in what passed for the Regional Mage's Office. With only Sorcerer Alfred in residence, Kathy was able to sleep in the office while Alfred returned to his house for the night.

Kathy informed Sorcerer Alfred about the possibility of additional Changed Ones in Franconia and where they might be employed. Sorcerer Alfred told her that he would certainly conduct a more thorough search in the coming days, after admitting that he had not considered visiting the few high-end shops in Weaton in his search for Changed Ones.

After an uncomfortable night's sleep, Wizard Kathy left early the next morning, leaving a note behind for Sorcerer Alfred. After flying all day and into the evening, Kathy was relieved to finally make it to her hometown of Baize before it was fully dark. Most cities in the kingdom were not especially safe for attractive women to walk alone in after dark. She secured a room at the Baizian Arms Inn and retired for the night. It would not do to disturb the King at this hour, and Kathy needed a good night's sleep before the unscheduled meeting tomorrow.

The next morning, Kathy woke, had a light breakfast at the Inn, and then proceeded into the city. She was unsurprised that nothing had changed in the year that she had been away. Things always happened *slowly* in Baize. To drive home the point, the guard at the gate to the palace allowed her to enter unchallenged. He merely said, "Hello, Mage Kathy, it's nice to see you again." *Typical.* Kathy decided to start by visiting the Court Wizard's Office. If Wizard James were in, he would surely know where the King was and secure her an audience.

She knocked on the Court Wizard's office door and was greeted by Mage Juliet, Wizard James' former assistant when he held the post of Chief of Army Wizardry. "Kathy! What brings you back to Baize? I thought you moved to Franconia." "I did, but my husband, Wizard Edward, who is now the Chief of Military Wizardry in Franconia, discovered some troubling news about the dragons that he wanted me to share with Wizard James and King Donald," said Kathy.

"James is in a meeting with the Regimental Commanders at the moment, but they should be about done. Would you like to wait?" asked Juliet. "Absolutely. In fact, the information I have may be of interest to the commanders if Wizard James would like…" Mage Juliet frowned, but said, "I'll just go ask him." "Thank you."

A few minutes later, Juliet returned and said that Wizard James would be happy for Kathy to join the meeting, especially if she had new information about their dragon enemies. Juliet escorted Kathy down the hall to the conference room and knocked softly. "Come in," said Wizard James through the door. Juliet opened the door and allowed Kathy in. The five Regimental Commanders all rose from their seats as Kathy entered, and Wizard James said, "Everyone, you remember Mage Kathy, formerly the Assistant Court Wizard, now residing in Franconia. Kathy, welcome back. I understand that you have some news to share with us about the dragons?" asked James.

"Yes," said Kathy, "and it is Wizard Kathy now, I took and passed the Wizard's Test four days ago at the Franconian Wizards Academy." This news shocked the assembled men, but James simply said, "Congratulations! Now, what is this news?" Kathy related the details of the dragon attack on

Three Forks and how all five clans of dragons participated in the assault.

"Have the dragons ever cooperated like this before?" asked one of the Regimental Commanders. "Never," replied Kathy. "We suspect it is because of the way that Sorcerer Donovan foiled the Snow Dragon attack on the town of Snowton. As you recall, Donovan transformed into a Great Dragon and killed or injured six of the ten attacking Snow Dragons. It seems that the dragons have decided to cooperate to prevent another occurrence like that," said Kathy.

"And you came all the way here just to tell us that?" asked James mildly. "No, James, I also needed to inform you that the dragons have learned that human magicians have learned how to transform into dragons, and that our well-kept secret has been compromised." There were murmurs amongst the assembled leaders at this disturbing news. "How do we know this?" asked James.

"After the battle of Three Forks, Sorcerer Donovan determined that one of the Sorcerers in the Franconian Regiment assigned to the city was a Fire Dragon Changed One. Under questioning, the Changed One admitted to abandoning his post during the fight, and disclosed our ability to one of the dragons that survived the battle. Since the Changed One was questioned under Truth Serum, we must believe it to be true."

"This is troubling news, and must be told to the King. Is there anything else, Kathy?" asked Wizard James. "Yes, but it is of a more *administrative* nature and would not really be of interest to your commanders," replied Kathy. "I see," said James. "In that case, you gentlemen are dismissed. Please return to your commands. If additional intelligence is obtained concerning the dragons, it will come through magical channels." The five Regimental Commanders filed out of the conference room, and Wizard James came over and took Kathy's hand. "Congratulations again, Kathy. I'm happy for you and your promotion."

Kathy said, "Thank you. I know it's something I would never have attained in Baize." James nodded his head and said, "Sit down, please, and let me explain something to you. Do you know how many Wizards there are in Baize?" Kathy shook her head. "There are eight. There can only be eight, *ever*. One is the Court Wizard, then the Chief of Army Wizardry and the Chief of Naval Wizardry, and the five Wizards assigned to the five Baizian Regiments. The Wizard's Test is only given when a new Wizard is required because one of those posts is vacant. The next Wizard candidate will not likely be selected and tested until Wizard Timothy dies or retires."

"Who replaced you when you advanced to the Court Wizard position?" asked Kathy. James shifted uneasily, "Wizard Ruben holds that position now," "RUBEN? That swaggering idiot?" asked Kathy. "Yes," admitted James. "He was selected after three other candidates failed the Wizard's Test." "Were any of the other candidates women?" asked Kathy. "No. None were put forward. That is one of the reasons that I prevailed on the King to release you, since you would have been the most qualified mage, and being overlooked would have upset you."

"Well, you were right about that. What about Mage Juliet? Was she even considered?" asked Kathy. James shook his head. "No. You know that that is not our way here in Baize. The Wizards have always been men." "That is a mistake," said Kathy. "It may well be, but centuries of tradition are difficult to change. Anyway, the decision has been made and is unchangeable. So, what is the *administrative* issue you wished to discuss with me?" asked James.

While she was seething at the injustice of the Baizian promotion system, Kathy put her anger aside and told James about how the previous Franconian Minister of Internal Security had systematically raided the Franconian Treasury, and how the Royal Expeditionary Force had been sent out to conduct an audit of all of the treasuries in the Kingdom. "Did they discover any missing funds?" asked James.

"Yes. In several cities. The magicians assigned to the Expeditionary Force were able to recover or replicate most of the pilfered gold, but not all. About a hundred golds just vanished," James whistled, "A hundred golds! But surely, *our* treasuries could not be short that much! After all, you were the one conducting the audits," exclaimed James.

"You are correct. I audited every treasury that Wizard Louis allowed me to. It has occurred to me that he never sent me to Oceanside or Seaside. Both of those cities have substantial treasuries. But Louis claimed that it would be like sending me on a beach vacation. If I were you, I would send my former staff to audit those two cities immediately," said Kathy. "What about here? Did you ever audit the treasury in Baize?" asked James, worriedly. Kathy smiled, "Yes. Several times, in fact. There should be no shortages in the Royal Treasury." James smiled at the news.

"This has been most informative, Wizard Kathy. Is there anything else you would like to share?" asked James. "Yes, there is one other thing. Edward is proposing that the Franconian Navy blockade the Coral Islands, which is the home of the Sea Dragon colony. He hopes that we can strike them hard enough that they will reconsider a peace treaty to end their role in the conflict." "I thought Franconia had a truce with the Sea Dragons, and that a peace treaty was being drafted!" exclaimed James. "It was, but King Henry's advisors and ministers made a mess of it. They composed a 37-page treaty, which the dragons refused to sign. It seems that dragons can't read. We should have thought of that," said Kathy.

"So, what happened?" "The dragons accused us of stalling for time while we made more Seabows, cancelled the temporary truce, and began attacking Franconian ships and port facilities again," said Kathy. "Is there no hope of another truce?" "The first truce was arranged after the Sea Dragons suffered a terrible loss in battle. That is what Edward is hoping for again."

"I understand," said James. "Now tell me, what is a 'Seabow'?" Kathy frowned; she had just given away a military secret. Deciding that it was best to inform James of the invention, Kathy explained that a Seabow was a crossbow, enlarged to four times its normal size, attached to a swiveling pedestal, and mounted on the sides of Franconian warships. She said that it required a crank system to draw the heavy steel bow, and that the iron bolts were the size of harpoons, but that the weapons were very effective against Sea Dragons.

"We have also begun mounting a stationary version on the battlements and towers of our garrisons and palaces," confessed Kathy. They have not been tried yet, but they might be useful in a pinch." James sat back in his chair, "Thank you for your trust, Kathy. I will inform the King and request that he attempt to purchase some of these Seabows for our use. I suppose they are very cumbersome to transport?" asked James. Kathy smiled, "Not after you reduce them to pocket size." James laughed, "Of course! That's brilliant!"

"So, is that all?" asked James. "No," said Kathy. "Wizard Edward would like Baize to attack the Fire Dragon colony in the Grey Mountains."

Chapter Nine:
A WINTER WONDERLAND

Donovan and Rachel flew quickly through the night. They followed the Sapphire River, which would lead them to the town of Hayford, then Three Forks. As they approached Hayford, the snow began to fall. The snowfall began gradually, but increased in intensity the farther north they flew. By the time they landed in the Three Forks garrison courtyard, there was almost a foot of snow on the ground, and it was still coming down.

Donovan and Rachel transformed back into humans and got dressed quickly. "My father wasn't kidding about the snow," said Donovan. Rachel shivered as they picked up the squawking Messenger Hawk and his cage and rushed inside the building, where they found Major Gerald pacing about impatiently. "There you are! At last! What kept you so long? I expected you back days ago!" said Major Gerald.

"I'm sorry, sir," said Donovan, "we ran into some 'dragon trouble' while we were in Kingston. We can tell you all about it on the road. My father, who has returned to Franconia and been appointed as the Chief of Military Wizardry, wants the Royal Expeditionary Force to leave immediately and make our best possible speed to Frostberg, then commandeer a ship to travel to Sundock, Eastport,

Grotton, and then home to Kingston. Here is the order from Marshall Guzman," said Donovan, handing over the written order from the Marshall.

"Let me inform the men. They should all be standing by already. We'll leave within the hour," said Major Gerald gruffly. He hurried out to notify the company commanders to assemble the men and get the wagons hitched for an immediate departure. While Major Gerald coordinated the departure, Donovan and Rachel returned to their room and packed up their few possessions, then placed them in their wagon, which had a lot more room now that they were almost finished distributing the Concealment cloaks to all of the magicians in the kingdom. Once the wagon was loaded, they hitched Stam, Donovan's white Caperian horse, to the tracers.

"It's really coming down out there. Maybe we should put on his horse blanket," said Donovan. Rachel agreed, and the Concealment horse blanket was quickly put on Stam (inside out), for his protection from the snow. As they were finishing up, Mages Gregory and Roark entered the stables. "Leaving so soon?" asked Mage Gregory.

"Yes. My father, the new Chief of Military Wizardry, ordered us to get to Frostberg as soon as possible," said Donovan. He and Rachel quickly explained what they had learned in Kingston, and advised Mage Roark to search for additional Dragon Changed Ones among the high-end merchants, and also the blacksmiths and undertakers. "By the way, thank you for your recommendations. We certainly never expected to be promoted to mage so quickly," said Rachel.

"No thanks are necessary," said Gregory. "You two deserve the promotion for your efforts here. Without your warning and help, this city might have been destroyed." Donovan smiled as he pulled out two Concealment cloaks with the Mage's emblem embossed on the front from the remaining cloaks in the wagon, and handed one to Rachel. "I wonder how long it will take for Major Gerald to notice the new cloaks," said Rachel impishly.

Just then, Major Gerald entered the stable and asked, "You two mages ready to hit the road?" "I guess not long at all," quipped Donovan. Mages Roark and Gregory told Donovan that they had already informed Major Gerald of the message they sent to Kingston, so it was no wonder that he anticipated their promotions.

Donovan and Rachel shook hands with the mages and climbed up onto their wagon. "Oh, we brought you a replacement Messenger Hawk from Kingston. He's in the foyer. The mages waved their acknowledgement as Rachel maneuvered the wagon out of the building into the falling snow. The rest of the Royal Expeditionary Force was already assembled and ready to depart. The Garrison guard opened the gates, and the force moved quickly out of the Three Forks garrison and onto the road to Frostberg.

Once they were out of the town and on the road, Donovan asked Rachel, "What say we put up a couple of Weather shields to get our men out of this snow? I know we don't normally use them outside the Academy, but these guys already know we're magicians." Rachel thought it over and agreed that there was no harm in it, just as long as they didn't tire themselves out too much.

Donovan erected the largest Weather shield he could, covering the leading half of the column of mounted soldiers, while Rachel's shield covered the back half. Once the shields were up, snow was no longer falling on the soldiers. The soldiers looked up in wonder, grateful for the reprieve, and Major Gerald rode back to the mage's wagon. "That's a neat trick," he said. "How long can you keep it up?"

"A Weather shield doesn't take much power to maintain, Major," said Rachel. "As long as we don't have to conjure more powerful spells, we can probably maintain them until we stop for the night." Major Gerald smiled. "I had no idea that magicians could cast Weather spells." "It's something we don't usually use outside of the Wizards Academy," explained Donovan. "Because it marks us out as magicians, but we decided that everyone here already knows we're magicians, so it doesn't matter. How long do you think it's going to snow?"

"Who can say? I hope it ends soon. It's piled up pretty good on the road already. What can you two do to clear the road if the snow gets too deep?" Donovan and Rachel pondered the question. "In Kingston, Academy students are paid by the crown for snow removal services. We can use Wind, Remove, or Heat spells to move or melt the snow. Those spells require a lot more energy, so we would have a hard time maintaining them for very long."

"Let's hope it doesn't come to that then," said Major Gerald. "By the way, congratulations on your promotion. Mage Gregory informed me of his and Mage Roark's recommendation to Wizard Noland." "Thank you, sir. It was quite unexpected, I admit," said Donovan.

Major Gerald smiled, "Wizard Noland told me that he nearly promoted you to mage after what you did during your Sorcerer's Test, but he didn't want to set a bad precedent for future students." "I had no idea," said Donovan. "Although, Wizard Mira did seem overly surprised when I extinguished Wizard Dylan's fireball while holding a shield."

"Well, keep the Weather shields up as long as you can without tiring yourselves out too much. I doubt that we'll run into any trouble on the road, especially in this weather, but you never know." The Major rode off to check on the rest of the Expeditionary Force and the rapidly deteriorating condition of the road ahead.

The snow lessened somewhat during the afternoon, and the Major called a halt earlier than usual to account for the miserable weather conditions. He rode back to the magician's wagon and asked if there was anything they could do to protect the force overnight. "If we pull the men in tight, we might be able to erect a Weather dome over the campsite," said Donovan. "The Weather shield will only stop rain, sleet, or snow, so if someone shoots an arrow, or even throws a rock at us, the shield won't stop it."

Major Gerald considered the idea, then ordered the men to camp in close formation, surrounding the three wagons, which were in the center of the bivouac. Once all of the tents were erected and the campfires arranged, Donovan and Rachel erected a dome-shaped Weather shield over the encampment.

"Please tell the men not to walk through the shield," said Donovan. "If they do, they'll break it and we'll have to cast it again." Major Gerald nodded his understanding and passed the word among the soldiers. There was some grumbling, but most of the troops were very, very happy about not having to stand guard while being snowed on. The wood that the men gathered for the fires was cold and wet and was difficult to ignite, so Donovan and Rachel used Fire spells to help get the campfires started.

There was immediately a problem. Smoke from the campfires rose to the top of the Weather dome, then descended as more and more smoke was generated. As the soldiers began coughing from the smoke, Donovan released the Weather shield, which allowed the smoke to rise into the night sky.

Major Gerald approached and asked, "Can you make a hole in the shield for the smoke to escape?" Donovan shook his head, "No, Major. Shields don't come with holes. I can create a flat, *angled* shield, which will allow the smoke out, and the men can walk out the sides or back to gather more firewood, or use the privy," said Donovan. "It won't be as warm though." "It's still much better than anything we've ever had before while campaigning in winter. Let's try the angled Weather shield."

The angled Weather shield was much easier to maintain, and the smoke from the campfires rolled up the sloped shield and out without choking the men below. Donovan agreed to take the first watch and wake Rachel a little after midnight. Rachel crawled into the wagon, lowered the front and rear flaps, and cast a warming spell to heat the air inside. She wrapped herself in her cloak and was asleep in minutes.

Donovan was very tired. He and Rachel had flown to Three Forks from Kingston, then immediately departed, casting and maintaining huge Weather shields all day. Now, he was holding a shield over the camp. He walked to the nearest campfire and sat down on a large stone, his head drooping. "Here, sir. It looks like you need this," said one of the cooks, handing him a steaming cup of tea. Donovan nodded his thanks and slowly sipped the scalding-hot tea. After a minute, he rose and walked around the camp, speaking to the men on guard duty. To a man, they were all exceedingly grateful to Donovan and Rachel for the Weather shields.

"I wouldn't mind winter field maneuvers if we always had these shields," said one man. "And that trick with the fire was pretty slick too. There have been many times when we couldn't get the fire lit and had to sit in the cold all night." Donovan assured them that the Fire spell was easy, and the Expeditionary Force would never have that particular problem again.

An hour after midnight, Donovan climbed wearily into the wagon and gently shook Rachel awake. Rachel grudgingly left the wagon and cast a Weather shield to replace Donovan's, which evaporated as he fell asleep.

The snow continued to fall sporadically throughout the night, and when the sun rose, there was a considerable snow drift piled up at the bottom of Rachel's Weather shield (the falling snow had simply slid down the angled shield and piled up at the bottom). "How are we going to get through all that?" asked a soldier in 1st Company. "Easy," replied Donovan, "the road is that way," he said, pointing in the opposite direction of the large heap of snow.

The Force had a chilly breakfast, then remounted and got back on the road, which was barely visible under the mounting snow. At least the sky was clear and it had stopped snowing (for the moment). As they moved slowly down the road, Donovan mounted Rachel's chestnut-colored horse, Ginger, and rode to the front of the formation. The lead riders were struggling through the deep snow.

"Let me see what I can do," said Donovan. He first tried a strong Wind spell. While the wind blew the snow off the road, it swirled around in the breeze, creating a blizzard condition for the men riding behind the first few riders. "I guess Wind isn't the answer," said Donovan. Next, he tried the Heat spell to melt the snow, but quickly abandoned that effort. The melted snow turned the road into deep mud, and the melting of so much snow was very tiring.

Next, Donovan tried the Remove spell, which worked a little better, but had to be constantly re-cast as the force advanced along the road. After a while, Donovan tried the

Reduce spell, which had served him so well in previous situations, but the individual snowflakes, being pretty small to begin with, did not shrink much under the Reduction spell. Running out of ideas, Donovan tried conjuring a protective shield in front of himself and pushing the snow off the road, but the weight of the accumulated snow quickly became too heavy to push, and Donovan abandoned the effort.

Frustrated, Donovan resumed his use of the Remove spell, and the force advanced slowly. Around mid-morning, Rachel rode up to the front of the column and asked Donovan how he was doing. "I'm tired," confessed Donovan. "The constant use of the Remove spell is wearing me out." "What other spells have you tried?" asked Rachel. "Wind, Reduce, Heat, and for a while, I tried using a shield to push the snow off the road, but it's too heavy."

Rachel thought for a second, then asked, "Have you tried Dig?" Donovan shook his head, "Dig is not one of the spells we used to clear the snow in Kingston," he replied. "Of course not," said Rachel. "That's because many of the students ended up digging too deep and damaging the cobblestone roads in the city. Out here, I think we're OK. We might dig up some of the compacted dirt on the road, but that shouldn't be a problem. Let me try."

Rachel cast the Dig spell, and a long stretch of the road was suddenly clear of snow. Donovan leaned over for a kiss and said, "You're a genius. Can you take over for a while? I'm beat." Rachel smiled at the compliment and said, "Sure. Why don't you go take a nap in the wagon? Healer Bone is driving it. I can handle this for a while. It's much easier to dig in snow than in dirt."

"DRAGON MESSENGER ARRIVING!" Andrew shook his head to clear it. *Where was he? Oh, in his cabin.* How he got there was another matter entirely. The last thing he remembered was a big Sea Dragon crashing into the mizzen mast, and his rushing toward it to finish it off before it regained consciousness. He took a drink from the water jug on his table, and quickly ate a couple of the hard crackers that passed as snacks on a ship, then headed topside to see which Dragon Messenger had arrived, and with what news.

As he came up on deck, the cold wind out of the north stung his face and brought him to full wakefulness. He headed aft to find the Commodore talking to Sorceress Anne, one of the two magicians in the Royal Navy who were used as Dragon Messengers. "Ah, awake at last are you?" asked Commodore Matthews. Andrew nodded grimly, "Yes, sir. I'm awake. How long have I been sleeping?" "Almost four days, lad. You've got to stop overdoing it. Although, I understand from the crew that the illusion that made the dragon crash head-on into the mizzen mast was quite a trick."

"That one was cutting through anything on the deck with a fine spray of water. I wasn't sure I had enough strength left to hold a shield against it," said Andrew. "Seemings take almost no power, and I figured that if the dragon hit the mast, it might kill it, or at least knock it out." The Commodore grinned. "That it did. Then you cut off its head before you passed out on the deck. It's a good thing that there weren't any more of them."

Andrew nodded. "All of the others had already flown off. I think the last one just wanted to do a little more damage after dropping his load of rocks. What were our casualties?" "We had one dead and three wounded. There was also a civilian on deck who was crushed by a tree trunk. Do you know anything about him?" asked the Commodore.

"Yes, sir. He and two companions tried to sneak up the gangplank and onto the ship, figuring we were all asleep. When I confronted them, one man jumped overboard, and the other tripped and fell head-over-heels back down the gangplank and onto the dock. The last one swung a cutlass at me, so I paralyzed him. That was just before the dragons attacked. I was so busy fighting dragons that I forgot to release my Paralysis spell. The poor man couldn't take cover and was an easy mark for the dragons," said Andrew sadly.

"Humph," said the Commodore. "Well, it served him right. We probably would have had him keel-hauled for an attack on a Royal Navy magician anyway. Good work with the dragons by the way." "Thank you sir, but in the future, we need to leave a magician on each ship. The VICTORY was too far away from me and Sorcerer Marvin for either of us to provide much protection."

"I thought that might be the case," said Commodore Matthews, "since they took the most damage in the attack." Andrew nodded his understanding, then turned to address Sorceress Anne. "Hello, Anne. What brings you out this way on this fine day at sea?" he asked.

"I have a message for you from the admiral. I also have one for the other two squadrons, so I can't stay long," said Anne. She handed one of the three message pouches that she was carrying over to Commodore Matthews.

The Commodore opened the pouch and extracted the message. It was brief and to the point. "We are ordered to return to Sundock and complete the re-fit of our Seabows. Once all of the ships in the Fleet have the new Seabow upgrade, we are to stand by for further orders for attacks against the Sea Dragons."

"That sounds simple enough," said Andrew.

"I wonder if I could talk with them, maybe make them see reason, before we attack?" asked Anne. "There's nothing in my orders that speaks to that," said the Commodore. "I figure it'll take about two weeks to get the modifications done on all of the ships, then we will most likely be ordered to sail for the Coral Islands."

Anne thought about the baby Sea Dragon that she had played with during her brief stay in the Sea Dragon colony. She resolved herself to try and prevent another bloodbath like the last one, even if it went against the admiral's orders.

Chapter Ten:
THE BEST INTENTIONS

The Royal Expeditionary Force rode into Frostberg two weeks after departing Three Forks. The men were cold and tired, as were Donovan and Rachel. They'd made very good time, considering the circumstances, but it was still a long, cold trip. As the men settled into the sparse barracks in the Frostberg garrison, Donovan and Rachel went in search of Sorcerer Stewart, the lone magician in the town. They found him in the town's Healing Clinic, magically healing a child's broken arm.

"There, that should do it," said the older-than-normal Sorcerer. Stewart was short, about five feet tall, with black hair and a short beard. He looked up as Donovan and Rachel entered. "And how can I help you two this fine day?" Stewart asked cheerfully. "I'm Mage Donovan, and this is my wife, Mage Rachel. We're the magical support for the Royal Expeditionary Force, and we just arrived in town. Are you Sorcerer Stewart?" asked Donovan.

Stewart rose from his chair and greeted Donovan and Rachel warmly, "I am indeed, sir. How can I help you? I don't think we were expecting the Royal Expeditionary Force, but welcome! Is this your first time in Frostberg?" "It's the first time for Rachel. I visited here some years ago with my father, Wizard Edward," replied Donovan. "Well, come on in and have a seat. If you just rode into town, you must be frozen! Would you like some tea? I have some in the back."

"Anything hot would be wonderful," said Rachel. "Is it always this cold here in the winter?" Stewart emerged from the back room with three steaming mugs of tea, which he placed on the table. "It's always cold here," said Stewart. "It's just *colder* in the winter, which has just begun, by the way. It will get much colder before it starts to warm back up again in about three months." Rachel shuddered. Sorcerer Stewart laughed, "Believe it or not, you get used to it. After five years here, I think I'd find it uncomfortably hot in Southport, or even Kingston."

"I understand that you're the only magician in town?" asked Donovan. "Yes, sir, but it's not that bad. I have two Enforcers, Toby and his twin brother Colby, but there's really not much crime in Frostberg. It's just too cold for sculking around, and there's really not much here to steal. The only trouble is usually when one of the townsfolk gets drunk and starts a fight. In the winter, drinking is about all there is to do around here, so it can get pretty rowdy sometimes."

"I understand," said Rachel. "Anyway, the reason we're here is that the King sent the Royal Expeditionary Force on an inspection tour of all the cities and towns in Franconia. He wants us to audit the Treasuries to make sure everything is in order. You know how King Henry is." "Not really," said Stewart with a frown, "I was posted here just before his coronation. What's he like?"

"He's a young man, given a difficult job, with a lot of power, and he often receives conflicting advice from his Ministers and advisors," replied Donovan diplomatically. Stewart frowned, "So he's like a spoiled child with no supervision…" "No. It's not that bad. He usually listens to Marshall Guzman and Wizard Noland. He did get some very bad advice from Victor, the Court Wizard, though." "Why would the Court Wizard give the King bad advice?" wondered Sorcerer Stewart.

That began the long explanation about the dragons, how they could change into human form, how to detect them, and all of the other news from around the Kingdom. "I had heard that Mage Edward was killed by a dragon, but nothing else. Frostberg is so far out from the capital that it takes forever for us to get news here. So, you're saying that Mage Edward was *not* killed, and he is now a Wizard, and the Chief of Military Wizardry in Franconia?"

Donovan grinned, "That's right. I should also mention that he's my father." "Well then, I guess you would know," said Stewart. "So, you want to inventory the treasury? We'll need to find the Mayor for that." Donovan yawned, "Actually, we'll save that for tomorrow. I'll also issue you your Concealment cloak tomorrow. We just came by to make your acquaintance and let you know we were here."

"How long will the Expeditionary Force be in Frostberg?" asked Stewart. "Only a couple of days," said Rachel. "I imagine the troops need a short rest, then we have to find a ship heading to Sundock." "Hmmm," said Stewart. "The 2nd Squadron was in port yesterday, but I don't know how long they'll stay. They're usually only in port for a day or two. It might be a good idea to have your commander head down to the port and see if they're still there. Otherwise, it might be a long wait. We don't get many ships here in the winter."

With the information that there was a squadron of Royal Navy ships in port at the moment, Donovan and Rachel took their leave of Sorcerer Stewart and hurried back to inform Major Gerald. "I guess I'd better get down to the port then," grumbled the Major. "We sure don't want them leaving without us, and stranding us here for weeks." The Major put his boots back on, took his cape from the hook where it was drying, and headed back out into the snow.

Major Gerald returned an hour later, considerably happier. "You were right! The 2nd Squadron, under the command of Commodore Lang, is in port and scheduled to depart in two days. Can you two be finished with the treasury inventory tomorrow?"

Donovan looked at Rachel, "We should be," she replied. "I mean, I don't imagine there will be that much gold in this town." "You might be surprised," said Major Gerald. "The principal export from Frostberg is crabs, and they fetch a hefty price. There may be more here than you imagine." Donovan shrugged, "We'll get it done, sir. Besides, there's no garrison here to check and we already met the Regional Sorcerer, and he's not a Changed One. Having a squadron here also means that we can issue Concealment cloaks to the magicians aboard."

"I like it," said the Major. "I'll let Commodore Lang know, and inform the men that we'll begin loading the day after tomorrow. How are you doing, Donovan? Any more 'bad feelings'?" "Not in Frostberg, but the Regional Mage in Sundock is probably a Sea Dragon Changed One," said Donovan. Major Gerald groaned. "How on earth would you know that?"

"It's a little trick I picked up while we were in Kingston," said Donovan. "You see…"

"So, Franconia wants us to attack the Fire Dragon colony?" asked King Donald. "Yes, Your Majesty," replied Kathy. "We will be launching an attack on the Sea Dragon colony in the next few weeks and hope to bring them to heel in order to negotiate a binding Peace Treaty with them." "I thought that such a Treaty was already in the works," said the King.

"The first attempt failed, sire. King Henry and his Ministers insisted on a lot of additional terms in the Treaty, like fishing rights, and what constituted a 'vessel.' The final document ended up being 37 pages long, and the Sea Dragons rejected it completely. It seems that dragons can't read, which is something we never considered. The dragons wouldn't agree to a Treaty that they couldn't understand. They wanted a simple, 'We won't attack you, if you don't attack us,' agreement, and that was not what King Henry offered. The Sea Dragons rejected the Treaty and also canceled the temporary truce with the Franconian Navy. They have begun attacking Franconian ships and port facilities again, dropping heavy stones on ships from high in the air, while they're under Concealment spells. It's a difficult attack to counter," explained Kathy.

"I imagine so," said King Donald. "What is King Henry doing about it?" "We have magicians on every Royal Navy ship, and they're using Sight Enhancements to scan the skies for distortions that might be Concealed Dragons. Then, they either fire Blast spells at the falling stones or erect shields to try and deflect them. They've had limited success, and, frankly, not inflicted very many casualties on the attacking dragons," said Kathy.

"So, we can probably expect the same type of attacks on our ships," mused the King. "That is certainly a possibility, sire. Although Baize is quite a distance from the Coral Islands. Another thing I should mention: when Franconia was negotiating the Treaty with the Sea Dragons, they made it very clear that any Treaty would only apply to Franconia, since they very rightly stated that King Henry did not speak for the Kingdom of Baize."

"These dragons are no fools," said Wizard James. "That is certainly true," said Kathy. "We are most concerned about the new combined-clan attacks, like the one the dragons launched against Three Forks." "Why is that?" asked the King. "It appears that the dragons have learned that our magicians can change into dragons, and a Sea or Snow

Dragon is no match for a magician who has transformed himself into a Great Dragon. By sending Great Dragons of their own with the Sea, Snow, and other dragons, they reduce their vulnerability."

Wizard James nodded. "I understand. And you say that the dragons are aware of our ability to change into dragons?" "Yes," said Kathy. "They learned about it after the attack on Three Forks, three weeks ago. I do not know how far this information has spread amongst the dragons, though."

"You also told Wizard James that there may be more Dragon Changed Ones than we anticipated?" asked the King. "Yes, Your Highness. When the Regional Mages in Franconia conducted their searches for Changed Ones, they only looked among the military and the nobility in the kingdom. They overlooked the merchants that provided expensive goods to wealthy clients, since magicians seldom have the opportunity to patronize those shops or taverns. Also, a neutral Changed One told us that many of the blacksmiths in Franconia are actually Fire Dragons, while the undertakers are often Stone Dragons. The Changed One, Alfred, said that there were "several dozen" Changed Ones in Kingston alone, but he would not help us find them."

The King looked troubled. "That is disconcerting," he said. "Yes, sire, and there are probably more Changed Ones in Baize than there are in Franconia," said Kathy tactfully.

"Why do you believe that?" asked James. "It's because of how our magicians are dispersed and what their missions are," explained Kathy. "In Franconia, each town and city has a magician assigned, usually a mage. These 'Regional Mages,' as they are called, are there to assist the local Enforcers in maintaining law and order, but also to seek out citizens with the spark of magic. If a Regional Mage discovers what they call a 'rogue magician,' they are detained and sent, usually unwillingly, to the Wizards Academy in Kingston, where they are held until they pass the Sorcerer's Test. That is not how it is done in Baize."

"Indeed not," said James. "Here, those with the spark seek out the local magicians in order to be tested and enrolled in a local school for magical instruction." "Exactly so," said Kathy. "That means that a Dragon Changed One, who must have the spark, is much more likely to be discovered in Franconia. No one in Baize is looking for them. At least, not until lately."

Now the King and his Court Wizard looked troubled. The thought of dozens of potentially hostile Dragon Changed Ones in every city in Baize was a frightening thought. "What can we do?" asked James.

Kathy considered the problem for a moment, then said, "You might try using the military magicians to search the towns where they're stationed, looking for any Changed Ones. They need to be prepared, though, if the Changed One is hostile. You both saw what happened with that Stone Dragon."

When Wizard Edward had first visited Baize and informed King Donald of the threat posed by the dragons, the King had ordered what he thought was a thorough search of the palace. However, his magicians neglected to inspect the palace servants, and a Stone Dragon, disguised as a night baker, had eluded the search. Later, that servant had transformed into a Stone Dragon and attacked the King. Fortunately, Wizard Edward was there to enclose the dragon in a protective shield, suffocating it, but it had been a near thing.

"Quite right," said the King, "James, will you send out an order immediately. I want all of our military magicians to conduct a careful search of the towns they are posted to. Their mission is to discover, and either kill or bind any Changed Ones they find." "I will send the message at once, Your Highness," said James.

"It has been good to see you again, Wizard Kathy. James has informed me of your promotion, and I'm happy for you. Before you leave, I will provide you with a document authorizing Franconia to negotiate on our behalf with the Sea Dragons, so that any Peace Treaty would apply to both our kingdoms. With regard to any attack on the Fire Dragon colony in the Grey Mountains, we will certainly consider your request, but I would expect some assistance from our magical friends in Franconia in any such an attack. I believe that Fire Dragons are much more formidable than Sea Dragons, and I would hesitate to attack without the assistance of our allies."

Major Gerald was right about there being more gold in the Frostberg Treasury than Donovan expected. There was almost five thousand golds; an enormous amount for such a small town. "It's the crabbing industry, you see," explained Josh, the Mayor of Frostberg. "Crabbing takes a lot of money. The ships are constantly being damaged by the ice floes, crab pots are lost at sea, and the fishermen have to pay very high salaries to their employees. I mean, crab fishing is *dangerous!*"

"Throughout the year, crab boat captains are constantly asking for loans to pay for repairs, equipment replacement, or other expenses. We happily loan out the money to support what is really the only industry in Frostberg. But, we don't get our money repaid until the crab harvest is in, packed, and shipped, and the payments are received. In winter, the payments take a bit longer to collect, since there are fewer merchant ships that will brave the dangerous waters to get here to pick up a load of crabs," explained the Mayor.

Despite the large amount of coin in the treasury and the complicated loan arrangements, it seemed that everything was in order, and there were no significant shortages. At the end of a very long day, Donovan and Rachel returned to the garrison and knocked on Major Gerald's door. "Come! Ah, you're back. Is everything in order?" he asked. "Yes, sir.

We're done with the audit, and everything seems to be as it should," replied Donovan. "Good! That means we can leave tomorrow. We'll start loading an hour after dawn. I have to warn you, the Commodore says that the sea can be a little rough this time of year."

"Anything to get somewhere warmer," said Rachel. "I hope the King *never* assigns us anyplace this far north!" Major Gerald laughed and dismissed them for the night, informing them that dinner would be served an hour after sunset, which came earlier than usual this far north. "What's for dinner, sir?" asked Donovan. "Crabs, of course," said Major Gerald.

Donovan and Rachel retreated to their room, which was freezing cold, and Donovan was all too eager to conjure a Heating spell which warmed the air in the room. Rachel stopped shivering and said," Thanks. I was hoping that you'd do that." Donovan leered and said, "And *I* was hoping we could find another way to keep warm."

As Azure landed outside Bruce's hut, she heard, "That curly line is an 'S,'" said Bruce patiently. "S?" asked Richard. "Yes. It sounds like sss," said Bruce, making a hissing sound. Richard had discovered a cache of children's color books in a corner of Bruce's makeshift bookcase and was trying to understand what all the 'squiggly lines' meant.

Bruce explained that they were letters, which formed words, which made up sentences, that told a story.

Richard was fascinated. He had never considered any form of communication other than the spoken word (Why would he? He was only a year old). Azure changed into human form quickly and got dressed. She entered the hut to find both Richard and Annalise sitting at Bruce's feet while he read them a story and helped them learn their letters. "You are teaching them to read?" she asked.

Bruce smiled, displaying his stained and crooked teeth, "I'm trying. Richard found this old stack of children's books and started paging through them. He asked me what the symbols in the books meant." "And where is Gek?" she asked. "I think he went out to catch some fish for dinner," said Bruce, as the children became restless at Azure's interruption.

"I will leave you to it then. Thank you, Bruce," said Azure. She walked carefully into the back room and laid down on the cot that she slept on when in human form. Azure was weary after the long flight from Acropo and was grateful that she didn't have to entertain the children for a while. She was asleep in minutes.

"Wake up sleepyhead." Azure roused slowly. It was dark outside, and Gek was standing in the room next to her. She had slept all day. "What time is it?" Azure asked. "Just after sunset," replied Gek. "Bruce was trying to teach the children how to read, and I figured that you needed your rest, so I let you sleep. There is fresh Sea Bass in the kitchen if you are hungry."

Azure yawned, then said, "Sorcerer Donovan and his wife, Sorceress Rachel, both survived the dragon attack on Three Forks last week." Gek's jovial mood evaporated. "How do you know this?" he asked. "A Sea Dragon Changed One named Wood arrived on Acropo while I was there with a message from the Fire Dragon, Cinder. Cobalt ordered Wood to kill Sorceress Rachel as soon as she returns to Three Forks."

"We'd better hope that she is successful. Some of these magic-users are hard to kill," said Gek. "I know," said Azure. "Are we certain that this is the same 'Donovan' we are bound to protect?" asked Gek. "Not entirely, but Cobalt does not think we can take the chance. If it is not the right 'Donovan,' there is no harm done. There is simply one less magic-user for us to fight."

Gek nodded at the truth of Azure's observation. "Did Cobalt have any suggestions as to where we could move to?" "No, but he said that he would make inquiries among the Sea Dragon Changed Ones along the coast. One of them may have a useful suggestion." "Just as long as it is not Grotton," said Gek. "I know that many Changed Ones settled there, but Mage Charles is not a magic-user to trifle with. It is a miracle that Beau and the others have eluded him for so long."

"There are many smaller hamlets and settlements along the coast. We might even find a suitable place across the river. After all, Ig and his family have lived there for years without detection," said Azure. "That is true, but they did not have a human child. I worry about Richard. How can we teach him what he needs to know to be a successful human? That is one reason that I encouraged Bruce to teach Richard this 'reading' thing. It is something that all humans can do. Richard will need to learn if he ever needs to move about among the humans."

"It is not such a bad skill for a dragon to learn either," replied Azure. Gek humphed, "Anna just does not want her brother to be able to do something that she cannot. This is one instance where sibling rivalry works in our favor," said Gek.

Azure thought for a moment, then asked, "Why do we have to leave here? We can ask Bruce to help us build our own hut to live in! He certainly has enough driftwood gathered, and he might appreciate the challenge and the privacy." "That is an excellent idea!" said Gek.

Miss Woods, the Sea Dragon Changed One, landed on the playground behind her school in Three Forks and made a disturbing discovery. The decomposing body of Cliff was laying in the sawdust near the back door. *So much for not violating the Binding spell,* she thought. But now she had a dilemma: *What to do with Cliff's body?* She couldn't very well call the city Enforcers; Mage Roark would undoubtedly accompany them, and she couldn't risk being discovered as someone with the spark, much less a Dragon Changed One.

If only I knew the Dig spell, she thought. This was a problem. She had been gone for several days, and Mage Roark was surely looking for Cliff's whereabouts by now. When his body was discovered, the magic-users would most likely deduce that he had broken his Binding spell and died as a result. They would not know *what* he had done to violate the spell, but it would make them curious. *His body could not be discovered here*, she thought.

Fortunately, much of the city of Three Forks was still damaged from the dragon attack, and the magic-users and city Enforcers had their hands full with containing the lawlessness that had briefly engulfed the city in the aftermath of the attack. *Perhaps she should move his body to someplace that would draw suspicion away from her, and onto someone else.* While she considered her options, she needed to get the body out of sight. She quickly moved the corpse into the schoolhouse, depositing it (temporarily) in the school's supply room.

After moving the body, Miss Woods left the school and wandered around the city, looking for someplace appropriate to dispose of Cliff, where it would not lead anyone back to her. During her tour of the city, she learned that the Royal Expeditionary Force had departed a few days ago, headed for Frostberg, so her attack on Sorceress Rachel would have to wait a few days. As Miss Woods walked, the snow continued to fall heavily, and she had the idea that all she had to do was drop Cliff's body in the street and it would be covered by the snow in less than an hour.

But where? She wondered. *It could not be anywhere near any of the Changed Ones she knew to be living in the city.* There was a woodlot behind the Mayor's house, but there was currently an awful lot of activity around his residence. She finally decided to simply drop Cliff's body in the Sapphire River and let it drift downstream, away from the city.

After disposing of the corpse, Miss Wood turned her thoughts to how to eliminate this Sorceress Rachel, who was assigned to the Royal Expeditionary Force. She knew from conversations she overheard in town that the Force had left Three Forks some time ago, and that they were heading to Frostberg. She also knew that every soldier in the outfit was armed with a deadly crossbow. She would need to plan her attack carefully. Taking on a magic-user was perilous for a Sea Dragon, especially one surrounded by soldiers with crossbows.

The dragon knew that the heavy snowfall would slow the Expeditionary Force's progress, but attacking them alone was still risky. Ultimately, she decided to fly to Frostberg and await their arrival. She would watch for an opportunity there.

Chapter Eleven:
SCHEMES AND PLANS

Damn this heavy snow! Thought Miss Wood, the Sea Dragon Changed One. She didn't mind the cold, the ocean depths were colder than this. It was the heavy, *clingy* snow. It coated her wings, making flying difficult and slow. She had tried to fly above the clouds, but they were higher than usual, and the thin air and biting cold at that altitude made it more miserable than flying lower and enduring the snow.

To make matters worse, the Expeditionary Force had seemingly not been slowed much by the snow. She had expected to find them shortly after leaving Three Forks, but by the time she located them, they were almost to Frostberg. No matter, she wasn't planning on attacking them on the road anyway. Her plan was to wait until the female magic-user was alone and eliminate her then. A dragon was nothing if not patient.

She landed on the outskirts of Frostberg, changed into human form, and donned her heavy coat and winter clothing before trudging into town through the deepening snow. She took a room at a boarding house near the Frostberg military barracks, where she assumed that the Expeditionary Force would be staying, and settled down to wait for their arrival.

Two days later, a column of mounted soldiers arrived and quickly occupied the garrison buildings. As she watched from her window, she saw the soldiers lead their mounts to the stables, while the two magic-users rode into town alone. Thinking that this might be the opportunity she was waiting for, Miss Wood quickly put on her coat and hat and ventured out, following the two magicians.

They went to the Frostberg Healing Clinic (whatever that was). As she waited outside (under a Concealment spell) in the still falling snow, she heard one of the occupants of the house telling the magic-users that there were ships in port which could provide transport to Sundock if they completed their business in town quickly, before the ships had to leave for Sundock.

What a stroke of luck! It would certainly be easy enough for a Sea Dragon to sink one of those puny human ships, or better yet, use a blast of water to knock a careless Sorceress off the deck and into the freezing water. Once in the water, the magic-user was *dead!* She would either freeze to death in a matter of minutes, or Wood could always grab her and drag her to the bottom of the sea.

Circling high over Grotton, Wizard Edward (in Great Dragon form) spied the naval warehouse that was used by the Dragon Messengers. He descended rapidly and landed softly in the spacious interior of the warehouse. He released his Concealment shield and transformed back into his human form. Once dressed in his new Wizard's robes, he re-cast his Concealment shield and exited the warehouse, heading for the Naval Headquarters building.

Edward released his Concealment shield before entering the building and approached the receptionist's desk. The young receptionist looked up from her paperwork and said, "Good morning, sir. How may I help you?" Edward smiled and said, "I am Wizard Edward Francis, the newly appointed Chief of Military Wizardry, and I'm here to see Admiral Cross and Wizard Lake, please."

The receptionist blinked hard, then regained her composure and said, "At once, sir. If you'll just follow me." Edward followed the somewhat flustered receptionist down the hallway to the admiral's office. She knocked timidly. "Yes, Page, what is it now?" came the gruff voice of the admiral from behind the door. Opening the door slightly, the young woman said, "Sir, a Wizard Edward Francis is here to see you and Wizard Lake."

"The new Chief of Military Wizardry? Well show him in, show him in!" Page opened the door for Edward, who strode into the office of the Chief of Naval Operations and said, "Forgive me for arriving unannounced, Admiral, but we have some urgent matters to discuss." The admiral rose from his desk and came over to greet Wizard Edward.

"I'm at your disposal anytime, sir," he said, offering his hand, "Admiral Hector Cross, at your service." Edward shook the admiral's hand warmly and proceeded further into the spacious office. "Page, dear, go fetch Wizard Lake and tell him that the Chief of Military Wizardry is here. Then bring us a pot of tea, please."

"At once, sir," said the receptionist, who closed the door hurriedly and practically ran down the hall to inform Wizard Lake of Edward's arrival. "Your facility for receiving Dragon Messengers is most impressive and discreet, Admiral. I had no trouble locating it, and I would never have suspected such a dilapidated structure was used for anything so vital to the Navy." The admiral beamed at the compliment and said, "Thank you, but it was actually Sorceress Anne who suggested using that old surplus warehouse as a landing pad for Dragon Messengers. Then she and Wizard Lake emptied and refurbished the inside of the building in less than a day."

"Impressive, and as I said, a most clever subterfuge," said Edward. Just then, Wizard Lake knocked and cracked open the admiral's door. "Come in, Wizard Lake! This is Wizard Edward, the new Chief of Military Wizardry," said the admiral, making introductions. "Hello, Bill," said Edward, "it's been a long time. How are you?" The two Wizards embraced briefly.

"I'm fine, Edward. I must say, I was very relieved when we heard that you had *not* been killed by that dragon a few years ago. Where have you been keeping yourself lately?" "Well, after the fight with the dragon, the King assigned me to go to Baize with the Royal Expeditionary Force to conduct a punitive raid on the city of Springfield, in retaliation for the dragon attack on Weaton. Then I got delayed in Baize when King Donald asked me to help them with the problem of the expanding Salt Flats in eastern Baize. I only returned a short time ago."

"You always did have a knack for finding trouble," laughed Wizard Lake. "Admiral, Edward and I were classmates at the Wizards Academy." "Indeed? Well, that must have been a banner year for magicians. Sit down, sit down. Page should be here any minute with tea. So, Wizard Edward, what brings you to Naval Headquarters?"

"Several matters, actually," began Edward. He stopped as the receptionist, Page, brought in the tea cart. After the tea was poured and Page had departed, Edward continued, "We've learned several concerning things about these dragons recently, and I thought I'd pop over and give you an update. Have you heard about the attack on Three Forks?"

"Three Forks? No. The last report I received was about attacks on Sundock and Eastport by invisible dragons, dropping stones on our ships. What happened at Three Forks?" Edward related the details of the attack and the troubling new combined-clan attacks. He also informed them that, at least some of the dragons were aware that magicians could transform into dragons.

"Wait, you're saying that two sorcerers from the Royal Expeditionary Force changed into Great Dragons and killed six of the attacking dragons? That sounds like someone grossly exaggerating their military prowess!" said the admiral. Edward smiled. "One of the sorcerers was my son, Donovan, and the other was his wife, Sorceress Rachel. I know it sounds incredible, but I did receive confirmation from Battle Mage Gregory and Regional Mage Roark, both of whom were present."

"Your son? I thought you told me once that he didn't believe that he had the spark!" said Wizard Lake. Edward smiled, "He has reconsidered. In fact, he graduated from the Wizards Academy in just over three and a half years, faster than anyone in history. After the battle of Three Forks, I promoted both him and Rachel to Battle Mage, making them the youngest mages in Franconia."

"Even younger than Mage Andrew on the HMS VALOR?" asked the admiral. "Yes. Andrew is three years older than his cousin, Donovan," said Edward with a smile. "Cousins? Your family certainly has some strong magical genes!" said Wizard Lake.

"I suppose," said Edward modestly. "But I didn't come here to brag about my son and nephew. I have convinced the King that we need to blockade the Coral Islands in order to bring the Sea Dragons back to the negotiating table. He's ordered the entire 1st Fleet to undertake this operation. We need to take the Sea Dragon Clan out of the fight, then concentrate our efforts on the Fire Dragons."

"We could have done that already if the King hadn't mucked up the first treaty!" said Admiral Cross angrily. "I know," said Edward, "but signing that treaty would have been a mistake." "How can you say that?" asked Wizard Lake. "I've read the first treaty, and it says that the dragons will not attack our sailors and port facilities." "Exactly!" said the admiral. "It would have spared the Navy any further attacks!" "Yes, but we need the treaty to say that the Sea Dragons will not attack any *humans*, not just *sailors.* I think it was a trick by the Sea Dragons to lull us into a false sense of security, then they could attack our forces on land with impunity."

The admiral and Wizard Lake sat back in their seats, considering Edward's words. Finally, the admiral said, "You're probably right. I should have seen that." "These dragons are cunning," said Edward. "It's similar to our last treaty, where they promised not to eat people. They didn't promise not to *kill* them, just not to *eat* them."

"You're saying that we have had a treaty with the dragons before?" asked Wizard Lake. "Yes. About two hundred years ago, we signed a treaty to provide the dragons with 20,000 head of cattle every two years, and they promised not to eat people. A Binding spell was even cast to ensure compliance." "So, what happened?" asked the admiral curiously.

"We gave the cattle slow-acting poison before we gave them to the dragons. Then, as the dragons died from the poison, the Army and the magicians of that time were sent in to finish them off." Wizard Lake whistled. "That's devious. Effective, but devious." "I agree," said Edward. "There may have been no other way, but it still seems evil."

"So, what does King Henry want the new treaty to say?" asked Admiral Cross. "Simply that we will not attack the Sea Dragons, and Sea Dragons will not attack humans. We cede the Coral islands to them but retain the right to shelter up to one squadron of ships in that cove on the northernmost island. Nothing in writing, just their Clan Chief's word with a Binding spell on top," said Edward.

"Do you think they'll agree to that?" asked Wizard Lake. "I hope so," said Edward. "After all, the Sea Dragons are the clan most likely to agree to a treaty." "Why do you say that?" asked the admiral. "Because the Sea Dragons do not lack prey, like the other dragons. There are plenty of fish in the sea. The Fire Dragons may eat fish, but I imagine that they have a hard time catching them. Gentlemen, the primary resource we're fighting over here is *food*. Dragons only eat meat or fish, and they need a lot of food to survive. The Sea Dragons do not suffer from hunger like the other clans. We need to use that to our advantage. That's undoubtedly one reason they would not agree to any restrictions on *fishing rights.*"

"So, what's the plan?" asked Wizard Lake. "We blockade the Coral Islands with 1st Fleet. How did you get them to attack the last time?" Wizard Lake grinned, "Mage Andrew and the other sorcerers in 1st Squadron set fire to the southernmost island. That got the dragon's attention pretty quickly." "I imagine. Let's hold off on that tactic, at least initially. The goal is to make peace. We can always resort to stronger measures if they won't cooperate."

"How long do we have?" asked the admiral. "I would like to move as soon as possible. These invisible attacks are hard to anticipate and counter. I should know. The Fire Dragons did the same thing to us in Baize. They also seem to be able to target our magicians with these rocks."

"Do we have time to install the new Seabow modifications?" asked the admiral. "I'm sorry, what modifications are you talking about?" asked Edward. "The arms merchant, James, developed what he called a Compound Seabow. It uses a system of pulleys so that the Seabow can be drawn by just one sailor, instead of two. He was making the modifications to the Seabows on the HMS VICEROY when the dragons attacked and he was killed."

"James is dead?" asked Edward. "I'm afraid so. Did you know him?" "Yes, we were neighbors in Kingston before he moved to Fairview. Damn! If James is dead, who's making the modifications?" "Apparently, his daughter is the only one who knows how. She's working on them, with magical protection. Her husband insisted on it after James's death."

"You're saying that Maria is modifying our Seabows?" asked Edward. "Yes. In fact, most of 1st Fleet already has the modified Seabows. Only 1st Squadron has a few left to be upgraded," said the admiral. "I ordered the fleet to get every ship the modified Seabows as soon as possible and assemble in Sundock."

"Please ensure Maria's safety. Maria is also a friend of mine and Donovan's," said Edward. "She's also a relative," said Wizard Lake. "How can that be?" asked Edward. "Because Maria married Mage Andrew after her father was killed. He's the one who insisted that a magician guard her while she works." Edward smiled.

"Next, Wizard Lake and I need to have a conversation with your Regional Mage. It seems that there may be a lot more Dragon Changed Ones in the kingdom than we anticipated…"

The new hut was finished. It was really no more than a square shack, made out of driftwood, with an eating area and three separate bedrooms. Since they had no need for a kitchen or a fireplace, the construction had been relatively easy. The three doors were each wide enough for a dragon to enter without knocking anything over. Bruce had collected a surprising amount of furniture over the years that had washed up on the shore, which he used to furnish the hut.

"That should about do it," said Bruce. "It's not fit for the King, but as long as the roof doesn't leak too badly, I think it'll do." Gek walked around the structure, looking for obvious flaws. "Are you sure it will hold up in a storm?" he asked.

Bruce considered the question for a moment, then replied, "I think so. The walls and roof are held together with baling wire, so they should stand up to most weather. Still, if we have a real blow, everything will collapse together. Of course, you could say the same thing about my hut, and I'd be much worse off than a dragon if my roof fell on me."

"I was thinking about Richard," said Gek. "He could be badly injured or even killed if the roof falls on him." "You're right. So, if we get a big storm, you might want to keep him in your room, just to be safe."

"That is a good idea," said Azure. "I guess we should move in immediately." "There's no rush," said Bruce, "but also no sense in waiting. It's not like you have a lot of luggage." Bruce laughed at his own joke. As they spoke, Annalise walked over and examined the hut. "What is this for?" she asked. "This is our new home," said Gek. "Really? Which room is mine?" "The one over here with the bigger outside door," said Azure. "Your brother does not need a dragon-sized door yet."

"Yet?" asked Anna. "We hope that he will learn how to change into a dragon someday, but it may be several years from now." "I see. What kind of dragon will he be?" Gek considered the question and said, "He will probably be able to change into either a Great Dragon like me, or a Sea Dragon like your mother." "But *not* a Great Sea Dragon like me?" asked Anna. "Probably not," said Azure. "Richard will probably have to choose one or the other at a time. You are unique." Anna smiled, "I like that."

"Just don't think your uniqueness will last forever, we will undoubtedly have more children in the future," said Gek. "Will they be dragons or humans?" "We shall have to wait and see," said Azure.

The new hut was about a hundred yards up the beach from Bruce's shack, and, like his, was set back from the beach, above the high tide mark, and in the tall grass and brush where it would not be seen by anyone walking along the shoreline. While it might not be a long-term solution to their housing problem, it was certainly the best compromise they had come up with. Bruce was happy for the company, but disliked being awakened during the night whenever a dragon came tromping through the house. Even the recently constructed 'back door' had not completely solved the problem (but it had certainly helped).

Richard waddled up to the new hut, munching on a mango. He looked over the structure and asked, "Ours?" "Yes, Richard. This is our home now. We will sleep and eat here. You can visit Bruce when he is at home." Richard walked into the driftwood shack and sat down in Anna's bedroom. "Mine?" "No, Richard. This is Anna's room. Your room is over here," said Gek, escorting the child to the bedroom with the smaller, human-sized doors.

"But that room is bigger!" wailed Richard. "No," said Azure. They are the same size, only the door going outside is bigger. Anna needs more room to get in and out. Dragons are bigger than humans." "But I want that room!" Gek sighed. "When you are old enough to change into a dragon, we will make your door to the outside bigger." "How long will that be?" "I do not know. Probably a few years from now," said Gek. "But, I want it now!"

Gek despaired of arguing with a year-old child (who looked like he was three). "I said, 'No.' If you do not like your room, you can always sleep outdoors." Richard stuck out his lower lip and glared at his sister, who smiled back smugly.

Chapter Twelve:
WARNINGS

"You can't be serious!" exclaimed Mage Charles. "How could there be dozens of Dragon Changed Ones in Grotton? Besides those old rogue magicians at the Cannery, we haven't found anyone with the spark in months!" "I'm not sure there are *dozens* of Changed Ones in Grotton," said Edward, "but there are certainly more than we thought. While interrogating a Changed One in Kingston, we learned that many of these Changed Ones have secured employment with merchants who provide high-end goods and services to wealthy clients. The one we caught was a waiter at the King's Table Tavern. He said that he avoided detection for five years because magicians do not frequent that establishment because they can't afford it."

Edward and Wizard Lake were seated in the Grotton Regional Mage's Office and were bringing Mage Charles up to date on recent developments. Mage Charles paused to consider Edward's words. Finally, he admitted, "You may have a point, sir. We have not made a thorough search of the wealthiest merchants in Grotton. While there are not many of them, I suppose it's possible for some of those with the spark to have eluded us by working in those types of shops."

"You're not alone. It never occurred to me either. Have you checked any of the Blacksmith shops in the city? We've also learned that Fire Dragon Changed Ones often seek employment as blacksmiths, and Stone Dragons prefer work as morticians or undertakers." Mage Charles looked thoughtful, "No, I have not searched in those places either. We always assumed that if anyone of low estate had the spark of magic, they would come forward voluntarily in hopes of improving their lot in life by becoming a magician."

"That's a common opinion among the Regional Mages in Franconia. One that we must change. If the waiter in Kingston is correct, there may be hundreds of undetected Changed Ones in the kingdom. Not all of them will be hostile, but I have seen the destruction that a single Stone Dragon can cause. It's not something I wish to re-visit," said Edward.

Mage Charles nodded his understanding. "Now, the few *prosperous* Changed Ones that we have identified have all accepted Binding spells, and promised never to change back into a dragon, and never to harm a human. I suspect that this is because their lives as humans are much better than the common man (or dragon). Those in less desirable jobs have generally been unwilling to agree to a Binding spell and had to be killed," said Edward.

"I understand," said Mage Charles. We will begin searching immediately." "I recommend that you start with the lower classes first: the blacksmiths, tanners, refuse collectors, and undertakers. Those Changed Ones are likely to be the most hostile," offered Wizard Lake. Mage Charles nodded in agreement.

"Now I need to tell you both something that is of concern, but by no means certain. It appears that my son, Mage Donovan, may be able to conjure the spell of Foresight, and he has foreseen an attack on Grotton by multiple fire-breathing dragons. He has no idea when such an attack may occur, but I must take his prediction seriously," said Edward.

"The spell of Foresight? But that hasn't been effected in over a century!" exclaimed Wizard Lake. "I know," said Edward. "But Donovan, who is assigned as magical support to the Royal Expeditionary Force, correctly anticipated an ambush on the road outside of Colton and the recent dragon attack on Three Forks. Donovan was never taught the spell, but informed his commander that he 'had a bad feeling' about both Colton and Three Forks. When we met in my office a week ago, I asked him to scan a map of Franconia and tell me if he had similar bad feelings about any other city in Franconia. He identified Sundock and Grotton."

"Just because he has a bad feeling about Grotton doesn't mean there is an imminent dragon attack!" said Mage Charles. "You are correct," said Edward. "However, Wizard Nolan and I informed Donovan of the incantation and gesture required to conjure the spell of Foresight. Once Donovan employed them, he saw the dragon attack. Unfortunately, Donovan cannot say *when* such an attack may occur. It may be soon, or years from now. We know so little about this spell."

"So, how do you recommend we prepare for this future attack?" asked Wizard Lake. "First, I recommend installing

Stone Dragon roof tiles on all of the key buildings in Grotton. These dragon scales are fireproof and can stand up to a magician's Blast spell. The roofs of the palace in Kingston have already been covered with them. I brought you one to replicate." Edward handed over a grey Stone Dragon scale. "While we have been able to replicate and reduce these in size, we have not been able to make holes in them. I believe that the carpenters in Kingston used tar to attach them to the roofs."

"Second, make sure that all of your magicians know how to change into Great Dragons. Donovan and his wife, Mage Rachel, have proven that Great Dragons can kill Snow and Sea Dragons easily, and Fire Dragons with some effort," said Edward. "What about Stone Dragons?" asked Mage Charles. "You need to encase them in a protective shield. First, that prevents them from destroying anything, and eventually, it suffocates them." Both magicians nodded their understanding.

"Now, the Royal Expeditionary Force is currently making a nationwide tour of Franconia. They should be in Frostberg by now. From there, they will use water transport to visit Sundock, Eastport, and then Grotton before returning to Kingston. Donovan has predicted that the Sundock Regional Mage is a Dragon Changed One. He will investigate such when they arrive in a couple of weeks. If his prediction proves true, I would say that he has the gift of Foresight."

"Why is the Expeditionary Force making such a sweeping tour of Franconia? I would have thought a position closer to Baize…" mused Wizard Lake. Edward looked around, then cast a Silence spell around them. "It seems that former Minister of Internal Security, Jasmine Onyx, used the Remove spell to vanish about ten thousand golds from the Kingston Treasury. The Expeditionary Force is conducting inventories of all the other Treasuries, just in case Jasmine had accomplices in other cities and towns." The two magicians gasped, *"TEN THOUSAND GOLDS! That would be ruinous!"* said Wizard Lake. "Indeed," said Edward. "It was most fortunate that the theft was discovered and the missing gold replicated while the King was away in Southport."

"Should I inspect the Grotton Treasury?" asked Mage Charles. "No," said Edward. "Major Gerald, the Commander of the Royal Expeditionary Force has an order signed by the King and the Minister of Finance, authorizing their audit. Without such a document, I doubt the treasurer would allow you access to the vault. You might discreetly make sure that the Treasurer is not a Dragon Changed One, though."

The Expeditionary Force began boarding the ships of the 2nd Squadron just after dawn. It was cold (naturally) and overcast, but the soldiers were only too happy to be leaving this frigid town. "I'm sorry to have to split up your command, Major," said Commodore Lang, "but these aren't cargo ships. There just isn't enough room in our holds for fifty men and horses."

In order to transport the entire Royal Expeditionary Force, one wagon had to be tied down on the deck of each of the three battleships: the HMS SEAHAWK, the HMS SEASPARROW, and the HMS SEAGULL; and the men were dispersed among the battleships and the frigate, the HMS ABLE. Once the horses were walked into the holds, the men quickly boarded and began stringing hammocks in the crowded and chilly space remaining.

Two of the 2nd Squadron sorcerers, Henry and Owen, agreed to share a cabin on the SEAGULL, allowing Donovan and Rachel to use Sorcerer Owen's cabin on the HMS SEASPARROW. Major Gerald rode on the SEAHAWK with Commodore Lang, Captain Smith rode on the SEAGULL, and Captain Fletcher found a bunk on the ABLE.

As soon as the force was loaded, the ships cast off, leaving Frostberg behind and heading out into the open sea.

Onshore, Miss Woods watched the loading, trying to determine which ship the sorceress got on, but the blowing snow and the milling about of the soldiers blocked her view, and as the ships departed, she had no idea which ship Rachel was on. She decided that it was undoubtedly one of the bigger ships with a wagon lashed to the deck, but beyond that, she had no idea. She would just have to keep a close watch and strike when the opportunity presented itself.

The VALOR's mizzen mast exploded spectacularly, spraying splinters across the deck. The mast fell backwards, striking the rudder and obliterating the aft Seabow. The ship listed to starboard as the mast sank into the water, pulling the ship towards the churning ocean. Andrew ducked and quickly erected a shield as the wood splinters rained down on the weather deck. The ship slowed as the mast acted as a sea anchor, still attached to the ship by the lines and rigging.

"CUT IT FREE! QUICKLY!" shouted the commodore. Crewmen rushed aft, grabbing axes and cutlasses. They struggled along the tilted deck and began furiously hacking through the ropes connecting the broken mast to the ship. Andrew recovered and said, "STAND BACK!" Using the Remove spell, Andrew rapidly cut the lines holding the mast to the ship. Once free of the mast, the ship settled back to an even keel, and the mast sank out of sight.

"MAN OVERBOARD!" shouted the first mate. Andrew rushed to the broken stern railing and spied the crewman who'd been swept overboard in the confusion. Casting a Tether spell, he seized the struggling seaman. "LAUNCH THE LONGBOAT!" shouted Commodore Matthews. While the crew wasted no time in lowering the lifeboat and reaching the sailor, by the time he was brought aboard, he was in shock from the submersion in the cold water.

"Get him to my cabin, quickly!" ordered Andrew. The sailors quickly carried their shivering shipmate to Andrew's cabin. Andrew entered and conjured a spell to heat the air in the cabin, attempting to warm the freezing sailor quickly. It wasn't enough. Hypothermia had already taken hold, and the man was fading rapidly. "Can't you do anything?" asked the commodore, who was standing behind Andrew.

"There's one last thing I can try," said Andrew, "but it might kill him." "Hurry, man! He's turning blue!" *"THERMO INTENSIF,"* murmured Andrew, attempting to warm the sailor's blood just enough, but not too much. The blue tint faded from the sailor's lips, and his breath came easier. Andrew wrapped him in blankets before taking a drink of water and then raising the temperature in the cabin a bit more. The sailor opened his eyes and said, "Uncle?" "You'll be all right, Sam. Just rest a bit." The sailor nodded and fell asleep.

"Uncle?" asked Andrew. The commodore nodded, "Yes, Seaman First Class Sammuel is my nephew. I'm very grateful, Andrew. I thought he was a goner. In all my years at sea, I've never seen anyone saved after going overboard in water this cold. Most men go down in seconds." "I tethered him, which kept him on the surface until the longboat could get there," said Andrew. "Still, it was a near thing. His body temperature was very low by the time we got him out of the water."

"What did you do there at the end?" "I used a temperature spell to warm his blood. I've never tried that before. You see, too hot and he dies, not enough and he dies.

I must have gotten it just right on my first try," said Andrew as he slumped into his chair. "Andrew!"

"Sorry, sir. I'm just tired. Do masts often just shatter like that?" The commodore humphed, "No. I suspect we have that dragon to thank for that. Colliding with the mast must have weakened it, and this damn gale out of the north did the rest. That was quick work getting those lines cut. We might have lost the ship."

"What do we do now?" asked Andrew. "I'll have the VICTORY tow us to shore, and then we'll find a nice tall tree to fashion into a mast. We have spare sails, spars, and lines in the hold, and I'm hoping you can repair any damage to the rudder. Why don't you get some rest, lad? I'll wake you when we get where we're going. It's just going to take us a little longer to get to Sundock."

Edward landed back at the Wizards Academy marina. He transformed and dressed quickly. *We should probably leave a footlocker here with some robes in it*, he thought. That would make changing easier and avoid having naked magicians streaking across the academy grounds. He opened the portal and proceeded to Wizard Noland's cottage. Wizard Faith met him in the courtyard.

"We should probably find a way to adjust the alarm in the gatehouse so that it only alerts you when someone opens the portal from the inside," said Edward. "We thought of that, but Michael said that he wants to know whenever anyone arrives, so it will have to stay as it is," said Faith. "How was your trip to Grotton?"

"I'm not sure that Mage Charles believes that Donovan can conjure the spell of Foresight, but he's concerned enough to step up his search for Changed Ones. The admiral is all for blockading the Coral Islands and has issued orders to the Fleet."

As they walked across the courtyard, Wizard Noland opened the door to his cottage. "Edward! Welcome back! How was Grotton?" "The same as always, Michael, humid and smelling of fish. I ordered Mage Charles to expand his search for Changed Ones, and he admitted that they had made the same mistake as all of the other Regional Mages, and neglected to search both the elite and the lower-class establishments. I was just telling Faith that the admiral is all for blockading the Coral Islands and was sending orders to the fleet as I departed."

"Excellent! Kathy returned earlier this morning, so she should be either at home or in your office." Edward smiled, "Speaking of *home*, I promised Kathy that we would look for a new house once she passed her Wizard's Test. Do you have any suggestions?"

Wizard Noland replied immediately, "Why, yes, now that you mention it. Do you remember Duke Draper?" "The one who married Dutchess Simpson? Of course. What about her?" "Well, the Duke died a little over a year ago, and apparently the Dutchess fled the city. At least, no one has seen her in the last year. I understand that her villa is currently in receivership and can be purchased for the very reasonable price of one hundred golds."

"Did you say a *hundred* golds? You must have mistaken me for the King!" Wizard Noland laughed, "Now Edward, I know you have money, and I sincerely doubt that you told Donovan where *all* of it was hidden. Besides, your new position pays handsomely. Add in Kathy's salary, and the two of you can easily afford it."

Edward thought for a minute. Michael was right, he did have over a hundred golds on deposit at the Kingston National Bank, and he had not touched it in years, so it had surely grown while he was in Baize. "Now that you mention it, what is my salary as the Chief of Military Wizardry?" "I looked it up in the old records. Wizard Raymond, the former Chief, drew a salary of one gold a week. I think Kathy deserves at least half that amount." Edward frowned, "Three golds a month is more like it." "Done!" said Noland with a smile.

"Now, go find Kathy and head over to Kingston Realty before someone beats you to the villa. I hear it's magnificent." Edward smiled. "I shall certainly take your advice. Since tomorrow is Endday, I would like to convene a meeting after Mentor Testing to discuss what we should offer the Fire, Great, Snow, and Stone Dragons in our next treaty. I would like the academy faculty, Wizard Cassandra, and a Changed One from each of the clans to attend. Do we have one from each clan at the academy?"

Wizard Noland thought, "Yes, Level Three Vida is a Fire Dragon, Level Three James is a Great Dragon, Level Three Sandra is a Snow Dragon, and Level Two Rufus is a Stone Dragon Changed One. However, there are concerns about whether Rufus will be able to pass his test for advancement to Level Three."

"That will be fine," said Edward. "We should probably release them all from the Binding spell, never to transform back into dragons. As long as they are still bound not to injure humans, we'll be safe. We need to consider sending those four as emissaries to their respective clans."

Wizard Noland considered the idea. "That would certainly be to Rufus's liking. I know that both he and his Mentor are worried that he will not be able to advance and will end up having his spark removed. He's a good boy, just not very bright." Edward nodded. "I understand that that is a trait common among Stone Dragons. We'll discuss it tomorrow. Please bring them to my office after lunch." "We'll be there," said Noland. "Now hurry along and buy your pretty wife an estate."

Chapter Thirteen:
DIRE STRAITS

"Close that damn door!" shrieked Rachel. Donovan hurriedly entered the cabin and closed the door firmly. "No need to shout, Miss Grumpy-pants. Are you planning to spend the whole voyage here?" "You bet I am! It's FREEZING out there! And it's not much better in here when you keep opening the door and letting the cold air in! I'm tired of warming the air in here just for you to let it out!"

Rachel was curled up in the bed, under three blankets and her Concealment cloak, which, for the record, was *not* designed for warmth. With the onset of winter, the ice pack had moved south of Frostberg, and the 2nd Squadron was currently plowing through it in a single file. "*Someone* has to blast or remove the blocks of ice from the water in front of the ship! Forgive me if I come back to warm up once an hour. And for the record, I KNOW IT'S FREEZING OUT THERE!" shouted Donovan. "Sorry," whispered Rachel. "I'm just not used to this weather. How do the sailors stand it?"

"Well, for one thing, they have warmer clothes. When we left Kingston, we didn't pack our winter gear (if we even have any). I know it's cold, sweetheart, and I'm sorry for shouting. Just give me a minute and I'll head back up on deck."

"DRAGON MESSENGER ARRIVING!" "Now?" asked Rachel. "Of course, now," grumbled Donovan. I wonder whether it's Anne or Phillip. I'd better go check. Be back later." Donovan gave Rachel a quick kiss and hurried out of the cabin, closing the door as quickly as he could.

The blue Sea Dragon was waiting on the aft deck as Donovan approached. "Anne?" he asked. "Hello, Donovan. Fancy meeting you here. Yes, it's me, Anne. Forgive me for not transforming, but being naked in this weather is not conducive to my health. If you could just take this message pouch and give it to Commodore Lang, I'd appreciate it."

"I can't," said Donovan. "You landed on the wrong ship. The commodore's on the SEAHAWK, two ships back." "Damn!" said Anne. "OK, I'll take it back to him." "How much further before we get to some warmer weather?" Donovan asked. "Quite some ways, I'm afraid. The weather doesn't break until you're almost to Sundock. That's where you're headed, right?"

"Yes," replied Donovan, shivering. "How much more ice is there ahead of us? I'm getting tired of blasting or removing it." "You have about ten more miles of ice ahead of you on this course. Have you tried casting a shield in front of the ship? That's what Mage Andrew did, and apparently, it moves the ice away before it hits the ship. It might slow you down a bit, but I understand it's much less taxing than blasting or removing the ice."

"Thank you very much!" exclaimed Donovan. "Anything else we should know about?" "Well, I think I saw a Sea Dragon swimming alongside your ships." "What! Where?" "It was off the port side, but it went deep when I approached," said Anne.

"I wonder what it's doing. If it was going to attack, I think it would have already done so." "Maybe it's just tracking your progress," suggested Anne. "It might not be hostile at all." "Do you think I should get the Seabows manned?" "In this weather? They'd be frozen in no time. Will the Seabows even work when it's this cold?"

"Yes. Battle Mage Link told me that they'd all been 'winterized,' whatever that means, before they headed to Frostberg. They should work if we need them. I hate to ask, but could you make a quick search around the squadron before you leave? It'll only take a minute," said Donovan.

"OK, but just one lap, and I'm *not* going underwater!" Anne made a quick lap around the four ships but saw nothing to be concerned about. She yelled to Donovan that all was "Clear," before landing on the HMS SEAHAWK and delivering her message pouch. She remained on deck only briefly before taking off again, heading back south. She failed to notice the Sea Dragon, which was hiding under the keel of the HMS SEAGULL.

Donovan quickly cast a protective shield in front of the bow of the SEASPARROW and immediately noticed the change. The ice floes no longer hit the ship. Their speed decreased somewhat, but the ride was certainly smoother. On the plus side, while Donovan had to maintain the shield, he didn't need to be on deck to do it, and as Anne had said, holding a shield was much less taxing than blasting and removing icebergs.

Donovan headed below deck to the Captain's cabin. He knocked firmly. "Come!" said the voice of Captain Caine, the commander of the HMS SEASPARROW. "Oh, come in, Mage Donovan. Was that a Dragon Messenger I heard being piped aboard a while ago?" "Yes, sir. It was Sorceress Anne. She landed on the wrong ship with a message. I sent her back to the SEAHAWK." The Captain nodded his understanding. "Are we through the ice pack already? I don't feel any collisions."

"No, Captain, Sorceress Anne says that we still have about ten miles to go before we break clear of the ice, but she told me that Mage Andrew from 1st Squadron used a shield across the bow of his ship to push through the ice pack, and it was much easier and smoother. It's certainly easier on the magician, but it has cost us some speed." The captain smiled, "No matter. We're not in that big of a hurry. I'll take a smoother ride any day. Is that what you came down to tell me?"

Donovan nodded, "Well, that, and that Sorceress Anne thinks she saw a Sea Dragon following the squadron." "WHAT? WHERE?" "She said it was off the port side, but when I asked her to fly around and locate it, she couldn't find it. She said there was only one."

"What do you think?" asked the captain. "Sir, *one* Sea Dragon is not a threat to four warships equipped with Seabows, even in this weather. I really can't imagine what one dragon is hoping to accomplish alone. Still, it might be prudent to uncover a couple of the Seabows and have crews on each side standing by."

"In this weather, the men will get frostbite quickly if I order them on deck," mused the captain. "Sir," said Donovan reluctantly, Rachel and I could erect Weather shields around the Seabows. Weather shields will at least keep the wind and the sea spray off the men. You'd still have to rotate them frequently, but we could try it for a short while." "I like it. Please ask Sorceress Rachel to man the Seabow amidship on the starboard side, and you take the one on the port side. I'll get the men." Donovan groaned. He was going to pay for this.

The villa was magnificent. It had eight bedrooms, complete with private baths, an enormous kitchen, a covered patio, a spacious family area with two fireplaces, and a detached carriage house with a stable, with stalls for four mounts, and expansive gardens. It was certainly a bargain at one hundred golds, but the upkeep and maintenance would be costly. "This is wonderful!" said Kathy. Edward humphed. "This is certainly more than Mrs. Haywood could keep clean, only coming in one day a week."

"Yes, well, we'll obviously need some staff. A live-in housekeeper, a cook, and probably at least one gardener." *A staff,* thought Edward. That was something he'd never envisioned needing.

"The Duke and Dutchess maintained a staff of five," said Mr. Jackson, the realtor. "They had a maid, a butler, a cook, two gardeners, and a coachman." Edward groaned. "I don't suppose any of them are still available?" asked Kathy, hopefully. "Alas not. The property has been vacant for over a year now," said Mr. Jackson.

Kathy and Edward strolled around the villa. It certainly needed some repairs, but nothing they couldn't magically fix. Except for the lawn and gardens, which were choked with weeds and overgrown with some sort of creeper vines. The carriage was similarly in need of repair and was currently undrivable. That was something they would have to contract out for, *if* they made the purchase.

The villa was on the north end of town, on a hill overlooking the Sapphire River, quite a distance from their office in the palace. "I don't know," said Edward. "This is much larger than I had envisioned, and I hadn't anticipated the need for a staff of employees. It's also quite a way from our office. Why, just furnishing a place this large would cost twenty golds." Mr. Jackson looked crestfallen. "The furnishings come with the purchase," he said desperately, "and am I correct in assuming that you have a house in town that you'll be selling? That sale will offset the purchase cost and reduce the agency's fees."

"Hmm," said Edward, "I suppose that's true. Why don't you do an assessment of our current house, and we'll make our decision then. We'll want to keep some of our furnishings, but certainly not all of them." The realtor looked relieved and promised to have an assessment done on Edward's house by the end of the day. Edward told him the address and replicated a key for him.

"Now, we have a meeting this afternoon. We'll come by your office tomorrow morning and see if we can work something out," said Edward. Mr. Jackson looked elated. The villa had been on the market, with no one interested, for several months.

Edward and Kathy rode back to the palace, had lunch in the palace dining hall, and then returned to their office. "Do you really think we can afford the villa?" asked Kathy hopefully. "We are certainly buying the villa," said Edward with a wink. "I'm just trying to get the best price. After we finish this afternoon, we need to start looking for our staff. I think Mrs. Haywood and her husband would make an ideal maid and butler, if they're interested, but I don't know anything about hiring gardeners, cooks, or coachmen."

The Sea Dragon, Wood, was having no luck. She had been following the ships of the 2nd Squadron for two days now, and she was exhausted. Unlike the ships, she could not make it all the way to Sundock without rest and sleep. *I will give it until sundown,* she thought. *If I do not find the*

Sorceress by then, I will fly to Sundock and make my attack there.

She had been surveilling the ships since they left port, trying to determine which ship the Sorceress was on without success. It seemed that *all* of the ships had at least one magic-user on board. She decided that her target was most likely on one of the ships with a wagon lashed to the deck, but which one was a mystery. She had moved closer to the ships as the time went on. It was difficult to make anyone out with the sea spray and the fact that all of the humans were bundled up in heavy winter clothes. The floating blocks of ice did not help either. She was alarmed when another Sea Dragon landed on the first ship in line and spoke to one of the magic-users aboard. She decided that it must be a human magic-user in dragon form.

When the imposter took off and circled the ships, Wood had hidden beneath one of the larger ships to avoid detection. She finally decided to focus her attention on the lead ship in the formation. It was only a few hours until sunset.

"What do you mean, I have to go up on deck?" asked Rachel. "It's freezing up there!" "I know," said Donovan, "I've been up there for most of the last two days. Anne thought she saw a Sea Dragon off the port bow, and the captain wants us to man the two Seabows in the middle of the ship, one on each side. The crew is uncovering the Seabows as we speak. We are to erect Weather shields and warm up the weapons in case they're needed. It should only be for a little while."

"Define 'a little while,'" said Rachel. Donovan winced, "Probably no more than a glass. If we don't see anything by then, we'll come back inside." Rachel pouted. "Stop pouting," scolded Donovan, "it's unbecoming of a Battle Mage."

Rachel rose from the bed and put on another shirt over the top of the one she was wearing. "Let me see your Concealment cloak, and I'll see if I can make it warmer," said Donovan. Rachel handed over the cloak with a skeptical look. Donovan laid the cloak on the bed, then placed one of the fleece blankets on top of it. "*FIRMENTO,*" he said, while pinching the thumb and index finger of his left hand. "There," he said, handing the cloak back to Rachel. "It should be warmer now." Rachel put on the cloak and smiled, "You're a genius." "I try."

The two mages headed up to the weather deck, bracing for the icy wind and freezing temperatures. They cast full-coverage Weather shields once they reached their assigned Seabows. The Weather shield stopped the wind and the sea spray, but did nothing about the cold. Still, the Seabow crews were very appreciative.

Rachel and Donovan scanned the tumultuous sea, but saw nothing. Donovan's protective shield was still keeping the blocks of ice from colliding with the ship, and he noticed the power drain. Not wanting to pass out again, he took a drink from his water bottle, grimacing at its ice-cold temperature.

Something was happening aboard the lead ship. Wood noticed that sailors had removed the canvas covers on the weapons on the sides of the ship and were busy loading the weapons. *I must have been seen,* she thought. As she watched the sailors, she spied a heavily cloaked magic-user moving to the weapon on the right side of the ship. *But who was it?* As the magic-user crossed the deck towards the weapon, the wind blew the hood of her cloak back, and Wood saw that it was a female magic-user! This must be the sorceress she was ordered to kill!

Wasting no time, the Sea Dragon swam close to the hull of the ship, rose up and fired a blast of water at the female magic-user, knocking her down and blowing her across the icy deck towards the waiting sea on the left side of the ship.

Rachel screamed as the jet of water struck her. She was knocked to the deck and went skidding across the ship. She tried to arrest her progress, but she was headed straight for a gap in the ship's railing. *"NERVO,"* shouted Donovan, casting a Tether spell on Rachel before she went sliding overboard. Rachel's perilous journey stopped, but she was still injured and confused.

"FIRMENTO," murmured Donovan, adhering Rachel to the wet and pitching deck. Rather than attend to Rachel immediately, Donovan conjured a Sight Enhancement and began searching the sea for the Sea Dragon, which he assumed was coming under the ship to catch Rachel when she fell into the water. "Sir," shouted the Seabow crewmen, "Your wife is injured!" "I know," said Donovan through gritted teeth. "But if that Sea Dragon pops up again, she might be killed!"

I got her! thought Wood. *Now to finish her off.* She submerged quickly and swam under the ship, planning to catch the sorceress when she fell into the water. She scanned the water, but did not see a human in the churning waves. The blocks of ice were obstructing her vision. *Could she have landed on an iceberg?* Deciding to make sure of the kill, Wood stuck her head above the surface and looked around quickly.

Donovan was waiting when the dragon's head broke the surface, and he triggered the Seabow instantly.

Unfortunately, just as he fired, the ship entered a trough between the waves, and the ship's bow dipped sharply. *The bolt is going to miss,* thought Donovan, but he forgot about the size of a dragon. The Seabow bolt shot through the water and struck the Sea Dragon three feet above the end of its tail.

Wood screamed when the iron bolt hit her. She quickly dove beneath the waves and attempted to swim away, but quickly discovered that swimming was nearly impossible with the iron bolt protruding through both sides of her tail. She thrashed about painfully, then decided that her only hope of escape lay in flying. She headed for the surface and the safety of the air.

"You hit him, sir!" shouted the Seabow crewman. "Yes, but only in the tail! Reload! Quickly!" The new Compound Seabow took much less time to reload, and Donovan began scanning the wavetops for the injured Sea Dragon.

The dragon broke the surface about a hundred yards from the ship and began flapping her wings madly, the Seabow bolt creating a drag on her as she moved through the water. As her tail emerged from the water and the drag lessened, Wood thought she had accomplished her mission and was about to make her escape. Before she rose more than a dozen feet in the air, another iron bolt struck her in the back, between the wings.

As she died, her last thought was that she did not believe that anyone could have made that shot.

"So, what are we looking for, exactly?" asked Andrew. The Bos'n grinned, "A tall, generally straight, white pine tree, about fifty feet tall. The mizzen mast should be about three-quarters the size of the main mast from the deck up. It doesn't have to be exact, but close."

Mage Andrew and a party of five sailors had come ashore on the sandy beach in search of a tree that they could use to replace the shattered mizzen mast. The sailors all carried small hand axes, and they had a large, two-man saw. Eventually, the Bos'n found a tree that would do. It was a tall eastern white pine with a straight trunk and branches only on the topmost section of the tree.

As the sailors got ready to begin sawing, Andrew asked, "Would you gentlemen like some magical assistance? I'm sure that I can bring this big boy down much faster and easier than sawing." The crew eagerly accepted Andrew's help, and using the Remove spell, he cut a wedge in the tree to make sure that it fell where they wanted it, then another Remove spell on the opposite side of the tree, and it fell (spectacularly) into the open area along the beach. The sailors cheered.

The sailors ran forward to begin chopping off the branches and shortening the tree to the right size, but again, using the Remove spell, Andrew completed the process faster than they could have. "What now?" asked Andrew. "Now we need to strip the bark off the tree. Any magical spells that will do that for us?" asked the Second Mate. Andrew thought for a moment.

"Well, I can't use the Remove spell, that might take too much wood off, let me think…" While Andrew pondered the problem, the sailors got busy with their axes, 'gently' stripping the bark off the enormous tree. This was going to take a while. Then Andrew came up with a solution.

"Hold it, men, I have an idea. Stand back." The sailors retreated from the tree, and Andrew murmured, *"REDUCTO,"* while pinching his right thumb and forefinger together. The fifty-foot tree shrank to about five feet in length. "Now, strip the bark off it, and I will enlarge it when you're done, so we can check to make sure we got all the bark off," said Andrew. The bark was stripped from the much smaller tree in short order.

"OK, stand back while I enlarge it again," said Andrew. *"DILATA,"* he muttered, performing the 'Enlarge' gesture. The tree lengthened back to its trimmed size, and the crew inspected it, removing a few lingering pieces of bark that they'd missed. Once the tree/mast was constructed to the Bos'n's satisfaction, Andrew asked how they were planning to get it back aboard the VALOR.

"We'll just roll it into the surf, then tow it back to the ship with the longboat, sir. Then, we rig the hoist and pull it aboard for installation. You've seen how that works." Andrew grimaced, remembering how the last mast-replacement operation had resulted in his skinned forearms that were covered with splinters. "I have a better idea. How about I just reduce the mast again, and we carry it aboard in the longboat?"

As the longboat was hauled aboard the HMS VALOR, Commodore Matthews approached and said to the Bos'n, "That was fast. But where's the mast?" The Bos'n grinned and replied, "Mage Andrew's got it in his pocket."

The Sea Dragon dispatched, Donovan raced to Rachel's side. He knelt down next to her and cast a weather dome over them and heated the air inside. "Are you OK?" he asked. Rachel bit her lower lip as tears leaked from her eyes, "No. I think the dragon broke my neck. I can't move my arms or legs. Do you have any Healing Serum handy?" Donovan smiled, "There's some in our cabin, but I don't think your neck is broken. *CODA, FIRMENTO,*" he mumbled. "How's that?"

Rachel tentatively raised her left arm, wincing as she did, then her right arm, and then she shifted her legs. You mean that you glued me to this cold, icy deck?" she asked. Donovan nodded, "Yes, I thought that was better than your falling into the cold, icy water next to an angry Sea Dragon."

Rachel smiled. "I heard you shout the Tether spell, but I didn't hear the incantation for the Adhere spell." "Didn't you scold me once for shouting an incantation, Mentor? I admit I may have said the Tether spell too loudly, but I did manage to get the Adhere spell right. I was rather busy trying to kill a Sea Dragon with a Seabow, after all."

"Did you get it?" "That he did, sorceress," said a nearby sailor. "And it was the finest shot I've ever seen. I could barely see the dragon when it jumped out of the water and tried to fly away. I didn't know these Seabows had that much range…" Donovan grinned, "I may have used a touch of magic to make that shot. Plus, the new Compound Seabow has more power than the original version. Why don't you men get those Seabows back under cover and get below? I'll take care of Rachel."

The seamen quickly replaced the heavy canvas covers over the two Seabows and hurried below deck. "Are you ready to get up?" Donovan asked Rachel, "Or are you planning to rest outside in the fresh air for a while longer?" Rachel slapped his arm, gently, "Help me up! I've had enough *fresh air* for now." As Donovan helped Rachel to her feet, she asked, "Sweetheart, how many spells are you holding right now?"

Donovan considered the question, then replied, "I have a Weather shield over us, and I'm heating the air inside it. Why do you ask?" "What about the shield over the bow of the ship?" "You're right, I'm holding that one too." "THAT'S THREE SPELLS AT ONCE! Only a Wizard should be able to do that!" Donovan put his arm around Rachel's waist as she draped her arm over his shoulder, "I won't tell my father if you don't," he said.

Once in the cabin, Rachel lay down on the bed, her left shoulder was bruised from where the dragon's jet of water had struck her, and her right shoulder was bruised from her slamming into the deck. Donovan removed her Concealment cloak and held it up. The back of the cloak was frayed and torn in several places, a result of her sliding across the deck of the ship.

"Well, you're going to need another cloak. This one's ruined. I hope Wizard Noland will waive the one-gold replacement cost, given the circumstances. Are you ready for some healing?" he asked. "You drink some water first, and maybe eat something. I don't want you passing out again! That would mean *me* having to go back up on deck to maintain the shield over the bow, and it's still too cold out there."

Seeing that Rachel was in no immediate danger, Donovan sat down at the small table in the cabin and ate an apple and had a cup of warm tea. He gave Rachel a cup of tea also, knowing that if she ate anything before she was healed, she would likely sick-up, which would not be good in this small space.

"Ready?" he asked. Rachel nodded. "Minor wounds, or Major? It doesn't appear that you need Mortal Wound-level Healing." "Minor Healing should be fine," said Rachel. "I think I just have some bruises on my arms and shoulders, and some abrasions across my back. If Minor Wound Healing isn't enough, you can try Major later."

"You got it," said Donovan. He crouched down next to the bed, placed his right hand on Rachel's right shoulder, and said, *"ALIEVIO."* Then he fell unconscious, striking his head on the bed frame on his way to the floor.

Chapter Fourteen:
PROBLEMS AND SOLUTIONS

Rachel conjured a Strength Enhancement spell and gently lifted Donovan into the bed. She had no idea why a simple Minor-wounds Healing spell had rendered him unconscious. He probably should have released the shield in front of the ship before healing her, but she knew that he had done more magic for longer without passing out. *Maybe it was the strain of holding three spells at once earlier,* she thought.

After Donovan was under the covers and resting comfortably, Rachel donned her tattered Concealment cloak and went to talk with the Captain. As she walked along the passageway, she felt a jolt as an iceberg struck the bow of the ship. She would need to hurry. She knocked on the Captain's door and heard "Enter!"

Rachel entered the Captain's cabin and said, "Sir, I just came by to let you know that Mage Donovan overexerted himself again and is currently asleep in our cabin. I'll re-establish the forward shield immediately. I just came by to let you know." "Are you completely recovered, sorceress? I heard what happened up on deck," said Captain Caine.

"Yes, sir. I'm fine. Donovan healed me before he passed out. He probably should have released the shield in front of the ship before he conjured the Healing spell. He often overestimates his own strength," said Rachel.

"Or, he was still fatigued from putting two incredible shots into the Sea Dragon a while ago," opined the Captain. "Two?" asked Rachel. "Yes. Apparently, the first shot hit it in the tail. The dragon tried to swim off, but I guess it was too hard to swim with a Seabow bolt through its tail, so it tried to fly away. Mage Donovan killed it almost as soon as it came out of the water. It's like he knew where it was going to emerge. I understand it was a remarkable shot." "Hmm," said Rachel. "When Donovan spars with a staff, he uses magic to anticipate where his opponent's next strike will come from. Maybe he did something similar with the Seabow."

"However he did it, I'm grateful. If you could reestablish the forward shield, that would be much appreciated. It should only be for a little while. I figure we'll be out of the ice pack in under an hour." "I'll go up and put up a shield right now," said Rachel. "Then I'll be in my cabin if you need me."

Rachel made her way up to the deck and quickly cast a shield across the front of the bow. Once the shield was in place, she retreated to their cabin and conjured a Warming spell to take the chill out of the air. She sat on the bed and stroked Donovan's hair. "You really have to get better at managing your power expenditures," she whispered.

The Wizards Academy faculty (less Wizard Faith), Wizard Cassandra, and the four Dragon Changed Ones from the Academy took their seats in the Chief of Military Wizardry's Conference Room. Edward and Kathy entered and sat down. "Thank you all for coming," said Edward. "This is the first in what will likely be several strategy meetings to discuss how we can bring about the end of this conflict with the dragons."

"Before we get too far along, let me bring you up to date on the current situation: The 1st Franconian Fleet, under the command of Vice Admiral Jordan, is currently assembling at our port in Sundock. 3rd Squadron is already in Sundock, while 1st Squadron is headed there from Eastport, and 2nd Squadron is sailing south from Frostberg. I expect all ships to be in Sundock within a week. Once assembled, the remaining ships will be retrofitted with the new Compound Seabows, which enable them to be drawn by a single crewman. I expect these modifications to take no more than a week."

"Once the Fleet is ready, their orders are to sail to and establish a blockade of the Coral Islands, with the intent of bringing the Sea Dragons back to the negotiating table. They rightfully rejected the first peace treaty that we proposed, so we will offer another, simpler treaty. *We will not attack them, and they agree not to attack humans. We will also cede ownership of the Coral Islands to the Sea Dragon Clan, with the stipulation that up to five Franconian ships may take shelter in the cove on the northern island. No human is ever to set foot on any of the islands.* Comments?"

"What if they do not agree?" asked Wizard Noland. "Then we use the Naval magicians to set the central island, I believe they call it Herma, on fire, and fight the Sea Dragons when they emerge. If this does not elicit a response, we move to attack their home island of Acropo. Sooner or later, we will bring the Sea Dragons to battle, or to the negotiating table."

The assembled wizards nodded, while the four Changed Ones looked uncomfortable with the discussion.

"I have hopes that we can come to a reasonable accommodation with the Sea Dragons," said Edward, "Although I suspect that their earlier treaty proposal was a ruse, agreeing not to attack our *sailors* or *port facilities.* Had we agreed to this treaty, the Sea Dragons would still have been free to attack our cities, like Three Forks, without violating the treaty."

"Speaking of Three Forks, in case any of you have not heard, the city was recently attacked by dragons from all five clans. This type of combined-clan attack has never been seen before." The four Changed Ones looked surprised by this news. "Wait," said Vida, "You're saying that Fire Dragons attacked alongside Sea and Snow Dragons?" "Yes," replied

Edward. "This cooperation between clans has me very concerned."

"We know that the Sea Dragons are generally pacifists, and that prey is not a concern for them. The question is, what can we offer to the other clans to get them to end the hostilities?" Edward looked at the four Dragon Changed Ones.

Finally, Sandra, the Snow Dragon Changed One said, "Generally, the Snow Dragons just want to be left *alone.* They are content to remain in the Snow Fields, even though prey is often hard to find. We find it uncomfortably *warm* anywhere south of Three Forks, unless we are in human form. The gradual creep of human settlements into the Caperian Mountains is distressing to the Snow Dragon Clan, since much of the prey they rely on inhabits those mountains."

"That's very enlightening, Sandra. Thank you," said Edward. "What can we offer the Fire Dragons, Vida?" Vida, the Fire Dragon Changed One, said, "I suspect it is the same issue for the remaining clans, and it is what started the last war: *food.* Dragons need copious amounts of meat in order to survive. The Fire and Stone Dragon Clans moved to the west side of the Amber River to minimize the intra-clan fighting over food. Even so, the amount of prey available is limited. Eastern Baize is dominated by the Great Salt Lake, where there is little prey, and in the west, there is a vast desert, almost completely devoid of prey."

"This means that the Fire and Stone Dragons vie for the limited prey that inhabits the area between the Green and Red Rivers in Baize. It is fortunate that neither clan is large, or they would all starve to death. This is why it is not uncommon for dragon parents to consume their children when prey becomes scarce," Vida concluded.

"So it's about food," mused Wizard Noland. "It has *always* been about food," said Rufus, speaking for the first time. "I was not alive during the last war, but my father told me that, even the 10,000 cattle promised to us each year were probably not enough to sustain the dragons. I mean, that is only a little over 3,000 head of cattle a year for each of the four meat-eating Clans (the Sea Dragons eat fish); hardly enough for them to survive and multiply. Frankly, that is why so many of the Changed Ones prefer to remain in human form."

The magicians sat in silence, considering the dilemma. Then Edward had an idea. "Maybe that's the solution! We permit— no, wrong word, we *encourage* dragons to change into human form to sate their hunger. They can live in dragon-form, but if prey becomes scarce, they can alleviate their hunger by changing into humans! There would have to be conditions and limits; safeguards to protect both humans and dragons. What do you think?"

The four Changed Ones considered the idea. It was new and revolutionary, but it might work. "I want each of you to consider this idea. We will meet again next month and discuss the advantages and disadvantages, and how it might be presented to the Dragon Council. Wizard Noland and I have discussed amending the Binding spell in order to permit you four to change back into dragon form and act as emissaries to your respective clans at the appropriate time. That is something else for you to consider. In the meantime, Level Two Rufus, your test for advancement to Level Three has been postponed indefinitely." Rufus looked immensely relieved.

As the magicians left the office, Wizard Noland remained behind. "Do you think that this outlandish idea will actually work, and you can sell it to King Henry?" "It might work," said Edward. "Selling it to the King might be a harder matter. Maybe we should socialize it with Sorceress Celeste first. In any event, I find it odd that it was a Stone Dragon who came up with the idea."

Richard walked out of the door to his room. He still wanted his sister's room; it had a bigger door and was closer to the living room, but his parents were unwilling to discuss the matter further. He wandered up the hill, through the tall grass, found a secluded area, and took off his diaper. He *hated* that thing! He relieved himself behind a Juniper bush and buried the diaper in the loose sand before returning to the hut.

Gek took notice of his son's return and the missing diaper. "Richard, where is your diaper?" he asked. "Gone.

Not needed," replied Richard. "Really? That is wonderful!" exclaimed Gek. "Does that mean I can have Anna's room now?" asked Richard hopefully. "No. There is nothing wrong with your room," said Gek. Richard frowned.

The new hut was taking some getting used to. Gek, Azure, and the children had grown accustomed to Bruce's hut. Since both huts were made from driftwood, there were gaps in the walls that let in rays of sunlight. Since dragons slept most of the day, they had learned where to lay their heads to avoid the sunbeams. The new hut had bigger gaps in the wood and fewer places that remained in the shade as the sun moved overhead in the sky.

"Tonight, I have to take your sister to visit grandma. Then your mother and I must go away for a few days while you stay with Bruce," Gek told Richard. "Can I sleep in Anna's room while you are gone?" asked Richard. Gek sighed, "What is wrong with your room?" "There is a big hole in the wall that lets in the sun. It wakes me up very early every day."

"Well, that is something we can fix," said Gek. "Come, show me this hole." Richard waddled around to the east wall and pointed to a large gap in the driftwood. "I see. I will talk to Bruce this morning and see what we can do about it."

Later that day, Gek asked Bruce how to patch a hole between the driftwood slats. "Most folks use mud," said Bruce. "The problem is, there's no mud around here. Just sand." "What is 'mud'?" asked Gek. "It's just dirt mixed with a little bit of water. You mix dirt and water until you get a kind of paste, then you slap the mud over the hole. Once it dries, it usually sticks to the wood. It won't last forever, though. A good, hard rain can wash it away," explained Bruce.

Gek thought, then asked, "Where can I find this 'dirt'?" "Just fly inland a little way, away from the sand, then dig a hole. You can't miss it," said Bruce. "Very well. I will look for some later today. By the way, we need some new clothes for Richard. He threw his diaper away this morning and says that he does not need it anymore."

Bruce smiled, "Your children grow faster than any I have ever seen before! Let me think, I seem to recall a chest washing up on shore a few years ago that had some children's clothing in it. I had no use for them, so I put the chest in the back of the shed. I'll look for it while you are out digging in the dirt, and see what I can find."

Later that evening, the hole in Richard's wall was patched with mud, and he had some new/old clothes to wear. It was just a shirt and trousers, but Richard was ecstatic. Gek bid Azure and Richard goodbye, and he and Annalise flew off into the night sky, headed for Acropo.

Anne was also headed for Acropo. After delivering her message to Commodore Lang and the 2nd Squadron, she flew south until she reached a point on the mainland that she was certain she could reach Acropo from. She had no desire to try swimming in Sea Dragon form, and she certainly didn't want the Sea Dragons knowing that she could change into a dragon. She settled down for the day in a secluded valley, deciding that she would leave just after midnight in order to reach the island while it was still fully dark.

While she was a dragon-friend and known to many of the dragons on Acropo, Cobalt, the Sea Dragon Clan Chief had certainly been unhappy with her during their last meeting when the Sea Dragons had rejected the proposed peace treaty. She was also worried about how Admiral Cross would react to her warning the Sea Dragons about the impending attack by the Franconian Navy. She was certainly walking a very fine line.

As the Gibbous moon rose over the water, Anne took her bearings and headed for the Coral Islands. She hoped that she could find them in the dark, with only the moon and stars for illumination. The air was cold and felt 'thin' somehow. At least she had to flap her wings more vigorously to maintain her altitude. After two hours, she was sure that she must be getting close. Just as she was beginning to despair, she saw a dark void, surrounded by the shimmering sea.

She landed on the eastern side of the island, happy to find that she was on Acropo, and not one of the other islands in the chain. Once on the ground, she quickly transformed and put on her white "parley" robes. She slung her canvas Navy duffel bag over her shoulder and headed for a spot on the cliffs above the entrance to the Sea Dragon colony where she hoped a friendly Sea Dragon would find her in the morning.

She gathered some firewood and made a small campfire to keep warm. It wasn't nearly as cold on the island as it had been in the air, and certainly not as cold as it was over the waters near Frostberg, but it was still uncomfortably chilly.

She waited patiently, hoping that her mission would not be in vain. She had, however, forgotten how she was going to explain to the Sea Dragons how she got to the island without a boat.

Donovan woke slowly. He had no idea why he had passed out (again). Sure, he was holding a protective Shield spell in front of the ship, but that wouldn't explain the debilitating power drain he'd experienced from the simple Minor-Wounds Healing spell he'd cast on Rachel's bruised shoulders.

As he looked around, he saw Rachel, asleep in the chair beside the only bed in the cabin. She was bundled up in two blankets and her tattered Concealment cloak. Donovan noted that the ship was not being struck by ice blocks, so either Rachel had cast a Shield spell to replace his, or the ships were out of the ice pack. Figuring that he'd been asleep for several hours or days, and since Rachel was clearly sleeping, he figured that the squadron had cleared the ice pack.

He rose quietly and magically heated the teapot that was sitting on the small table near the bed. The smell of freshly brewed tea awakened Rachel. She yawned and asked, "Are you feeling better?" "Yes," said Donovan. "But I can't imagine why I passed out again. I had tea and an apple before I healed you. A simple Healing spell should not have been that taxing."

"I can't explain it either, unless it was because you used so much power fighting with that Sea Dragon. You did admit to casting three spells at once, if you remember." "I remember, and, frankly, in order to hit that Sea Dragon as it tried to flee, I may have actually cast four spells at once. But that doesn't explain why I passed out when I healed you! I was only holding the shield in front of the boat then!" said Donovan.

"Are you feeling OK? Maybe you're coming down with the flu or something. We have been out in the cold a lot lately," speculated Rachel. "I don't think so," said Donovan, "I feel fine. Am I running a fever?" Rachel put her hand on Donovan's forehead. "No. You don't feel warm to me."

"Well, that's a problem for another day. How long was I out for this time?" asked Donovan. Rachel smiled, "Only about eight hours this time." "Are we out of the ice pack, or are you holding a shield?" he asked.

"We cleared the ice pack about seven hours ago, thank you very much. The Captain says that we should be in Sundock in about two more days if the wind stays out of the north." "Have any more Dragon Messengers arrived while I was sleeping?" "No, but I don't expect any. Phillip is undoubtedly delivering messages for the 2nd Fleet in the Low Sea, and Anne just left us a day ago."

"I'm worried about Anne," said Donovan. "Why?" "She seemed *overly* concerned that we were going to attack that Sea Dragon. It almost seemed like she wanted to warn it or something. She certainly tried to convince me that one Sea Dragon wasn't a threat. Boy, was she wrong!"

"That is strange," said Rachel. Suddenly, the ship dipped into a deep trough between the waves, and Rachel hurled chunks of semi-digested apple all over Donovan. "Nice!" Donovan complained. "What brought that on?" he asked, wiping his face and hands on a nearby towel, "Are you sea-sick?" Rachel shook her head 'No,' then hurled again. This time, Donovan was quick enough to erect a shield over his face, and the vomit splashed harmlessly to the floor.

A quick Remove spell cleaned up most of the mess, except for the smell. Rachel rose and raced for the weather deck, holding her hand over her mouth. Donovan rushed after her. After emptying what was left in her stomach and drinking some water to rinse out her mouth, Rachel allowed Donovan to lead her back to their cabin.

"Here, drink some of this," said Donovan, handing her a vial of Healing Serum. "I'm fine, really," insisted Rachel. "Honey, you just threw up all over me and the cabin. You are definitely not *fine*." Rachel reluctantly took a small sip of the Healing Serum, grimacing at the eucalyptus taste common with all such serums.

"Better?" asked Donovan. Rachel nodded. "We've traveled a lot by ship lately, and you've never been seasick before," observed Donovan. "I know," said Rachel. "The rocking of the ship actually feels soothing to me. I can't imagine what's wrong with me."

A hopeful thought occurred to Donovan, and he held his right hand out, fingers spread, towards Rachel and said, *"SENSUS."* Rachel looked alarmed and asked, "Why did you just cast the Sensing spell? You never use that one!" Donovan smiled, "I know why I passed out yesterday, and why you were sick a moment ago. You're pregnant!"

Chapter Fifteen:
HOME IMPROVEMENTS

THE DRAPER VILLA

"So, James, how is the search for these Dragon Changed Ones progressing?" asked King Donald. "Our magicians have identified dozens of these impostors, sire. In most cases, the Changed Ones are only too happy to agree to the Binding spell, never to transform back into dragons, and never to bring harm to a human. However, we have had to kill at least a dozen dragons who would not agree to the Binding spell, and I'm sorry to say, we've had three sorcerers killed during our search. Also, several suspected Changed Ones have fled their cities before they could be confronted."

The King sighed. "It appears that Wizard Edward was right again. I would never have believed that there could be so many dragons, hiding right under our noses!" "Don't blame yourself, sire. This has seemingly been going on for decades, long before you took the throne."

Donald humphed. "That may be, but it is *my* problem to fix. If it becomes known, the people will certainly blame me for this problem, not my predecessors." "That is unfortunately true, sire," said James.

"So, where have we found these Changed Ones?" asked the King. "Everywhere, sire. In every city and town in the kingdom. To make matters worse, it seems as if every blacksmith shop in the country employs at least one Fire Dragon Changed One, and most of them are the ones refusing the Binding spells. We may need to start a training program and increase the pay of our smiths to encourage more apprentices in that career field."

The King shook his head sadly, "We might have been better off leaving them alone," he said. "No, Your Majesty! The risk of them becoming hostile and attacking our citizens without warning was too great a risk! No matter how many dragons we discover, we must continue."

"I suppose you're right," said the King, "but it's still disheartening. James, let me ask you something. How are magicians promoted in Baize? I find that my knowledge is lacking in this area."

Wizard James said, "As you know, sire, apprentice magicians are trained in local 'Schools of Magic,' which we have in every major city in the Kingdom. When the headmaster of the school feels that the apprentice has mastered all, or most of the 38 spells, and can produce the nine serums, they are promoted to sorcerer. After their promotion, the Court Wizard is informed and assigns them to either the Royal Army or Navy, depending on the needs of the kingdom at the time."

"Once a sorcerer is able to cast and hold two spells simultaneously for three glasses of time, their military superior informs me, and they come to Baize to undertake the test to become a mage," said James.

"And how does one achieve the rank of wizard?" asked King Donald. "As I explained recently to Wizard Kathy, there have only been eight wizards at any one time in the kingdom. There is one for each regiment in the army, the Chief of Naval Wizardry, the Chief of Army Wizardry, and the Court Wizard. When a wizard dies or retires, a slate of candidates is put forward by the remaining wizards, and the top candidate is given the Wizard's Test, which requires the candidate to cast three spells concurrently and hold them for one hour. It sounds simple, but it is an exceedingly difficult test. After Wizard Louis was killed, the first three candidates tested all failed the Wizard's Test."

"Are eight wizards enough?" asked the King. James was taken aback by the question. "Sire, that has always been the number. It has been so for centuries." "I understand. What I'm asking is: Are eight wizards enough? It seems to me that more wizards are better than fewer. If we have capable magicians, it seems like we would be better served by having additional wizards. I'm sure we could find jobs for them."

James hesitated. *This is because of Kathy,* he thought. "Sire, as I said, the first three mages we tested all failed the Wizard's Test. I'm not sure that testing the other candidates would have resulted in more being successful…"

"I understand," said the King, "and we certainly don't want to lower the standards and have incompetent wizards in the kingdom. Tell me, were any of the candidates women?" James shifted his feet. "No, sire. All of the mages recommended for testing this time were men." "Has there ever been a female wizard in Baize?" asked the King.

"I do not believe so, sire." "Why is that?" "Statistically, there are more male magicians in the realm. With fewer female apprentice magicians, there are, naturally, fewer female sorceresses and mages; therefore, fewer candidates for wizard," said James diplomatically.

"Has there *ever* been a female *candidate* for wizard?" "Not that I am aware of, sire, but I have only been the Court Wizard for a short while. It may be that there were some in the past that I'm not aware of." The King stared at Wizard James. "I would like you to go through the records and determine if there has ever been a woman considered for promotion to the rank of wizard."

"There is no need to go through the records, sire. As I explained to Kathy during her last visit, traditionally, wizards in Baize have always been men, and centuries of tradition are hard to change," said James.

The King sat in thought for a time. Finally, he said, "In one week's time, I want you and the other two wizards in the city to come up with a list of other positions in the kingdom that would benefit from the appointment of a competent wizard, beyond the eight that we normally have. Then I want a list of all of the mages in the kingdom, with a notation as to how long they have been mages. This war with the dragons is going to take *all* of our magical resources! I will not let tradition stand in the way of our survival."

"The other wizards may resist this change, sire," said James. "I DON'T CARE! It seems to me that Mage Juliet and that mage we met in Springfield, Elaynia?" "Elianna," said James. "Yes. Elianna. She and Juliet might both be able to pass the Wizard's Test. Times change, James. We must adapt, or we may come to regret it later. You are dismissed."

"WHAT DO YOU MEAN, 'I'M PREGNANT'?" shouted Rachel. Donovan looked at her quizzically. "You know, you are 'with child,' 'expecting,' 'eating for two,' you have 'a bun in the oven,' *pregnant*," said Donovan. "That's why I passed out yesterday; I was healing both of you. Is it really that hard to understand?" Rachel sat down. "I won't say 'How could this have happened?' because I know *how*, it's just unexpected!"

Donovan came over and put his arm around her. "So, are you ready to become a mother, Mrs. Francis?" Rachel looked up and smiled. "Yes, I am!" They shared a passionate kiss, then Donovan said, "Now, I have two rules for you while you're pregnant: number one, no more changing into a dragon for you. I have no idea what that would do to the baby." Rachel nodded, "OK. What's rule number two?" "No more throwing up on me!" Rachel laughed.

"When should we tell Major Gerald? Do you think he'll ask for a replacement magician?" Donovan considered the question. "We should probably tell him as soon as we get to Sundock, certainly before you start to show. We also need to let him know about rule number one. As to requesting another magician, we probably have several months before you'll need to curtail your magical exertions. We should certainly be back in Kingston by then."

"What about your vision of the attack on Grotton?" asked Rachel. "I will certainly need your assistance then. I just hope Mage Charles and the 5th Regiment's Battle Mage can change into dragons when the time comes. Now, Mrs. Francis, you get in that bed and get some rest. I know you've been sitting in that chair all night."

"Yes, sir," said Rachel. Donovan beamed.

The villa was purchased for the sum of 71 golds, after deducting the sale price of Edward's house, and adding the realtor's fees and taxes (of course). Mr. and Mrs. Haywood were overjoyed to be offered positions in Edward's household staff, and Mrs. Haywood knew a horticulturist, Sarah, who was looking for work. All they needed now was a cook (urgently) and a coachman (less urgently).

"Where does one find a cook, I wonder," said Kathy. "I have no idea," replied Edward. "I don't think there's a cooking school in Kingston. We'll have to ask around. We can probably check the stables in town and see if we can find an Ostler/carriage driver. That's not a priority, though."

"What about that cook whom you healed? He might be interested, or at least know someone." "That's an excellent idea! And if I remember correctly, Burt works here in the palace!" Edward and Kathy headed down to the palace kitchen. They found a bustling operation, as a dozen cooks, chefs, and serving girls moved about preparing for the lunch crowd. Edward marched straight back into the kitchen area, ignoring the "Staff Only" sign on the door, and was immediately confronted by the Head Chef.

"Hold it right there, buddy! Can't you read the sign? It says "Staff Only," and you are definitely not on my staff." "You are correct, Chef," said Edward. "I am Wizard Edward, the Chief of Military Wizardry, and this is my wife and deputy, Wizard Kathy. We are looking for Burt. Is he around?"

Completely cowed, the head chef apologized profusely, afraid that Edward was going to exact some sort of magical revenge for his slight. "Yes, sir. I'm sorry, sir. I meant no insult. Please follow me. Assistant Chef Burt is in the back, overseeing the baking. I'll take you right to him."

As they entered the baking area, which had several large ovens, several tables, and racks with trays full of baked goods, Edward was relieved to see that the six barrels of flour were safely stored in a pantry, well away from the ovens. "Burt! There's someone here to see you! Look lively, man," said the head chef.

Burt recognized Edward immediately, and after a word to the pastry chef, he came over. "Good morning, sir. How can I help you?" The head chef excused himself, stammering something about needing to get back to the 'front end.' Edward and Kathy took Burt aside and told him about their recent purchase and the need for a live-in cook. "Are you interested in the position, or do you know anyone who might be?" asked Kathy.

Burt looked thoughtful, "Well, sir, I might be interested, depending on the pay and the size of your staff. I have to tell you that I'm more of a baker than a chef. If you're looking for someone to make elaborate, fancy dishes, that's not my skill set." Edward smiled, "No, Burt, we don't need anything fancy, just good plain food. How much do you make here?"

Edward was shocked by the low wage that Burt was paid, then he remembered how miserly King Henry was. He immediately offered him three times what he was currently making, plus room and board in the villa. Burt was overjoyed. "When would you like me to start?" he asked. "Not for a few days. I need to get the house cleaned and ready. It hasn't been occupied in over a year. Say two weeks?" "That would be wonderful, sir. Thank you so much! When you have the villa cleaned, please remember to hire a chimney sweep. Those things tend to end up with birds nesting in them if they sit unused for a long period of time."

"An excellent suggestion! Thank you, Burt. Now all we need to find is an Ostler who knows how to drive a carriage," Edward said to Kathy. Burt overheard the comment and said, "Excuse me, Sir Edward, but I know someone like that who is desperate for another chance." "Another chance? What does that mean?" asked Edward.

"Well, you remember when King Henry's parents were killed in the carriage accident?" Edward nodded. "Well, Anthony was the driver. He swears that he did nothing wrong, that an enormous wind came up out of nowhere and blew the Royal Carriage over the edge of the cliff, and there was nothing he could do about it. He managed to jump clear, so he survived the accident, but now, no one will hire him. It's a sad case."

"Anthony's right. The wind was conjured by a magician in order to kill the King and Queen. He did nothing wrong. I would be more than happy to hire anyone experienced enough to be the Royal Coachman. Where can I find Anthony?"

Burt brightened, "He's in the alley out back. I admit that he looks disheveled right now. Being unemployed, he survives on the kindness of others. I slip him day-old bread when I can. He cleans up nice though, if you give him a chance." Edward nodded his understanding. "Take us to him."

Anthony was as Burt described him, wearing little more than rags, and thin as a rail. He rose as Burt and the two magicians approached. "Tony, this here's Wizard Edward and his wife, Kathy. He wants to hire you as his carriage driver and Ostler!" Tony stood and removed his ragged knit cap respectfully. He was a surprisingly young man, only about twenty-five, Edward estimated. "Hello, sir, Miss. I'm Anthony Williams, and I really need a job. I'll work for just room and board. Please forgive my appearance, but times have been hard lately."

"I understand, Anthony. My wife and I recently purchased the villa that was previously owned by Dutchess Draper. Do you know where it is?" "The one on the hill overlooking the river? Yes, sir, I know it well. The Queen used to visit fairly regularly."

"Good. I've looked at the carriage, and while it may have been opulent once, it has fallen into a state of disrepair over the last year. Do you know anything about carriage repair?" "Of course, sir. Every coachman has to maintain his or her own vehicle. I'd be happy to repair and upgrade the carriage. You'll also need a matched pair of horses to pull it. You can't just use any two random mounts; they need to be trained to work together and respond to the reins."

"Well, it seems you're the man we're looking for," said Edward. "Can you start today?" Anthony practically leaped for joy. "Of course, sir. Thank you very much!" "Now, here are two golds, go clean up and purchase some appropriate attire. We'll discuss your salary later. Then head on up to the villa. Our housekeeper, Mrs. Haywood, and her husband, our new butler should be there already, cleaning up the place. It's been vacant for over a year, you know. Take a look at the carriage and help them with the cleaning, and whatever else they need. Our new gardener, Sarah, might be there as well."

Anthony took the coins with shaking hands. He could scarcely believe his incredible luck. He moved briskly towards Mrs. Thomas's bathhouse to clean up. Edward approved of his priorities. "Well, Burt, we'll see you in two weeks. If you hear about a pair of carriage horses for sale, let Anthony know. Now we have to get back to work."

As they entered their office, Edward said, "Well, that was certainly easier than I expected." Kathy smiled, "You know what you've done, don't you?" Edward shrugged, questioningly. "You have hired a staff that will be completely loyal to you. Not just employees, working for a wage." "Is that important?" asked Edward. Kathy laughed at his naivety, "During my time in Baize, I encountered many, many instances of employee theft, idleness, and disloyalty among the staff of various nobles. If a servant is only working for the coins they can get, they can be bribed or tempted into dishonest actions. I don't think we'll ever have to worry about that."

Chapter Sixteen:
FEMALE ISSUES

Gek spotted the campfire from miles away as he and Anna flew towards Acropo. It was on the cliffs above the submerged entrance to the cavern system that was home to the Sea Dragon Clan. "Anna, there is a human on the island above the entrance to the caves. Stay behind me. I will deal with this."

Gek swooped in, roaring and spewing fire. The human sitting beside the small campfire erected a shield, which protected her from the shower of burning inferno. "GEK! STOP! IT'S ME, ANNE!" she shouted. Gek ceased his attack and landed on the hilltop near the shielded sorceress. "Anne! What are you doing here?" he asked.

"I came to speak with Cobalt. The Franconian Navy is planning to blockade and attack the islands. I was hoping to prevent more bloodshed," said Anne, releasing her shield. Anna landed behind Gek and began growling at the strange human.

"No, Anna. This is Anne. She is a Dragon-friend, like Bruce." "How many dragon-friends are there?" asked Anna. "There are three that I know of," answered Gek, "Bruce, Sorceress Anne here, and her identical twin sister, Sorceress Celeste." "What does *identical* mean?" asked Annalise.

"It means that my sister and I look exactly alike," said Anne, "and who is this?" "Anne this is my daughter,

Annalise." "It's nice to meet you Annalise," said Anne. "Who is Bruce?" As Anna started to respond, Gek said, "Bruce is no one you need to concern yourself about. You are fortunate that I found you. Another dragon might have killed you."

Anne gulped, "Since I have healed so many members of the Sea Dragon Clan, I judged it a reasonable gamble that I would be found by you, Azure, Cobalt, or one of the dragons that I healed and placed under a Binding spell, not to injure humans. I was aware of my risk, but, if I can, I would like to avoid the results of the last confrontation between humans and Sea Dragons."

Gek considered her words. "I will go find Cobalt and inform him that you are here. It will be his decision whether to allow you entrance. Anna, come with me." Gek and Annalise jumped off the cliff and entered the submerged opening that led to the caverns occupied by the Sea Dragon Clan. They emerged in the grotto, and Gek said, "Grandma is most likely in her cave. You know the way. I will come speak to you after I talk with Cobalt."

Anna plodded down the passageway to the chamber her grandmother, Aqua, usually slept in, while Gek took a side corridor, looking for Cobalt, the Chief of the Sea Dragons. He found him in a small, secluded chamber on the lower level of the cavern system. "Cobalt! Why are you way down here, and in this small, little sleeping chamber? You are the clan chief, shouldn't you have the largest, most accessible sleeping chamber?"

Cobalt groaned (a *very* unbecoming sound for a dragon). "I am here because I am hiding from some of the members of my Clan. They give me no peace, constantly badgering me, urging me to approve more, and making greater attacks on the humans. I am tired of arguing. I have already lost many friends, and I am not sure if it is worth it anymore."

"Well, then you are not going to like my news. Sorceress Anne is on the cliffs above the entrance. She said that she has come with a warning about an imminent attack by the humans. She hopes to prevent further conflict."

Cobalt looked startled. "It is a good thing that you found her then. Other members of the Clan would have killed her on sight." "That is what I told her." "How did she get here? There have been no ships seen approaching the islands. I would have heard about them." "I do not know. I did not think to ask her that. I was distracted by Annalise."

"Why did you bring Annalise here? Oh, it is almost time for the next Dragon Council. How time flies. Where is Azure?" asked Cobalt. "Azure is on the mainland with Richard. We plan to leave him with our friend Bruce while we both attend the next Dragon Council meeting."

"Will he be safe?" "Yes. If anything, it is Bruce who may be in danger if Richard learns any more magic spells." Cobalt laughed. "Have you decided on a new place to live yet?" "We built a hut near Bruce's. Bruce is teaching the children to read. I had my doubts, but it is something that Richard will need to learn if he ever needs to live among the humans. Anna has taken an interest because she does not want her brother to be able to do something that she cannot."

"Hmm. Reading might prove to be a useful skill someday. From talking to some of the Sea Dragon Changed Ones, reading is something all of them had to learn in order to blend in with the humans."

"Back to Anne. How could she have made it to our island?" wondered Cobalt. "Perhaps she is one of the magic-users who has learned how to change into a dragon," speculated Gek. "She is one of the few humans who has seen a dragon and lived to tell about it." "That must be it," said Cobalt. "I wonder why she did not simply swim down into the caves and seek me out."

"Maybe she hopes to conceal her knowledge from us," said Gek. "Then we should not let her know that we are aware of her ability. Do not ask how she got to the island. We will let her think she has fooled us."

The 2nd Squadron arrived in Sundock just after dawn. It had been a cold, cramped trip for the members of the Royal Expeditionary Force. With only one independent Company (the 13th) in Sundock, there was no garrison compound big enough to accommodate the Expeditionary Force. Fortunately, there were several, mostly empty, warehouses near the dock. The merchants normally shipped out most of their goods before winter, even in Sundock, and Major Gerald was easily able to find a merchant willing to rent out his empty storage facility to the Royal Expeditionary Force (for a small fee, of course).

As the men settled into the new place, Donovan and Rachel found Major Gerald in the warehouse manager's empty office. "Sir, can we have a word?" "Any time," said Major Gerald with a smile. "By the way, I understand that you made an incredible shot with one of the new Compound Seabows. Captain Caine was most impressed and grateful. Now, what's on your mind?"

Donovan waited for Rachel to deliver the news, "Well, sir, it seems that I'm pregnant," she said, blushing. "Really? CONGRATULATIONS!" Major Gerald rose and gave Rachel a hug, then shook Donovan's hand enthusiastically. "I'm so happy for both of you!" "Thank you, sir. We just wanted to let you know before it became obvious. It's early yet, but there have been signs," said Rachel quietly.

"Morning sickness?" asked the Major. Rachel nodded. "I surely hope it only happens in the mornings!" said Donovan. Rachel slapped the back of his head. "Easy!" complained Donovan. "I was unconscious yesterday!"

"Again?" asked Major Gerald. "Yes, but it wasn't my fault," pleaded Donovan. "During the encounter with the dragon, Rachel was injured. When I healed her, we didn't know she was carrying. Healing two people at once is more than twice as taxing, and I wasn't expecting it. So now, I have another scar on my forehead." Gerald smiled, "So, once you're settled in, we need to take care of the reason we're here."

"As soon as we stow our things, we'll head over to the 13th Company Headquarters and deliver the Concealment cloak to the company sorcerer, then have him escort us to the town treasury. We'll visit the Regional Mage tomorrow." "That's fine. We'll likely be here for a few days. I need to contract with a merchant ship for transport to Eastport, then Grotton. I'm not inclined to use Navy ships again. I don't like splitting up the force, and the men and horses were cramped on the trip here."

Donovan nodded. As they prepared to leave the office, Donovan said, "Dirk, Lance, my wife's condition is a secret. I don't want anyone in the Expeditionary Force treating her any differently. You take my meaning?" Both Dirk and Lance lowered the hoods of their Concealment cloaks. "Understood, sir. Congratulations." "Thank you," said Rachel, "that goes for you too, Corporal Knox."

Rachel and Donovan left the office and found their wagon in the warehouse. "I guess it'll be warmer and more private just to sleep in the wagon bed," observed Donovan. He picked up a sorcerer's Concealment cloak, then took one of the few remaining mage's cloaks out of the wrapping. Here," he said, handing it to Rachel. "I can't have my wife wandering around Sundock wearing rags." Rachel smiled and said, "But *this* rag is warm. Give me a minute to fix the new one," Rachel took the new cloak and spread it out on the floor of the wagon, then she magically removed the fleece blanket that Donovan had adhered to the inside of her old cloak, and attached it to her new one. Without the fleece lining, the old Concealment cloak really did look like a tattered rag.

"We should probably look into adding liners like this to the other soldiers' cloaks," said Rachel. "That's a great idea. We should have thought of it earlier. The next time we head up north in the winter, we should definitely do that. Since we're headed to Eastport, then Grotton, they don't really need the linings now," said Donovan.

The 13th Company Sorcerer, Paul, was human. He knew about the dragons, since Sundock had been attacked by Sea Dragons twice. The news about how to kill a Stone Dragon was news to him, as was the new Concealment cloak and the ability of magicians to change into dragons. After a brief conversation with Sorcerer Paul, the three magicians headed into town to see the mayor and the town treasurer.

"What can you tell me about the Regional Mage?" asked Donovan, nonchalantly. "Mage Lisa? She's OK, I guess. I don't really see her much around town. I guess she goes out with her Enforcers regularly, but I've only spoken to her a couple of times in the year since I was posted to the 13th Company. I do know that she received a sorceress as her assistant, but almost immediately, she sent her to the Royal Navy to replace one of the magicians who was killed during the first dragon attack."

"That would be Sorceress Anne," said Donovan. "She was the first woman ever assigned to a ship in the Royal Navy. She was instrumental in the truce we briefly had with the Sea Dragons. She was later appointed as a Dragon Messenger to the Royal Navy."

"What does that mean?" asked Paul. "She relays messages between Naval Headquarters and ships at sea, like Messenger Hawks do for us on land." "Amazing!" said Paul. "Yes. It's the first time in history that we can send messages to ships at sea. Anne works with the 1st Fleet, while Sorcerer Phillip is assigned to the 2nd Fleet in the Low Sea. It would be much too difficult for one magician to carry missives to both fleets."

They arrived at the town hall and proceeded in. Henry, the mayor greeted them warmly. "Sorcerer Paul! What brings you to the city hall this early in the morning?" "Mayor, allow me to introduce Mages Donovan and Rachel. They're with the Royal Expeditionary Force and are here to inspect the treasury."

The mayor was somewhat taken aback by this news. "The treasury? Why? What's wrong?" "Nothing, we hope, sir. It's just the King. He sent the Expeditionary Force on a sweeping tour of all of the towns and cities in Franconia. From here, we're headed to Eastport, then Grotton before heading home to Kingston." The mayor looked relieved (somewhat).

"I'm sure you'll find everything in order. Come along, I'll take you there myself. Good to see you again, Sorcerer Paul. Stop by anytime."

As the Mayor predicted, everything was in order in the Sundock Treasury. For a port city, there was not as much money in the treasury as Donovan expected. "It's because there's no industry in Sundock. They're a port city, sure, but other than some dry docks for repairing damaged ships, they don't really produce any goods here," explained Major Gerald.

"How do you know that, sir?" asked Donovan. "Because this is my hometown. I came up through the ranks in 13th Company, then was transferred to the 5th Regiment in Grotton. That's where I got my battlefield promotion, during the Grotton rebellion." "A rebellion?" asked Rachel. "Yes. The wealthy merchants got tired of paying the King's taxes, so they convinced the city council to withhold the annual payment to the crown. I can tell you that King Henry X was not amused."

"I imagine not," said Donovan. "What happened?" "Well, several Couriers and Messenger Hawks were intercepted by the rebels, so it was some months before the regiment even knew anything was amiss. When we finally received word, we marched on the port to put down the rebellion. My commander thought he could talk reason to the rebels. They killed him and the four battalion commanders he foolishly took with him to the meeting. We had to charge the wharf area, which had been barricaded and fortified. My company commander was killed while going over the barricade. As the senior sergeant, I assumed command, and we broke through and ended the rebellion in a single day of fighting. It was a sad thing," said Major Gerald.

As they finished speaking, a bell in the harbor began ringing. Looking out the window, Major Gerald said, "Ah,

1st Squadron is arriving. It's going to be really crowded along the piers this week. I wonder why the entire 1st Fleet is here at once. They must be up to something."

"I think we should go down to the dock and see if we can find Andrew," said Donovan. "With your permission, sir?" "Go. I still have to find a commercial vessel to take us to Eastport. We're not leaving for a few days."

As they reached the port area, Donovan spied a familiar face, "Maria! What are you doing in Sundock?" "Hello, Donovan. My father and I came here a few months ago to see about shipping some steel from Smithville to Fairview by way of Sundock. The city taxes in Eastport were just too high for us to make a profit." "Where is your father?" asked Donovan, scanning the crowd. "He was killed in the last dragon attack. An invisible dragon dropped a stone on him while he was modifying one of the Seabows on the HMS VICEROY."

"I'm so sorry, Maria. I had no idea. By the way, this is my wife, Mage Rachel. Rachel, this is my friend and former neighbor, Maria." "It's nice to meet you, Maria. I'm sorry for your loss." "Hello," said Maria. "I had heard that Donovan graduated from the Wizards Academy and had gotten married."

"Who told you that?" asked Donovan. "I did," said Andrew, coming up behind them. He gave Maria a big kiss and said, "Miss me?" "Terribly," replied Maria. "Donovan, Rachel, this is my husband, Andrew."

"Your *husband*?" asked Donovan. Andrew showed him his adorned ring finger. "It was a very rushed engagement. About three hours, actually. Then Commodore Matthews married us the day before we had to leave port. What brings the Royal Expeditionary Force to Sundock?" asked Andrew.

"We've been auditing all of the treasuries in the kingdom and distributing Concealment cloaks along the way. From here, we'll head to Eastport, Grotton, and then home," explained Donovan.

"I'd love to hear all about it," said Andrew. "Let's head over to our house and you can fill us in." "Andrew," said Maria, "There's something important I need to tell you." "Me too," said Donovan. "I think Mage Lisa is a Changed One," said Maria and Donovan simultaneously.

"So, Anne, why have you come?" asked Cobalt. They stood in a large chamber on the upper level of the cavern system. Anne had just dried herself off after a cold dunk in the water leading to the Sea Dragon's lair. Gek, who had brought her in, stood in the doorway.

"I came in the hopes of preventing further suffering and death," said Anne. "The King realizes that he made a mistake with the first treaty we proposed, and would like to try again." "And, what does your king propose this time?" asked Cobalt.

"It is very similar to your first proposal," said Anne, hopefully. "He will cede control of the Coral Islands to the Sea Dragons and agree that our forces will not attack you. You agree never to attack humans, and, like before, to allow up to five of our ships to take shelter in the cove on the north end of Acropo during a storm. No human will ever set foot on one of your islands. However, we would ask that, if an unfortunate human were shipwrecked or fell overboard and made their way to one of the Coral Islands, you grant them mercy and allow us to retrieve them."

Cobalt considered the offer, then said, "This is not the same offer. The previous treaty was between the Sea Dragons and your Navy. You ask that we expand our agreement to *all* humans. We will need to consider this and discuss it with the Dragon Council. How would such a treaty be enforced?"

"A Binding spell, such as the ones I cast during my last visit, might be employed," suggested Anne. "And your king would agree to such a spell?" asked Cobalt.

Anne paled, "That would not work. Binding spells only work on those of us with the spark of magic, and the King does not have the spark." "You ask for much, while offering little in return. Who among the humans would be bound by this spell?" asked Cobalt.

"I would offer myself," said Anne. "Unacceptable. You are already named a dragon-friend, and under our protection, as is your sister. If we were to agree to such a pact, we would need someone much more senior among your magic-users.

The Court Wizard, or the head of your Wizards Academy, for example."

"One or both of them might agree to your terms," said Anne.

"You told Gek that your Navy is planning to 'blockade' our islands. I am unfamiliar with this term. What does it mean to 'blockade'?"

"Our ships will surround the Coral Islands. No one will be allowed to enter or leave." Cobalt laughed. "Your ships could not stop us from entering or leaving! We would simply swim under or fly over them! It would be a pointless exercise, which I assure you, we would exploit."

"If the blockade is not successful, they might set fire to another island, as they did before," said Anne. "Hmm," said Cobalt. That would be an inconvenience, nothing more."

"I know. That is why I had to come, to try to make peace between us before more drastic measures are employed by either side."

"I will consider your words. In the meantime, *for your safety*, I must insist that you remain here with us. It would not be safe for you on the island above if your magic-users were to set fire to it or employ other *drastic measures*. I will instruct my clan to allow you to remain here unharmed, but no one will assist you in returning to the surface until we have made our decision. I hope you like fish, because that is all we have to eat here."

A growing sense of panic engulfed Anne. "Remain? But I can't! Please, Cobalt, I have other duties to perform! The admiral will be looking for me!" "I am sorry, Anne, but you brought this upon yourself. As a dragon-friend, I am bound not to let harm come to you if I can prevent it. By keeping you here, I am keeping you safe while we consider your peace offer. It should not be long; I believe your king took three cycles of the moon to review the first treaty. We should certainly be able to decide in that amount of time."

"But—" "No further discussion, Anne. Gek, go and fetch Emerald and ask her to keep Anne company while we consider this peace offer. She is not to harm her, but to keep her here to ensure her safety." Gek headed down into the cavern system to find Emerald, the green Sea Dragon who had lost her mate in the last battle. *She* would certainly not be very sympathetic to any pleas for assistance from Anne.

Maria

Chapter Seventeen:
MAGES

"*SILENTIUM,*" said Andrew, casting a Silence spell around himself, Maria, Donovan, and Rachel. "What do you mean, you think Mage Lisa is a Changed One?" asked Andrew, confused. Donovan was shocked that Maria had the same idea, but since she lived in Sundock and had met the Regional Mage, he let her explain first. "When I went by the funeral home to arrange for my father's burial, I noticed that Mr. Stone, the Mortician, didn't use any contractions. Then the handkerchief he gave me smelled like a lizard. I immediately reported this to Mage Lisa and asked her to investigate. She went to the morgue and told me the next day that she had determined that Mr. Stone could, in fact, use contractions, and that the smell on the handkerchief was just embalming fluid."

"So?" asked Andrew. "So, I noticed that Mage Lisa also didn't use any contractions, and I find it suspicious that Mr. Stone had to leave town suddenly because of a death in the family." Andrew nodded, "Yes, that's certainly suspicious. Donovan, tell me why *you* suspect Mage Lisa."

Donovan looked around, despite the Silence spell, then asked quietly, "Have you ever heard of the spell of Foresight?" "AUGURIM?" asked Andrew. "Yes, I've heard of it. But no one has been able to cast that spell in decades!"

"Well, I can. I used it in my father's office and found a dragon in the Sundock Regional Mage's Office. It must be Lisa." "Edward is back in Franconia?" "Yes. He and Mage Kathy returned a short while ago. The King promoted him to the Chief of Military Wizardry, so he has a very nice office in the palace now. By the way, Kathy passed her Wizard's Test. She is now the Deputy Chief of Military Wizardry."

Andrew shook his head. "Things are sure happening fast lately. By the way, you and Rachel are wearing the wrong Concealment cloaks. The ones with the crest on the pocket are for mages." Donovan smiled, "We know. We had to replace our old ones after we were promoted."

"You're mages? How in the world… Never mind. Congratulations! Now, what should we do about Lisa?"

"Why is the entire 1st Fleet in Sundock?" asked Rachel. "It seems like a risk, having all of the ships here at once." "The fleet has been ordered to complete the upgrade to the Seabows as quickly as possible and proceed to the Coral Islands. We're going to blockade the islands in an attempt to bring the Sea Dragons back to the bargaining table," replied Andrew.

"How are you going to blockade islands full of Sea Dragons?" asked Donovan, "Won't they just swim under you, or fly over the fleet. We know that they can cast Concealment shields!" "I raised the same points with Commodore Matthews. He said, "Orders are orders." We may have to set fire to the islands again in order to lure the dragons out. That's why we need the Seabow modifications."

"How many are left to modify?" asked Maria. "Just the four on the VALOR. It would have been three, but the aft Compound Seabow was destroyed when the mizzen mast shattered and fell on it." "Is that the one the dragon ran into?" asked Donovan mischievously. "How did you hear about that?" asked Andrew.

"I was in my father's office when the Messenger Hawk arrived with news about the attack on Eastport. That trick with the Seeming was pretty slick." "Thanks, but after I removed the dragon's head, I passed out. When I came to, we were already at sea. I never thought about checking the mast for damage. We nearly lost the ship when it broke and fell over the side, dragging the ship with it. The mast acted like a giant anchor. If I hadn't been able to remove the lines fast enough, the whole ship would have rolled over on its side."

"Then I guess it's a good thing you woke up when you did," said Rachel. "Now, back to the matter at hand, what do we do about Mage Lisa?" "Well, I need to get Maria working on the Seabow modifications, and I insist that a magician remain with her as she works, just in case a Concealed Dragon tries to drop a stone on her," said Andrew. "Rachel will stay with her," said Donovan, earning him a scalding look from his wife. "Me? Why?" asked Rachel.

"You know why," said Donovan softly. "Andrew and I can handle one Dragon Changed One, and Maria needs protection." Rachel glared, but eventually nodded. "Let's go tell the Commodore. How long do you think it will take to make the modifications?" Andrew asked Maria.

"At least three days. I'll need to make another kit. I didn't anticipate one being destroyed." "You should probably make a few spares," suggested Donovan. "If the fleet gets into a fight with the dragons, there will probably be more Seabows damaged or destroyed." "That's an excellent point. Let's go talk to the Commodore," said Andrew.

After a brief conversation with Commodore Matthews, it was decided that, in addition to the four Compound Seabows that were needed immediately, the Navy would pay for five additional replacement Compound Seabows. "Once we return from dealing with the dragons, we're going to need you to train our ship's carpenters how to install the Compound Seabows. We can't keep rushing back to Sundock whenever one breaks. Plus, I think the plan is to have 2nd Fleet swap oceans with us, so they can get the new Seabows also."

"I'm happy to help, sir," said Maria. "Good! Where are the new kits now?" asked the Commodore. "They're still in the blacksmith shop. I'll get a wagon and bring them down right now so I can get started," said Maria.

"Sir, while Maria and Rachel are doing that, Mage Donovan and I have some business to take care of in town." "Fine," said the Commodore. "I have to go report to Vice Admiral Jordan and let him know the plan and receive any orders."

"Sire, here is the list of mages you requested," said Wizard James. "There are a dozen or so who have been mages for at least ten years and *might* be able to pass the Wizard's Test." The King reviewed the list of fourteen names. He was not surprised to find that eight of the names were women. The King sighed. "So, this discrimination has been going on for decades…"

"Sire—" began James. "It's all right, James. I don't blame you. We were all blind to the injustice we perpetuated. I want all of these mages tested as soon as possible. Please let me know the results of the testing." James nodded uncomfortably. "And James, please ensure that these tests are *identical* to those given to all other mages. If I find that any *unnecessary impediments* are introduced into the testing, I will replace the wizard, or wizards who conducted the tests."

"Of course, sire. I understand completely," said James. "Have you given any thought to where the new wizards might be placed?" asked the King.

"Well, sire. It has been pointed out to me that the Royal Navy has no one of wizard rank assigned, other than the Chief of Naval Wizardry; we might assign some there. I would like to point out that women are not currently assigned to any ships in the Baizian Navy. There is also the possibility of promoting the headmasters or headmistresses of our biggest schools of magic to the rank of wizard. The schools in the cities of Oceanside, Seaside, Springfield, Middleberg, and here in Baize come to mind. There is also the Assistant Court Wizard position, that has been previously filled by a mage."

The King's eyes narrowed. "I understand where this is going, and I will go along with any such recommendation, as a step in the right direction. I want the Army Command and the Navy Admiralty to begin exploring ways to integrate female magicians into their ranks, from sorceress through wizard. I'm not saying we'll make changes immediately, but I want to see options."

"I will inform them at once, sire," said James. "Now, what are your thoughts on the attack on the Fire Dragon colony that Franconia has requested we conduct?"

"Before we consider any such attack, we will need to determine the exact location of the entrance to the colony," said James. "Wizard Edward's description of a 'narrow glen' on the east side of the Grey Mountains is hardly specific enough for us to target. We would need to conduct some reconnaissance first, then plan an attack. The attack should probably be conducted by both magicians on the ground, and magicians transformed into dragons, attacking from the air."

"How many magicians do you think will be required?" asked the King. "Dozens, sire. We have no idea how many Fire Dragons there are, and what we might be facing. I would say that it is also unlikely that we will be able to sneak up on the colony from the ground without being spotted by the dragons."

"Unless we had some of those marvelous Concealment cloaks," mused the King. "I will request a number of them from King Henry, as a condition of our attack. Surely he'll see that as a reasonable request. What about magical support from Franconia?" James looked doubtful. "Sire, I know you told Kathy that we would not consider attacking without assistance from our allies in Franconia, but I hesitate to recruit many of their magicians."

"Why is that?" "While it might be appropriate to request a small number of skilled magicians from Franconia, we would not want it known that we needed too much of their help. The citizens might start to wonder why we couldn't handle it ourselves. We won't be able to cover up Franconian assistance the way we did with the Great Salt Lake."

"Very well. I will send a Messenger Hawk to King Henry today, asking for several dozen Concealment cloaks to be used by our ground assault forces. Please handle the other matters we discussed and get me a plan of attack as soon as you can."

"Henry, have you given any more consideration to Wizard Edward's concerns about our wedding?" asked

Celeste. "Yes, my love, I have, and while I share Wizard Edward's concerns about security, we simply cannot elope, or have some small, sparsely attended Royal Wedding. It simply isn't done." "So, what *can* we do?"

"There are two possibilities: one, we have a small, private ceremony in the palace, followed by a grand reception in the main ballroom, and we invite, no, *we insist,* on the attendance of every magician in the Wizards Academy, or; two, we have a large wedding in the palace cathedral, and skip the reception altogether. The first option costs more coin, but might be more secure; the second costs us virtually nothing."

"Do you have a preference?" "Frankly, my dear, I'm inclined to choose the second option, and not just because of the cost savings." "Why no reception?" asked Celeste. "Frankly, I've never been comfortable around so many people. Believe it or not, I abhor Royal Balls, which is why I make my excuses early and leave before everyone gets drunk and rowdy."

"Option two it is then," said Celeste with a smile. "I'm sure that Wizard Edward will approve." "It's not *his* approval I need, beloved." Celeste smiled. "What about a date?" she asked. "Is tomorrow too soon?" asked Henry, jokingly. "Yes. Definitely too soon, darling. How about the first day of spring? That's only about two months away. That should give us plenty of time to plan everything."

Henry smiled, "The first day of spring it is! I'll have my scribes begin making the invitations. You need a wedding dress, and some bridesmaids! I will have the Queen's crown cleaned and re-sized for you, and arrange for the officiant. The seating chart will be the most complicated thing we have to do. All of the nobles have to be seated by seniority, you see. What about your parents?"

"They passed away some years ago. Sorceress Anne is my only family. As a Dragon Messenger, I'm sure she'll be able to make it." "Of course. Plus, all of your friends and instructors from the Academy. That should give us adequate security, as long as we carefully screen everyone who enters. I would not like a Dragon Changed One to get into the cathedral."

"I guess that's settled then," said Celeste, smiling. "One more thing, dear, there's no need to bother the scribes. Once we have a single invitation, I can replicate as many as we need." "That sounds excellent, and very prudent," said Henry.

"So, *Mage* Donovan, how do you want to confront Mage Lisa?" asked Andrew. "Well, *Mage* Andrew, how about if I just stop by to deliver her new Concealment cloak? She doesn't know me. If you go in first, she might be suspicious. Especially if she thinks that you've talked to your wife."

"I think that's a good idea. By the way, why did you insist that Rachel remain with Maria? Any of the ships' sorcerers could have provided security for Maria while she works." "Because Rachel is pregnant, and I'm not sure I want her confronting a Dragon Changed One right now."

"Rachel's pregnant? Congratulations!" "Thanks. By the way, if Maria ever gets pregnant, and you try to heal her, just be aware that you'll be healing for two. I passed out when I tried it on the way here. That was before I knew she was expecting," said Donovan.

"Is Rachel OK?" "She's fine. Just some morning sickness so far. However, I've told her not to change into a dragon until after the baby is born. We just don't know what would happen to the child if she changes." "Hmm. Yes, that's something that's never come up before. But she can still do magic, right?"

"Sure. I just don't want her overdoing it or taking any unnecessary risks," said Donovan. "Now, what can you tell me about Mage Lisa?" "She's the only magician in the Sundock Regional Mage's Office. Sorceress Anne was assigned as her assistant, but she was transferred to 1st Squadron to replace the sorcerer who was killed aboard the HMS COMFORT during the first dragon attack. At the time, I didn't think anything about it. We needed a magician, and it was either Lisa or Anne," said Andrew.

"It must have been a big relief for her when Anne was assigned to the Navy, Lisa would not have wanted another magician in the office who might have identified her as a Changed One," said Donovan.

They walked down the street to the Regional Mage's Office. The whole town of Sundock was abuzz with business and rumors as to why the entire 1st Fleet of ships was in port at the same time. "I hope Lisa is in her office. I'd hate to have to look all over town for her," said Andrew.

As they approached the brick building that housed the Regional Mage's Office, Andrew said, "I'll wait out here and watch the street. If she's in there, paralyze her quickly before she can change. The last thing we need is another dragon tearing up the town." Donovan nodded his understanding and walked up the stairs to the office.

As he entered the building, Donovan immediately noticed the smell. The office smelled like cinnamon. The young man at the receptionist's desk said, "Good morning, sir. How can I help you?"

"I'm Mage Donovan with the Royal Expeditionary Force. We got into town yesterday with the 2nd Squadron. I just came by to meet Mage Lisa and issue her her new Concealment cloak. Is she available?"

The receptionist shook his head, "I'm sorry, sir. It's Midweek, the mage's day off. You see, most of the trouble in town happens on Endday, so Mage Lisa makes sure that she and all of the Enforcers are in the office then. I'll make sure she gets the cloak..." Donovan shook his head, "I'm sorry, but I'm under strict orders only to give these cloaks to their intended recipients. There are some instructions that go with the cloaks, and they have to be signed for. I can either take it to her house or come back tomorrow."

"Well, Mage Lisa has a house on the south side of town, down by the river. It's number 7, Canal Street. She might not be home, though. The mage usually does her errands and shopping on her days off." "I understand," said Donovan. "If I don't see her today, I'll be back tomorrow."

Donovan left and found Andrew under his Concealment cloak across the street from the office. "Mage Lisa is off today. She'll be back in the office tomorrow if we want to come back, or I have her home address in town if we want to look for her there." Andrew lowered his hood and frowned, "Going to her house might make her suspicious. Let's just come back tomorrow."

They returned to the VALOR to find Maria hard at work, stringing one of the new Compound Seabows as Rachel stood beside her, scanning the sky. "Did you find her?" They both whispered. "No. Apparently, the Regional Mage is not in the office on Midweek. We'll need to go back tomorrow. How much longer is this one going to take?"

"I'm almost done," said Maria. This makes two so far. I'll modify the next one in the morning. The stern Seabow is going to take longer since the pedestal is missing." "Oh, right. I forgot about that. The mast did a thorough job of destroying that one," said Andrew.

"Well, you'll need to replicate a new pedestal for me tomorrow, so I can mount the new Seabow. Then I'll be done. You might also like to know that the blacksmith in town is *not* a Changed One."

Donovan slapped his forehead. He had totally forgotten that many of the blacksmiths in the kingdom were actually Fire Dragon Changed Ones. He couldn't believe that he'd been so foolish as to send Rachel and Maria there. "I'm sorry, I should have thought of that," he said. "Thought of what?" asked Andrew.

"We've learned that most of the blacksmiths in Franconia are actually Fire Dragon Changed Ones. It seems that it's an occupation that Fire dragons are drawn to," said Donovan. "I thought all of the Fire and Stone Dragons lived on the west side of the Amber River," said Andrew.

"It seems that many of the Fire Dragons have disregarded that rule," said Rachel. "We also discovered that there may be a lot more Changed Ones in Franconia than we anticipated. Many of them have taken jobs in high-end shops that are not frequented by magicians, or as refuse-haulers, tanners, or undertakers. The Regional Mages are all taking another look for Changed Ones in their towns and cities."

"That's just great," complained Andrew.

Mage Lisa was having her own problems. Over the last week, the entire 1st Fleet of ships had arrived in Sundock. That meant that at least eleven magicians were wandering around the town! She needed to stay out of sight until the fleet departed, and it was safe for her to return to her office. *I guess I can tell that lacky of a receptionist that I am ill,* she thought. That should buy her a few days' grace. At least until the fleet left for wherever they were headed.

She quickly composed a short message, informing her Chief Enforcer that she had come down with a case of the flu, and that she would be remaining in her home for the next few days until she was feeling better. She asked him to inform her clerk about her illness. Walking over to her neighbor's house, she paid a copper to the twelve-year-old boy of the house to deliver her message, then returned to her home and barred the door.

When Donovan and Andrew returned to the Regional Mage's Office the next morning and were informed of Mage Lisa's illness, they weren't buying it. "She's hiding. Probably from all of the magicians in town," said Andrew. "Then I guess we'll have to do this the hard way," said Donovan.

They donned their Concealment cloaks as they approached Mage Lisa's cottage. It was a small log cabin near where the Emerald River met the sea. There were only a few houses on her street, and no one was outside any of the dwellings. "What do you think?" asked Donovan quietly. "Well, we can't just walk up and knock on the door; she'd probably attack us," replied Andrew.

They stood across the street and considered their options. There was a thin whisp of smoke coming out of the chimney, so someone was definitely home. Then Donovan said, "I have an idea. See that tree in the backyard? Wouldn't it be a shame if that large branch broke off and landed on Lisa's roof? I'll bet that would bring her outside to investigate."

"I like the way you think. Let's get closer and be ready to tether her the minute she comes out." "What if she's in dragon form?" asked Donovan. "If she's a Sea Dragon, Blast spells will work, and if Stone, a shield. I think it's most likely that she's a Sea Dragon," whispered Andrew.

"I hope you're right. Ok, here goes the branch." Using a Remove spell, Donovan cut through the large tree limb that hung over Lisa's cabin. The limb fell straight down with a resounding boom, breaking through shingles, wooden slats, and rafters. The two mages waited long minutes to see what Lisa would do. Eventually, she opened the front door a crack and looked out.

Not seeing anyone, Lisa came out the door and looked at her roof. The damage was significant, but nothing a magician couldn't fix in short order. Using the Remove spell to vanish the offending tree branch, Lisa walked around to the side of the cabin to see how much damage had been done to her roof.

She had only gone a few steps when she was seized by a powerful Tether spell cast by Andrew. The two mages lowered the hoods of their Concealment cloaks and approached the struggling Changed One. "Release me at once!" screamed Lisa, "or I will kill you both where you stand!"

The two mages laughed, "I doubt that very much, Mage Lisa. You see, we think you're a Dragon Changed One. So, unless you can convince us otherwise, your life is going to change dramatically in the next few minutes." "How could I possibly convince you of something I am not?" asked Lisa.

"Just say 'can't'" said Donovan. "What?" asked Lisa. "We have discovered that dragons don't use contractions, so please use one to convince us you're human. Otherwise, you have two options. Option one: you can submit to a Binding spell, never to change back into a dragon, and never to harm a human, or, option two, you can die."

"What happens to me if I submit to the Binding spell?" asked Lisa. Andrew looked at Donovan and shrugged. "You resume your duties as the Regional Mage, although I must tell you that cooperating with other Changed Ones, like Mr. Stone, for instance, would be considered 'harming humans' and trigger the spell." Lisa stood, considering her choices. There really didn't seem to be much of a decision here.

Finally, she decided that her life as a mage wasn't so bad, and she agreed to the Binding spell. Once cast, Andrew removed his Tether spell. "Sorry about your roof," quipped Donovan, "but I'm sure you'll be able to fix it quickly. I recommend the Enlarge, Replicate, and Adhesive spells."

As Andrew and Donovan made their way back into town, Donovan said, "Did you notice how Lisa did not deny that Mr. Stone was a Changed One?"

Chapter Eighteen:
DRAGON PROBLEMS

"So, Lisa is still the Sundock Regional Mage?" asked Maria. "How can that be? She's a Dragon Changed One!" "I know," said Andrew, "but we placed a Binding spell on her that will prevent her from ever changing back into a dragon, or ever harming a human. It's a choice we've been offering all of the Changed Ones we find, that we don't have to immediately kill."

Andrew, Maria, Donovan, and Rachel were seated in Andrew and Maria's cottage, discussing the day's events. "Did she mention Mr. Stone?" asked Maria. "Well, she didn't deny that he's a Changed One, and we warned her that if she warns or assists him in any way, that will violate the Binding spell," said Donovan. "What happens if she violates the Binding spell?" asked Maria. "She dies," said Rachel.

"Humph," said Maria, "and just how many Changed Ones violate their Binding spells?" "That's a good question. I actually have no idea. I can't imagine why a Changed One would risk it," replied Andrew.

"Anyway, I understand that congratulations are in order, Rachel." Rachel blushed, and Donovan beamed. "Wait, you're pregnant?" asked Maria. "Yes," confessed Rachel, "but it's only been a few weeks now. We just discovered it on our journey from Frostberg." Maria gave her a hug and said, "Congratulations."

"It just occurred to me," said Andrew, "now that you're carrying another descendant of Wizard Amanda, you and the baby should be covered by the dragon's Binding spell, not to harm any of her prodigy." "I suppose that's true," said Donovan. "Assuming that the dragons know that we're married. Although I'm not sure how they could have learned that."

"Hmm," said Andrew, "your wedding was common knowledge in Kingston. I suppose an undiscovered Changed One could have heard about it and spread the word to the dragons." "I guess that's possible," said Rachel. "Which reminds me, we need to send a Messenger Hawk to my parents tomorrow!"

"I'll send one to my father and have him give them the news. It's unlikely that we'll be back in Kingston for a couple of months yet," said Donovan. "Besides, we still have the problem with Grotton to deal with."

"What's wrong with Grotton?" asked Andrew. Rachel grimaced, "Donovan has foreseen a large dragon attack on the city." "When?" asked Andrew. "That's the problem, I have no idea when. It could be tomorrow or next year. The spell of Foresight doesn't give me any idea *when* events will occur," said Donovan.

"So, tell me about this spell," said Andrew. Donovan explained about what had happened to the Expeditionary Force on their way to Colton and Three Forks, and how he foresaw the dragon in the Sundock Regional Mage's Office, and the attack on Grotton. "So, what are we doing to protect Grotton?" asked Maria.

"I think my father was headed there to warn them. It just doesn't make any sense, though." "What doesn't make sense?" asked Andrew. "Three Forks has an entire Regiment stationed there. That's four sorcerers and a Battle Mage, plus the Regional Mage and the three sorcerers in his office. The dragons took a beating by attacking a city with so many magicians in it. Grotton has even more magicians because of the magicians in the Naval Headquarters, even more if a squadron of Royal Navy ships is in port! If I've learned anything, it's that these dragons aren't stupid!"

"Maybe they don't know how many magicians are in Grotton," speculated Maria. "Or, maybe there are a lot of undetected Changed Ones in the city that are going to aid the dragons in their attack," said Donovan darkly.

"And you have no idea when this attack will happen?" asked Andrew. "None. Although I didn't see any snow on the ground, being so far south, Grotton doesn't get much snow anyway."

Rachel yawned. "That's our cue," said Donovan. "We need to get back to the warehouse. I think we'll be leaving the day after tomorrow. Just as soon as Major Gerald arranges commercial transport for us to Eastport. When is the fleet leaving?" "Now that all of the ships have the new Compound Seabows, I imagine we'll be leaving soon as well. We'll see you both tomorrow. Don't forget about that Messenger Hawk," said Andrew.

As Andrew saw them out, Donovan whispered to him, "If the dragons learn that Maria is your wife, they might target her to prevent our line from spreading. I don't want to rush you two, but the sooner Maria's pregnant, the safer she'll be."

The Fire Dragons Sear and Broil landed in the mountains that made up the western border of the kingdom of Baize. The trip had been grueling; there was almost no prey in the desert between the river and the mountains. Only a few small desert foxes, not nearly enough to sustain three adult Fire Dragons. In order to survive the trip, Sear had killed the smaller dragon, Fry, and he and Broil had eaten his carcass. There had been a decided lack of trust between the two surviving dragons ever since.

The mountains had plenty of prey, and both dragons had eaten their fill. "Do you think there are other dragons in these mountains?" asked Sear. "Surely not many," replied Broil, "or there would not be so much prey about. We will search for others after we have rested and regained our strength."

Over the next several days, the two dragons foraged freely among the hills and valleys of the mountain range. It was a paradise for a dragon. Plenty of prey, an abundance of water, and no humans anywhere in sight. "I am beginning to see why none of the dragons who ventured out here ever returned," said Broil. "Yes. It is unfortunate that Fry is not with us," said Sear. "That was *your* doing!" said Broil, angrily. "You know very well that if I had not acted, none of us would have survived the journey through that desert!" "I still say that it was harsh!" "I did not say it was not. I only said that it was *unfortunate* that all three of us could not complete the trip together."

"It has always been so," said a gravelly voice behind them. Both dragons turned quickly to find an enormous Stone Dragon behind them. "Who are you?" they asked. "I am Rock, chief of the dragons who inhabit these mountains. Who are you?"

"I am Sear, and this is Broil," said Sear. "How many dragons live in the mountains? We have not seen any in the days since we arrived." "I know, but we have seen *you*," said Rock. "Why have you come?"

"We were sent by our Clan Chief, Rose, to seek out any of our dragon kin who live in these parts, in order to ask for their assistance in our war with the humans," said Broil.

Rock, the Stone Dragon laughed, "Why would any dragon here wish to make the perilous journey back across the desert, just to fight with the humans? Here, we have a utopia! Plenty of prey for the few dragons who were brave enough and clever enough to reach this place, no humans to fear, and a temperate climate. No. I fear that you will find no dragons here who wish to return to the place you came from."

"Is there no way back across the desert?" asked Sear. "Well, I suppose if you traveled far enough north along these mountains, you would come to the Snow Fields. You *might* be able to make your way back by that route. I believe that there is at least some prey in the Snow Fields. Or, I suppose a Sea Dragon could follow the mountains south to the sea and swim back. It is a long way, though, weeks of travel, I would guess, and there are no Sea Dragons here."

The two Fire Dragons looked at each other and shrugged. Rock laughed again, "Come, Sear, Broil, meet some of the other Fire Dragons in my clan. I think you will find this a much more pleasing place to live than where you came from."

Ig roamed about the city of Oceanside, unafraid of being detected as a Great Dragon Changed One. The people here all acted as if they were on some sort of holiday. There were a few magic-users in the city, but they paid Ig no mind. Unfortunately, so far, there had been no Changed Ones with any interest in reverting to dragon-form or fighting the humans.

"Why would we wish to fight the humans, Ig? We have a good life here," said Zard, another Great Dragon. Unless something changes, I doubt that you will find any of our kin who would choose to go back to the hunger of being a dragon.”

“But surely, there must be some whose human lives are less than desirable, or who long for vengeance for the wrong that was done to us!” insisted Ig. “That was long ago, Ig, and many have forgotten the old wrongs. You may be correct that there are some who would join you, but they are generally unreliable as humans, and probably would be no better as dragons.”

“It was much the same in Lakeshore,” said Ig sadly. “Well, I must return for the Dragon Council, which meets soon. I fear that they will not like my news.” Zard said, “Impress upon the Council that, not only will most of us in Oceanside not fight against the humans, but some of us might choose to fight *with* them if our families are endangered by dragon attacks.”

Ig considered Zard’s words. They were troubling on many levels. He slipped out of the city unnoticed and headed for the lake. He had just enough time to visit his family on the east side of Lake Ford before he must fly north to the quarry where the Dragon Council met.

Anne was wet. It was dark and damp in the Sea Dragon cavern, so she had to keep using wind spells to keep herself warm and dry. The Sea Dragon, Emerald, was not very good company. She rarely spoke to Anne, despite the sorceress's attempts at conversation. All Anne had learned was that Emerald's mate had been killed when the dragons attacked after the 1st Squadron had set fire to Perfo.

Anne had tried casting a Concealment shield around herself while Emerald slept, hoping that she could fool the dragon into thinking she had escaped. The dragon had simply smiled and said, "Nice trick, but it will not work, human."

Anne knew that she could escape any time she wished. She could dig a hole through the floor or the walls, paralyze the Sea Dragon guard, or even kill her if she must. But that was not why she came here. She only hoped that the next Dragon Council meeting was soon, and that they would see reason.

Hopefully, by now, the Admiralty was looking for her. But she doubted that they'd look *here.* "Dinner," said Emerald, tossing a sea bass into the cavern. That was another thing, Anne was *tired* of eating fish. Nonetheless, she scooped up the fish and cleaned it using magic, vanishing the guts, then started a small fire and cooked her dinner. Emerald watched and listened closely, attempting to learn new magic spells. Anne usually mumbled the words to the spells she cast, but sometimes she forgot.

Anne had no idea how long she had been imprisoned in the Sea Dragon colony. There was no sun or moon, and the dragons had no calendar that she could discern, other than the cycles of the moon (which she couldn't see).

One day (or night), Emerald said, "You have a visitor." Annalise, Gek's daughter, came into the cave and sat down. "Hello, Annalise," said Anne. "Hello. Are you comfortable?" Anne frowned, "No. I am definitely not comfortable. The floor is damp and hard. It is difficult to sleep on. Where is your father?"

"He left for the Dragon Council several days ago. He should be back soon. Then I can go home and see my mother and my brother." "How is your mother?" "She is well, but a little sad about what happened to my father," said Anna.

"What happened to Gek?" "He was injured by the humans and now cannot change back into a human. Richard is very upset that he cannot." "I imagine," said Anne. "How was your father injured?" "He was fighting in someplace called Three Forks, and a human magic-user struck him with a spell that cut off part of two of his fingers. The Change spell will no longer work for him."

"That is enough, Anna," said Emerald. "Run along now. You can come back another day." Anna paddled away softly. "Goodbye, Anne." "Goodbye, Anna, thank you for coming."

The beginnings of a plan began to form in Anne's mind.

The Fleet sailed at dawn, and most of the town came down to the docks and waved to the sailors as they departed. It was a rare event for the entire fleet to be in port at once. Donovan, Rachel, and Maria stood on the pier until the HMS VALOR disappeared over the horizon. "When will you two be leaving?" asked Maria.

"Tomorrow at midday," replied Rachel. "Major Gerald has booked us passage on the FS IRONSIDES, which is transporting a load of coal and some passengers to Eastport." With all of the 1st Fleet headed toward the Coral Islands, and no Navy ships available for convoy duty, the captain of the IRONSIDES was only too happy to transport the Royal Expeditionary Force (and its two mages). He even reduced his normal asking price. The Expeditionary Force would begin loading in the morning, and the ship would sail with the noon tide.

Donovan, Rachel, and Maria walked through Sundock, headed for Maria's house. The town seemed empty with all of the sailors gone. Most of the shops were open, but there was very little foot traffic. As they passed the Regional Mage's Office, Donovan stretched. As he looked up, he was startled to see two large stones falling from the sky.

"DRAGON ATTACK!" he shouted, casting a shield over himself and the two women. The first stone bounced harmlessly off his shield, landing in the street next to them. The second, larger stone smashed through the roof of the Regional Mage's Office.

Donovan, Rachel, and Maria rushed into the office and found a shocked, but otherwise unharmed, receptionist cowering under his desk. The stone had crashed through the ceiling above Mage Lisa's desk, striking her fatally. As Donovan attempted a Healing spell, Lisa whispered, "Dragons can be very vindictive if they think they have been betrayed…" The Healing spell was useless; Mage Lisa was dead.

"How could the dragons have known that she consented to the Binding spell?" asked Rachel. "I'm not sure they did," said Donovan. "They may have just been targeting the Regional Mage's Office. Sorceress Anne told me that the Sea Dragons have lost contact with most of their Changed Ones, who moved to the mainland. They may not have realized that Lisa was one of them."

They left the office and checked on the receptionist. He was shaken, but uninjured. "A Concealed Dragon dropped a stone on the office," said Rachel. "I'm sorry, but Mage Lisa is dead." "How could this have happened?" asked the man.

"I'm not sure. Maybe the dragons intentionally targeted this building. Or maybe it was just a random chance. Did Lisa have any family?" asked Donovan. "No, she was an only child and her parents passed some time ago," said the receptionist. "What should I do?"

"Go to the mortuary and arrange for her body to be picked up, then make arrangements for her funeral. Use the funds in the Regional Mage's Office to pay for her burial. I'll contact Sorcerer Paul in the 13th Company and let him know that he will need to help your Enforcers until a replacement mage is sent," said Donovan. "Was Mage Lisa working on any active cases?"

"Not really. The Enforcers have been busy for the last week, what with all of the sailors in town, but I'm not aware of anything *magical* that she was investigating." Donovan nodded his understanding, and the three of them headed back out into the street. The large stone had already been moved to the side of the street by the local shopkeepers.

They proceeded to Maria's house with no further incidents and sat down in the living room to have tea and discuss the situation. "What are your plans, Maria?" asked Donovan.

"Well, I need to get back to Fairview eventually and check on Prestige Arms. We've been gone for months now. We have an able assistant, Ben, but the other three workers are fairly new. Ben can keep the shop open and operating, and there are orders for crossbows still coming in. I can't stay here forever," said Maria.

Donovan drank his tea and thought. Finally, he asked, "Could you move the business to Sundock, or, better yet, open a branch here?" Maria considered the idea, "We'd have to purchase some additional land for a warehouse and our supplies. You know, lumber, steel stock, coal. Plus room for finished products and an office where we could display our wares. We'd also have to probably purchase the blacksmith shop across the street and hire some additional smiths. Mr. Smith is a hard worker, but he'd need some more help," said

Maria, warming up to the idea. "We might even have to expand the current blacksmith shop, get a couple more forges and anvils, plus additional tools. It would be quite an undertaking…"

"What is that devious mind of yours thinking?" Rachel asked Donovan. "I was thinking that Andrew has been in the Navy for over two years now, so he's about due to rotate out. Once this peace treaty is signed with the Sea Dragons, he could be assigned here as the Regional Mage. I have some influence with the Chief of Military Wizardry, you know."

"Hmm, that will still leave Sundock without a Regional Mage for some months," mused Rachel. "I know, but it will take months for my father and Wizard Noland to find another mage and get them here anyway." "It's an inspired idea," said Rachel.

Maria looked doubtful. "Do you really think Edward would assign Andrew here?" "I can only suggest it. I don't have visibility on the needs of the rest of the kingdom. I mean, we already need a mage in Colton, and I'm sure there are other needs elsewhere that I'm not aware of. It's just an idea. But I think my dad might go for it."

"There's a lot of prep work required to make this happen," said Maria. "At least it will give you something to do while you wait for 2nd Fleet to arrive for the upgrades to their Seabows," said Donovan. "Don't spend a lot of money yet, but you can certainly make inquiries about purchasing land and the smithy. I don't believe that there is another arms merchant in Sundock," said Donovan, "and the taxes would certainly be lower than in Fairview."

"Yes, and we might be able to get that steel from Smithville without shipping it all the way from Eastport to Fairview," said Maria. "I'll give it some thought and look into the costs. This all assumes that Andrew stays here."

"Well, it wouldn't be forever. I believe that Regional Mages get rotated every few years, too," said Rachel. "Once we have the branch office set up, I wouldn't have to stay here," said Maria. Donovan said, "If you hire any new blacksmiths, just make sure they can use contractions." Maria nodded her understanding.

"We'd better head over to the Message Center and get a Hawk off to Kingston," said Rachel. "We sail tomorrow."

Donovan and Rachel headed to the Sundock Message Center, a small, one-story building situated next to the Regional Mage's Office. Upon entering, the attendant said, "Can I help you?" "Yes. I am Mage Donovan, and this is Mage Rachel. We need to send a Messenger Hawk to the Chief of Military Wizardry in Kingston, please."

The clerk frowned, "We don't have any hawks trained for that destination. Will the Wizards Academy do?" Donovan smiled, "Yes. That will do nicely." The clerk handed over the message parchment and said, "I'm sorry it's so small, it's the weight, you know." "I understand, said Donovan. He wrote:

Sir,

As expected, Lisa was a Changed One. She was killed by a falling stone. Sundock needs a new Mage. Recommend Andrew once the treaty is complete, as Prestige Arms may be moving to Sundock. Andrew married Maria.

Mage Donovan Francis, REF

Donovan murmured the spell to prevent changes to the message and sealed it with the wax seal provided by the clerk. "I'll send this out immediately," said the clerk.

As Rachel and Donovan left the Message Center, she asked, "What was that spell you cast on the message? I've never seen that one before."

Chapter Nineteen:
COUNCILS

Gek, Azure, Sky, and Cobalt landed in the rock quarry just north of Colton for the Dragon Council meeting. The Fire Dragons, Rose and Fern, and the Stone Dragons, Jasper and Basalt, were already present. The Snow Dragons, Bliz, and Ice arrived a few minutes later, followed by the Great Dragon, Ig.

"Now that we are all here," said Cobalt, "we need to discuss recent events and our path forward. As you all know, our attack on Three Forks was not as successful as we hoped." "Successful! It was a disaster!" shouted Fern. "My Clan cannot keep losing our best fighters in these fruitless attacks."

"Nor can we," said Jasper. "What went wrong, Bliz, Gek? You two were the only survivors!" Gek deferred to the older Snow Dragon to answer.

"As we made our attack, we were set upon from behind by two Great Dragons. The two Sea Dragons were killed quickly, and the other Snow Dragon, Hale, was killed by a human-fired iron arrow. The two Fire Dragons were similarly attacked and killed by the much larger Great Dragons. I do not know how the two Stone Dragons died," said Bliz.

"The Stone Dragons were killed by two human magic-users, who encased them in some kind of shield. Once inside the shield, our Stone Dragon cousins were unable to attack the humans with teeth, talons, tail, or fire. I believe they suffocated," said Gek.

"And just where were *you* while all this was happening?" asked an enraged Fern. Gek shifted his feet, then said, "I had circled around, hoping to attack the humans from behind. I knocked over a large building on top of the two magic-users who were fighting the Stone Dragons, and another magic-user who was nearby. They were all buried under the rubble, which I then doused with flaming inferno. Then I was struck by a magic-user's spell and injured," said Gek, holding up his injured hand.

"Bliz and I retreated back to the rock quarry just north of the town." "Who were these Great Dragons?" asked Rose. "More Changed Ones?" "No," said Gek. "After the battle, a Fire Dragon Changed One named Cinder arrived at the rock quarry and informed us that human magic-users have learned how to transform into dragons. Cinder also mentioned that one of the sorcerers in Three Forks was Donovan." There was shock among the members of the Dragon Council. "Humans can change into dragons? Has Donovan left the wizard's school? Are we certain this is the same magic-user? How will we track him now?"

"I do not know if it is the same Donovan, but we must assume it is," said Cobalt. "I received a report from one of our Sea Dragon Changed Ones in Three Forks that indicates that, not only did Donovan survive the attack, which is fortunate for those of us under the Binding spell, but he has taken a mate. In order to prevent any more offspring, I ordered his mate to be killed immediately, before they could have any children. It could be that even an *unborn* child might trigger the Binding spell if the child were harmed."

"How are we to counter this new threat?" asked Jasper. "It all depends on how far this new knowledge has spread among the human magic-users," said Gek. "In order to change into a dragon, one must know what a dragon looks like! There are only a few human magic-users who have seen me." "Exactly how many is that?" asked Rose.

Gek thought *there were Andrew, Anne, Celeste, and Donovan that he knew of. Plus, the magic-users in Three Forks who had witnessed the attack.* "I know of four magic-users for sure, Andrew, Donovan, and the dragon-friends Anne and Celeste, but several more may have seen me during the attack on Three Forks." The Council was disturbed by this news.

"So, what are we to do? We seem to be undone," said the Snow Dragon, Ice. "Well, for one thing, we do not attack a large human city with several magic-users in it again," said Gek. "If we had chosen a smaller town to attack, there would have been fewer magic-users to deal with."

"Even one Great Dragon would be a problem," said Bliz. "Where is Ard?" asked Rose. "I expected to see him here." Gek swallowed, "Ard passed away some months ago." "That is sad news," said Rose, "Ard was a ferocious fighter in his youth, and a wise counsel." Looking at Ig, Rose said, "That means that you, Ig, are now the Chief of the Great Dragon

Clan, and either Gek or your mate is the Great Dragon representative to this Council."

Ig said, "My mate is busy raising our children. Gek has been a member of the council for some time, and I choose for him to remain a member." Gek nodded his acceptance.

"Very well," said Cobalt. "Ig, you were asked to investigate the number of Changed Ones in southern Baize and determine if they would help us in our fight. What have you discovered?" "My news on that front is not good," said Ig. "While I have located a dozen or more Great Dragon Changed Ones, none of them are willing to go to war with the humans."

"*None of them?*" asked Fern. "Correct. Every dragon I spoke with was perfectly content to remain in their human form, unless they or their families were somehow personally threatened by the humans. Some even said that they would fight against us," said Ig.

"What about the Stone Dragons you contacted?" asked Jasper. "I did not approach any Changed Ones that were not of my Clan," said Ig. "If there are Stone Dragon Changed Ones in Baize, then a Stone Dragon will need to be the one to contact them. I suspect the answer will be the same though."

"This is troubling," said Fern. "We had counted on some assistance from our Changed One brothers." "Do you know how many Fire Dragon Changed Ones there are?" asked Gek. Fern looked doubtful and said, "I assume there to be dozens, spread across the country, but I do not know the exact number," the Fire Dragon confessed.

"What about the three Fire Dragons that were sent to search for dragons in the far west? Have any returned with news?" asked Cobalt. Rose shook her head, "No. We have had no word from Sear, Fry, or Broil. I do not know if this is because they perished in the desert, or if they have simply not had time to find any more of our kin and return."

"We seem to be running low on resources," said Bliz, the Snow Dragon Clan Chief. "I must tell you that many in my Clan are skeptical about how to move forward with this conflict. Snow Dragons can easily kill humans, but we cannot fight against magic-users changed into Great, Fire, or Stone Dragons. If we lose many more of our Clan, we may be forced to withdraw from this fight."

The assembled members of the Dragon Council all looked concerned and doubtful of a path to success. Cobalt said, "I must also inform you that a fleet of ships is currently approaching our islands in an attempt to bring the Sea Dragon Clan back to the negotiating table to secure a truce between us and the humans."

"I thought you had a treaty," said Rose. "One that would allow you to kill humans on land, but not at sea." "No. I would not sign what the human king proposed. He wanted us to sign a 37-page document, which none of us could read! I rejected it utterly."

"What was in it?" asked Jasper. "Who knows? I heard something about *fishing rights!* As if we would ever consider a restriction on where we could catch prey!" said Cobalt.

"So, why have they returned?" asked Fern. "It seems that they have a new proposal. *They will not attack us if we agree not to attack humans,"* replied Cobalt. "That is a completely different treaty!" said Rose. "Yes. It is," said Cobalt, "but one I may eventually have to agree to. The number of male Sea Dragons still willing to fight is dwindling. There are some aggressive females whose mates have been killed or injured by the humans who have volunteered to fight, but not many. Our most effective attack has been dropping heavy objects on the humans, but we can only kill a few at a time that way."

"What are the human ships doing?" asked Bliz. "It seems that their plan is to surround our islands. I am not sure to what end. We can always swim under them or fly over them. The worst thing they could do would be to set fire to one or both islands. That would be inconvenient, but nothing more."

"They must have something else in mind then," said Sky, "but I am not sure what."

"I have a suggestion," said Gek. The other dragons perked up, hoping for a plan that could swing the balance of power back to their side. "What if we focus our attacks, not on the humans' military or magic-users, but on their commercial centers?"

"What do you mean?" asked Rose. "If the human navy is surrounding the Sea Dragon's islands, they cannot be guarding their merchant ships! Those ships do not have magic-users on board and are more vulnerable targets. I have also heard of ships in the North Sea that fish for crabs. They would be prime targets for Snow Dragons! In the summer and fall, we could burn their crops! Why, a single Fire Dragon could cause severe damage to their economy if we divert our attacks to their food supply!"

"What about the humans on the west side of the river?" asked Jasper. "We need to target a town or city that has few magic-users, but significant commercial value. Do you know of such a place?" asked Gek. Jasper thought, then said, "The human city of Middleberg sits at a fork in the river. I have heard that there is much trade there, but few soldiers or magic-users. It might be a good target for the Fire and Stone Dragon Clans."

"I like it," said Cobalt. "Which human port on this side of the river handles the most trade, and should be attacked by the Sea and Great Dragons?"

"Grotton," said Gek.

"Did you get all that?" whispered Wizard Noland. Edward nodded, "Yes. It seems that Donovan was correct, the dragons will attack Grotton soon." Wizards Edward and

Noland were under both Concealment cloaks and shields, and had cast Silence spells and Hearing Enhancements in order to listen in on the Dragon Council's deliberations. They were hidden on the ledge at the top of the rock quarry and had been in place for three days, awaiting the arrival of the dragons.

"Now, we just need to wait until they all leave so we can get out of here. This rock is uncomfortable," said Edward quietly. Noland grunted. The Stone and Fire Dragons left first, heading west into Baize, followed by the Snow Dragons, who flew north, back into the Snow Fields. That left the Sea and Great Dragons in the quarry.

"Cobalt," said Gek. "I have an idea that I did not wish to bring up before the entire council, but I would like you and Ig to consider." "What is it?" "Once before, I suggested that we might want to let the humans know about our ability to understand their language and change into human form. I know it is a radical idea, but hear me out. It might be a way to get the humans to push our Changed One brothers into joining our cause. If the humans begin searching for, or killing Changed Ones…"

"You are suggesting that we intentionally endanger other dragons, in the hopes that they will abandon their lives as humans, and attack the humans in self-defense?" asked Ig. "Yes. That is the gist of it."

"I am not sure I like this idea. Why did you not bring it up before the entire Dragon Council?" asked Cobalt. "You know how hot-headed Fire Dragons can be! They might have agreed immediately and convinced their Stone Dragon neighbors. It is just an *idea,* and I admit, a radical one," said Gek.

"Let us keep that idea as a last resort," said Cobalt. "I like the idea of targeting the human trade and food supplies, as long as we do not lose too many dragons in the process." "I have one more question," said Gek. "How does this war end?"

"I do not understand," said Ig. "I do not think that we can kill all of the humans, everywhere," said Gek. "Eventually, they may retreat into strongholds that we cannot overcome, or develop new and even deadlier weapons. I am reminded of Ard's last words. He said, *'If we can win the war, but only with unacceptable consequences, then we must consider an imperfect peace.'"*

Ig and Cobalt considered Gek's question. Neither had an answer, but both knew he was correct. Finally, Cobalt said, "You ask hard questions, son. I do not know how this war ends, but it must end with our ability to survive and flourish, with access to prey and an end to the hunger. Eventually, we may have to negotiate with the humans."

"This Great Dragon is too smart for his own good," whispered Edward. "If the dragons start attacking our food supplies..." "Then we are lost," finished Noland. "That means that we must end this conflict before the next fall harvest. The dragon is correct; there is no way for us to guard all of the fields and crops in Franconia or Baize. Once we get back, we need to warn the crab fleet in Frostberg to have at least one magician who can transform into a dragon with every flotilla of ships that heads into the crabbing area. We also need to warn Rachel of the threat to her."

"I'm concerned about his comment about 'endangering the Changed Ones.' By seeking them out *vigorously*, we may push them into joining the hostile dragons," said Edward. "I'm also concerned about the public's reaction if the dragon's ability to speak and change into humans becomes common knowledge," said Noland. "That's something we have no control over," said Edward. "Fortunately, it sounds like the older dragons are reluctant for this knowledge to come out, except as a last resort."

"It sounds like we need to convene a Wizards Council," said Edward.

Vice Admiral Jordan opened his operating orders from Admiral Cross. They had been delivered by Dragon Messenger Anne while they were on their way to Sundock with explicit instructions that they were not to be opened until the fleet arrived at the Coral Islands.

The Fleet Commander wondered again where Anne could be. She had delivered orders to the 2nd Squadron when they were in the ice pack, sailing from Frostberg to Sundock, then she had vanished. He had other magicians at his disposal who could change into dragons and relay messages, but they had other duties.

The orders said:

Vice Admiral Jordan,

You are to position your fleet on the east side of the Coral Islands, then have your magicians transform into Sea Dragons and patrol underwater from your line eastward. Your mission is to drive off the Sea Dragon's food supply. We know that there are few fish between the islands and the mainland. By driving the fish away from the islands, we hope to deprive the Sea Dragons of prey and bring them to the bargaining table. You know the treaty conditions. Make sure to keep some of your magicians aboard at all times. I expect the Sea Dragons to react violently when they realize what you are doing.

Good Luck,

H.C. Cross, Commander,

Royal Franconian Navy

"Summon the fleet magicians," said the admiral. "I have new orders for them. And signal the fleet to make a line from north to south on the east side of the Coral Islands. I want 1st Squadron in the north, 2nd Squadron in the south, and we'll take position in the center."

When the fleet was arranged as ordered and the magicians gathered on the HMS SENTRY, the admiral read the orders to the assembled magicians. When he finished, he said, "I want two magicians from each squadron on deck at all times, one resting, and one in the water. I know that won't be possible for 1st Squadron, so they just need one magician on deck. Our mission is to drive the schools of fish away, herd them south, since there is no food for them in the deep water. Watch out for Sea dragons. Once we clear this area, we'll move east and re-form the line. Make sure all the Seabows are ready for action, and if anyone sees Dragon Messenger Anne, please tell her that I need to speak with her at once. Dismissed."

The magicians quickly changed back into Sea Dragons and returned to their ships, passing along the admiral's orders to their respective Captains.

Andrew landed on the VALOR, changed back into human form, and informed Commodore Matthews of the admiral's orders. "What do you think, Andrew?" asked the commodore.

"I think the Sea Dragons are going to be very unhappy, sir. This is probably going to provoke an even bigger attack than last time, once they figure out what we're up to, which will probably only take a couple of days," said Andrew.

"If that's the case, then I want you in the water first, I'll have Sorcerer Marvin on the VICEROY on deck, and Sorcerer Roger can get some rest. The rotation will be Sea Dragon, rest, then deck duty, until further notice," said the commodore. "Aye, Aye, sir."

Andrew went to the aft deck, removed his garments, and changed into a Sea Dragon. "Here goes nothing," he said, before diving over the side. The water did not feel as cold as he feared, and, surprisingly, the salt water did not burn his eyes the way it did when he was in human form. Andrew swam down and looked around. He could clearly make out the hulls of the ships in the first two squadrons.

Swimming east, he found a large school of codfish, which started and scattered at his approach. Andrew had to slow his speed in order not to overtake the frightened fish. He understood immediately that Sea Dragons were much faster than their prey. He circled around the school and drove them south and east as well as he could. It was difficult. The cod did not *want* to go south, but they realized their peril from the Sea Dragon.

Andrew swam for hours, herding various schools of fish south until he reached the next magician-turned-Sea-Dragon, who took up the task. Andrew circled back to the north, looking for more fish. He occasionally came across a large shark or other leviathan in the waters, but all of them swam away quickly, afraid of the Sea Dragon.

As the sun began to set, Andrew headed for the surface and the VALOR. Making the transition from swimming to flying was harder than expected, and he failed to gain any altitude before splashing back into the water. Eventually, he learned to use his tail to get his wings above the wavetops, then flap vigorously to get into the air.

He landed on the aft deck of the VALOR and transformed. *Now* he was cold (and wet). Andrew quickly dried himself off and got dressed. The commodore was standing by, as was Sorcerer Marvin. "It's not as cold as I expected," Andrew said to Marvin. "The fish are afraid of Sea Dragons, but they really don't want to leave. They keep circling back. You need to herd them all the way to the next magician in order to keep them moving south." Marvin nodded his understanding and headed aft.

"We're going to need some way to tell magicians from actual Sea Dragons, sir. We all look the same after all." "Right," said the commodore. "Well, give it some thought. It would be unfortunate if one magician attacked another, or let themselves be attacked by an actual Sea Dragon."

A splash from the water got their attention, as Sorcerer Marvin landed back on the deck and transformed. "What's wrong?" asked Andrew. "I can't see a thing down there!" said Marvin, "It's too dark!" "Hmm," said Andrew, "I wonder how the Sea Dragons hunt at night. Maybe they use their sense of smell to find the fish."

"I thought of that, but everything just smelled like seaweed to me," said Marvin. "Then I guess we'll have to restrict our underwater activities to daylight hours," said the commodore. "Marvin, why don't you fly over to the other ships and see if they're having the same problem. Then head to the SENTRY and inform the admiral that I'm going to keep you all onboard except during the day."

Marvin changed back into dragon form and flew off to deliver the message. "I wonder what's keeping Anne?" mused Andrew.

Chapter Twenty:
REVELATIONS

Anne was getting very tired of her captivity. The Sea Dragon, Emerald, was not pleasant company, and the baby dragon, Annalise, had not been allowed to visit her again (yet). "Emerald, when am I going to be able to leave?" she asked.

"That is not up to me. When Cobalt returns from the Dragon Council meeting, he may have a decision," said the disagreeable green Sea Dragon. "So, the Dragon Council is meeting now?" asked Anne.

"I suppose so," replied Emerald. "At least Cobalt, Sky, and Gek left a few days ago and said they would be gone for several days. Which means that they either went to a Dragon Council meeting, or to attack your ships or people. Or both," said Emerald smugly.

"Which means that you have no idea where they went," said Anne, "for all *you* know, they went to visit Richard." "Who is Richard?" "Richard is Gek and Azure's human baby," said Anne.

"Azure has a human child? You are lying to me!" said Emerald angrily. "Why would I do that? In fact, I helped deliver Richard. Ask Annalise if you don't believe me." "I will certainly do so the next time she is permitted to visit, and if you have lied to me, you will get no dinner!"

"Why would you care if Gek and Azure have a human child?" asked Anne. "Because it could cause divided loyalties!" said Emerald. "Particularly for someone on the Dragon Council!" "Gek is on the Dragon Council? Isn't he a little young for that?"

"Yes. He is decades too young, but there are few of his kind left. You humans killed off most of the Great Dragons!" "I'm sorry. I had no idea. That was centuries before I was born," said Anne.

"Perhaps so. But that is no excuse. Oh, hello, Annalise. Tell me, how is your brother?" asked Emerald. "Richard was fine when we left. How do you know about him?" asked Anna.

"So. It is true. You have a human brother?" "Yes. He is weak, but not useless. In fact, he saved me from being eaten by a mountain lion once." Emerald was shocked, both by the admission and by Anna's acceptance of such a sibling.

"How could a human baby possibly save you from a cougar?" asked Emerald. "Richard can do magic. He put the big cat to sleep after it pounced on me." "He knows the Sleep spell?" Anna giggled, "Yes, mother and father tried to use it on him once, when they had to leave for a few days, but it would not work on him. Instead, he learned the word and the motion and started putting our human friend, Bruce, to sleep over and over again. It was hilarious!"

Emerald looked very uncomfortable with this revelation. Finally, she said, "You may go in and visit for a short time. Anne, I apologize for accusing you of lying. Lies are abhorrent to dragons. It is cause for immediate expulsion from the clan if a dragon is caught lying, even in the smallest matter. It is a matter of honor."

Anne nodded her understanding, having learned something valuable from the conversation with the now *less* disagreeable Sea Dragon. "Hello again, Annalise. How are you doing today?" "I am fine, Anne. My grandmother took me fishing today, and we caught a Manta Ray! It was delicious!"

"I'll have to take your word for that," said Anne, "I've never eaten Manta Ray before." "Would you like some? I think we have some left." "No, thank you. You should have it. After all, you caught it. So, tell me more about your brother."

"Richard? He is small and has a blue streak in his hair. Bruce says that he has learned to walk and talk much faster than a normal human child." "If he can walk and talk, then he is certainly growing faster than any human child I have ever seen," said Anne. "Most one-year-old human babies are still learning to crawl."

"That is what Bruce says." "Who is Bruce?" asked Anne quietly. "Bruce is the human we live near. He is my parents' friend. He has a driftwood house on the beach." "ANNA!" shouted Emerald, "You were told not to tell this human anything about Bruce!" "But why not? He is a dragon-friend too, is he not?"

"He is," said the adult dragon, "but that is not something Anne needs to know about. I think it is time for you to go back to your grandmother." "OK," said Anna softly. As the baby dragon walked away, Anne said, "When you see your father, tell him that I might be able to fix his hand."

Edward and Noland landed back at the Academy marina. It was a two-day flight from the rock quarry above Colton, and they had stopped to rest by the western shore of Crystal Lake. "What would you like to do first?" asked Noland.

"I need to get to my office and cast a Seeing spell to determine where everybody is right now. If you could send a Messenger Hawk to Frostberg and warn the crab fleet, that would be helpful. Then we need to send out invitations to our key magicians, asking them to come to Kingston for a Wizard's Council," said Edward.

"Who should we invite?" asked Noland. "All of the Wizards and Regional Mages. We will also need a representative, preferably of at least mage rank, from each Regiment and Naval Fleet. We should also probably invite some of the magicians from Baize since this concerns them too."

"When would you like this Council to convene?" asked Wizard Noland. "How about *yesterday?*" Edward grinned. "It must be before the next full moon, in case the Dragon Council meets again. It will take a few days to get the Messenger Hawks to their destinations, and for the magicians to get here, especially those coming from Baize. Let's say three weeks from today. It's going to be quite a crowd. Can we use the Lecture Hall?"

"Surely. It should be empty during Endday Mentor testing," said Noland. "OK. If you send out the invitations, I'll head over to my office and determine where everyone is. I'll let Kathy know what's going on. I may need to send her to Baize, but I hate to keep doing that. Now that the dragons know that we can change, our Dragon Messengers are not as safe as they once were."

When Edward returned to his office, Kathy was waiting. She rose and gave him a kiss. "Welcome back! Did you learn anything interesting at the Dragon Council?" she asked.

"Several things, some more disturbing than others. First, the dragons know that we can change into dragons; second, they know that Donovan has left the Academy and is married to Rachel. The Sea Dragon Clan Chief has ordered Rachel to be killed to prevent Wizard Amanda's line from spreading further. Another Great Dragon reported that none of the Changed Ones in Oceanside or Lakeshore would help them fight us. Lastly, they plan to start attacking our commercial industries and merchant ships, while the Navy is busy around the Coral Islands. They also discussed sending Fire Dragons to burn our crops in the summer and fall."

"Wow! That's a lot of news for one meeting!" "Indeed. I have asked Wizard Noland to send out invitations for a Wizard's Council meeting. We need to gather all of the Wizards and Regional Mages to discuss our plans. The meeting will take place at the Wizards Academy in three weeks. Right now, I need to cast a Seeing spell and determine where all our key pieces are on the board," said Edward.

He moved to the map on his wall and took his truncheon from its holster at his waist. Holding it before the map, he cast the Seeing spell. He found the 1st Fleet, with Mage Andrew, in a line just east of the Coral Islands. Donovan and Rachel were in the Eastern Ocean, just a little way south of Sundock; King Henry was in Southport with Sorceress Celeste (of course); Dragon Messenger Phillip was in Grotton, presumably at Naval Headquarters; and Dragon Messenger Anne was on the northernmost of the Coral Islands.

"I wonder what Anne is doing on the Coral Islands," said Edward. "Maybe the Sea Dragons are ready to negotiate?" speculated Kathy. Edward humphed, "Not based on what I heard two days ago. They seemed generally unconcerned with our fleet surrounding their islands. They're going to be *very* unhappy when they realize why the fleet is there."

"By the way, you received a Messenger Hawk from Sundock yesterday. It was delivered to the Academy. It's quite short," said Kathy, handing over the message. Edward took a brief sniff of the parchment, then read:

Sir,

As expected, Lisa was a Changed One. She was killed by a falling stone. Sundock needs a new mage. Recommend

Andrew once the treaty is complete, as Prestige Arms is moving to Sundock. Andrew married Maria.

Mage Donovan Francis, REF

Edward shook his head. "That's putting an awful lot of information in a very short message. It means that Mage Lisa was a Changed One, as Donovan Foresaw; I'm not sure who dropped the stone on her; Mage Andrew married James's daughter, Maria; and she is moving Prestige Arms to Sundock, and Donovan thinks I should appoint Andrew as the Sundock Regional Mage."

"How much longer is Andrew's tour with the Navy?" asked Kathy. "Hmm, Magicians normally rotate assignments every three years, so he is almost due for a new assignment. Once the new treaty is negotiated with the Sea Dragons, it will be a good time to move him. Donovan may be on to something, but it leaves Sundock without a mage until a new treaty is agreed to," said Edward.

"How long would it take to get a mage there normally?" asked Kathy. "That depends on where the mage is coming from in Franconia. Let's not forget, Colton also needs a mage. Let's see, I think we should move Mage Ben from Westport to Colton, and promote Sorceress Candice to be the Westport Regional Mage if she can pass the Mage Test. Sorceress Karen, who was the mentor's supervisor at the Academy, is on her way to Smithville, which frees up Sorcerer Christopher to replace Sorceress Candice in Westport. I'll announce the new assignments at the Wizard's Council."

"So, how do we warn Rachel?" asked Kathy. "I'd send Sorceress Anne, but she's not available. I guess I'll have to go myself. That's a long way, though," said Edward. "Speaking of flying around, we need to invite Wizard James and the other wizards from Baize to this Wizard's Council meeting. I also heard that the dragons are planning to attack Middleberg. Should we send a Messenger Hawk, or do you think one of us should go in person? I hate to keep sending you back there."

"What else do we need to warn Baize about?" asked Kathy. "After the Dragon Council meeting, Gek, the Great Dragon, made a suggestion to the Council Chair that *maybe* they should inform our citizens of the dragon's ability to change into human form," said Edward. "To what end?" "If it caused the local citizens to go on a hunt for Changed Ones, the friendly or neutral Changed Ones might reconsider their position and join the fight against us. We need to be careful not to let that happen."

"That's probably too complicated a message to send by Hawk. I should probably go," said Kathy. Edward sighed, "I was afraid you were going to say that. Well, you're not leaving today. By the way, how's the villa coming?" said Edward, changing topics to a more pleasant subject.

"The place is clean, and your furniture is moved into the villa. We're going to need some new beds and other furniture soon. The chimneys are clean, and some of the minor repairs are underway. Anthony wants to talk to you— something about the carriage. He's been working on it, and he found a matched pair of horses. Burt starts tomorrow, as you recall."

"You've gotten a lot done in a short while," said Edward. "The staff is *very* motivated and appreciative. I think the biggest challenge is going to be the grounds. Those gardens are a mess!" "I'm sure Sarah can sort it out," said Edward. "Anthony's been helping her when he has the time," said Kathy with a suggestive wink.

Edward thought for a minute, then said, "You know, if we're going to keep running off like this, we're going to need a receptionist. If only to collect messages and keep the office clean." "Do they have to be a magician?" asked Kathy. "No. I think that would be a waste of magical assets. Do you have someone in mind?" Kathy nodded, "Yes. Do you remember the Caterer who was killed by the Stone Dragon at Donovan's reception? Well, her mother has had a hard time making ends meet since her daughter was killed. I understand that Wizard Noland has been helping her a little, *financially*, since the wedding."

"Can she read and write?" asked Edward. "Yes, her father was a librarian. I think it would be a great help to her. We might also be able to eventually explain how her daughter was killed. I'm not sure that she believes that one of her daughter's heating elements exploded." Edward thought it over and agreed. He asked Kathy to make the job offer, then said he was heading home to get some sleep. They both have a busy day tomorrow.

When Edward arrived at the villa, Anthony immediately ran up and said, "Sir, can you help me with something? There's something wrong with the carriage." Edward sighed but walked over to the carriage house with his new coachman.

"What seems to be the problem?" asked Edward. "This carriage is too heavy," said Tony. "I don't understand," said Edward. "See these leaf springs?" asked the coachman, pointing to the heavy steel slats that were stacked above the coach's axles. "Yes, I see them," said Edward, confused.

"Well, sir, they're practically new. The springs keep the ride smooth, so you don't feel every bump in the road. The problem is they should be holding the carriage much higher!" "You've lost me," said Edward.

"This is a standard Wilkinson Carriage, sir; it weighs about 180 stone," said Tony. "OK, so?" "So these springs are compressed like they're carrying 250 stone! Where's all the extra weight coming from?" "I have no idea," said Edward. "I've looked everywhere, and the only place it can be is in the storage compartments under the seats," said Tony. "Storage compartments?" "Yes, sir. You see, these seat cushions lift up and there's a compartment under them for storing tools, luggage, or other valuables."

"So, the extra weight must be in the storage compartments," said Edward. "Exactly right, sir, but I can't open them!" said Tony. "Is there a secret lock or something?" asked Edward, intrigued. "Not one that I can find, and I've looked everywhere."

Edward grabbed the seat cushion and tried to lift it, but, as Anthony said, it wouldn't budge. He conjured a Strength Enhancement, but still the compartment refused to open.

Edward decided that the compartments must be held closed with magic. *"MAGNUS,"* he murmured. The two coach seats began to emit a blue-green glow.

"CODA, FIRMENTO," muttered Edward, releasing the Adhesive spell. He opened the compartments and was stunned by what he saw. Both compartments were filled to the brim with gold coins. "Oh, my," said Edward, "no wonder the Dutchess fled." "Sir?" asked Tony, craning his neck to see what was in the boxes. "Several thousand gold coins came up missing from the Royal Treasury recently. I think we just found them."

Donovan and Rachel stood on the deck of the FS IRONSIDES as it plowed its way through the relatively calm waters. They were both very glad to be out of the icy waters near Frostberg. The weather got warmer the farther south they traveled. In a few days, Rachel was going to have to remove the fleece lining that she had adhered to her Concealment cloak. Donovan put his arm around her, "Feel better?" he asked.

Rachel nodded without opening her mouth. "At least you didn't hit me this time," said Donovan. The morning sickness was *not* going away with the cold weather, but at least she was on deck this time. The few Expeditionary Force soldiers who saw her said nothing (mercifully). They just assumed she was seasick.

A Great Dragon suddenly came swooping down out of the clouds. Soldiers and crewmen screamed in fright, yelling "DRAGON!" The soldiers rushed to retrieve their crossbows from below deck. Donovan and Rachel braced themselves for the coming fight. "Remember, no Changing. No matter what happens," said Donovan. Rachel nodded.

Donovan conjured a Sight Enhancement and looked at the approaching Great Dragon. Then he smiled, "STAND DOWN!" he shouted. "IT'S A FRIENDLY! CLEAR THE AFT DECK!" The men cleared space on the stern of the ship, making a space for the dragon to land on. The Great Dragon landed gently, still holding the white robes in its talons.

"DAD!" yelled Donovan, as the dragon changed into Edward. He quickly donned the white robe he had been carrying. "Hello, son. Thanks for not shooting at me," said a grinning Edward as he came forward and embraced Donovan and then Rachel. "How are you two doing?" "We're fine," said Donovan, "glad to be out of the cold. So, what brings you to the FS IRONSIDES this fine day at sea?"

"I was looking for you two," said Edward. "Is Major Gerald around? I should probably speak to him as well." As he spoke, the Commander of the Royal Expeditionary Force walked up, accompanied by Senior Specialists Dirk and Lance (uncloaked). "Gentlemen, it's good to see you all," said Edward. "Is there someplace we can talk?"

"There's no cabin big enough for the six of us if that's what you mean," said Gerald. "How about we talk on the fo'c'sle?" "That will be fine," said Edward, walking forward. When he reached the deck forward of the main sail, Edward cast a Silence spell over the six of them and said, "I just came by to let you know what the dragons are planning."

"How would you know that?" asked Donovan. "Wizard Noland and I eavesdropped on the last Dragon Council meeting. It was quite informative." Donovan shook his head and said, "And you call *me* impulsive." Major Gerald and the two Specialists laughed. "Anyway, after their ruinous attack on Three Forks, the dragons have decided to concentrate their efforts on attacking our commercial activities, avoiding our Navy ships and magicians. Specifically, they're planning an attack on the crab fleet out of Frostberg, and then a massive attack on Grotton, while the Navy is busy blockading the Coral Islands."

Donovan whistled, "That's a change." "Yes, and it gets worse. They're also considering burning our fields and crops once they're ripe next fall, and there's no way we can protect them all," said Edward. "I've sent a warning to Frostberg, and a single sorcerer, who can change into a Great or Fire Dragon, can easily drive off a pack of Snow Dragons, so our risk there is manageable. Sorcerer Stewart knows how to make the Change, right?" "Yes," said Donovan. "Frankly, he's a bit old for a sorcerer, but he seemed capable."

"That's good. Now, besides attacking our trade and merchant ships, there was a suggestion made to spread the word to our citizens about how the dragons can change into humans." "Why would they do that?" asked Rachel. "I think the idea is to rile up the populace and get the people accusing their neighbors of being Changed Ones. You see, most of the Changed Ones they've tried to recruit are not interested in fighting. That might change if they feel threatened."

"I think they're right about the Changed Ones. The majority of those we've found have accepted the Binding spell," said Donovan. "So, tell me about Mage Lisa. Who dropped a rock on her?" asked Edward. "It was a dragon," replied Donovan. "She had accepted the Binding spell, so Andrew and I left her in place as the Sundock Regional Mage. After the fleet departed, two stones fell out of the sky as we were walking through town. One nearly hit us, but I deflected it. The other crashed through the Regional Mage's Office, killing Lisa."

"Do you think you were targeted intentionally?" asked Edward. "I don't know, but it's hard to imagine that it was just a coincidence that the only magicians in town both had rocks dropped on them," said Rachel. "I agree," said Edward. "When the dragons dropped stones on us in Baize, they hit my tent and Mage Elianna, who was in the latrine. It does seem that they can specifically target us. Which brings me to the next issue."

"The dragons know that you were in Three Forks and that you're married to Rachel," Edward said to Donovan. "How could they possibly know that?" asked Donovan. "I don't know, but Cobalt, the Sea Dragon Clan Chief, reported such to the Dragon Council," said Edward. "It must have been Sorcerer Cliff. He must have sent a message to the Sea

Dragons somehow, but wouldn't that violate the Binding spell?" wondered Donovan.

"I'm not sure," said Edward, "if the spell decided that such information constituted 'harm' to humans, then it would have triggered. We'll have to find Sorcerer Cliff and ask him."

"So, the dragons know that I'm no longer at the Academy. So what?" "They also know that you're married, son. Cobalt told the Dragon Council that he had given orders for Rachel to be killed in order to prevent Wizard Amanda's line from spreading." Rachel looked shocked.

"That explains the Sea Dragon," said Donovan. "Explain," said Edward. "While we were on our way from Frostberg to Sundock, Anne arrived and said that she thought she saw a Sea Dragon shadowing the squadron. She landed on the wrong ship, looking for Commodore Lang, and told us about the dragon. We uncovered the Seabows and watched the water."

"What happened?" asked Edward. "A Sea Dragon hit Rachel with a blast of water, trying to knock her into the ocean. I tethered her to keep her from going overboard, then adhered her to the deck, while I killed the dragon with a Seabow." "Wait, you glued your wife to the deck?" Donovan reddened, "Well, I didn't want her falling into the freezing water, and I was a little busy with other matters at the time." Edward grinned.

Rachel said, "I thought the dragon had broken my neck and paralyzed me since I couldn't move my arms or legs."

Edward laughed, and Donovan smiled. "After he was done playing with the Sea Dragon, Donovan put a Weather shield around me and warmed the air. This was while he was holding a Protective shield around the bow of the ship to keep the icebergs away," said Rachel.

"You said you wouldn't tell," said Donovan. Rachel stuck out her tongue. "Well, a Weather shield doesn't take much power. So, I don't think I need to promote him to wizard just yet," said Edward.

"Anyway, after he removed the Adhesive spell and got me below. He healed my bruised shoulders, then passed out again." "Again?" said Edward, shaking his finger at Donovan. "I had a good reason!" protested Donovan. "Really?" asked Edward, "and what might that be?" "I was healing for two!"

It took a second for Donovan's words to sink in, then Edward smiled widely, "Congratulations!" "Thank you. Is there a Healing spell for morning sickness?" asked Rachel. "No! And you need to go easy on any other Healing spells. Each time you're healed while pregnant, the baby gets bigger! Trust me, you don't want to give birth to a twenty-pound baby." Rachel shuddered at the thought.

Both Specialists came over and offered Rachel their congratulations. Lance said, "I forgive you for throwing up on my cloak." Rachel grinned, "Is that why you're not wearing it?" "Yes. I was downwind of you earlier." "What's your excuse, Dirk?" "Mine is still airing out from yesterday," said Dirk slyly. The others laughed.

"The last thing I need to tell you is that there is going to be a Wizard's Council in two weeks, in the Lecture Hall of the Wizards Academy. All wizards and mages in Franconia and Baize are invited," said Edward. "Rachel won't be able to make it," said Donovan. "Why is that?" asked Edward. "Because Rule number one is that she is not allowed to change into a dragon until after the baby is born."

"A wise precaution," said Edward.

Edward laughed, "No, son. Most of it needs to go back to the Kingston Treasury. I'm just not sure how to explain it. I mean, we replicated all that Victor and Jasmine stole and told the King we found it in Jasmine's house. We can't very well tell him we just found thousands more, and it would be a waste to just vanish it. Anyway, we're not going to do anything with it until *after* the Royal Wedding. Otherwise, King Henry might squander it all on decorations."

"You know, with that much money, we could afford to start putting Compound Seabows on most of our larger merchant ships..." mused Donovan. "That's an interesting idea, but how would we explain it to the King?" asked Edward. "We tell him that we *sold* the Seabows to the traders, and give the extra gold to the treasury. We'd have to charge them something, but we could subsidize some of the costs. We'd also have to run it by the Admiralty. I'm not sure how supportive the Royal Navy will be of our arming merchants."

"If it relieves them of convoy duty, they might buy it. I'll bring it up with Wizard Lake at the council meeting. On that note, I must be off," said Edward. He quickly changed into a Great Dragon, and flew west, heading back to Kingston.

Sorceress Cindy was finally beginning to feel safe again. She had fled Haven immediately after Mayor Moss had informed her that there was a Sorceress Rachel from the Royal Expeditionary Force, along with a Specialist, who were there to conduct an audit of the town's treasury. As soon as the Mayor left, Cindy rushed over to the Exchequer Building, where she tore out the last few pages of the General Ledger of Haven. Without those pages, it would be difficult for anyone to reconstruct the financial records of the town.

Not bothering to return home, Cindy ran to the riverbank, where she had secretly stashed a small rowboat. She certainly couldn't be seen flying away in dragon form. It had taken weeks to reach Sundock. Cindy was not a skilled boatman, and the river was winding and ever-changing. In some places, it was a wide, smooth waterway; then the banks narrowed, and the current picked up. There were also several rapids that she had to traverse.

By the time she reached Sundock, Cindy was cold, wet, and hungry. She took a room in a cheap boardinghouse, not wanting to draw attention to herself. She had no idea if she was being pursued. She still had most of the forty golds that she had taken from the Haven Treasury, but it would not do to flaunt her wealth. At least not yet. She eventually decided to book passage on a commercial ship, the FS IRONSIDES, which was headed to Eastport, which she thought would be far enough from Haven to be safe.

She cursed her luck when, to her surprise, the entire Royal Expeditionary Force boarded the ship after she had settled into her cabin. Now she was trapped. At least until the ship made port in Eastport. Cindy dared not go up on deck, or even to the galley, for fear of being discovered. She had brought some food with her, but not enough for the entire voyage. Sooner or later, she was going to have to find something to eat (she was still a dragon after all).

Two days into the voyage, Cindy heard a cry of "DRAGON!" and thought that she had been discovered. She retreated to the far wall of her cabin, and prepared to transform into a Fire Dragon. Before she affected the Change, she heard someone shout, "STAND DOWN! IT'S A FRIENDLY! CLEAR THE AFT DECK."

Cindy was confused. As far as she knew, there were no 'friendly' dragons. Certainly, none that would stop to visit a Franconian merchant ship in the middle of the ocean. Her curiosity was piqued, but her caution won out, and she remained secluded in her cabin. A few hours later, looking out the porthole in her cabin, Cindy saw a Great Dragon, flying west. *Had the Great Dragons betrayed them?* she wondered.

Cindy decided that she needed to get off the ship before she ran out of food or was discovered by one of the human magic-users on board. She decided that it would be best to wait until nightfall, when there were fewer people up on deck. She knew the Concealment spell, and decided that she would conceal herself, then make her way up on deck. *I might need to push someone overboard to create a distraction,* she thought. She would make that decision when the time came.

As she made her plans, she heard two soldiers in the passageway outside her cabin talking. "I think Mage Rachel is pregnant," said the first man. "Are you sure?" asked the second. "Well, she's been up on deck, hurling her breakfast each of the last two days." "Maybe she's just seasick." "Nah, she's sailed with us before, and never had a problem. Besides, she's starting to show a little."

The voices faded as the soldiers moved down the hallway. *Rachel?* thought Cindy. *The magic-user who had been looking for her in Haven?* That couldn't be good. She had no interest in whether this Mage Rachel was with child or not; she had her own survival to consider.

Cindy waited patiently until just after midnight, then cast her Concealment spell and headed up on deck. She hated leaving her gold behind, but she would have no use for it as a dragon. She stepped on deck quietly and headed aft, stepping in a puddle of water as she crept toward the stern.

There was only a single crewman on the stern, and he was star-gazing. A quick shove, and he was over the side, headed for the water below. Cindy quickly dropped her Concealment, changed into her true form, and leapt off the deck. She flew low, barely above the wavetops, as she made her escape. Behind her, she heard the cries of "MAN OVERBOARD!" from the sailors on deck.

A few minutes later, when she was over the coast and safe, she climbed, gaining altitude as she searched for a good place to hide for the day.

"I tell you, I didn't *fall* overboard! I was pushed!" shouted the drenched crewman. "I was standing my watch at the stern rail, and someone pushed me from behind!" "Who?" asked the Captain. "When we got to the stern, there was no one there! You're fortunate that the mage was able to see you in the dark and get a Tether spell on you."

Donovan walked around the aft deck. There was certainly something strange about the sailor falling overboard, and his claim of being 'pushed' bothered Donovan. He scanned the deck closely, then called the Captain over. "Captain, was there anyone else posted on deck this evening?" "No, why?" asked the Captain. Donovan pointed out a still-wet footprint on the deck, "Because *somebody* left that footprint, and I don't think it was your crewman. It's too small. It looks like a woman's print."

The Captain got down on his hands and knees and examined the footprint. "You're right," he said finally. "Other than my wife, are there any other women on board?" "Just one," said the Captain. "A woman booked passage from Sundock to Eastport before the Expeditionary Force contacted me about passage. Come to think of it, I haven't seen Cindy since we left port."

"Cindy?" said Dirk as he lowered the hood of his Concealment cloak. The Captain started and nearly fell overboard himself, but Donovan grabbed him and steadied him. "Th—that's what she said her name was, Cindy. She said she was going to Eastport to visit family, and she paid a gold for passage."

"Please take us to her cabin," said Dirk. As they headed below deck, Donovan signed *Cindy?* Dirk nodded and signed, *It sounds like the Haven Treasurer who escaped us with forty golds. She's probably a dragon.*

A search of Cindy's cabin turned up a bag of gold coins, but no Cindy. There was also no luggage, only a few scraps of food and a half-eaten bag of beef jerky. "Well, if it was her, she's gone now," said Donovan. "Captain, are there any other passengers you've failed to mention?"

"No. Cindy was the only other passenger, and no one asked me if the Royal Expeditionary Force was my only passenger on this voyage. Other than you and Cindy, all I'm carrying is a load of coal for Eastport."

Donovan and Dirk headed back up on deck, and the Captain returned to his cabin. "We're lucky that Cindy didn't think to set that load of coal on fire before she fled. She might have sunk the ship," said Dirk. "You're right," said Donovan quietly. "In the future, we need to make sure we know if anyone else is on board with us. We were fortunate this time."

"How many of the mages passed the Wizard's Test?" King Donald asked Wizard James. "Eight of the fourteen, sire. I must admit, I was very surprised by the success rate." The King smiled, "So, where are you assigning them?"

"Wizard Elianna will remain in Springfield, and prepare to take over when Wizard Timothy retires, in the mean time, she is in charge of the Springfield School of Magic; Wizard Franklin will be assigned to the Navy facility in Oceanside; Wizard Tristan will head up the Navy Facility in Seaside; Wizard Neal will be assigned here in Baize as the Headmaster of our School of Magic; Wizard Matthew will take a new position as the Chief of Naval Wizardry; Wizard Doris will be assigned to Minister Williams office and be in charge of magical construction projects; Wizard Beatrice will be in charge of magical support to our Research and Development Center; and Wizard Juliet will remain as the Assistant Court Wizard, Your Majesty."

"Has there been any grumbling?" asked the King. "Nothing that I couldn't handle, sire. In fact, most of the male wizards were more than happy to relinquish some of their additional duties to the newly promoted wizards," said James.

"Very good," said the King. "As more candidates become ready, I expect them to be tested expeditiously. I think more wizards are better than fewer." "I agree completely, Your Majesty," said James.

"Your Highness, there is a Wizard Kathy here, who requests an audience," said the door warden. The King said, "Kathy? Why, she was just here! Show her in, show her in! She must have more urgent news about the dragons. James, please summon Wizard Juliet and join us."

James left quickly as Kathy was ushered into the throne room. "Wizard Kathy! Welcome back! I'm surprised to see you back so soon. Is there a problem?" "No more than usual, sire, but I do have some news about the dragons that will be of interest."

James entered quietly, followed by Juliet, wearing her new wizard's robes. "Come, sit down, everyone," said the King. "Wizard Kathy has news. Kathy?"

"Earlier this week, Edward and Wizard Noland, the Headmaster of the Franconian Wizards Academy, positioned themselves above the rock quarry where the Dragon Council meets and listened in on their deliberations," said Kathy.

The King and the two wizards were shocked. "Wasn't that extremely dangerous?" asked Juliet. "Potentially, yes," said Kathy, "but since they knew *where* the dragons usually meet, and that they meet on the night of the full moon, they deemed it worth the risk."

"What did they learn?" asked King Donald. "First, the Dragon Council was informed of our ability to change into dragons ourselves. That made them very uneasy." "I should hope so," said James. "Next, they are debating whether to cease their attacks on our military and concentrate on the commercial enterprises in both our kingdoms. They specifically discussed attacking merchant ships, especially in Franconia, because the Franconian Navy is currently blockading the Coral Islands, where the Sea Dragons make their home."

"They also discussed sending Fire Dragons to begin burning our fields and crops next summer and fall. This is particularly concerning because we lack the ability to protect all of the farmers and ranchers." "Indeed," said the King. "What else did they learn?"

"The dragons are planning an attack on the Franconian crab fleet that sails out of Frostberg, the port of Grotton in Franconia, and the city of Middleberg in Baize," said Kathy. "Why Middleberg?" asked James. "Apparently, the Stone Dragon colony lies somewhere in the desert just west of Middleberg. The dragons also believe it to be a key hub for commercial traffic."

"Do we know when these attacks will occur?" asked the King. "No Sire, but Wizard Edward indicated that this appeared to be just a planning session, and that the actual attacks would not take place until some time after their next Council meeting, three weeks hence." "Then we have time to prepare," said James.

"The most concerning topic was brought up after the Dragon Council meeting adjourned, when one of the Great Dragons suggested that the dragons consider letting our people know about their ability to understand human speech and transform into humans." "Why would they do that?" asked Juliet.

"As I understand it, the dragons have been searching for Changed Ones to help them in their fight against us, but most of the Changed Ones are content with their lives as humans and have no interest in joining the hostile dragons. If these

Changed Ones suddenly feel threatened, they may change their minds. We don't think this disclosure is imminent, but it is concerning, and something that we have absolutely no control over."

"So, what should we do? Do we redouble our efforts to identify and bind these Changed Ones, or do we cease our search and hope for the best?" wondered the King. "This is a topic which Edward would like to discuss, sire. He has called for a Wizard's Council to meet at the Franconian Wizards Academy in twelve days. All wizards and mages in Franconia and Baize are invited. That's the main reason I've come. The explanation was far too lengthy for a Messenger Hawk."

"Twelve days doesn't give us much time," said James. Kathy nodded, "The date is driven by the phases of the moon, which we have no control over. Edward thinks that we should meet before the next Dragon Council meeting."

"Thank you very much for bringing us this news and the invitation, Kathy. I will certainly send representatives to the Wizard's Council. Perhaps not all of my wizards and mages, but those that I can. It might interest you to know that we have recently promoted an additional eight mages to the rank of wizard, doubling the number of wizards in Baize, and that four of those promoted were women. Wizard Juliet here is one of them."

Kathy smiled, "Congratulations, Wizard Juliet. If I may be so bold, I think this was a wise decision, Your Majesty."

"Thank you, *Wizard* Kathy. Safe travels back to Franconia." The King rose, indicating that the meeting was over. Kathy shook Juliet's hand on her way out of the throne room. Once Kathy was gone, the King sat back down.

"What are your thoughts, James, Juliet?" "Wizard Edward certainly has balls," said James. "To spy on the Dragon Council?" he shivered. "Indeed," said the King. "What else?" "We need to get more magical support to Middleberg, and quietly prepare them for what's coming," said Juliet. "Why quietly?" asked the King.

"Because there are undoubtedly Changed Ones in Middleberg, who will disclose any of our preparations if we're not circumspect," said Juliet. "An astute observation," said James. "What about our merchant ships?" "That is more of a problem for Franconia, I think," said the King. "*Our* Navy is not blockading the Coral Islands. I wonder what King Henry is thinking. How does one blockade an island when the dragons can simply fly over, or swim under the Navy ships?" James and Juliet shrugged.

"Next, who should we send to this 'Wizard's Council'?" "I think I should go," said James, "and Wizard Elianna, and perhaps Wizard Matthews." "Just three of you?" asked the King. "Three will be enough, sire." "Very well, how will you inform Wizard Elianna?"

"I believe that she's still here in Baize, sire. She just passed her Wizard's Test this morning. I will speak with her before she departs."

"Good. Perhaps we should ask to send a wizard to the next meeting of the Dragon Council as well. I want you to discuss that at the Wizard's Council." "By your command, sire," said James.

Chapter Twenty-Two:
EASTPORT

The FS IRONSIDES pulled into the dock in Eastport, and the Royal Expeditionary Force began disembarking. "I'm sorry that I can't take you all the way to Southport, or even Grotton," said the Captain. "But we need to get back to Sundock and pick up another shipment of coal. We short-loaded this trip to accommodate your men, and my buyer is waiting for the rest of his order."

"I understand, Captain. Thank you for the ride. I'll put in a good word with the King for you," said Major Gerald. "I appreciate that, Major."

Once the Expeditionary Force was off the ship, they headed for the 8th Battalion's garrison. If the entire battalion was in town, it was going to be a tight fit in the barracks. *At least it's not snowing here,* thought Major Gerald.

The garrison was on the west side of Eastport, and one of the companies was out patrolling the road between Eastport and Grotton, freeing up room in the garrison stables for the Expeditionary Forces' mounts. "Your men can sleep in the mess hall, training room, and the supply warehouse," said Captain Steele. "I'm sorry, we don't have bunks for all of them. I imagine that you and your officers will want to stay at one of the Inns in town. I recommend the Eastport Lodge, and not the Eastport Inn. How long will you be in town?"

"That depends on how long it takes to inventory the town's treasury, and when we can book passage for Grotton," said Major Gerald. Captain Steele said, "Good luck with the Treasurer, Mr. Cash! He's a real stickler. Do you have some kind of authorization from the King?" "Yes, and it's cosigned by the Minister of Finance. Is he going to be a problem?" asked Major Gerald. "He might be," said Captain Steele. "Well, I've dealt with his kind before. Where is the treasury, anyway?"

"It's right next to the town hall, you can't miss it. It's probably closed by now, though. I recommend going by first thing in the morning." After the Force was settled in the garrison and the officers had secured lodging in the Eastport Lodge, Donovan and Rachel headed over to the Regional Mage's Office.

They found Mage Les in the office. "Good afternoon. How can I help you today?" asked Les. "I'm Mage Donovan, and this is Mage Rachel. We're with the Royal Expeditionary Force, which just arrived in the city. The Expeditionary Force has been visiting all of the towns and cities in the kingdom."

"So I heard," said Les, "come in and have a seat. Can I offer you some tea?" "That would be lovely," replied Rachel. The three magicians took seats around the small table in the outer office, and the office clerk brought out a pot of tea. Rachel nodded gratefully.

"Have you heard about the upcoming Wizard's Council in Kingston?" asked Donovan. "As a matter of fact, I just received the invitation this morning," said Mage Les. "Any idea what it's about?" Les's use of a contraction immediately put Donovan and Rachel at ease, and Donovan said, "Yes. My father, Wizard Edward, and Wizard Noland apparently concealed themselves and eavesdropped on the last Dragon Council meeting a couple of weeks ago. What they learned was so concerning that they decided to call a Wizard's Council to let everyone know what the dragons are planning."

Mage Les said, "Wait, Wizard Edward, the Chief of Military Wizardry, is your father?" "Yes," said Donovan. "I heard he was killed by a dragon a while back..." "No. He was just injured, and his Healing spell rendered him unconscious for a couple of weeks. We certainly thought he was dead. It's fortunate that we didn't bury him."

Mage Les nodded in understanding. "Do you have any idea what the dragons are planning?" "My father mentioned that they're considering a plan to start attacking our commercial centers and trading vessels, avoiding our military and magicians," replied Donovan.

"That could be a problem," said Les. "Yes. If they start burning crops, I'm not sure how we'll be able to protect all of the farms and ranches in the kingdom," said Rachel.

"So, how are things in Eastport? I have to admit that, while I've traveled extensively, I've never been here before," said Donovan. "Eastport is mainly a shipping port for coal and steel coming down from Smithville. There's a small fishing fleet also, but the main industry here is orange growers. There are extensive groves north and west of the city. Part of the city is still rebuilding after the big storm we had last fall. Quite a few buildings were damaged, some severely. Sorceress Mabel and I were kept pretty busy helping with some of the repairs," said Les.

"I understand from a friend that the city taxes on exports are rather high…" said Donovan. Mage Les frowned, "Yes. That's one of the chief complaints I get from the merchants here: high taxes. Unfortunately, other than oranges, there's not much commerce in Eastport, so the primary source of income is taxes."

Just then, Sorceress Mabel entered the office, followed by two of the city's Enforcers. "Mabel! Come meet Mages Donovan and Rachel. They just arrived with the Royal Expeditionary Force," said Les. "Donovan, Rachel, this is my assistant, Sorceress Mabel."

The magicians shook hands, and Les asked, "So, Mabel, anything interesting happening today?" The sorceress shook her head, "No, sir. The FS IRONSIDES docked and offloaded some coal and the Royal Expeditionary Force, then left quickly, heading back to Sundock to pick up another load of coal; there was a bar fight in the Westend Tavern, but no one was seriously injured. Other than that, it was a quiet day."

"I'm glad to hear it," said Les. "So, Donovan, why is the Royal Expeditionary Force touring all of Franconia? That seems like a long mission." "It has been," said Donovan. "Fortunately, we're on the homeward leg. After Eastport, we just have to visit Grotton, then we head home to Kingston. In answer to your question, King Henry wanted us to audit all of the Treasuries in the Kingdom.”

“Why?” asked Mabel. “Have you heard about Minister Jasmine?” “The former Minister of Internal Security? We heard that she died and was replaced by her assistant, Katelyn, but nothing more,” said Mabel.

“She was a Dragon Changed One,” said Donovan, “Wizard Noland turned her into a marble statue. After her death, it was discovered that she had stolen several thousand golds from the Kingston Treasury.” The two Eastport magicians gasped. “Was the gold ever recovered?” “No,” whispered Donovan, “the Wizards Academy faculty had to replicate gold to replace the shortage. Without letting the King know, of course.”

“So, when Wizard Noland reported the theft to the King, he told him that he was concerned that Jasmine might have had other accomplices in other cities in the kingdom. The king sent us out at once to check all of the Treasuries,” said Rachel.

“Have there been any shortages?” asked Les. “Some. Not as many as we feared. Captain Steele indicated that the Eastport Treasurer might resist opening the vault for us...” said Donovan.

Mabel laughed, “He just might. He’s quite *anal* about his vault, but I think he’s generally honest. I doubt you’ll find any shortage here.” “That’s good to know. While we’re on tour, we also decided to distribute the new Concealment cloaks to all of the magicians in the kingdom. Here are yours," said Donovan, handing Mage Les and Sorceress Mabel their cloaks. "Concealment cloaks?" asked Les.

"Yes. With this cloak on, you'll be practically invisible, so you don't have to use a Concealment shield. That will allow you to cast an extra spell. After we visit Grotton and distribute their cloaks, every magician in Franconia will have one, and each new sorcerer will be issued one upon graduation from the Wizards Academy," said Rachel.

"Just remember where you put them," cautioned Donovan, "if you put them down somewhere and forget where, you may never find them again. We recommend turning them inside out when you're not wearing them, just in case. There's a one-gold replacement fee if you lose yours. They also have a Secrecy spell on them, so they can't be Replicated."

Mage Les and Sorceress Mabel accepted the cloaks appreciatively. "How long will you be in Eastport?" asked Mabel. "Just long enough to audit the treasury; assuming we can book passage on a ship headed to Grotton soon," said Donovan.

Mabel bit her lower lip, "That might be a problem. I don't think there are any ships due in port for the next two weeks. It might be faster to ride to Grotton. The road is pretty well maintained, and there's not much traffic at this time of year." "No ships?" asked Rachel. "No. You've arrived during our low season. The orange crop has already been shipped out, and there's not much coal or iron mining going on in the mountains during the winter months."

"That's going to slow us down," said Donovan. "Plus, I have to get to the Wizard's Council in Kingston." "How are you planning to get there in time?" asked Mage Les. "I'll just change into a dragon and fly, I suppose," said Donovan. "You have to land at the Academy Marina. That's the only place with enough space outside the Academy. Now that I think of it, there's going to be a lot of traffic there."

This led to a discussion about how one changes into a dragon and the intricacies of flying. In the end, Donovan had to take the two magicians out behind the Mage's Office and transform, since neither of them had seen a dragon before. "Didn't the Sea Dragons attack Eastport once?" asked Donovan.

"Yes," replied Les, "but they were concealed, and they just dropped stones from the sky onto a few of the Navy ships in port. We didn't really see them. I understand Mage Andrew killed one, but the crew threw the carcass overboard, and it sank to the bottom of the harbor before we got there."

"Well, we'd better get back to the Lodge. We've got a full day tomorrow," said Rachel. They left the Regional Mage's Office and returned to the lodge. Unsurprisingly, dinner was fish with an orange glaze.

Cobalt, Sky, and Gek landed back on Acropo together, just as the moon was rising. Azure had returned to the hut near Southport to check on Richard. She hated imposing on Bruce, who was not a young man anymore, and Richard could certainly be a handful at times. As the three dragons emerged into the underwater cavern, they were met by Blue, a particularly disagreeable Sea Dragon.

"The humans have returned," said Blue angrily. "We saw," replied Cobalt. "And what are you going to do about it?" asked Blue. Cobalt sighed, "First, I am going to get some rest, then we will try to determine *what* the humans are doing. From what I saw, their ships are in a line, about a thousand fathoms from our islands. They probably can't even *see* us from their current position. What harm could they possibly do from so far away?"

"I do not know," conceded Blue, "but they are certainly up to *something*. They have not surrounded the islands, only formed a line to the east. They have not moved in two days, except perhaps, to move *farther* east. It does not make sense."

"Well, without knowing why they are there, it would be imprudent to jump to any conclusions. I will have some of the Clan begin monitoring their activities. Once we know what they are doing, we will be able to respond accordingly," said Cobalt.

Blue moved off, grumbling about the lack of action to this new threat. Cobalt did his best to ignore him. Once in Cobalt's chambers, Gek said, "Blue is right. The humans must be up to something, but I cannot imagine what." "Maybe we should ask Anne," suggested Sky. "After all, she did warn us that they were coming."

"Anne said that the humans were planning to surround our islands, but we saw no ships on the north, south, or west side," said Cobalt. "*No,*" said Gek, "Anne said that the fleet was going to *blockade* the islands. I do not believe that 'blockade' is the same as 'surround.'"

"You may be right, but that does not explain what they think they are doing. We are all tired from the long flight from the rock quarry. I suggest we get some sleep while other members of the Clan approach the humans underwater and try to determine what they are up to," said Cobalt.

Before retiring, Cobalt found three of the younger male Sea Dragons and ordered them to approach the human ships and try to determine what they were doing. They were not to expose themselves and risk being struck by the spear-throwers that were so deadly to dragons. The scouts dispatched, Cobalt settled down for an uneasy sleep.

When Cobalt rose the next morning, the three Sea Dragons had returned with a report that the humans were not doing *anything.* They had observed them all night and detected no activity on any of the eleven ships. "Hmm," said

Cobalt, "perhaps they were sleeping. Send out three more to observe them during the day. It may be that whatever they are doing, they need daylight for."

Cobalt roamed the cavern system, speaking with the other members of his Clan. They were all concerned about the arrival of the humans, but unsure what to do about it. "Should we conceal ourselves and drop stones on them?" asked Gek.

"We may consider that option," said Cobalt, "but I would really like to know what they are doing before I launch an attack." "Would you like me to fly over them to see if I can determine anything?" asked Gek. "Let's see what the sky looks like first. It would be too dangerous if the skies are clear."

"What are you going to do about Anne?" asked Gek. "We cannot keep her here forever." "I know, and I have not decided what to do with her yet. From talking to Emerald, she has behaved herself during her confinement. We both know that, as a magic-user, she could probably break out of her chamber using the dig spell, or even attack her guard, but she has not done either of these things," said Cobalt.

"She told Annalise that she might be able to heal my hand, enabling me to change back into a human again. I have not spoken with Anne yet, but I assume that there will be conditions to this healing," said Gek.

"You must not accept the Binding spell that she placed on the other members of the Clan that she healed," said Cobalt forcefully. "You are a member of the Dragon

Council, and one of the few Great Dragons remaining. We need you in this fight." "I know," said Gek. "Perhaps she will trade this healing for her freedom…"

"Before we discuss that, let us go outside and see what the clouds are doing," said Cobalt.

Gek and Cobalt swam through the grotto, and up to the surface. They walked up the beach and observed the overcast sky. "With these clouds, you should be able to fly over the human ships without being seen. Do not endanger yourself. I am not sure what you will be able to detect from the air, but you may notice something that will be helpful. At least, try to determine which ship is the VALOR, so we can avoid it if we need to attack and drive the humans away," said Cobalt.

Gek took flight, quickly rising above the clouds and heading east, toward the line of Navy ships.

Dragon Messenger Phillip was tired. With the unexplained absence of Sorceress Anne, he was doing double-duty, running messages for both fleets, and there had been a *lot* of messages lately. Now he was heading for 1st Fleet, which was positioned just to the east of the Coral Islands. That was a long way from Grotton, even for a Dragon Messenger.

From the air, it was easy to see the eleven Royal Navy ships in a line from south to north, about a mile east of the islands. He located the flagship, the HMS SENTRY, and headed for the aft deck, screaming that he was a Dragon Messenger, and for the sailors not to shoot. One of the sailors on the HMS GUARDIAN, the closest ship to the SENTRY, apparently didn't hear Phillip, and shot a crossbow bolt at him. It missed (by a lot), but made Phillip swoop left and out of range. "CEASE FIRE! DRAGON MESSENGER ARRIVING!" boomed the voice of Battle Mage Vance, the mage on the SENTRY. Mercifully, there were no more shots fired at Phillip before he landed and transformed.

Vice Admiral Jordan approached Phillip and said, "Sorry about that. The men are a little jumpy, being this close to the islands, and some of them have never seen a Dragon Messenger before." "I understand, sir," said Phillip, handing over the message pouch.

"Let's go below so I can read this out of the wind," said the admiral. Sorcerer Phillip and the commander went below to the admiral's cabin, where he opened the message pouch and read the orders from Admiral Cross and Wizard Lake.

Vice Admiral Jordan,

Wizard Edward, the Chief of Military Wizardry has called a Wizard's Council to be held at the Wizards Academy in two weeks, on Endday. He requests that at least one mage from your fleet attend this council. I believe this Council will discuss our strategic plan for dealing with the dragons. Which mage you send is at your discretion.

H.C. Cross,

Commander, Royal Franconian Navy

"Who's the most junior mage in the Fleet?" the admiral asked Mage Vance. "That would be Mage Andrew, aboard the HMS VALOR," said the Fleet Battle Mage. "Very well, Sorcerer Phillip, please hop over to the HMS VALOR and inform Commodore Matthews that he'll have to do without his Battle Mage for a few days. Mage Andrew needs to attend a Wizard's Council in two weeks at the Wizards Academy. I know the timing could be better, but orders are orders."

Sorcerer Phillip returned to the aft deck, disrobed, and changed back into a Sea Dragon. He took flight and made the short trip to the VALOR, where he reversed the process to deliver his message to Andrew and Commodore Matthews. Gek watched the entire process from high above.

Once the message was delivered to the VALOR, Phillip changed back into a Sea Dragon and took off for his return trip to Naval Headquarters in Grotton. Before he had cleared the fleet, Gek swooped down and coated him in burning inferno. Dragon Messenger Phillip screamed and dove for the water, trying in vain to put out the burning inferno. He didn't make it.

The sailors watched in horror as Phillip plunged to his death. Most of them had not seen what happened, but instinctively knew that their Dragon Messengers were no longer safe.

"I don't care what that paper says, I'm not letting you into the treasury!" said Mr. Cash, forcefully. They had been arguing for almost a glass, and Rachel was fed up with the obstinate Treasurer, *"INCOGITA,"* she murmured, making the required gesture. Nothing happened.

"Is that supposed to mean something to me?" asked Mr. Cash. Donovan and Rachel shared a glance, and Rachel signed: *Mr. Cash has the spark of magic, so the Sleep spell won't work on him.* "It means that you have the spark of magic and should have been sent to the Wizards Academy before you turned twenty," said Donovan. "How long have you known that you had the spark?"

Mr. Cash grimaced, "I've known since I was a child. My parents didn't want to lose me to your school of magic, so they helped me hide it from the Regional Mage. Are you saying that I'm too old for the Academy now?"

"Yes," said Donovan, "no one over twenty can be admitted, which means that we need to place a Binding spell on you not to hurt anyone with magic, and never to counterfeit coins." "What happens if I violate this Binding spell?" asked the now-worried Treasurer.

"If someone violates a Binding spell, they die," said Rachel. "And, what happens if I refuse to submit to it?" "You die sooner," said Donovan coldly. Mr. Cash gulped and said, "OK, cast your oppressive Binding spell."

"Say, 'I, your full name, of Eastport, promise never to hurt another human with magic, and not to counterfeit any currency for as long as I live.'" As Mr. Cash repeated the oath, Donovan drew his finger along the floor, saying *"PROMISA,"* and a shower of sparks descended and enfolded the Treasurer.

"There. That wasn't so bad, was it?" asked Donovan. "I suppose," murmured Mr. Cash. "Now, we still need to audit the Eastport Treasury. You can be present as an observer, but the audit must take place." "I SAID 'NO!'" said Mr. Cash. *"LIGARE,"* muttered Rachel, making a fist with her left hand. Mr. Cash froze, paralyzed.

"I'm sorry it's come to this, Mr. Cash, but the King gave us explicit orders not to take 'No' for an answer. While you may have the spark, it only protects you from the Sleep spell. Now you just sit right here, while we inventory the treasury," said Rachel.

The audit took several hours, and in the end, the vault was short thirty-one golds. Too much for it to be an accounting error. Rachel and Donovan returned to the outer office, where they had left the paralyzed Treasurer. "I think we're going to need some Truth Serum for this," whispered Donovan. "Just to make sure we get the truth about the missing golds." Rachel nodded and took out her vial of Truth Serum. The vial was nearly empty.

"We're going to have to make some more of that before we leave Eastport. How is our stock of Healing Serum?" asked Donovan. "I've got a full vial," said Rachel, but it's almost expired, and I think your vial is empty." "You're right," confirmed Donovan. "I hope the Regional Mage has some serum ingredients handy. Anyway, let's dose Mr. Cash and get to the bottom of this missing gold."

Rachel added the rest of her Truth Serum to a mug of water and took it to the table where the angry Treasurer was sitting. She set the mug in front of him on the table and removed the Paralysis spell.

"Mr. Cash, I apologize for the Paralysis spell," said Rachel, "but our audit was *not* optional. Here is a glass of water. Paralysis victims are often parched after the spell is lifted."

Mr. Cash glared at the two mages, but eagerly drank the water. After a few seconds, Rachel said, "So, Mr. Cash, you have kept excellent records of all of the transactions involving the Eastport Treasury account. However, there are thirty-one golds missing from the vault. How can you explain this shortage?"

Mr. Cash sat silently for a time, then said, "I loaned thirty-five golds to Miss Bozeman, the Headmistress of the Easton Orphanage. During the big storm last fall, the roof of the orphanage was partially torn off, and there was other structural damage. The Bank would not extend her any credit, since the orphanage generates no income. They only receive a small stipend from the crown each month for operating expenses. Miss Bozeman appealed to me for help. I have been repaying the loan out of my personal salary as I can."

Donovan and Rachel looked shocked. Given the Truth Serum, what Mr. Cash said *had* to be true. "Did you ask the Regional Mage or his assistant for help?" asked Donovan. "I did," replied the treasurer, "but Mage Les said that they would have to wait their turn. There were other homes and businesses damaged during the storm that had a higher priority."

"Still, thirty-five golds seems an extravagant amount for roof repairs," said Rachel. "I'm sure it was," said Mr. Cash. "But all of the construction companies were charging extra because of all of the damaged homes. I complained that it was usury, but they just laughed and said that I could always wait for the Regional Mage to get around to it in a couple of months. By then it would have been winter!"

Donovan and Rachel sighed at the injustice of the situation. *He seems like an honest fellow,* signed Donovan, *why don't we give him the coins we confiscated from Cindy?* Rachel considered the idea, then signed, *You really are a good guy. I approve.* Donovan smiled, "OK, Mr. Cash, we believe you. As luck would have it, we recently confiscated thirty-seven golds that were stolen from the Regional Mage in Haven. You may have them to repay the *undocumented* loan you made to the Eastport Orphanage, and some of what you contributed from your personal funds."

Mr. Cash was visibly relieved, "Thank you so much! I was so afraid that, if the shortage was discovered, the king would take it out on the children by garnishing the orphanage's stipend until the money was repaid." "I understand," said Donovan, "and we'll speak to Mage Les before we leave. Hopefully, he'll give the orphanage a higher priority if this ever happens again."

"I do not know what the ships are doing, but they are using magic-users to change into Sea Dragons to deliver messages between their ships," said Gek. "I caught one just after he left the VALOR and killed him."

"Are you sure it was not Celeste?" asked Cobalt. "Positive. It was a male magic-user I killed." "I hope so," said Cobalt. "It would not be honorable to kill someone who saved your life." "I know," said Gek. "I saw him land on one ship and transform, then transform again and fly to the VALOR, where he transformed again and delivered a message to Andrew. Then he changed back into a Sea Dragon and was attempting to return to the mainland. We will not be troubled by that magic-user ever again."

"Good, but we still do not know what the humans are doing out there," said Cobalt. "No," said Gek. "There was almost no activity on the decks of any of their ships that I could see. There are men posted near the spear-throwers, but they did not seem to be doing anything, other than watching for a dragon attack."

As they spoke, one of the young dragons that Cobalt had tasked with scouting out the ships returned. "Cobalt, we have a problem."

As Sorceress Mabel predicted, there were no commercial ships scheduled to arrive in Eastport for at least two weeks, and the ship that was expected was probably too small to carry the entire Royal Expeditionary Force.

"So, I guess we should just ride to Grotton from here," said Major Gerald. "With the lack of shipping, we could be in Grotton before a ship big enough to accommodate us gets here." "Sir, would it be possible for us to delay here for a few days?" asked Donovan. "I have to be in Kingston for the Wizard's Council in two weeks, and after what I've foreseen, I really don't want you arriving in Grotton without me. Rachel and I also need to make some more serums. Our supply of Healing Serum is low, and what's left is almost six months old, so it's about to expire."

Major Gerald considered the request, then asked, "When do you think this attack on Grotton will occur? We can't stay here indefinitely." Donovan replied, "I've been thinking about it, sir, and so far, everything I've foreseen has happened when I was in the city I had the 'bad feeling' about: Colton, Three Forks, and Sundock. It could be that I'm seeing something that will happen while I'm in that particular place."

"So how long should we wait?" asked the Major. Donovan did some quick calculations, "It will take me a day to fly to Kingston, one day for the Council, then a day to get back; the Council meeting is in two weeks, and it will take two weeks for the Expeditionary Force to get to Grotton from here; so, if we stay here three or four days, that should give me time to rejoin you before you get to Grotton. My father should have already warned the forces in the city, so hopefully, they're already making preparations for the attack."

"OK, we'll wait here for four days. Go see about making your serums. I'd recommend that you make a bunch of Healing Serum, if we're gonna be in a big fight soon."

Donovan and Rachel left immediately and headed for the 8th Battalion's sorcerer's office. They found Sorcerer Matt in his office, replicating crossbow bolts. "Good morning, sir," said Sorcerer Matt. "What can I do for you two today?" "We need to make up some more Healing Serum," said Donovan. "Ours is about to expire, and you never know when you're going to need some."

Sorcerer Matt smiled, "That's certainly true. Come with me, and I'll take you to what passes for a Serum laboratory around here." Sorcerer Matt led Donovan and Rachel along the covered walkway to the garrison dining hall. They entered and walked to the kitchen area.

"The kitchen?" asked Rachel. "Yes," said Matt. "It's the only place where I have enough secure storage for my ingredients." He led them to an ordinary-looking pantry and quietly said, *"CODA, FIRMENTO."* With the Adhesive spell removed, he opened the pantry door, exposing an array of Serum ingredients, cauldrons, and measuring spoons. "Here you go. I've been stockpiling ingredients lately, so there should be plenty. How much Serum are you planning to make?"

Donovan looked at Rachel, and she said, "A chest-full. We're expecting an attack on Grotton soon, so we need a lot." Sorcerer Matt whistled, "I'm not sure I have enough supplies for that much Healing Serum," he admitted. Donovan smiled, "No worries, we'll just replicate what we need. I don't want to leave you short."

"Replication! Of course! Why didn't I think of that? I could have saved the crown a lot of gold over the years. Some of these ingredients are quite costly, you know." Rachel smiled and said, "Don't feel too bad, I don't think anyone else has thought of using the Replication spell either. I hate to think how much the Wizards Academy spends on Serum ingredients. It's just that my husband is sneaky." "I prefer to think of it as *inventive*," said Donovan, blushing.

"Do you need any help?" asked Matt. "No. We can manage. I saw that you were replicating crossbow bolts. I know that's taxing. We're going to be here for a few more days. Once we get these serums made, we'd be happy to help you." Matt brightened and said, "That would be very helpful! Thank you! I'll leave you to it then. Please secure the pantry door when you're finished. I don't want the cooks accidentally adding belladonna berries to the stew tonight."

Sorcerer Matt returned to his office, and Donovan and Rachel got to work making Serum. They had to replicate several cauldrons and burners in order to make several batches of Serum simultaneously. "We should probably make a couple of vials of Truth Serum too, and maybe even some Death Serum, just in case," said Rachel. "Yes, Dear," said Donovan, earning him a slap on the back of the head.

Chapter Twenty-Three:
FISH IN A BARREL

A ndrew paced the deck sadly. "We should have been using Great Dragons as messengers," he said. "Poor Phillip never had a chance." Despite their best efforts, the crew had been unable to retrieve Phillip's body. It had sunk to the ocean floor, and even in Sea Dragon form, none of the sorcerers had been able to dive deep enough to get to it.

"It wasn't your fault, Andrew," said Commodore Matthews. "We were using Sea Dragons because of the truce. We never stopped to think that there was a Great Dragon in the vicinity, or that they would know that we were using magicians to deliver messages to ships at sea. These things happen in war."

"We'll need to let Anne know. I wish I knew where she was. For all we know, she's dead too." "I thought she was a 'Dragon-friend,'" said the commodore. "So was Wizard Amanda, but that didn't save her," said Andrew.

"Who is Wizard Amanda?" asked Commodore Matthews. Andrew explained about the end of the last dragon war and how Wizard Amanda had befriended the sick and dying dragons after they were poisoned. Unfortunately, the dragons learned that they could perform magic spells by watching and imitating Amanda. Once she discovered what she'd done, Amanda tried to flee the dragon colony to warn the people of Franconia, but the dragons killed her before she could make her escape.

"Huh, so what you're saying is that being a 'dragon-friend' only goes so far." Andrew nodded.

"Getting back to the mission," said the commodore, "How are we doing with scaring the fish away?" Andrew put aside his sadness and said, "Most of the larger schools of fish have moved off to the south. There are some smaller groups, but they're not really worth pursuing. I'm not sure how far away we need to drive them. I'm afraid that if we chase the fish too far south, they'll double back on us and we'll be right back where we started."

"So, you recommend that we just stay here?" asked the commodore. Andrew nodded, "Yes, sir. I think we've accomplished the mission of driving away most of the Sea Dragon's food supply. Unless I'm mistaken, we'll get a reaction from them pretty soon."

"What do you think they'll do?" Andrew considered the question for a few moments, then said, "They'll probably start by dropping rocks on us, and if that doesn't work, they'll attack from underwater. If they know that we can change into Great Dragons, I doubt they'll try a direct assault from the air. Between the Seabows and our magicians changing into Great Dragons, they'd suffer significant losses."

"So, how do we protect our ships underwater?" "We could try magicians, changed into Sea Dragons, but I don't like our chances," said Andrew. "Why do you say that?"

"Because these dragons *live* in the sea! They are undoubtedly much better swimmers than we are, and there are only eleven of us. There could be dozens of Sea Dragons," said Andrew.

"So, you're saying that we need more magicians," said Commodore Matthews. "More like *more* dragons," said Andrew. "Maybe we could conjure Seemings of Sea Dragons," he mused. "What's a Seeming?" asked the commodore. "A Seeming is an illusion, sir, like the birds I used to blind the dragon that crashed into the mizzen mast. I'm not sure I can conjure one underwater, though."

"Why not?" "A Seeming takes intricate hand gestures. It's not something I could do with dragon claws," explained Andrew. "Well, put your mind to it. We need something to attack Sea Dragons underwater, and, as you said, we may not have much time."

The commodore moved off to inspect the Seabows, leaving Andrew standing on the deck. *Something that can attack Sea Dragons underwater,* thought Andrew. *But what?*

"What do you mean by 'we have a problem,' Blue?" asked Cobalt. "We have determined what the humans are up to. They are driving away the prey," said Blue. "How can they do that?" asked Cobalt. "These are not fishing trawlers with nets to catch fish, they are warships."

"The magic-users are changing into Sea Dragons, and chasing the schools of fish to the south. The prey that was once near, is now leagues away, and moving farther south each day," said Blue. "Then we will just swim south to find it," said Cobalt.

"The farther south we go, the more likely we are to encounter the human fishing fleets with their nets," said Blue. "What about the sea to our north?" asked Cobalt. "You know the water gets very cold, very quickly, and there is little prey in those icy waters."

"And the waters between here and the mainland are almost devoid of prey already," said Cobalt. "You are right, Blue. This is a problem. Where is the VALOR?" "It is the second ship in the line, on the northern end of the human ships," said Blue.

"Then we attack the ships on the southern end," said Cobalt. "If we can sink several of the ships, we will be able to reach the prey more easily. Inform the clan, we will attack after the moon rises tonight. Begin gathering the stones."

Cobalt walked down to the chamber occupied by Gek and said, "Gek, we have determined what the humans are up to. They are attempting to drive our prey away. You were right, the magic-users are changing into Sea Dragons, and they have already forced the schools of fish far to the south. I have ordered the clan to prepare to attack the human ships at moonrise."

"Do you need my help? I was planning to take Anna back to Azure this evening," said Gek. "We will be concealed when we drop our stones on the human ships, so I do not believe that your help will be needed tonight. Have you spoken with Anne yet?" asked Cobalt.

"Not yet, but I should before we depart. Is she awake?" "I have noticed that she sleeps very little. Come, we will speak to her now." Cobalt and Gek walked up to the chamber where Anne was being held. "Emerald, you may take a break. I know it has been a while since you went outside. We will speak to Anne for a time, then I will remain until you return."

Emerald nodded gratefully and headed toward the grotto and the open sea. "Hello, Anne," said Gek, "Annalise tells me that you think you might be able to heal my claw."

"No. I said I might be able to *fix* it. Once removed, a body part cannot be healed," said Anne tiredly. "I do not understand," said Gek. "Your body has already *been* healed, or you would still be bleeding," said Anne. "I might know a way to *enlarge* your stumps, which *might* allow you to make the Change spell work again."

"I see," said Gek. "I assume there are conditions for such help?" "I would like to leave," said Anne.

"I am sorry, Anne, but it would not be safe for you right now," said Cobalt. "Your ships have come. They could set fire to the island at any minute, and you would be killed. I promised to keep you safe, so I cannot permit you to depart yet." "Then when?" asked Anne.

"I do not know," said Cobalt. "How long are your ships likely to remain?" "Probably for as long as it takes for you to reopen negotiations for a peace treaty, Cobalt. We gain nothing by fighting with the Sea Dragon Clan! The King does not care about these islands! You were willing to have peace before. Was that just a trick so that you could attack us on land? How many more of your brothers will you sacrifice needlessly?" asked Anne.

Cobalt looked down. He was disturbed by the truth in Anne's words, but could not go back on his word to the Dragon Council. Finally, he said, "I will consider your words, Anne. I realize that, as a magic-user, you could use magic in an attempt to escape, but you have not done so. You have always treated us honorably, and that is appreciated."

As they turned to leave, Anne said, "Gek, come here please. I will do what I can for you as a sign of good faith, asking nothing in return." Gek approached cautiously.

"DILATA," murmured Anne, making a concealed gesture. The two stumps on Gek's injured hand enlarged, until they were normal size, but he had no knuckles or talons on either finger.

"That is the best that I, or anyone, can do for you, Gek. I don't know if it will work, but I have done my best." Gek gulped and said, "Thank you, Anne. I hope you will be released soon."

Gek left the cavern and headed for the chamber where Aqua and Anna were sleeping. It was time to go home.

"We'll be leaving tomorrow," Donovan said to Mage Les. "The inventory of the treasury was a little short. Apparently, Mr. Cash made a personal loan to the Eastport Orphanage in order to pay for repairs to their facility after the storm last fall. I asked him why he didn't come to you for help, and he said that you had 'other priorities.'"

Mage Les said, "That man! I told him that we had to make repairs to the town prison, which was severely damaged, so that none of the prisoners could escape; then we had to repair the Infirmary; and then the Easton Retirement Center, which houses our elderly who do not have any family! I told him that the orphanage would have to wait a couple of days before we could get to it. I think Mr. Cash is enamored with Miss Bozeman, the Headmistress of the orphanage, and was trying to impress her."

Donovan laughed. "I'd hoped that there was a good explanation. Not to worry, we recently confiscated a sum of gold from a criminal, and were able to repay the loan, so no harm done." Mage Les looked relieved, but still rather angry.

"I would suggest that you have two people conduct all future audits of the treasury accounts, just to make sure that Mr. Cash doesn't make any other personal loans to anyone," said Rachel.

"That's an excellent idea," said Les. "I heard that you also helped Sorcerer Matt replicate several dozen crossbow bolts, and re-filled his supplies of serum ingredients. You've certainly been a big help to the town in the short time you've been here."

"We're glad we could help," said Donovan. "Before we go, do you know where I can purchase some eggplant? I suddenly have a craving for it," said Rachel.

Andrew sat in his cabin thinking, *What could he use to kill Sea Dragons underwater?* He knew that Wizard Edward had used barrels of flour to kill two Fire Dragons. They had blown the flour into the air with a Wind spell, then ignited it with a Fire spell. *That won't work underwater,* thought Andrew

What if I sealed some flour in a glass jar, then tossed it over the side and ignited the flour inside the jar with a fire spell? The flour would burn, and the gas and smoke would likely expand and shatter the glass! It would have to be fairly close to the ship, though. Would shattered glass penetrate dragon scales? Probably not. And anything forceful enough to hurt the dragons would undoubtedly damage the ships.

Andrew discarded the flour idea as unworkable. He heated the teapot on his table and thought. He filled his strainer with dry tea leaves and carefully lowered it into the glass teapot. He absently watched the brown tea slowly emerge from the strainer. *Hmm, what if I put Belladonna berries into large barrels with holes in them? We could lower the barrels over the side, and the poison juice would contaminate the water beside the ships. The seawater would dilute the poison quickly, but it might be enough to sicken a few dragons or drive them away. That is, if belladonna berries were even poisonous to dragons.*

Deciding that it was at least worth a shot, Andrew headed down to the commodore's cabin to tell him about his idea. He was going to have to replicate a *lot* of Belladonna berries to make this work.

"What's this, I hear about a Wizard's Council, Edward?" asked King Henry. "Yes, sire. Wizard Noland and I infiltrated the last Dragon Council meeting and learned quite a bit about the dragon's plans. So much, in fact, that I thought it would be prudent to inform all of the magical leaders in the Kingdom, and I have even invited a few from Baize, since they are affected also. The Council will take place at the Wizards Academy, a week from today," said Edward.

Edward had flown to Southport to inform the King about the Wizard's Council and what he and Wizard Noland had learned during their mission to eavesdrop on the most recent

Dragon Council meeting. Sorceress Celeste was seated at the King's right and was listening intently.

"Please tell me what the dragons are planning, and what you will propose at this Council meeting," said the King.

"Sire, the first thing that you need to know is that the dragons are aware that our magicians have learned how to change into dragons. This news was very concerning to them, and they are planning to strike us before this knowledge spreads throughout our magical community. Next, they discussed their unsuccessful attack on Three Forks, which saw seven of the nine attacking dragons perish. They discussed making their next attacks on the smaller towns and cities in the Kingdom, which would have fewer magicians to defend them."

"That would certainly pose a problem for us," said the King. "It would, sire, but, in the end they decided on a potentially more destructive option," said Edward. "Which was?" "To attack our commercial centers, many of which do not have military or magical protection. I believe that the Snow Dragons will attack our ships that sail from Frostberg, searching for crabs soon. They also discussed burning our crops and fields next fall."

"That would be ruinous!" exclaimed the King. "I agree, Your Majesty, that's why I believe that we need to bring this conflict to an end before that happens. The dragons are correct: there is no way we could protect all of our farms and ranches from the destruction that even a single Fire Dragon could cause," said Edward.

"Was there any good news?" asked the King. "Yes. Apparently, the dragons have also been searching for their Changed Ones, whom they have lost contact with over the years. One of the dragons who had been searching in Baize reported to the Council that none of the dozen or so Great Dragon Changed Ones that he had met with was willing to join their fight against us. Another dragon said that he had discovered the same problem here in Franconia," said Edward.

"Interesting," said Sorceress Celeste, "but what use can we make of it?" "It tells me that, as long as we do not threaten these neutral or friendly Changed Ones, we need not fear them. Our Regional Mages need to know to proceed cautiously in their hunt for those with the spark of magic, which would include any Dragon Changed Ones in their areas of responsibility," said Edward.

"Was there anything else you learned?" asked the King. "The Sea Dragons know that our fleet is heading towards the Coral Islands. They discussed a plan to attack Grotton, since they have correctly identified it as a key trading city, and they believe that it is unguarded, with our fleet in the Eastern Ocean. They are also planning an attack on the Baizian city of Middleberg, in western Baize."

The King looked troubled. "How will we defend Grotton?" he asked. Edward smiled, "Sire, Grotton is even better defended than Three Forks was. Not only is there a regiment of troops with their magical support, but we can move some of 2nd Fleet to guard the port. Naval Headquarters is also in Grotton, and Wizard Lake is very capable. I will also move additional magicians to Grotton before the dragons attack."

"Do we know when this attack will take place?" "Not precisely, sire. But I believe that it will not occur until *after* the next meeting of the Dragon Council, which will happen in two weeks. The Dragon Council only meets once a month, on the night of the full moon."

"Which is why you have called this short-notice Wizard's Council…" said the King. "Yes, sire. I believe it is vital that we meet and discuss our options before the dragons act." The King smiled. "I agree completely. Has there been any word from 1st Fleet?"

"I know that they have reached the islands and begun their operations, sire. They should see results in the coming days," said Edward. "Do you really think the Sea Dragons can be reasoned with?" asked Celeste. "I do," replied Edward. "Also, during the Dragon Council, the Sea Dragon Clan Chief, Cobalt, already knew what our new treaty proposal was. I'm not sure how he came by that information. We may have a spy in our midst."

The King's mood darkened, "How could they have learned such a thing?" "I'm not sure, sire. The condition not to attack *humans* was certainly discussed at Naval Headquarters and elsewhere. I admit that it is a troubling development, but I have had other things on my plate and have not had time to investigate this leak yet."

"Please do so at your earliest convenience," said the King. "We cannot have these dragons learning about *our* plans." "Of course, sire," said Edward.

As Edward left the audience chamber, Celeste followed him and asked, "Wizard Edward, has there been any news about my sister?" Edward grimaced and said, "She has not been heard from in some time. I know that she is alive, but the last time I looked for her, I found her on the Coral Islands. Do you have any idea why she would go there without orders?" Celeste frowned, "No. Unless she went to try and persuade the Sea Dragons to make peace."

"I didn't say anything to the King, but I fear that Anne is the one who leaked our Peace proposal to the Sea Dragons. I hope she has a good explanation for her actions," said Edward.

Andrew was exhausted. He had flown to each of the other ten ships in the fleet, replicating Belladonna berries and constructing barrels full of the poisoned fruit. He had cautioned the sailors on each ship not to touch the barrels without wearing gloves, and not to lower them into the sea unless Sea Dragons were close to the hulls of their ships. The poison would dissipate rapidly in the saltwater, and each ship only had six barrels, three on each side. He didn't even know if the nightshade juice would deter the dragons, but it was all that he'd been able to come up with.

As he completed the construction of the last barrel on the HMS SEAGULL, the last ship in the line, Andrew sat down and took a drink from his almost empty water bottle. The sun had set hours ago, and the moon was just beginning to rise. Working in the dark with the deadly Belladonna berries had been risky, but he had a feeling that the dragons were going to act sooner rather than later.

As he prepared to change back into a Great Dragon and head back to the VALOR, a large stone crashed into the deck near the port side Seabow. "DRAGON ATTACK!" he yelled, "BATTLE STATIONS! ALL HANDS ON DECK! SORCERER HENRY, SHIELDS!" Sailors rushed to man the Seabows, cranking and loading the cumbersome weapons, while Andrew and the ship's sorcerer scanned the dark sky for distortions that would indicate Concealed Dragons, or unidentified falling objects, which were hazards.

It was almost impossible to detect the dragons against the overcast sky. If the magicians were lucky, they were able to get shields in place to deflect the falling stones and tree trunks. While the men were focused on looking *up*, submerged Sea Dragons began ramming the ships from below, surfacing periodically to fire jets of high-pressure water at either the men on deck or the hulls of the ships near the water line.

"DEPLOY BARRELS!" shouted Andrew, hoping that he was not too late (or too early). Six barrels splashed over the sides of each ship. The barrels were tethered with heavy rope to keep them from sinking too far below the keels of the ships.

Andrew saw several Seabow bolts launched into the sky, missing their targets badly. It was hard enough to hit a dragon in flight, but doing so in the dark, while they were concealed, was proving impossible for the gunners. "SEABOWS, CONCENTRATE FIRE ON THE DRAGONS IN THE WATER! MAGICIANS, FIGHT THE DRAGONS IN THE AIR!" he shouted, using a Voice Enhancement so that his words carried to all of the ships.

Andrew was racked with guilt about not being on the VALOR while his ship was under attack. He hoped that the dragons knew which ship was his and were avoiding the VALOR as they had in the past. The thought also occurred to him that, since he wasn't on the VALOR, he was as subject to attack as everyone else was. *I guess that's fair,* he thought.

Rocks, stones, and other heavy objects continued to rain down on the ships. *They must be picking up more,* thought Andrew. Taking an idea from the last attack, he conjured an immense Seeming of a ship just to the south of the SEAGULL, and was relieved when it vanished in a flash of light a few moments later, as a large stone passed through it.

He cast another Seeming, knowing that he couldn't keep doing this while simultaneously shielding the SEAGULL from falling rocks. At least the submerged attacks seemed to have stopped. Andrew didn't know if it was because of the barrels of poison or some other reason, but he was relieved.

As quickly as the attack had begun, it ceased. No more unidentified falling objects fell from the sky, and there were no attacks by submerged Sea Dragons. As the crew of the SEAGULL was attempting to retrieve the barrels from the water, Andrew realized the danger and ordered, "DO NOT BRING THE BARRELS BACK ON DECK! CUT THE ROPES!" It would not do to have poisoned Belladona juice (even diluted) splashing about on the deck.

As the sun rose, the fleet was able to assess the damage. Seven ships had been hit by the aerial attack, and all had suffered damage from the surface attack. Eight of the precious Seabows were either damaged or destroyed, and Andrew didn't know how to make the new Compound Seabows. Across the fleet, there were forty men killed and twice that wounded. At least none were missing.

As the magicians went about healing their wounded comrades, Andrew considered the attack. As far as he could tell, they had not successfully engaged any of the concealed flying dragons, and he had no idea if they had killed or wounded any of the dragons that attacked from the water. *I guess we'll just have to wait and see.*

Cobalt led the air assault, while Sky attacked the ships from the water. For this attack, Cobalt mustered all of the adult males and any female Sea Dragons that did not have children to care for. Over a hundred dragons would attack the fleet. This would be the largest Sea Dragon attack in history.

Cobalt split his forces evenly, with fifty dragons attacking from the air and fifty from the sea. He decided to avoid the HMS VALOR, leaving ten ships to attack. That meant five Dragons from the air, and five from the sea for each ship. Since the male Sea Dragons were generally bigger than the female of the species, and could carry heavier loads, most of the air attack would be carried out by the males.

From the air, Cobalt felt that the attack had been generally successful, with several ships damaged by the dropped stones, while only one Sea Dragon had been hit by one of the iron spears. The hit had been fatal though, and Sapphire would not be returning to his mate.

When Cobalt returned to the grotto that was the entrance to the Sea Dragon Colony, he found quite a different story. Ten of the Sea Dragons that had attacked underwater were dead, including Sky, and almost all of the rest were hurt or wounded. Eleven had been struck by iron spears (large and small), and the rest were writhing about on the floor of the cavern in pain, with no obvious injuries.

Cobalt quickly did what he could for the six dragons that had been struck by the small spears. He now regretted letting Gek leave before the attack, since conjuring the Remove spell was impossible for a dragon. (A dragon's wrist did not flex that way.) He supposed that he was going to have to ask for Anne's assistance again, but he was unsure that she would be willing to help them again after her imprisonment.

As to the other twenty-nine dragons, Cobalt had no idea what was wrong with them or how to help them. All they could say was that they 'hurt.'

Cobalt quickly strode to the chamber where Anne was being held. He relieved Blue of his guard duty. Emerald had insisted on going out to fight to avenge her murdered mate. She was one of the dragons who were 'hurt.'

Anne was sleeping when Cobalt entered, and he roused her gently. "Anne," he said, "we need your help again."

Anne roused and said, "What has happened?" "We attacked the ships that were driving off our prey. The Sea Dragons that attacked from the air returned unharmed, but those of the Clan, mostly our females, who attacked from under the water are injured or dying. There are five with those long iron spears in them, but the rest have no visible signs of injury. I do not know what is wrong with them, they can only tell us that it 'hurts.'"

Anne shook her head sadly, "I begged you not to do this," she said. "I will require the same Binding spell as the last time for the five with the Seabow bolts in them. Then I will try to determine what is wrong with the others."

Anne quickly healed the five Sea Dragons that had been struck by Seabow bolts, then approached Sage, one of the female Sea Dragons who showed no visible injuries, but was clearly dying.

The dragon's eyes were dilated, and her mouth was dry (highly unusual for a Sea Dragon). And when coherent, Sage said that she had a headache. Anne was baffled. All of the Sea Dragons seemed to be suffering from the same affliction, but she could not begin to imagine what was causing it.

Finally, she told Cobalt, "I need to know more about the attack. Did all of these dragons attack the same ship?" "No," said Cobalt, "there were five dragons assigned to each ship." "I need to speak to one of the surviving dragons," said Anne.

Cobalt led her to Midnight, one of the dragons that he had healed. "Please tell me about your attack," he said. Midnight looked at Anne for a moment, then said, "We approached underwater. Once we detected that the air assault group had launched their attack, we began ramming the ships from below the waterline. The wood was too hard, so we started surfacing briefly and spraying the humans on the decks with jets of water. Suddenly, wooden barrels began being thrown over the sides of the ships."

"Barrels?" asked Anne. "Yes. They were attached to the ships by ropes, but we thought nothing of them. It was as if they were there to keep us away from the ships. Sky swam up and crushed one in his teeth. He immediately began convulsing, then suddenly sank to the bottom of the sea. Others broke the barrels with their tails or talons, and then many of us suddenly began feeling ill. We tried to continue the fight until the air attack ended, but some of the others returned to Acropo immediately."

Cobalt and Anne moved away from the recovering dragon. "It sounds like poison," said Anne softly. "Poison?" asked Cobalt. "Yes. The barrels may have contained a poison. When the dragons broke them open, the poison spread to the surrounding water, and the dragons ingested it." "Can you help them?" asked Cobalt.

"I'm not sure," said Anne.

Chapter Twenty-Four:
FREEDOM

The Royal Expeditionary Force rode slowly toward Grotton. Major Gerald was in no rush. He certainly didn't want to arrive before Donovan had a chance to get to the Wizard's Council and return. He didn't doubt Mage Rachel's prowess; he just knew that two Mages were better than one, and he was aware that asking Rachel to change into a dragon might endanger her unborn child.

Rachel's pregnancy was common knowledge now, and, if anything, the soldiers were even more protective of her than they had been before. Her morning sickness had subsided (somewhat), but she was generally more irritable than usual, and her dietary requests were driving Donovan crazy. "*Avocado?*" he asked, "Where am I supposed to find that? You know that I can't just conjure one out of thin air!"

However, Major Gerald had anticipated this request and had brought along a basket of avocados, as well as some tomatoes, cucumbers, and peppers (which he said his wife had requested when she was expecting).

Fortunately, the road to Grotton passed along the 'fruit basket' of Franconia. Most of the fruits in the kingdom were cultivated in the rich soil along the southern coast, so when Rachel requested strawberries, they were easy enough to find and purchase. "I just hope she doesn't want unicorn steaks next," groused Donovan one evening (out of earshot).

"I leave for Kingston in two days," Donovan said to Rachel. "Is there anything you would like me to bring you from home?" "No," said Rachel. "You should probably go see my parents and let them know about my condition. Ask my mother if she had any strange food cravings while she was pregnant. Then get right back here. And no talking to strange dragons on your way!"

Donovan nodded his understanding. The last time he had gone to Baize to see his father, he had thwarted a Snow Dragon attack on a small town in Baize, but had been scratched across the face during the battle. The scars had healed, but the memory remained.

At least their wagon was nearly empty now. Almost all of the Concealment cloaks had been issued to the magicians of Franconia. All that remained were the four cloaks for the magicians in the Grotton Regional Mage's Office, the five cloaks for the magical support to the 5th Franconian Regiment, and the two cloaks for Wizard Lake and his assistant at Naval Headquarters. The eleven cloaks took up almost no space, leaving plenty of room for Rachel to stretch out in the wagon bed when the mood took her.

"I've been thinking about the dragon attack on Grotton," said Donovan. "Oh?" said Rachel, "and what sneaky plan have you come up with this time?" "I was thinking about *Seemings,*" said Donovan, "and how Andrew used one to get a Sea Dragon to crash into a mast and knock itself out."

"What type of Seemings did you have in mind?" asked Rachel. "Well, during the attack, we could cast Seemings of fire, dragons, and other objects to confuse or disorient the dragons. I mean, if a Sea Dragon suddenly saw a Great Dragon flying towards it, it might veer off, or even flee." "Interesting," said Rachel, "and I assume you intend for *me* to be the one conjuring these Seemings?" "Well, if you shielded yourself, you could cast Seemings without using too much power. You wouldn't be the only one, of course—"

"Of course," said Rachel crossly, "I'm sure you'll be conjuring them too." "I expect to *be* a Great Dragon," said Donovan reasonably, "I was thinking about the magicians in the 5th Regiment, or the Regional Mage's Office. As I recall, Sorceress Laura was very good at casting Seemings."

"I see," said Rachel, only slightly mollified, "but why would we cast Seemings of fire?" "Well, if you were a Fire Dragon, would you waste inferno on a building that you thought was *already* on fire?" "I see what you mean," said Rachel, "so, when you had your vision of Grotton burning-" "I might have been seeing a Seeming," finished Donovan.

"Still, Grotton is a very big city…" said Rachel. "I know, but if we just cast Seemings around the critical buildings—" "We could divert the dragons to less critical parts of the town. That's *very sneaky*, but I doubt the people in those parts of town will appreciate your strategy." "So, we relocate them in advance," said Donovan. "We might not be able to spare their homes or businesses, but we might be able to save their lives."

"I like it. I'll speak to Major Gerald about it while you're gone," said Rachel. "And I'll bring it up at the Wizard's Council. Wizard Lake and Mage Charles should both be there, and maybe even Battle Mage Devon from the 5th Regiment. We need to make sure that there are no Changed Ones among the magicians in Grotton before we announce this strategy, though. We certainly don't want it getting out to the dragons," said Donovan with a yawn.

"I guess that means that it's time to turn in," said Rachel. "My thoughts exactly," said Donovan with a leer. "You can put that thought right out of your head, mister," cautioned Rachel, reading her husband's mind. "No, I really can't," said Donovan with a grin.

"BATTLE MAGE ON DECK!" shouted the Bos'n. "As you were, men." "Andrew! Welcome back!" said Commodore Matthews. "It's good to be back aboard, sir. I'm sorry I wasn't aboard during the attack. Is everyone OK?" asked Andrew. "We're all fine," said the commodore, "I guess the dragons knew which ship was the VALOR, because we didn't have a single stone dropped on us, or even get blasted by a dragon from underwater. We didn't even have to drop those barrels over the side!"

"I'm glad to hear that, sir. I'm not exactly sure how well the barrels worked, but I think that most of the underwater

Sea Dragons left after we dropped them in. I know darn well that we didn't have much success against the dragons in the air, though. It's really hard to hit a flying dragon with a Seabow, it's even harder to hit one at night. Throw in a Concealment shield, and it's almost impossible."

"How bad is the damage to the rest of the fleet?" asked the commodore. "We had seven ships hit by falling stones, and eight Seabows damaged or destroyed. There were forty sailors killed and about eighty wounded. All of the wounded have been healed, but two magicians are unconscious from their efforts," said Andrew.

"Did we lose any magicians?" asked Commodore Matthews. "Just one, Sorcerer Frank from the HMS WATCHDOG in 3rd Squadron. He was standing next to one of the Seabows that was destroyed," said Andrew. "Can we repair the damaged Seabows?"

"My *wife* might be able to, sir, but I can't. I'm sorry. I should have spent more time studying their construction. They're too complicated to replicate. We can always make more of the original model, but the new ones are going to have to be repaired or replaced in Sundock."

"Do you have any idea what Admiral Jordan is planning to do now?" asked the commodore. "Yes. He's planning to resume operations as before, sir. The attack by the Sea Dragons means that our operations are succeeding in driving away their food supply. If we can find a way to deal with these UFO attacks, we'll be well on our way to defeating the Sea Dragon Clan." "UFOs?" asked the commodore.

"Unidentified Falling Objects, sir," said Andrew. "Got it," replied the commodore.

Andrew yawned, "Sir, if you'll excuse me, I need to get some sleep. Replicating all of those barrels, then the battle has really worn me out, and we need to be ready for another round of attacks tonight. I also have to leave for Kingston tomorrow." "Of course. Go below and get some rest. You've done well, Andrew." Andrew nodded his thanks and headed below.

Anne racked her brain, trying to think of what she could do for the poisoned Sea Dragons. Cobalt said that he tried Healing, and that it hadn't worked. It would help if she knew what type of poison had been used. Whatever it was, it was a fast-acting poison, since Sky had died almost instantly, according to Midnight. "Well?" asked Cobalt.

What do you do to treat poisoning? Wondered Anne. Then she had it. "We need to move these sick dragons to the surface immediately and dig a deep hole in the sand," she said. "Why?" asked Cobalt. "I'm going to induce vomiting, and the last thing you want is a puddle of poison in your caverns."

Cobalt hurried to the grotto and began giving orders. Those dragons who could make it on their own were ordered to swim out of the cavern and crawl onto the island. "Blue, I want you to go first and dig a deep hole in the sand. Have the sick dragons lay next to the hole." The young Sea Dragon, Blue, left immediately.

Most of the dragons were able to drag themselves back into the water and swim for the surface, but Emerald, the largest of the female Sea Dragons, was in too much pain. "I cannot make it," she said to Cobalt. "Leave me and go tend to the others." "No. I will carry you to the surface," said Cobalt. Emerald smiled through her pain and said, "I appreciate the thought, but big and strong as you are, I am still too heavy for one Sea Dragon to carry that far."

"Then I will help him," said Anne. *"MORPHIUS,"* she said, clapping her hands together. Anne *rippled* and transformed into a large Sea Dragon. "Hurry now," she said to a stunned Cobalt, "she does not have much time."

Working together, Anne and Cobalt eased Emerald into the water of the grotto and pushed/pulled her down and through the underwater passage that led to the sea. They each positioned themselves under one of Emerald's wings and swam to the surface, depositing her on the beach.

Anne quickly changed back into her human form and hurried over to the poisoned dragons that were lying in the sand next to the big square hole that Blue had constructed using the Dig spell.

"I am going to use a spell that will cause each of you to empty the contents of your stomach. It is not pleasant, but it may save your lives. Please sick up into the pit, so that we can bury the poisoned liquid afterward." Without another word, Anne walked over to Emerald and said, *"NAUSEUM,"* while placing her left hand on her stomach.

Emerald vomited into the pit. The liquid was brown and sprinkled with purple chunks of Belladonna berries, half-digested fish, seaweed, and other crustations. It looked disgusting and smelled even worse. Anne was shocked by how much fluid a Sea Dragon had in its stomach. "Nightshade!" she said.

"What?" asked Cobalt, looking over her shoulder. "See those purple berries? That is Nightshade, a deadly poison. It's a miracle that any of these dragons have survived this long. We must hurry. After I purge their stomachs, they will need to drink water to dilute any poison that remains." Cobalt nodded his understanding.

One by one, the dragons emptied the contents of their stomachs into the pit, then headed back to the underground cavern and the freshwater spring inside to drink their fill. When all thirty-nine dragons had left the beach, Anne conjured a Sand spell to fill in the pit, burying the toxic sludge.

Anne sank down onto the sand and reached for her water bottle. After taking a deep drink, her color returned and she recovered. "I suppose I should have placed a Binding spell on them before I healed them," she said absently. "There is no need," said Cobalt. "Our war with the humans is over. I will accept the terms, and we will never attack humans again as long as they do not attack us. We will allow up to five of your ships to shelter in our cove during a storm, and will provide grace to anyone who washes up on one of our islands."

Anne was shocked by Cobalt's sudden change of heart. "What will the Dragon Council have to say about that?" asked Anne. Cobalt shrugged. "The Council is not binding on individual Clans; it is more of an advisory group. The other Dragon Clans may be unhappy with my decision, as may some of the adult males here, but we have suffered enough."

"I am sorry that I deceived you about my being able to change into a dragon," said Anne. Cobalt smiled. "We knew from the moment you arrived, Anne. How else could you get here? I will tell you that the Dragon Council also knows of this ability." Anne gulped.

"You are free to leave. Please tell your commander of our agreement and ask them to depart. We need the prey to return," said Cobalt. "I will tell them. Thank you, Cobalt."

"You are a true dragon-friend, as was Wizard Amanda. You and your descendants will be protected by the Sea Dragon Clan. This includes your sister as well. Return anytime. Farewell."

Cobalt dove back into the water, headed for the Sea Dragon colony. Anne quickly changed into a Great Dragon and headed east, looking for the fleet.

WIZARD DYLAN

Chapter Twenty-Five:
THE WIZARD'S COUNCIL

Donovan landed at the Wizards Academy boat dock in the early hours before dawn. He noticed that the marina area had been expanded, making more room for dragons to land. There was also a cabinet full of magicians' robes for those who forgot to bring clothing with them.

Once dressed in his finest forest green shirt and tan trousers, Donovan headed for the Mentor's quarters. He ran into Wizard Faith as he entered the courtyard. "Donovan, welcome back," said Faith. Donovan grinned, "You're going to have a very busy day if you go running every time someone opens the portal," observed Donovan. Faith laughed, "You're right about that. Starting this afternoon, I'm going to stay down here until the Council meeting tomorrow."

"So, who'll guard the gate?" asked Donovan. "Well, it is Foursday, so we don't anticipate any new students today. Mage Curtis is standing by in my cottage just in case someone comes by, but I don't expect anyone." Donovan nodded.

"Why are you here so early?" asked Faith. "I need to speak to Rachel's parents, and check on my house. We've been gone for months now," replied Donovan. "Where's Rachel?" asked Faith.

"She's still with the Expeditionary Force," Donovan explained. "We couldn't both leave, and since she can't change into a dragon for the time being, I was the logical choice to attend." "I don't understand," said Faith. Donovan grinned, "Rachel is pregnant, and I have forbidden her from changing into a dragon until after the baby is born. We don't know what changing will do to the baby."

"Congratulations!" said Faith. "I had no idea. How is she doing?" "She is irritable, heavy, and beautiful," said Donovan with a smile. "I just wish she could stop asking for strange foods. It's not like we're in a city, where I can run to the market and get a turnip for her."

"Turnips?" "Turnips, eggplant, zucchini, I swear, I feel more like a grocer than a magician lately," said Donovan. Faith laughed, "So, where are you headed this early?" "I was hoping to grab a bite to eat in the Mentor's dining room," said Donovan. "Being a dragon makes you hungry, you know."

"Hmm, we hadn't thought about that. Maybe we should make some sandwiches and have them at the marina for when everyone arrives for the Wizard's Council," said Faith. "That might be a good idea," said Wizard Noland, who appeared behind them.

"Good morning, sir, I didn't see you coming," said Faith. "I often walk around the Academy in the mornings, just to make sure everything's in order," said Wizard Noland.

"Donovan, I understand that congratulations are in order."
"Thank you, sir. Is my father back yet? I assume he's been traveling a lot recently," said Donovan.

"Edward returned from Southport last night, and you're right, it's been a busy couple of weeks. Let's go get something to eat while we talk. Faith, could you please inform the kitchens that we'll be needing some food taken to the marina today? You know what we need. Nothing hot, just something for the arriving magicians to snack on."

Noland and Donovan entered the Mentor's kitchen area, where a breakfast had already been prepared for Wizard Noland. "Martha, could you whip up something for Mage Donovan? He just arrived from Grotton." The elderly woman in charge of the Mentor's kitchen beamed, "Of course, sir. Welcome back, Mage Donovan. I'll bring it right out."

As Donovan and Wizard Noland found a table and sat down, Noland asked, "So how is Rachel coping with the pregnancy?" "She is grumpy all of the time, and has weird food cravings," said Donovan, "and my father advised me against trying to heal her morning sickness because it would make the baby grow." Noland nodded in understanding.

Martha brought Donovan a plate of eggs, ham, and biscuits, and left quickly. "Have you had any more 'bad feelings' about anything?" asked Noland.

"No, sir. I did have a thought about Grotton, though," replied Donovan. "Really? Please tell me." "I think I see things that will happen when I am *in* certain places, so the attack on Grotton will not occur until I arrive in the city. I don't know how long after my arrival, but I don't think it will happen before then."

"Hmm," said Noland, "Yes, that makes sense. Anything else?" "Yes, sir, I had the idea to cast Seemings of fire when the dragons attack," whispered Donovan. "To what end?" "Well, if I were a Fire Dragon, I wouldn't expend any of my limited amount of inferno, flaming a building that I thought was already on fire," said Donovan. "In my vision of the city, some of the fires I saw might have been Seemings."

"Even if it wasn't, I think using Seemings in this manner is a brilliant idea," said Noland. Donovan blushed at the compliment, "Plus, I can't have Rachel changing into a dragon. We have no idea if that would injure the baby."

Wizard Noland nodded, then said, "I have made some inquiries of the Changed Ones here at the Academy, and they inform me that Changing will not harm the child. Each time the mother transforms, the baby Changes also, from dragon egg to human fetus, and back again. The Changes take longer because she is changing for two, but as long as Rachel is not in dragon form when she gives birth, all should be well. You do *not* want her to lay a dragon egg!"

Donovan shuddered at the thought. "I understand, sir. We'll keep that as a last resort." The two magicians finished their breakfast, and Wizard Noland said, "Why don't you run along and see Rachel's parents? I have a million details to work out for this Wizard's Council tomorrow."

Donovan left the Academy and headed over to Mr. Turner's tailor shop, which wasn't open yet, so there shouldn't be a line of customers outside like Rachel described after her last visit.

Donovan entered without knocking and found the Turners at the breakfast table. *Donovan! How good to see you,* signed Mr. Turner. *Is Rachel with you? No,* Donovan signed, *Rachel couldn't make this trip. Is everything all right?* Signed Mrs. Turner. Donovan smiled, *Yes. Rachel is pregnant, so I asked her not to change into a dragon until after the baby is born. We should be back from our travels in about a month.*

Rachel's parents were ecstatic to learn of her pregnancy. *Do you need anything?* asked Mr. Turner. *No,* Donovan signed, *Rachel is doing fine. She only has morning sickness every other day now. She wanted me to ask her mother if there were any special foods she should eat or avoid.*

Mrs. Turner said, "She should probably avoid spicy foods. The last thing she needs is indigestion. Has she started to have cravings for certain foods?"

"Yes," said Donovan, "eggplant, cucumbers, tomatoes, and zucchini so far." "As long as it is bland, she should be fine," said Mrs. Turner. "I had cravings for all sorts of cheeses when I was expecting. Where is she now?"

"The Royal Expeditionary Force is on the road between Eastport and Grotton. After we finish our business in Grotton, we'll probably catch a boat back to Southport, then Kingston," said Donovan. *Well, I have to go see my father before our big meeting tomorrow, then I'll be heading back immediately. It was nice to see you both,* signed Donovan.

Donovan left the tailor shop and headed to the palace, hoping to find his father and stepmother, Wizard Kathy.

Gek and Annalise landed outside their hut on the beach. "Well, here goes nothing," said Gek. *"MORPHIUS,"* he said, clapping his hands together. He immediately changed into human form, but his left hand was stiff and misshapen. The index and middle fingers would not bend, and they did not have fingernails.

"I guess that is as good as I could have expected," said Gek. Annalise looked disappointed with her father's renewed ability to transform. She had enjoyed his being just a dragon for a while.

"Azure! We are home!" shouted Gek. Richard came bounding out of the hut at the sound of his father's human voice. "Daddy! You changed back!" Gek smiled, "Yes, son, a kind Sorceress fixed my hand so that I am able to conjure the Change spell again." Richard smiled, "So, not all humans are evil?"

"No, son," said Azure, emerging from the hut. "Some humans are kind like Bruce. Who healed you?" she asked. "Was it Anne or Celeste?" "It was Anne," said Gek. "Despite her imprisonment by Cobalt, she said that she would try to 'fix' my hand as a show of good faith."

"What do you mean *fix*?" asked Azure. "Anne said that my hand could not be healed, because it had already been healed. She used a different spell to lengthen the stubs of my fingers. They will not bend, and I have no fingernails, but I am able to conjure the Change spell. Anne was not sure that it would work, but she said that lengthening the stubs was all that anyone could do."

"Well, I am glad it worked. What is the Clan doing?" asked Azure. "When I left, they were preparing to attack the human ships that were positioned to the east of the islands. The magic-users on the ships were changing into Sea Dragons and driving the prey away from the islands," said Gek.

"And you did not stay to help them?" asked Azure angrily. "Cobalt said that they did not need my help. They were planning to attack from underwater and from the air, dropping stones on the ships. You know that I am not a strong swimmer. Relax, Cobalt had a good plan, and I am sure they were successful."

"I guess we will have to wait until the next Dragon Council to find out," said Azure. "How is everything here?" asked Gek. "I am worried. Bruce is failing. He is very old for a human, and living out here all alone, in a driftwood hut, is not conducive to his health."

"No, I suppose not," said Gek. "Is he sick?" "Not really sick," said Azure. "Just *old*. Like Ard was *old*."

Donovan entered the palace and proceeded to his father's office. He stopped in the hallway, sure that he had made a mistake. *Wasn't the door at the other end of the hall before?* he wondered. He stood before the door that said "Franconian Chief of Military Wizardry" on it, deciding whether he should knock or just go in. Ultimately, he just went in.

He found himself in a reception area facing an elderly woman seated behind a roll-top desk. "Yes? May I help you, young man?" she asked. "I'm looking for my father, Wizard Edward," said Donovan. "Is he available?" "Just let me check for you, sir," said the receptionist.

The woman knocked softly on the door and opened it a crack, "Excuse me, Wizard Edward, but your son is here to see you." "Please show him in, Harriet." "Right this way, sir," the receptionist said to Donovan. As Donovan entered, Edward came around the desk to embrace him. "How are you, son? Oh, this is Harriet, our new receptionist; Harriet, this is my son, Mage Donovan."

"It's nice to meet you, Donovan," said Harriet, closing the door to the office. Once the door was closed, Harriet picked up a glass from her desk and placed the top of the glass against the door with her ear on the bottom of the glass.

"When did you get a receptionist?" asked Donovan. "We decided that we needed someone to man the office and collect messages since we're gone so often," said Kathy. "Hello, Donovan, how are you?"

"I'm fine, just a bit tired from all the travel. It was exciting at first, but after a while…" Edward laughed, "I know exactly what you mean! So, where is the Expeditionary Force now?"

"They're about four-days ride from Grotton. Major Gerald wanted to make sure I had time to get here and back before they got to the city. We had to travel by the road, since there were no ships due in to Eastport for at least two weeks."

Edward nodded, "How is Rachel doing?" "She's grumpy and keeps asking for strange food, which I have to keep searching for. You don't know where I can find some water chestnuts, do you?" Edward laughed again, "As a matter of fact, I do. Have you had any more visions?"

"Just the same one, but I think I have a better understanding of it now." "Really? What have you deduced?" "I think that the attack won't occur until after I arrive in Grotton, that seems to be how it works, I see things that are going to happen to me," said Donovan.

"Hmm. That's interesting, and it may be exactly how that spell works. We just don't know. Anything else?" "Well, I told Rachel and Wizard Noland that I think we should use Seemings of fire when the dragons attack Grotton." "Seemings? Why?"

"We know that dragons have a limited amount of inferno, so if I were a Fire Dragon, I wouldn't bother expending it on a building I thought was already on fire," said Donovan. Edward smiled, "That's a great idea, son. We can discuss it with Mage Charles after the Wizard's Council tomorrow."

"What time is the Council?" "Ten in the morning. That will give those magicians that are close to Kingston time to fly in in the morning. We're going to have enough trouble finding rooms for all of the visiting magicians as it is." "Where are you putting them all?" asked Donovan.

"Most of them will be in the Level Three dormitory or the Mentor's quarters at the Academy, the rest we'll put up in town for the night."

As they spoke, Donovan noticed that Kathy looked a little pale. "Are you all right, Kathy?" he asked. Kathy nodded, but looked like she was about to be sick. Recognizing the symptoms, Donovan said, *"SENSUS,"* while holding his right hand out towards her, fingers spread.

Donovan nodded, his suspicions confirmed. He immediately retrieved the waste basket from under Kathy's desk and handed it to her. "Here. Use this." Kathy looked at him strangely, then threw up into the waste basket.

The Academy Lecture Hall had more magicians in it than Donovan had ever seen before. It seemed that every

Regional Mage, wizard, and even some of the sorcerers from the independent Companies were in attendance. His Father, Wizard Noland, and one of the Baizian wizards were seated on the stage, overlooking the crowd. The wizards were seated in the front rows, with the mages and sorcerers seated behind them. Sorceress Celeste was seated in the front row with the wizards.

"Ladies and Gentlemen," said Wizard Noland, "Welcome to the Wizard's Council. With me on stage is Wizard Edward, the Franconian Chief of Military Wizardry, and Wizard James, the Court Wizard of the Kingdom of Baize. We are here today to discuss the ongoing conflict with the dragons, our current operations, and to discuss a path forward in this struggle."

"First, I need to tell you that Wizard Edward and I snuck up and listened in on the last meeting of the Dragon Council, which meets in the abandoned rock quarry just north of Colton every month on the night of the full moon." There was murmuring among the assembled magicians.

"The dragons discussed their disastrous attack on the city of Three Forks. In case you haven't heard, nine dragons, two from each clan, except for the Great Dragons, attacked Three Forks about two months ago. Thanks to the heroic efforts of the soldiers and magicians of Three Forks, seven of the nine dragons were killed, but there were over 900 casualties, and many of the buildings in Three Forks were damaged or destroyed." More murmurs.

"The Dragon Council considered this a defeat, and discussed their mistake, which was in attacking a city with an entire Regiment of troops and a large Regional Mage's Office. They decided that if they had attacked a smaller town, like Farmdale or Hayford, they would have probably been able to raze the town and kill all of the people. We concur with this assessment." Now there were worried conversations among the assembled magicians.

"Fortunately, the dragons decided not to pursue this strategy, instead opting to attack our commercial ships and trade centers, believing that these merchant ships and towns had fewer military forces to defend them. They are also planning to send Fire Dragons to burn our crops and fields this summer and fall. Therefore, we must bring this war to a conclusion before that happens. The dragons are correct in believing that we cannot adequately defend all of the farms and ranches in Franconia or Baize."

"I believe the next attack will come from the Snow Dragons, who will strike at our crab fishing fleet that sails from the port of Frostberg. I have informed the local sorcerer and advised him that, by changing into a Great Dragon, he can drive off and defeat such an attack," said Edward. "The dragons are also planning to attack our city of Grotton, and the Baizian city of Middleberg. We need to plan for the defense of these cities."

"Next, the 1st Fleet was sent to the Coral Islands with the mission to attempt to drive off the large schools of fish that the Sea Dragons feed on. We are hoping to bring them back to the bargaining table. Mage Andrew, can you tell us how that operation is proceeding?"

Andrew rose and said, "The fleet has been successful in driving off most of the larger schools of fish that the Sea Dragons rely on for food. Two days ago, they attacked in force, dropping stones on our ships during the night while under Concealment shields. It was virtually impossible to hit a Concealed Dragon at night with a Seabow, and I doubt we inflicted any damage on them. We were also attacked from underwater, and I constructed several barrels for each of our ships and filled them with Belladonna plants. We lowered the barrels over the side as sort of a dragon-repellant. It seemed to be successful, but I have no confirmation of its effectiveness."

"Your poison barrels ended the war with the Sea Dragons," said Sorceress Anne, as she entered the Lecture Hall. "Forgive my tardiness, but I have just returned from the Sea Dragon colony. The Sea Dragons that attacked from underwater were mostly adult females. Of the fifty that attacked underwater, ten died, and all of the other forty were either wounded by crossbows, Seabows, or afflicted by the poison. After I had healed them, Cobalt, the Chief of the Sea Dragon Clan, said that their war with us is over. He accepted the conditions never to harm a human as long as we do not attack them." There were cheers from the crowd.

"Welcome home, Anne," said Wizard Noland. "We will discuss this further after the Council adjourns. Mage Andrew, it appears that not only were your barrels effective, but they have ended our conflict with the Sea Dragons. Well done!"

"Getting back to the Dragon Council," said Edward, "one of the Great Dragons reported to the Council that none of the Great Dragon Changed Ones that he approached in the Baizian cities of Oceanside or Lakeshore would join the dragons in their fight against us. It seems that, as long as we do not give these Changed Ones cause to fear for their safety, they may not join their dragon kin in their war against us."

"The next item I must inform you about is that the dragons know about our ability to change into dragons. Unfortunately, we learned about this too late to save Sorcerer Phillip, who was serving as a Dragon Messenger to the 2nd Fleet. While in Sea Dragon form, Phillip was attacked and killed by a much larger, fire-breathing, Great Dragon. In the future, if you transform into a dragon to deliver messages or attack other dragons, transform into either a Great or Stone Dragon. Does everyone here know how to kill a Stone Dragon?" There were murmurs of assent.

"The last thing that the Dragon Council discussed was the most troubling, and one that we have no control over. They are considering letting the populace know about their ability to transform into humans, believing that such knowledge will cause the citizens to turn on each other. If the dragons decide to pursue this course of action, there is nothing that we can do about it. We need to consider how we will respond to such a disclosure if and when it occurs," said Edward.

Wizard Dylan raised his hand. "Yes, Dylan?" asked Wizard Noland. "So, how do you propose we defend Grotton and Middleberg?" Edward smiled, "The dragons are mistaken if they believe that Grotton is only lightly defended. There is a Regiment of troops stationed in the city, two squadrons of the 2nd Fleet are headed there as we speak, Naval Headquarters, with their magical support, is also located in Grotton. Additionally, the Royal Expeditionary Force, with their two Battle Mages, are closing on the city and should be there within two days. Lastly, Wizard Mira and I will be flying to Grotton to aid in the defense of the city."

Wizards Noland and Mira both started at this last pronouncement, but stayed silent. "Wizard James, what can you tell us about Middleberg?" asked Wizard Daniel. James shifted in his seat, clearly not expecting to be called on. "Middleberg is situated at the fork of the Green and Yellow Rivers in Western Baize," he said. "It is the fourth largest city in Baize. We have a School of Magic in the city, where we train our apprentice magicians, and there is a mage in charge of that school. I believe there is a battalion of our soldiers quartered in the city, with a Battle Mage. Other than that, there is limited magical support in the city."

The assembled magicians again began muttering among themselves, many of them asking why they should have to defend a neighboring kingdom. Edward raised his hand, and the crowd quieted. "I believe that the attack on Grotton will occur first. Once that threat is dealt with, we will certainly send magical help to our Baizian allies to help defend

Middleberg." "But—" began a mage in the back of the room. "No 'buts'" said Edward forcefully.

"WE. WILL. DEFEND. HUMANS. AGAINST. DRAGONS! ALWAYS! UNDERSTOOD?"

Chapter Twenty-Six:
REASSIGNMENTS

The Wizard's Council went on through the afternoon and into the night. After a brief break for lunch, the magicians split up into break-out groups, with the Regional Mages gathering in the serums laboratory to discuss the various ways to detect and confront Dragon Changed Ones in their cities and towns; the magicians assigned to military posts met to discuss the best ways to kill, deceive, or incapacitate dragons; and the Wizards met to discuss strategy.

"I don't think the dragons will attack Grotton or Middleberg before the next Dragon Council meeting," said Edward. "My impression was that it was more of an idea for discussion than an attack decision. I'm less confident about the attack on our crab boats. It seemed like the other dragons didn't think that the Snow Dragons were pulling their weight in the conflict."

"I agree," said Wizard Noland. "Should we send additional magical support to Frostberg?" Edward considered the suggestion. He was hesitant to send anyone to Frostberg in winter, but the threat could not be ignored, and it might be too much for one sorcerer to handle. "OK. I'll send Sorcerer Colby from the 4th Regiment in Southport to Frostberg on a temporary assignment. I think he's one of the most capable of the military sorcerers, and the threat to Southport is minimal."

While the wizards discussed the threat of the dragons disclosing their ability to take human form, they were unable to come up with an effective counter to the problem. When the magicians reassembled, Edward announced that Sorcerers Ben, Celeste, Anne, Karen, and Candice were to report to the Forces Training Area, where they would be given the test for promotion to Mage. The five named magicians and Wizard Noland left the Lecture Hall immediately.

Next, Wizard Edward announced that the Official Dragon Messenger to the Navy positions were being eliminated. "With the death of Sorcerer Phillip and the peace treaty with the Sea Dragons, these positions are no longer required. If messages need to be conveyed between ships or Fleet Headquarters, the magicians assigned to the Navy will be able to change into Great Dragons and deliver them," said Edward.

Next, the assembled magicians adjourned to the Academy courtyard, where Edward asked Donovan to change into the various species of dragons, since he was one of the few magicians in Franconia who had seen them all.

Donovan changed into each type of dragon, and the magicians walked around him, examining each type of dragon, so that they would be able to change into one as needed. Once this exercise was completed, the magicians returned to the Lecture Hall, and Edward discussed the idea of outfitting a limited number of commercial ships with Seabows. As expected, Wizard Lake, the Chief of Naval Wizardry, was skeptical of the idea.

"I'm not sure I like arming civilian ships," he said. "If the Seabow technology gets out, we could end up with armed pirate ships preying on merchant ships." "I understand," said Edward, "and we would have to put Secrecy spells on these commercial Seabows, to prevent Replication. Our main concern right now is dragons, not pirates. Plus, it may relieve the Navy of some of its convoy escort missions."

"I suppose we could try it on a limited basis," said Wizard Lake.

Wizard Noland returned and announced that all five sorcerers had passed the Mage's Test and been promptly promoted. There was a round of applause for the new Mages.

Edward rose and announced, "Finally, I have some new assignments to announce: Mage Andrew is hereby appointed as the Sundock Regional Mage. He will be replaced by Mage Ben from Westport. Mage Karen will take over the Smithville Regional Mage's Office. Mage Anne will take over the Colton Regional Mage's Office and will be joined by Sorceress Mary as soon as Mary passes her Sorcerer's Test. Mage Candice will take over the Westport Regional Mage's Office, Sorceress Joyce has been assigned to replace Sorcerer Cliff in the Three Forks Regional Mage's Office, and Sorcerer Troy is going to the 6th Regiment in Three Forks. Sorceress Kelly is hereby assigned to replace Sorcerer Frank aboard the HMS WATCHDOG."

"This concludes the Wizard's Council meeting. I need a word with Mages Anne and Andrew before they leave for their new assignments. Thank you all for coming."

The magicians slowly filed out of the Lecture Hall, some heading for the Academy marina and home, others returning to their rooms for some sleep before they departed in the morning. Andrew and Anne remained behind.

"Mage Anne, why don't you go and talk with your sister while I speak with Andrew?" said Edward. "It may be a while before you see her again." Anne left, looking for Celeste.

"So, Andrew, first, congratulations on the dragon repellant. That was an inspired idea, and it led directly to the agreement with the Sea Dragons." "Thank you, sir. I'm just glad it worked," said Andrew.

"Here are your reassignment orders for when you get back to the VALOR. I'm sure that Commodore Matthews will be sorry to lose you, but the rotation of magicians is common among our military forces, and you've been there long enough. You are to report to Sundock as soon as Mage Ben arrives on the VALOR to relieve you. Besides, with the Sea Dragon treaty, there shouldn't be a need for your talents there," said Edward, handing over a set of reassignment orders.

"As the Sundock Regional Mage, your duties are supporting the Enforcers and seeking out those individuals with the spark of magic. I'll send you an additional sorcerer as soon as one becomes available. I understand that Maria will be moving Prestige Arms, or at least a branch of it, to Sundock, and that's a good thing. Please expedite the outfitting of the fleet with the new Compound Seabows, and be ready to begin installing the Mark One Seabows on merchant ships."

Andrew nodded, "I appreciate you assigning me to Sundock, sir. It will make married life much easier for us." "It was Donovan's idea," said Edward with a smile. "If the fleet has not left the vicinity of the Coral Islands by the time you get back, please tell them to head for the Low Sea as soon as all of their Seabows have been repaired. It would be good if at least one squadron reached Grotton before the dragon attack."

Andrew said, "I'll tell them, sir. Thank you again." Andrew left the Lecture Hall, and Anne entered immediately. "Come in, Anne," said Wizard Noland.

"First, congratulations on passing your Mage's Test. Next, I would like an explanation as to why you traveled to the Coral Islands without orders and remained there for so long. Your actions led directly to Sorcerer Phillip's death, and I do not take that lightly," said Edward.

Anne said, "I went to the Sea Dragons in an attempt to get them to accept the peace treaty before anyone else was hurt or injured, sir. I did not intend to remain, but Cobalt, the Sea Dragon Clan Chief, said that, since our fleet was approaching and would likely set fire to the island, he was obligated to protect me because I'm a dragon-friend. They kept me confined and would not let me leave."

Edward scoffed, "As a trained Sorceress, there were any number of ways you could have escaped such confinement!" "True, but not without revealing that I knew how to change into a dragon, sir! I didn't know that the dragons were already aware of our ability, and I didn't want to make them aware."

"Hmm. And just how did you explain your arrival on the island?" asked Wizard Noland. Anne looked down, "They never asked me how I got there," she said finally. "I just assumed…" "That you had tricked them?" asked Edward. Anne nodded.

"Your actions have had unintended consequences. After Wizard Noland and I eavesdropped on the Dragon Council meeting and heard that the Sea Dragons already knew what our next treaty proposal was, I informed the King. He is convinced that we have a traitor in our midst, giving the dragons inside information. He has ordered me to conduct an investigation into the matter."

Anne gulped. "Now, since you successfully convinced the Sea Dragons to accept the terms of our treaty, you are acquitted of the charge of Treason. DO NOT LET IT HAPPEN EVER AGAIN. Is that clear enough?" asked Edward.

"Yes, sir. Is that why you're exiling me to Colton?" "You are going to Colton because Dragon Messengers are no longer needed, and Colton needs a Regional Mage. This is not a punishment, it is an *opportunity.*"

Edward, Kathy, and the three wizards from Baize rode home with Edward, in his newly refurbished carriage. "Edward, I must thank you for insisting so forcefully that you will assist us against the dragons," said Wizard James. Edward nodded. "We have to stick together in this war. I hope I made that clear." James smiled. "That reminds me, here are eighteen Concealment cloaks for your magicians. We'll worry about telling King Henry later." James accepted the package of Concealment cloaks gratefully.

"Are you all right, Kathy?" asked Elianna, "You look a bit peaked." "I'm fine, Elianna, but I just found out that I'm pregnant. It's just a bit of morning sickness." "Congratulations!" said the three Baizian Wizards. Kathy nodded, keeping her mouth closed.

As they arrived at the villa, James observed, "The job of Chief of Military Wizardry in Franconia must pay very well, Edward." Edward laughed, "You mean the house? It belonged to Duke and Dutchess Draper. We suspect the Dutchess killed the Duke and fled Franconia before she could be arrested. The house sat vacant for over a year, and the bank sold it to us at a greatly reduced price. We've been repairing it with magic for weeks now. It's certainly in much better shape now than when we purchased it."

"So, what are you planning to do next?" asked Wizard James. "Tomorrow, I'll speak to my son, Mage Donovan, before he heads back to his post with the Royal Expeditionary Force. They're about two days from Grotton. Then I need to gather up Wizard Mira and head for Grotton myself."

"I heard you say that," said Elianna, "Why are you taking Wizard Mira?" Edward smiled, "Wizard Mira is the Seemings and Changes instructor at the Wizards Academy. One of the strategies we plan to use when the dragons attack Grotton is to create Seemings that make it look like the buildings are on fire. Mira is very skilled with Seemings."

"What good will that do?" asked Wizard Matthew, speaking for the first time. "Dragons have a limited amount of fire breath. We're hoping that, if the dragons believe that some of the buildings in Grotton are already on fire, they won't 'waste' their limited inferno on them."

"Hmm," said James, "If it works in Grotton, we may employ a similar tactic in Middleberg. When do you think the attacks will occur?" "Hopefully not before the next Dragon Council meeting," said Edward. "Although, I wouldn't be surprised if the Snow Dragons attack our crab fleet before then. I sent an additional sorcerer to Frostberg today to augment the magical support in the town."

"That was nice work, getting the Sea Dragons to agree to a peace treaty," said James as they entered the house. "I think that, between Mage Andrew's poison barrels and Anne's Healing, they saw that there was no point in continuing the struggle. After all, Sea Dragons don't want for food like the other dragon species," said Edward. "So, here we are. There are three guest bedrooms on the second floor, and Burt, our cook, should have dinner ready by now if anyone is hungry. I imagine that you'll want to get an early start back to Baize in the morning."

"Just one last thing, Edward, King Donald wanted me to inquire about the possibility of having one of our wizards join you the next time you eavesdrop on the Dragon Council," said James. "That would be fine," said Edward. "In fact, it would free Wizard Noland to remain at the Academy. He's working hard to fast-track the training of our apprentice magicians. Who would you like to send?"

"Wizard Elianna, who is currently posted in Springfield, would be the closest, and since she is known to you, would be an ideal choice," said James. "Very well, *Wizard* Elianna, I'll meet you in the Colton Regional Mage's Office three days before the next full moon, and we'll head to the rock quarry. Don't forget your Concealment cloak," said Edward with a wink.

The Baizian wizards departed early the next morning, headed home. Edward went to the Wizards Academy to talk with Wizards Noland and Mira, and Kathy went to the office to finish drafting and sending out all of the reassignment orders.

"Why do you want Mira to accompany you to Grotton?" asked Wizard Noland. "I'll need her help with all the Seemings we plan to cast to fool the dragons. I know that she's the best with Seemings." Wizard Mira blushed at the compliment.

"Could you use another Seemings expert?" asked Noland. "Who do you have in mind?" asked Edward. "Level Two Lisa is our most accomplished Seemings caster," said Noland. Wizard Mira looked shocked at the suggestion. "You would send a Level Two magician out to fight dragons?"

"Not alone," said Noland, "but you did say that she was your best student." Mira bit her lower lip as she considered exposing young Lisa to the horrors of war. "She can stay close to you," said Edward, reassuringly. "How will we get her to Grotton? She doesn't know the Change spell yet," said Mira.

"I guess she can ride on my back," said Edward. "That should be a great adventure for her." "I suppose," said Wizard Mira. "Who will take over my classes while I'm in Grotton?" "I had thought Kathy could handle them for a short while," said Edward.

"Doesn't she have other duties?" asked Noland. "Yes, but she won't be here all of the time. She'll be able to split her time between here and the office." "I guess that's settled then," said Noland.

"When will we be leaving?" asked Mira. "I don't expect the dragons to attack until after their next Dragon Council meeting. That reminds me, Wizard Elianna from Baize will be joining me on the eavesdropping mission next time, so you can stay here," Edward said to Wizard Noland.

"Just be ready to depart at a moment's notice once I return. Once they decide something, the dragons tend to move very quickly," said Edward. "I understand, and we'll be ready," said Wizard Mira.

With that settled, Edward headed over to his office, where he found Kathy drafting messages and sending out Messenger Hawks. "Almost done?" asked Edward. "Yes, I only had to send out three reassignment orders. The other magicians were here for the Council meeting," said Kathy tiredly.

"Are you all right?" asked Edward. Kathy nodded, "Yes, I'm alright, but being pregnant is harder than digging in the Salt Flats."

Just then, Harriet opened the door and let Donovan in. She closed the door quietly behind him.

"Do you have any orders for me before I go?" asked Donovan. "No orders, son, just information. After the next meeting of the Dragon Council, I, Wizard Mira, and Level Two Lisa will be flying to Grotton to aid in its defense."

"Lisa? Isn't she a little young for that?" asked Donovan. "Do you know her?" asked Kathy. Donovan nodded, "Yes. We were Level Ones together when I arrived at the Academy. She replaced my wardrobe with a Seeming my first night there."

"Wizard Mira says that she's the best Seemings conjurer at the Academy, despite her young age," said Edward. "I'm not surprised," said Donovan, "still…"

"One of the things I need you to do when you get to Grotton is find the best vantage point for Wizard Mira and

Lisa. They'll need to be in an elevated position, where they can see what's happening and cast their Seemings according to what the dragons are doing." "I understand," said Donovan.

"Now, I don't expect the dragons to attack until after the next Dragon Council meeting, but I don't think they'll wait very long. That means you and the Expeditionary Force have about three weeks to scout out your positions and prepare for the attack," said Edward.

"How is Lisa going to get to Grotton?" asked Kathy. "She's going to ride on my back," replied Edward. Donovan smiled, "Just make sure she climbs up *above* your wings. I'm sure she'll be a lot lighter than Specialist Lance was."

"One more thing before you go," said Edward, handing over a package wrapped in heavy paper. "What's this?" asked Donovan. "Water Chestnuts."

Harriet quickly sat back down at her desk, wondering how she could get this information to the dragons. *The wizards needed to pay for getting her daughter killed.*

Cindy landed outside the Fire Dragon colony. It had been a long trip from Eastport, and it took her a while to find the right canyon in the Grey Mountains. She had left the colony over fifty years ago, never planning to return. As she walked into the cave, she was met by a young male Fire Dragon who was guarding the entrance.

"Can I help you?" he asked. "Yes. My name is Cindy. My parents, Ember, Glow, and I left the colony many years ago. I have been living as a Changed One in the Franconian City of Haven, far to the east. I have returned with information for the Fire Dragon Clan Chief."

"Follow me," said the guard. "I will take you to Rose, the current Clan Chief." They walked down the narrow passageway to an open cavern with many side chambers that were occupied by Fire Dragons, most of which were sleeping. Winding their way deeper into the cavern system, they eventually came to a large chamber. "Wait here," said the guard. He proceeded into the chamber and spoke softly to the dragon inside.

Rose emerged from her sleeping chamber and said, "Welcome back, Cindy. It has been a long time. How are your parents?" "They both died several years ago as humans," said Cindy.

"I am sorry to hear that," said Rose. "Why have you returned?" "I was living in the town of Haven in eastern Franconia, when one day, a Sorceress arrived in the town looking for me and wanting to audit the treasury, which I was responsible for. I feared that I would be discovered, so I fled the city, making my way to the town of Sundock, where I boarded a ship headed for the town of Eastport. While on board the ship, I overheard the sailors talking; they were transporting the Royal Expeditionary Force, the very people who ran me out of Haven," said Cindy.

"Yes. We have heard about this group. They are sweeping across Franconia, looking for Dragon Changed Ones. You are saying that they are now in Eastport?" asked Rose.

"Yes, but I do not know how long they will remain there. I believe they are heading for the city of Grotton soon," said Cindy. "Interesting. Did you learn anything else about them?" "Only that one of their magic-users, Rachel, is pregnant." Rose cursed.

"What is wrong?" asked Cindy. "The magic-user, Rachel, is married to Donovan, who is a descendant of Wizard Amanda. Several of the members of the Dragon Council are under a Binding spell to spare Wizard Amanda's progeny. Rachel's child will be another magic-user we cannot kill."

"Can we kill her before she gives birth?" asked Cindy. "I thought that the Sea Dragon Clan was going to kill her before she became pregnant! It appears that they have failed, and now we have a problem. It could be that harming even an *unborn* child will trigger the Binding spell! I will have to discuss this development at the next Dragon Council meeting. You have done well, Cindy. Ferrari," she said, addressing the young Dragon guard, "show Cindy to a vacant sleeping chamber, then return to your post. Welcome home, Cindy."

BLIZ, THE SNOW DRAGON

Chapter Twenty-Seven:

FIRE AND ICE

Despite Gek's attempts at healing, Bruce continued to fade until eventually, there was nothing more that could be done for him. He told Gek and Azure that it was just his time, and that he appreciated their company and the time they spent together. He passed quietly in his sleep, and Gek buried him on the hillside where Ard had died.

"Now what?" asked Azure. "I am not sure," said Gek. "I guess we just continue living here until we figure out what to do. I do not think we should take Richard to the islands. He would not fit in with the other dragon children, and the humans may still be there. I guess we need to know how the attack on their fleet went, and what the Sea Dragons are planning next."

"The next Dragon Council is in two weeks," said Azure. "With Bruce gone, one of us will have to stay with Richard." "Since I am on the Council, I think I need to go," said Gek. Azure snorted, "If that is your argument, then you will *always* be the one going."

"You know, it might be best if we moved to a location closer to Acropo," said Gek. "With Bruce gone, there is no reason for us to remain here. We can build a hut from driftwood on any beach."

"True, but we would need the hut built before we move. It would not do for Richard to sleep outside in the rain. He is growing fast, but is still too young to sleep outside in the cold." "What about a cave along the coast?" asked Gek.

"If we are going to move into a cave, why not Cobalt's cave on Perfo? At least it has a freshwater spring," said Azure. Gek thought about it and finally decided that Azure was right. "You are right. Let us go and make a new home on Perfo. I will begin gathering Richard's things. There is nothing left for us here."

"So, James, how was the Wizard's Council?" asked King Donald. "It was very informative, Sire," said James. "The highlights are that the Sea Dragons have agreed not to attack humans as long as we do not attack them; the dragons are planning attacks on Middleberg and Grotton, which we already knew; the Franconians are anticipating an attack on their fleet of fishing vessels that sail from Frostberg in search of crabs; and Wizard Edward has invited Wizard Elianna to join him on his next mission to spy on the Dragon Council meeting."

"That's quite a lot for one meeting," said the King. "Well, they also used the opportunity to give the Mage's Test to several of their sorcerers, and Edward announced the reassignments for several of the magicians in the kingdom.

Also, Edward's son, Donovan, changed into all five species of dragons in the Wizards Academy courtyard, so that everyone at the Council meeting now knows what a dragon looks like, and how to change into one."

The King nodded, "That sounds like a good idea for us to copy. Anything else?" "Yes, Edward told all of the assembled magicians that Franconia will absolutely be providing magical assistance to us if needed. He was quite forceful about it."

The King smiled, "That's good to know. I'm sure there was some resistance to such an idea." "There was, but Edward quashed it immediately. He said that magicians should always aid each other in defense against dragons."

"So, do we know when the dragons will attack Middleberg?" asked the King. "Edward believes that the attacks on Grotton and Middleberg will not occur until after the next meeting of the Dragon Council, so we have some time to prepare. To that end, Edward gave me eighteen Concealment cloaks for our wizards. He told Elianna to bring hers to spy on the Dragon Council."

"Eighteen! Why, at ten golds a cloak, that's almost 200 golds worth of goods! Did he clear it with King Henry?" James smiled, "I doubt it, Sire. Edward gave me the cloaks *after* the Council meeting had adjourned, while we were on our way to his home for the evening. I doubt that King Henry will be informed of his generous gesture," said James.

"It seems that I was correct when I said that Edward would make a good friend, and a dangerous enemy," said

Donald. "So, back to Middleberg; how can we improve our defenses there?" "I need to travel to the city and inspect their defenses, Sire. You may recall that Wizard Elianna was formerly in charge of the Middleberg School of Magic, and Sorcerer Stephen, who is currently in charge, was her best student."

"Very well," said the King. "Also, I just received an invitation to a royal wedding. It seems that King Henry is getting married to a Sorceress Celeste, on the first day of spring." "Hmm, I suspect that Sorceress Celeste is one of the magicians that took and passed the Mage's Test at the Council meeting," said James. "I hope being married helps Henry settle down some," said the King.

"Being married to a magician might speed up that process," said Juliet, with a side-long look at Wizard James. "Are you going to attend?" asked James, ignoring Juliet's stare. "I'm considering it. Do you think it would be safe for me to travel to Kingston?"

James considered the question, "It should be, but I would recommend keeping your travel plans confidential. We can't risk the dragons learning about them. It's a two-week trip by boat, though, and even longer by land…" "I'll give it some thought," said the King, "I would like to attend if possible, but I am *certainly not* spending a month in a carriage getting there."

"How is the hunt for Changed Ones going, Mage Curtis?" asked Edward. Curtis was seated in the overstuffed armchair in Edward's office. He sipped his tea and said, "We've uncovered twenty-two Changed Ones so far. Almost every blacksmith in town had at least one Changed One working there, and most of them agreed to the Binding spell. We found almost a dozen more in the high-end shops and boutiques, and *all* of those dragons agreed to the Binding spell. So far, we've only had to kill five dragons."

"How is Mr. Turner doing?" asked Edward. "He's extraordinary," said Curtis. "That man can smell a Changed One from a block away!" "Is he troubled by the deaths of those that won't accept the Binding spell?" "Not at all. I think it's because his wife and daughter were almost killed by that Stone Dragon at Donovan's reception," said Curtis.

"That reminds me, I need to have a conversation with Harriet soon, and let her know how her daughter died," said Edward. "Harriet?" asked Mage Curtis. "She's our receptionist. Today is her day off. I'm sure you'll meet her another time. We hired her because she was having difficulty making ends meet after her daughter's death. Her daughter was Doris, the caterer who was killed at the reception."

"Anyway, we've searched most of the city. The last area for us to scour is the waterfront. I expect mostly Sea Dragon

Changed Ones down there, and with the peace treaty, they shouldn't be any trouble," said Curtis. "That's assuming they've *heard* about the treaty. Don't assume that they have, and I have *no* idea how you could convince them of the treaty, other than suggesting that they fly or swim back to the Coral Islands and ask Cobalt," said Edward.

"Hmm, that's a good point. This may not be as easy as I imagined. Not to worry, we'll manage." "Just keep Brian safe. Remember, he's deaf, so you can't just shout 'LOOK OUT!' and assume he'll duck," said Edward.

"There are always two of us with him, and Mr. Turner is exceptionally *observant*," said Curtis. "I expect so, just don't take anything for granted. If the dragons find out that he's helping us, his life would be in danger." Curtis nodded.

"Has there been any word from Frostberg?" "No, nothing yet. Sorcerer Colby should be there by now. I have no idea how frequently the crab fleet goes out, but they'll have a sorcerer with them every time they do. I just hope they keep their ships in sight of one another. I honestly have no idea how one fishes for crabs," said Edward.

"As I understand it, there can be quite a distance between boats," said Curtis. "They drop their crab pots over the side with buoys attached, let them sit on the bottom for a day or so, then grab the lines and bring the traps back up on deck. I imagine that if the traps are too close to one another, they would catch fewer crabs."

"That could pose a challenge," said Edward. "A single Snow Dragon could probably cover a small crab boat in ice pretty quickly…"

"Are we ready, Captain?" asked Sorcerer Stewart. "We are," grumbled the grizzled captain of the ICE MAIDEN, a forty-year-old crab boat which had certainly seen better days. "Are you sure you want to come along?" Sorcerer Stewart shivered and said, "I would rather be home in bed. But I have orders to go out with the crab fleet whenever they leave port until further notice."

"And just why is that?" asked Captain Brown. "The Chief of Military Wizardry believes that the Snow Dragons are planning an attack on our crab fishermen," answered Stewart. "I'm here for your protection."

"Well, I hope you brought warm and waterproof clothes," said the captain, "because it's gonna be a mite chilly and damp where we're goin'."

"And where is that, exactly?" "Today, we're headed up north of the ice pack, about four hours northeast of here. Once we clear the ice, we'll start droppin' the pots," he said, pointing to the square wooden crates that were neatly stacked on the deck. "Once we get 'em all laid, we'll head home, then come back tomorrow to see if we caught anythin'," said Captain Brown.

"How often do you do this?" asked Sorcerer Stewart.

"Once we get back to Frostberg, we gotta sort the crabs, weigh the load, then pack 'em for shipment. That usually takes a couple'a days. Then we repair any damaged equipment, and get ready to go out agin'. So, we usually sail out on Firstday, and Twoday, then sort and pack on Midweek, make repairs on Foursday, then take Endday off."

"So, you are only at sea twice a week," confirmed Stewart. "Unless the crabin's good," said the captain. "If we get into a mess of 'em, we might go right back on Midweek. You've got to strike while the crabin's good. You never know when the crabs will move to another spot. Nothin' worse than pullin' up a load of empty pots."

Sorcerer Stewart sincerely hoped that the crabbing was only marginal. He was used to the cold weather of Frostberg in winter, but he'd never gone out with the crab fishermen before. There were five boats in all (this trip), but the captain had informed him that the number of boats could be as high as eight or nine ships if the fishing was good. Two of the other boats were in port for repairs due to damage from the ice, and the other captains seldom ventured out during the winter months, unless the fishing was extraordinarily good.

Crab fishing was hard, cold work, and the fishermen were seasoned veterans. There were a few "greenhorns" (new crewmen), but they seldom lasted long. The lure of high pay for just a few days' work was enticing, but crab fishing was not a job for the weak, lazy, or sickly.

At least everyone on board knew that Stewart was a magician, so he had no reservations about conjuring a Weather shield to protect himself from the icy spray, rain, or snow. If the Snow Dragons were really going to attack, Stewart hoped that they would hurry up and get it over with.

"Is the clan prepared?" asked Bliz, the Snow Dragon Clan Chief. "They are," replied Ice. "Are you sure this is a good idea?"

"After our last two disastrous attacks, I am not sure of anything anymore," said Bliz quietly. "We should be fine. The small fishing boats are commercial ships and do not have magic-users on board. With ten of us, we should be able to quickly cover the humans in ice, which will sink their ships. With any luck, their disappearance will go unnoticed for weeks. It might even be attributed to bad weather or poor seamanship."

"How many ships do you expect to find?" "I have only seen the human fishing ships in these waters once before, when I was flying to Acropo to visit the Sea Dragons. There were six ships, all fairly close together as I recall."

"Where will they be?" asked Ice. "They normally do not stray too far from their port, and they will *not* be in the ice pack. It is too dangerous for their ships in there." "So, how will we proceed?" "We will find a large iceberg and land on it. Once we find their ships, we will strike quickly, then return home."

"And if a human magic-user transforms into a Great Dragon and attacks us?" "Then we flee. We are faster than the Great Dragons. We will have two members of our force stay high above us to watch for such an attack. I deem it unlikely, but we have suffered too many casualties already. I am beginning to regret ever agreeing to this war," said Bliz.

The boat rocked violently as yet another iceberg crashed into the hull. Sorcerer Stewart grabbed the railing to keep from being tossed overboard into the icy water. "Is this normal, Captain?" he asked. Captain Brown smiled, "We're just getting started, sorcerer!"

"How does the ship stand the pounding?" asked Stewart. "It's double-hulled," explained the captain, "designed for use in the ice pack. Don't worry, sir, we're not gonna sink."

Stewart decided that he *hated* this assignment. The boat was small, it smelled bad, and it was rocking violently with the heaving seas and the floating chunks of ice in the water. He was also cold, despite his Weather shield and what he thought were warm winter clothes. Stewart had lived in Frostberg for almost ten years, but he had never been this cold.

Most of the six-man crew remained below deck, out of the worst of the weather. There wasn't anything for them to do until they reached the area where they would drop their crab traps, so there was no point in standing on deck in the cold. Stewart was there to guard the boats from Snow Dragons, so going below wasn't an option for him.

Stewart found out early on that using a Wind spell to push the ice sheets aside didn't work. He could blast them, but if they were too big, that just meant that *two* blocks of ice hit the boat instead of just one. He tried removing the ice, and it worked a little. But the biggest part of the icebergs was underwater, and he couldn't remove what he couldn't see.

Stewart was also keenly aware that if he tired himself out blasting and removing ice, he might be too weary to fight Snow Dragons if the situation presented itself. Eventually, he decided to just blast the largest of the ice blocks, bracing himself for the collisions with the smaller ice floes.

After a little over an hour, the tiny flotilla of crab boats broke free of the ice pack, emerging into calmer waters. The captain turned the fleet northeast, heading for the area where he intended to start dropping the crab pots.

The captain ordered the crew to assemble on deck and prepare to start dropping the crab pots over the side of the ship. The crew was experienced and moved about the deck with precision. The other four boats took station about five hundred yards apart, each preparing to drop their traps over the port side of their boat.

Suddenly, a flight of eight Snow Dragons descended out of the clouds and began spraying ice at the boat farthest to the west. Sailors screamed and rushed for cover below the deck, abandoning the crab pots and the helmsman, who remained on deck to try and steer clear of the dragon attack.

The first ship was quickly covered in a foot of solid ice. The boat was instantly top-heavy and began rocking from side to side with each wave bringing it closer and closer to capsizing.

Sorcerer Stewart (in Great Dragon form) attacked the Snow Dragons, scattering them as they yelled warnings to their clan members. While Stewart was much larger than the Snow Dragons, he had not mastered fire breath yet and was struggling to bring fire to bear on the faster Snow Dragons.

Several of the Snow Dragons were struck by an unlit inferno and immediately recognized their peril. The attack on the crab ships was forgotten as the Snow Dragons circled and screamed at the Great Dragon in their midst.

Stewart caught one Snow Dragon that came too close and crushed it in his talons. The dead Snow Dragon fell from the sky, improbably striking another Snow Dragon on his way down. Both Snow Dragons fell into the sea. Neither resurfaced.

Bliz, circling high above the melee, decided that he had seen enough. "Retreat!" he shouted. "Back to the Snow

Fields!" The Snow Dragons heard their Clan Chief and slowly, reluctantly, ceased their attack and turned north. Their hesitation was fatal. Stewart finally mastered the trick of spitting inferno and igniting it, and he flamed the last two Snow Dragons as they turned for home.

Once the threat from the Snow Dragons was over, Stewart quickly flew to the ice-covered crab boat and used his dragon breath to try and thaw the ice on the deck, without catching the sails on fire. As the ice began to melt, the crew emerged, carrying hammers and axes. They attacked the ice, quickly removing the deadly coating, and the boat regained its seaworthiness.

As Stewart flew back to the ICE MAIDEN, the crews of all five ships cheered him. Then, unbelievably, they resumed dropping crab pots into the sea as if nothing had happened.

Harriet wandered through the streets of Kingston. She needed to find a Dragon Changed One who was *not* under a Binding spell, but she had no idea where to look. She knew from overheard conversations that dragons did not use contractions, and that they smelled "reptilian," but that wasn't much help.

She decided that dragons would most likely avoid the areas around the Wizards Academy, the Regional Mage's Office, and the army garrison, with its complement of magicians. That left the wharf area, the city square, with its multitude of merchant shops, and the neighborhoods where the citizens of the city lived.

The town square was too crowded. Even if she identified a dragon, it would be impossible to have a private conversation; the neighborhoods were a possibility, but there were few people on the streets, and Harriet did not fancy the idea of going door-to-door, looking for a dragon.

That left the wharf area. While there were quite a few sailors and merchants about, it wasn't nearly as crowded as the town square, and, by sitting quietly in a tavern, Harriet could listen to the conversations of her fellow customers to see if there was anyone who was not using contractions.

After consuming three pots of tea and a plate of oysters, she decided that the blond-haired man in the corner booth was a likely candidate. He was sitting alone, ordered nothing but fish to eat, and had not used a contraction that she could hear. Steeling herself, she approached his table and said, "Excuse me, sir. I wonder if you can help me. I'm looking for a friend of mine, *Cobalt.* Do you know where I might find him?"

The man started, looking around quickly. "Are you a magic-user?" he asked. "No," said Harriet, "but a magician killed my daughter, and I would like to help any friend of Cobalt's in order to get my revenge."

"And just how do you know Cobalt?" asked the man. "I have never met him," Harriet whispered, "but I understand that he is the Clan Chief of the Sea Dragons. I have an urgent message for him. Do you know how I can get word to him?"

"I might," said the man cautiously, "what is this message?"

"The wizards know when and where the Dragon Council meets each month, and are spying on the meetings. Whatever was discussed at the last meeting has been compromised. The Council should pick another place to meet in the future."

"How would you know this?" asked the man. "Because I am the secretary for the Chief of Military Wizardry."

Chapter Twenty-Eight:
SEA CHANGES

A ndrew landed back on the HMS VALOR, which was sailing toward Sundock. "BATTLE MAGE ON DECK!" shouted the Bos'n. Andrew said, "As you were, men," and he suddenly realized how much he was going to miss that announcement. He went below to find Commodore Matthews.

"Andrew! Welcome back! I take it you heard about the agreement with the Sea Dragons?" "Yes, sir. Mage Anne told us about it at the Wizard's Council," said Andrew.

"*Mage* Anne?" asked the commodore. "Yes, sir. Since almost all of the magicians in Franconia were present, Wizard Edward took the opportunity to give the Mage's Test to five of the sorcerers, including Anne and her sister Celeste. They all passed."

"Does this mean that Anne will no longer be a Dragon Messenger?" "I'm afraid so, sir. With the treaty with the Sea Dragons, Wizard Edward has discontinued the Dragon Messenger to the Navy positions, since any magician can transform into a dragon to deliver messages between ships now. Mage Anne has been assigned as the Regional Mage in Colton, effective immediately," said Andrew.

The commodore nodded knowingly, "And where are you going?" Andrew looked surprised by the commodore's perception, "I've been assigned as the new Sundock

Regional Mage, sir. I'm to report there as soon as Mage Ben arrives here to relieve me. Ben was the Regional Mage in Westport."

"I can't say I'm surprised. Most magicians rotate every three years, and you've been here longer than that. Besides, with the treaty with the Sea Dragons, we've been ordered back to the Low Sea, so 2nd Fleet can get to Sundock to be fitted with the new Compound Seabows," said the Commodore. "Did anything else interesting come out of the Wizard's Council?"

Andrew told the commodore about the dragon's plan to begin attacking commercial targets rather than military facilities, and about the expected attack on Grotton and Middleberg in Baize.

"Do we know when the dragons plan to attack Grotton?" "No, sir, but it probably won't be until after the next meeting of the Dragon Council, which will happen the night of the next full moon, which is in just a couple of days," said Andrew.

"Well, Andrew, you'll be missed around here, but I understand how these things happen. I'm sure Maria will be happy with your new assignment." "Yes, sir. I think she's planning on opening a branch of Prestige Arms in Sundock and keeping the one in Fairview. As you said, my assignment in Sundock won't last forever."

"Well, conjure us a good, strong wind and get us back to Sundock with all possible speed, mage." "Aye, Aye, sir," said Andrew.

Gek, Azure, and the children arrived on Perfo just as dawn was breaking. They had observed the fleet of navy ships sailing towards the mainland and wondered what had happened. Gek was weary from carrying Richard on his back and a crate of their possessions in his talons. Azure was also tired. Flying with Richard's mattress had been difficult, since the wind kept catching it and trying to rip it from her grasp.

"I hope we did not forget anything important," said Azure. "If we did, I will pick it up on my way back from the Dragon Council meeting," said Gek. The two dragon parents had brought along everything they could think of that Richard might need as he grew: larger human clothes, shoes, the reading books, a small folding table and chair, and his bed. This was going to be a difficult transition for Richard, so they tried to bring what they thought he would need as he grew. There was no telling when they would return to the mainland.

As the dragons settled into the cave, Richard asked again, "Where is Bruce?" Gek sighed and repeated, "Bruce is gone, son." "Like Ard?" "Yes. Like Ard." "Will he be coming back?" "No, Richard. Bruce will not be coming back." "I liked him," said Richard. "So did we, son," said Azure. "Now, which chamber do you want?"

Richard waddled around the cave and finally selected a smaller cavern near where he thought his parents would sleep. "I will take this one," said Richard. Gek and Azure transformed briefly and moved Richard's bed into the sleeping chamber he had selected. Annalise had already picked a cavern near the entrance. Once everyone was settled in, Gek said, "Now it is time to sleep. We will explore the island later this evening, then I have to leave for a few days."

"But you will be back, right?" asked Anna. "Yes. I will be back," said Gek. "Not like Bruce?" asked Richard. "No, not like Bruce. I will be back soon."

The children retired to their sleeping chambers, and Gek and Azure changed back into dragons. "The children really miss Bruce and Ard," said Azure softly. "I know. It is difficult to explain death to them."

"The human ships have left the islands," said Azure. "What do you think that means?" "I do not know," said Gek. "Some of the ships looked damaged, but not badly. I cannot imagine why they are returning to the mainland."

"I hope Cobalt is OK," said Azure.

That evening, Gek headed for Acropo. When he arrived and wandered through the cavern system, he noted that Anne was no longer in the chamber where she had been held. He found Cobalt in his den and was surprised to find Emerald sleeping with him. "Cobalt? Where is Anne?" asked Gek.

Cobalt roused, whispered something to Emerald, and walked out into the passageway to speak with Gek. "I let her go, once the threat from the humans had passed."

"How did that happen?" asked Gek. "As you know, we determined that the human ships were driving our prey away," began Cobalt. "Their magic-users were transforming into Sea Dragons and herding the schools of prey far, far to the south, towards the part of the sea that the human fishing fleets frequent. We could not permit this to continue, so we attacked the ships."

"What happened?" "I sent a hundred Sea Dragons against them, almost every adult dragon in the colony. The males attacked from the air, dropping stones on the ships, while the adult females attacked from underwater. I led the air attack, while Sky was in command of the undersea strike. It did not go well."

"Why do you say that?" asked Gek, fearing the answer. "The air attack went well. We damaged several of the ships and destroyed a few of the spear-throwers, and we only lost one member of the clan, to what was likely a lucky shot by the humans," said Cobalt.

"That sounds good," said Gek. "Yes, but the females did not have success. The humans lowered barrels of poison into the water beside their ships. We did not know what they were. Sky crushed one with his mouth and died instantly from the poison. Several of the clan were struck by the iron spears as they surfaced to attack the ships, and all of the dragons that attacked from the sea ingested some of the poison. We had ten killed, and the forty that returned were all injured by the spears, the poison, or both," said Cobalt sadly.

"Did you ask Anne to heal them?" "Yes, and she healed the five with the spears in them, requiring the same Binding spell as she insisted on before, but she was unsure how to help the dragons that were poisoned."

"What did she do?" asked Gek. "She had us all swim up to the island. Then she asked Blue to dig a large hole in the sand. Anne changed into a Sea Dragon and helped Cobalt drag me to the surface," said Emerald, joining the conversation. "Then she cast a spell that caused us to empty the contents of our stomachs into the pit, expelling the poison. It was not pleasant, but it saved our lives. Then she filled the pit with sand so that the poison sludge would not spread."

"Did she insist on a Binding spell?" asked Gek. "No. There was no time, and several of the poisoned dragons were incapable of responding. She helped us with no assurances," said Cobalt.

"Then what happened?" "I told her that our war with the humans was over; that I agreed that Sea Dragons will not attack humans if they do not attack us," said Cobalt. Emerald nodded.

"WHAT?" asked Gek, astounded. "You capitulated?" "Son, how many Sea Dragons have died already? How many more would have died if not for Anne? And what have we gained? I grieve for Liza, but the life of one dragon is not worth all of the pain and suffering we have endured during this conflict," said Cobalt.

"What will you tell the Dragon Council?" asked Gek. "I will tell them that the Sea Dragon Clan can no longer support our dragon kin in this war against the humans," said Cobalt. "But, you did not submit to a Binding spell!" insisted Gek.

"Gek, you should know that a Binding spell is not required for dragons. If we give our word, that is enough. It is a matter of honor. The humans may believe that a Binding spell is required to ensure that dragons keep their word, but it is not so. We keep our word because that is our nature."

Gek was disturbed and saddened by the surrender of the Sea Dragon Clan, but he understood Cobalt's reasoning. The Sea Dragons did not lack for prey as the other Dragon Clans did, and they had plenty of room to expand. It was logical, but troubling.

"Does this agreement apply to all Sea Dragons?" he asked, "Even Azure?" Cobalt nodded, "Yes. Although, I have not been able to get the word to all of our kin, everywhere. It may be particularly hard to inform all of the Changed Ones. However, since there is no Binding spell involved, if an ignorant Sea Dragon attacks a human, it may be explained, and hopefully, the peace agreement will continue."

"Azure is going to be angry," said Gek. "I know," said Cobalt, "but perhaps she will reconsider when she learns that Aqua was one of the poisoned dragons that Anne helped." "Is Aqua OK?" "Yes. She is resting in her chamber, and I must say, her attitude towards humans has softened somewhat."

"When will we depart for the Dragon Council?" asked Gek. "We must leave tomorrow night. With Sky dead, I have appointed Emerald, my new mate, as the second Sea Dragon member on the Council. She will accompany us." Gek took a moment to digest that news, finally deciding that Cobalt must have his reasons for taking a mate, and that it had been many years since Liza's death.

"Very well. I will speak to Aqua and be ready to depart with you tomorrow. By the way, our friend Bruce passed away, so we have moved into your old cave on Perfo. I do not know how well Richard will adapt to his new environment, but this seemed like our best option."

"I understand," said Cobalt, "and with our agreement, Richard has nothing to fear from the other members of the clan. I will see you tomorrow evening." Cobalt and Emerald returned to their sleeping chamber, leaving Gek alone in the passageway.

Donovan landed in the field beside the Royal Expeditionary Force just after dawn. They were about a day's ride from Grotton. Once he changed back into human form, he walked into the camp, looking for Rachel and Major

Gerald. He found Rachel sleeping in their wagon. He woke her gently and offered her a warm cup of tea.

"Wake up, sleepy-head. It's time to rise and shine." "It's about time you got back," Rachel grumbled. "I've only been gone three days," said Donovan, reasonably, as he handed her the cup of tea. "Get that away from me!" said Rachel. "You don't want tea?" asked Donovan. "No. It makes me sick. Just get me some orange juice."

"Where am I supposed to get orange juice?" asked Donovan. "You take one of those oranges," said Rachel, pointing to a sack of oranges in the corner of the wagon bed, "and you squeeze the juice into a cup." Donovan hurried to comply. He got almost as much juice on his hands and shirt as he got in the cup. "That's not enough," complained Rachel. Thinking quickly, Donovan used the Replicate spell to double the amount of orange juice in the cup before handing it to Rachel.

"Smart thinking," said Rachel. "So, how was the Wizard's Council?" "I didn't really learn anything that we didn't already know," said Donovan. I changed into all five dragon species so that everyone there now knows what the various dragons look like, and five sorcerers, including Celeste and Anne, were given and passed their Mage's Test."

Rachel nodded her understanding as she sipped her juice. "Anything else?" "Anne reported that the Sea Dragons have agreed not to harm humans if we do not harm them, so it appears that our conflict with them is over. With this new information, my father dissolved the position of Dragon Messenger to the Navy and assigned Mage Anne to the Colton Regional Mage's Office. He also appointed Andrew as the Sundock Regional Mage, and replaced him with Mage Ben from Westport," said Donovan.

"It sounds like it was a productive meeting," said Rachel. "Yes. My father said that he and Wizard Mira would meet us in Grotton to prepare for the dragon attack. They'll arrive after he listens in on the next Dragon Council meeting in three days."

"Why is Mira coming?" asked Rachel. "She's the best at the Academy with Seemings. I guess my father wants her help in casting Seemings of fire when the dragons attack," speculated Donovan. "Hmm. It's been a long time since Mira left the Academy. I hope she's up to it," said Rachel. "She must have served somewhere besides the Academy, but you're right, I don't really consider her a Battle Wizard," said Donovan.

As they talked, Major Gerald walked up to the wagon. "Welcome back, Donovan. Is there anything I need to know about that came out of the Wizard's Council?" "We apparently have a peace treaty with the Sea Dragons," replied Donovan. "As long as we don't attack them, they won't attack humans. My father doesn't think the dragons will attack Grotton or Middleberg until after the next Dragon Council meeting this week; and my father and Wizard Mira, the Seemings and Changes instructor at the Academy, will be meeting us in Grotton after the Dragon Council, which my father plans to listen in on."

"Well, then I guess we should get this show on the road and get into Grotton as quickly as possible. We'll need the time to set our defenses."

With that, Major Gerald gave the word for the Force to move out. The scouts from 1st Company moved out first along the road, with the rest of the Expeditionary Force falling in line behind them. Donovan drove his wagon, allowing Rachel to rest in the back. As the force neared the city, traffic on the road picked up, with farmers headed to or from the market, traders headed for Eastport, or the city Road Patrols who were looking for smugglers or bandits.

When the force entered the city, they proceeded immediately to the garrison that housed the 5th Franconian Regiment. "Tomorrow, you two need to inventory the treasury and distribute the last of the Concealment cloaks. Let's not forget why we're here," Major Gerald said to Donovan and Rachel. "While you're doing that, I'll be discussing this imminent attack with Major Adams, the Commander of the 5th Regiment. I hope you're right about this, Donovan. Otherwise, I'm going to look like a paranoid fool."

"The dragons are coming, major. You can count on it," said Donovan.

After settling in and seeing to their horses, Rachel and Donovan headed over to the Regional Mage's Office. They found Mage Charles in the office, along with the three sorcerers stationed in Grotton. "Mage Donovan! Welcome to Grotton!" said Charles.

"Mage?" asked Sorceress Laura. "How can you be a mage already? Hello, Rachel. It's good to see you again." Donovan and Rachel smiled, "Hello, Laura. How are you doing? Yes, we've both been promoted to Mage." Laura looked shocked, "I don't understand, Donovan spent less than four years at the Wizards Academy, which is surprising enough, but promotion to mage..."

"It's probably because I can cast two spells at once," said Donovan reasonably. "Three sometimes," said Rachel. Laura's mouth dropped open. "Anyway, we just came by tonight to distribute the Concealment cloaks to the three of you that don't have yours yet," said Rachel.

Donovan gave Mage Charles, Sorcerer Adam, and Sorceress Grace their cloaks (after smelling them to be certain that they weren't Dragon Changed Ones). "Tomorrow, we'll be inventorying the Grotton Treasury, then handing out the last five Concealment cloaks to the magicians assigned to the 5th Regiment," said Donovan.

"Are we going to have any trouble with the Treasurer?" Rachel asked Mage Charles. "Darrel? I wouldn't think so. Why? Have you had trouble with some of the other Treasurers?" Rachel grinned, "Yes. Usually, those whose accounts are short of coins, although the Fairview Treasury was accurate to the copper, but the treasurer still wouldn't let me in."

"What did you do?" asked Sorceress Grace. "I spelled him to sleep and conducted the inventory without him," replied Rachel. "The King was very specific. We are not to take 'No' for an answer."

"How many Treasuries have been short?" asked Mage Charles. "Only four so far," said Donovan. "Not including the Kingston Treasury, which was completely empty." The four magicians gasped. "Empty? How many golds were missing?" asked Laura. "About ten thousand. It took Wizard Noland and the Academy faculty almost a week to replicate all the missing golds."

"What do you think happened to them?" asked Sorcerer Adam. "Between Wizard Victor and Minister Jasmine, they either stole or vanished them. They were trying to ruin the Kingdom financially."

"Well, I certainly hope that you don't find that problem here," said Mage Charles.

"So, how are preparations for the dragon attack coming?" asked Donovan, changing the subject. "With the two of you and Wizards Edward and Mira coming, there will be 14 magicians in Grotton soon. That doesn't include any that will be on the navy ships if a squadron can get here in time. That would bring us up to three wizards, five mages, and eleven sorcerers. How many dragons do you think will attack?"

"I have no idea," said Donovan. "In my vision, the dragons are flying around too fast in all different directions, and some of them may be magicians in dragon-form." "Your 'vision'?" asked Laura.

"Yes. It seems that I can cast the spell of Foresight. In the past year, I've accurately foreseen attacks on Colton, Three Forks, and Sundock. I believe that Grotton is next, and based on what my father heard at the last Dragon Council meeting, I'm correct."

"Wait, you're saying that you can cast the spell of Foresight?" asked Mage Charles. "It seems so," said Donovan. "But the spell does not tell me *when* such an attack will happen. I'm assuming it's when I'm in that place. At least that's what happened all of the other times."

Charles whistled. "Do you know why Wizard Edward wanted Wizard Mira to come to Grotton with him?" "Yes. In my vision, much of Grotton was on fire. I came up with the idea of using Seemings to fool the dragons into believing that more of the city is on fire than actually will be. Dragons have a limited amount of inferno, the gel that they ignite and spit. If a dragon thinks that a building is already on fire, they may not breathe fire at it. Since Wizard Mira is the Seemings instructor…"

ROSE, THE FIRE DRAGON

Chapter Twenty-Nine:
PLANS

"What do you mean, you have made a peace treaty with the humans?" screamed Rose, the Fire Dragon Clan Chief. "Exactly what I said," replied Cobalt. "The Sea Dragons will not attack humans as long as they do not attack us! My clan has suffered too much during this conflict. We cannot continue."

"Nor can we," said Bliz, the Snow Dragon Clan Chief. "During our attack on their so-called 'defenseless' crab fleet, I lost another four of my best fighters to a magician who changed into a Great Dragon. I am not sure we sank even a single boat. This conflict has brought us nothing but sorrow."

"Did you sign a treaty with the humans? Either of you?" asked Jasper, the Stone Dragon. "No," said Cobalt, "but I gave a human magic-user, who is a dragon-friend, my word as a Clan Chief. I do *not* need anything on paper."

"I do not have any kind of agreement with the humans," said Bliz, "but I am telling you that the Snow Dragon Clan will not attack again. Every time we have attacked, even with Fire, Stone, and Great Dragons to aid us, we have suffered grievous losses. My clan is less numerous than any other, except maybe the Great Dragons. I cannot afford to lose any more of my clan."

"How will you survive?" asked Rose. "There is enough prey in the Snow Fields, and we require less to eat than any of you. We will be all right. We may need to move farther west in the Snow Fields, but there is enough prey to sustain us," said Bliz.

"Cobalt, my friend," said Rose desperately, "there must be some way that you can aid us in our struggle!" Cobalt thought about Rose's request. "I promised not to *attack* the humans as long as they do not attack us. We could still provide you with *information* about where the human ships are, and I can teach you the healing spells that we learned from Anne."

"Is that all you can offer?" asked Basalt, the Stone Dragon. "I suppose we could also fly reconnaissance missions, spying out the humans' positions; perhaps there might even be some of my clan who would be willing to change into humans and visit the human cities to determine where they are weak and vulnerable," said Cobalt.

"At least that is *something,* I suppose," said Rose. "Now, where should we attack next?" Rose asked Amber and Ig. "Middleberg is close to our Colony," said Jasper. "That is true," said Rose, "but Grotton is nearer to the Sea Dragons."

"The human mage in Grotton is formidable," said Gek. "Sending Sea Dragon Changed Ones into that city would be risky."

"Then we attack Middleberg first," said Rose. "I have other news, the Fire Dragon Clan has learned that the magic-user, Rachel, who is mated with Donovan, is with child. We dare not attack her now, lest Jasper, Cobalt, Bliz, Gek, and Azure perish for violating the Binding spell cast by Ard." There was grumbling among the non-bound members of the Dragon Council.

"Is the Binding spell still active, now that Ard is dead?" asked Fern. "No one knows," replied Cobalt, "and I, for one, do not wish to test it." "Where are Donovan and Rachel now?" asked Ice. "They were in Eastport with a group called the Royal Expeditionary Force, the last we knew, but they may be heading to Grotton," said Rose. "And Andrew? Is he still on the VALOR?"

"We must assume so," said Cobalt, "but that could change at any time." "We must locate these three magic-users," said Basalt. "Otherwise, we risk death to three members of the Dragon Council." "And my mate," said Gek.

"Cobalt, since the Sea Dragons can no longer attack humans, tracking these three magic users might be a good job for your clan," suggested Rose. Cobalt considered the request and finally agreed. After all, it concerned his safety as well as his family's.

"So, when should we attack Middleberg?" asked Gek. "The night of the next full moon," ordered Rose. "I will send ten Fire Dragons. Jasper?" "I will come and bring several Stone Dragons." "Gek and I will be there," said Ig, "as well as any other Great Dragons that I can find and convince to help us."

"Where should we meet?" asked Gek. "There is an oasis in the desert, just west of Middleberg. We will launch our attack from there," said Jasper.

Wizards Edward and Elianna remained hidden on the ledge above the rock quarry until all of the dragons had departed. "So, it seems that Middleberg will be attacked first," said Edward quietly. Elianna nodded worriedly. "We have been preparing for such an attack for over a year, but now that it is upon us, I'm not sure we're ready."

"I've never been to Middleberg. What are its defenses like?" asked Edward. "Before I left, we had constructed watch towers in several locations around the city and designated fire-proof shelters for the citizens to take refuge in. My apprentices and I made hundreds of vials of Healing Serum and distributed them to the Army and the city council. Unfortunately, it's all expired now, and with all of my students working in the Salt Flats for the last year, I doubt that any more has been made yet," said Elianna.

"We still have a little time," said Edward, "and I have a plan. Only the Sea Dragons and Gek the Great Dragon have seen Mage Andrew. We should start a rumor that he has been posted to Middleberg as a magical liaison between Franconia and Baize. That may make the dragons more cautious."

"I need to get back to the king and let him know what is about to happen," said Elianna. "Then I'll return to my office and determine what magical support I can send to Middleberg," said Edward. "Will you send Wizard Kathy?" Edward shook his head, "No. Since Kathy is pregnant, I will not risk her safety. Besides, her condition has left her weaker than normal. Our timing is *terrible*." Elianna smiled.

All was *not* as it should have been in the Grotton Treasury. "I just don't understand it!" exclaimed Darrel, the Treasurer. "How could a *thousand* golds be missing? I just inventoried everything last week with Sorcerer Beryl from the 5th Regiment! We counted six thousand, four hundred and sixteen golds, five hundred and eleven silvers, and eight hundred and twenty coppers. It should all still be here!"

"Was Sorcerer Beryl ever left alone in the vault?" asked Rachel. "Absolutely not! Except for the few seconds that it took me to put the ledger back in my desk before locking the vault door, I was with him every minute," said Darrel.

"It would only take a few seconds for a magician to remove a chest of gold," said Donovan. "But why would he do it? What's the point of stealing gold if you can't escape with it?" asked Darrel. "The point is to weaken Grotton and Franconia, financially. To undermine the people's confidence in our institutions. We've seen it before," replied Donovan.

"So, what happens now?" "Now, we go and have a conversation with Sorcerer Beryl. Maybe he simply *reduced* the chest and carried it out in his pocket. If we can recover it, we can probably use a spell to return the chest and the gold to its normal size," said Rachel.

Donovan and Rachel left the treasury and headed for the 5th Regimental Headquarters, stopping along the way to retrieve the last of the Concealment cloaks from their wagon. They entered the headquarters building and found Major Gerald talking to Major Adams, the Regimental Commander.

"Donovan! Rachel! Come meet Major Adams, the commander here in Grotton. I was just telling him about your premonition about an imminent dragon attack," said Major Gerald. Donovan winced at the news, "Sir, you didn't happen to mention this to any of the Regiment's magicians, did you?"

"Of course I did! We're going to need their help fighting these dragons after all." "Where's Sorcerer Beryl?" asked Donovan and Rachel together. "Why, I sent him out to the battlements to start replicating and installing Guardbows," said Major Adams.

Without another word, Donovan raced out of the office, headed for the garrison battlements. He arrived just in time to see a Stone Dragon flying south, away from the city. "I got him," said Donovan.

Donovan stripped off his garments and transformed into a Great Dragon. He leapt into the air and chased after the escaping Stone Dragon. Donovan caught the Stone Dragon in a few short minutes, and the two began grappling in the air. They coated each other in flaming inferno, they bit, clawed, and tail-whipped each other. Donovan was running out of ideas when he remembered that Stone Dragons can't swim.

Their battle had taken them close to the surface of the water, and Donovan twisted around and bit down on the leading edge of the Stone Dragon's wing, breaking the forebone. The Stone Dragon fell into the sea and sank all the way to the bottom. "Good luck walking back to shore," gasped Donovan. He watched for a few moments, but it was obvious that the Stone Dragon was probably crushed by the immense water pressure as he sank into the deep water.

Exhausted, Donovan flew back to Grotton. He landed on the battlements, changed back into human form, and collapsed. Rachel reached him a few moments later, "Donovan, are you OK?" she asked. Donovan nodded weakly, "Water," he gasped. Rachel quickly handed him her water bottle. It was full of orange juice. Donovan gagged on the acidic juice, but drank as much as he could.

Rachel took stock of his injuries; he had deep scratches on his back and left shoulder, his right hand appeared to be burned, three of his front teeth were cracked and bleeding, and he had a couple of broken ribs. *"SALV—"* Rachel began, before Donovan grabbed her hands. "Oh, no, you don't! You go get one of the other magicians to heal me!" "I can do it!"

said Rachel. "I'm sure you can," said Donovan, but this much healing would take too much power out of you! I won't risk our son!"

Rachel nodded and ran to find the Regiment's Battle Mage. Fortunately, Mage Devon was nearby, having stopped to watch the dragon fight from the watch tower. The two of them raced back to Donovan, and the Battle Mage conjured a Healing spell for major wounds, which healed Donovan's ribs and his mouth. A Healing Serum closed the deep scratches on his back and shoulder, and healed his burned hand.

As Donovan lay on the battlement, Majors Gerald and Adams approached. "Are you all right, Donovan?" asked Major Gerald. "I think so, sir." "You know, you could have just let him go," said Major Adams. Donovan shook his head, "No, sir. He knew too much about your defenses here. He would have been back with his dragon cousins. I couldn't risk that."

Major Gerald just shook his head. "Let's get you up and to the Infirmary. You need some rest." Donovan started to argue, but Major Gerald wouldn't take 'No' for an answer. Once Donovan was in bed in the garrison Infirmary, he said, "Rachel, take Battle Mage Devon and distribute the rest of the Concealment cloaks. Just make sure the other three sorcerers aren't Changed Ones."

"What about Mage Devon?" asked Rachel. "He's not a Changed One. I got a good whiff of him when he healed me," said Donovan. As Rachel headed for the door, she stopped and turned around, "So, we're going to have a son, are we?"

"It appears that Donovan was wrong," said Edward, "the dragons plan to attack Middleberg first, then Grotton. It seems that the Stone Dragon colony is in the desert just west of Middleberg." Edward, Kathy, Noland, and Mira were seated in Edward's office, discussing the Dragon Council.

"Edward, can you tell me why I'm here?" asked Mira. Edward shifted in his chair and said, "Mira, when the dragons attack, we're going to create Seemings of fire across the entire city of Middleberg and Grotton. Our thinking is that, given their limited amount of inferno, a dragon won't flame a building that he or she believes is already on fire."

"I see," said Mira. "You want me to cast as many Seemings as I can, to distract the dragons and keep them from destroying the city." "That's the gist of it," said Noland. "Wizard Elianna has informed me that Middleberg has constructed several stone shelters to protect the citizens of Middleberg. While I hope they're fireproof, I don't want to underestimate these dragons. Also, there are several watch towers that will have soldiers armed with crossbows in them. It would be best if the dragons didn't set the towers on fire. We should probably also send some Stone Dragon scales to Middleberg and Grotton to help them reinforce their roofs," said Edward.

"Edward, Headmaster, I'm flattered that you think I can cast so many Seemings at once, but—" "You won't be alone, Mira. There will be other magicians casting Seemings also, but some of us have to be conjuring Blast spells and enclosing Stone Dragons in shields. We're also thinking about sending Level Two Lisa with you."

Mira paled, "Lisa? But she's just a child!" "I know," said Noland, "but I understand that she's the best student at the Academy for conjuring Seemings." "Well, yes, but…" "This is war, Mira. Lisa can stay near you while you two conjure Seemings, but we need all the help we can get. I wouldn't ask if it wasn't important," said Noland.

"I will talk to Lisa," said Mira. "Do we know when this attack will happen?" "The dragons will attack on the night of the next full moon, four weeks hence. We need to be in Middleberg in time to plan for the defense of the city. I'll be recruiting additional magicians. If we can blunt this attack, we may be able to bring this war to an end," said Edward.

"YOU WANT US TO DO WHAT?" yelled Azure. "We need to determine where the magic-users Donovan, Andrew, and Rachel are," said Cobalt reasonably. "Since we cannot fight, this is the best way we can help our dragon cousins."

"I still cannot believe that you promised Anne that we would not attack humans if they did not attack us!" said

Azure angrily. "Azure, the Sea Dragon Clan has suffered too much already! Your father died, your mother almost died, and my friend Sky perished. It is not worth continuing!" said Cobalt forcefully.

"I WANT MY VENGEANCE!" shouted Azure. "At what cost?" asked Cobalt softly. "Gek's life? Mine? Your children's?" "We could have continued dropping stones on them!" said Azure.

"For how long? These human magic-users are not fools. What if they start flying over their ships as concealed Great Dragons? We cannot tolerate any Unidentified Aerial Predators (UAPs). I am sure the humans will think of that eventually. I thought it best to cease hostilities before we suffered a worse defeat," said Cobalt. "You may not agree with me, but as the Clan Chief, I have spoken."

"Do we know where Donovan and Rachel are now?" asked Azure. "The Fire Dragon Clan Chief said that they were in Eastport, but were traveling to Grotton soon. They may already be there," said Cobalt.

"Grotton? The city where Gek was discovered and taken? How can we go there?" asked Azure. "I understand that there are Changed Ones there that might help you," said Cobalt. "That is true," replied Gek quietly. "Beau and the other Sea Dragon Changed Ones might be willing to help us, and Beau has two human sons…"

"Who may be compromised already?" said Azure. "I thought you said that the Regional Mage was going to investigate the Cannery." "But we do not know the results," said Gek. "So, we would have to be cautious," said Azure.

"If I go into Grotton, that Regional Mage will recognize me," said Gek, "and this time he will not just try to send me to the wizard's school!" "Then I should go," said Azure. "He has never seen me. If I remain hidden in the Cannery, and Beau's sons seek out Donovan and Rachel, I should be safe. Besides, someone has to stay here with the children."

"I do not like this. Not one bit. You do not even know what Donovan looks like!" said Gek. "So tell me. You are the only one who has seen him," said Azure. "I only caught a glimpse of him in Three Forks," said Gek, "and that was just before I accidentally pushed a building over on top of him."

"What did he look like?" asked Cobalt. "He had shoulder-length blonde hair. He was of average height for a human. When I last saw him, he was wearing a red shirt and gray pants. That is all I remember, and it is not much to go on," said Gek.

"I am sure that Beau's sons will be able to find him, and they are humans, so they will not arouse suspicion from the Regional Mage," said Azure. "What do we do once we locate him?" asked Gek.

"We will need to inform the Fire and Stone Dragons of his location so they do not injure him or his wife when they attack Grotton. It would be best if they delayed their attack on the city until after Donovan and Rachel have departed. As you heard, they are planning on attacking the city of

Middleberg on the other side of the river first, then Grotton, and they will not attack Middleberg until the next full moon," said Cobalt.

"Just remember that Donovan can change into a Great Dragon. If he is in Grotton when the Fire Dragons attack…"

"I understand," said Cobalt. "Now, what can we do about Andrew?" "Andrew has seen all three of us, in both dragon and human form," said Gek. "He would recognize us immediately." "Then I will send Emerald," said Cobalt. "I may have to teach her the spell of change, but she will be less conspicuous."

"Why are we worrying about Andrew?" asked Gek. "If he is on the VALOR, and we do not attack it…" "We just need to know where he is. Sometimes, human magic-users move to different places. If he is still on the VALOR, that would make things much easier than if he were to move to say, Grotton."

"You know that was foolish, chasing after that Stone Dragon, don't you?" asked Rachel. Donovan nodded. "I thought I could just push him into the ocean," Donovan replied. "I tried to burn his wings, but they were fireproof. He was very slow, but very strong. I broke my teeth on his wing." "Is that how you got him into the water?" asked Rachel.

"Yes. Once I broke the forebone in his right wing, he couldn't fly. He hit the water and sank to the bottom," said Donovan. "Do you think that killed him?" "I hope so. The ocean there was pretty deep. The water pressure probably crushed him, but if it didn't, I don't think he could hold his breath long enough to walk back to shore. We were a long way out to sea."

"I'm glad to hear that," said Edward, walking up behind them. "Dad!" said Donovan. "What brings you to Grotton?" "I have news," said Edward, "but as soon as I arrived, Major Gerald told me that you were in the Infirmary again."

"Sorcerer Beryl, from the 5th Regiment, was a Stone Dragon Changed One. We think he vanished a thousand golds from the treasury. When I went to confront him, he changed into a Stone Dragon and flew off, over the water. I couldn't let him get away."

"So I've heard," said Edward. "What was your impression of the Stone Dragon?" "He flew very slowly. That was why I was able to catch him," said Donovan. "His scales were very tough and fireproof. I wasn't able to claw or bite through them. Fortunately, Great Dragon scales are pretty fire-resistant too, although he did burn my hand and clawed my back. I think his tail strike broke some of my ribs too," said Donovan.

"What happened to your teeth?" asked Edward. "I must have broken them when I bit the leading edge of his wing. I think I broke the bone. That's why he fell into the sea." Edward smiled, "That was good thinking, son. It was fortunate that he tried to escape by flying over the water. If he'd headed north…"

"I know," said Donovan. "I didn't think he would be so tough. Why are you here in Grotton?"

"After I listened in on the last Dragon Council meeting, I learned that the dragons are planning to attack the Baizian city of Middleberg on the night of the next full moon; then attack Grotton later. I came to tell you that I need you in Middleberg in the next two weeks to help defend the city," said Edward.

Donovan frowned, "But my vision—" "You said that the vision was probably going to happen while you were in Grotton. If you're in Middleberg, then Grotton is probably safe." "What if they attack both cities at once?" "I'm not sure that there are enough Fire and Stone Dragons left for that, son. We seem to be whittling them down."

"What about Rachel?" asked Donovan. "The Royal Expeditionary Force will remain in Grotton until after the dragons attack. There's no point sending them back to Southport or Kingston yet, and I can't get them to Middleberg in time. Don't worry, you'll be back in plenty of time," said Edward.

"Why me?" asked Donovan. "There must be many more senior Mages in Franconia." "Son, in all of Franconia, you and Rachel are the only magicians, besides me, that have killed a Stone Dragon. And you've killed three now," said Edward.

"Did you learn anything else at the Dragon Council?" asked Donovan. "Yes. The Snow Dragons are out of the fight. It seems that one of our sorcerers, either Stewart or Colby, killed several of them when they attacked the crab fleet. While we have no formal peace agreement with them, their Clan Chief told the Dragon Council that they could not continue," said Edward. "That reminds me, I need to send a Messenger Hawk to Frostberg, recalling Sorcerer Colby to 4th Regiment in Southport. I'm sure he'll be happy to get out of the cold."

"Oh, the Grotton Treasury is short about a thousand golds," said Rachel. "I suspect we have former Sorcerer Beryl to thank for that. I guess we should start replicating coins…" "No need for that," said Edward. "I'll bring a thousand from Kingston when I return. We still haven't decided what to do with all the gold that I found in my new carriage. I don't want the magicians here wearing themselves out replicating coins. They need to start replicating Stone Dragon scales and putting them on the roofs here."

Edward handed Rachel a Stone Dragon scale from his pocket. "Have them start replicating this one. You know what to do." "On that note, I need to get back to Kingston and check on Kathy," said Edward. "How's she doing?" asked Donovan.

"She's tired and grouchy, and is drinking a lot of tomato juice lately," said Edward. "Wait, is she pregnant?" asked Rachel. Edward looked at Donovan, "I thought you told her." "It must have slipped my mind in all the excitement," said Donovan sheepishly.

Emerald clapped her forelegs together and said, *"MORPHIUS."* Instantly, she changed into a naked human female with long blonde hair with green highlights. "Well, this is weird," she said. Cobalt looked on admiringly.

"Stop leering, and hand me that dress," she said. Cobalt reluctantly handed over a white gown that was a bit too short and a bit too snug. Emerald wiggled into the silk dress, saying, "This thing is too tight. I will need something else to wear if I am to move about among the humans without attracting attention."

Cobalt nodded and said, "Yes, I can see that." Emerald blushed, an unusual sensation for a dragon. "We will search for other garments for you if the need arises," said Cobalt. "Just remember to take off your human garments before changing back into a dragon, or you will shred the clothing."

The two dragons were on Acropo, and Cobalt was explaining to Emerald her mission to locate and track the movements of Mage Andrew. He described Andrew's appearance and the HMS VALOR, which, according to his clan, was sailing towards the port of Sundock. "I do not know how long the VALOR will remain in Sundock, or where it will go next," he said. "Most of the human ships are moving south, toward Eastport, but the VALOR and two other ships appear to be going to Sundock."

"You just want me to locate Andrew?" asked Emerald. "Yes. The Dragon Council needs to know where he is so that no one accidentally kills him. Five members of the Council are under a Binding spell to spare any offspring of Wizard Amanda. Right now, there are only two magic-users we need to be concerned about, Andrew and Sorcerer Donovan, but Donovan's mate is pregnant, so there will soon be three humans we must not injure."

"Are you one of the five dragons under the Binding spell?" asked Emerald. "Yes, as are Gek and Azure. The others are Bliz, the Snow Dragon Clan Chief, and Jasper, the Chief of the Stone Dragons," said Cobalt.

As they spoke, another Sea Dragon landed near them and approached. "Are you Cobalt?" he asked. "Yes. I am he. What do you want?" asked Cobalt.

"I am Jade, a Changed One who lives in the human city of Kingston, and I have news for the Dragon Council. It seems that the human magic-users know when and where the Dragon Council meets, and have been spying on your discussions."

Cobalt was shocked by this news, "Are you sure?" Jade said, "A human female who works for the Chief Wizard sought me out to give me this news. I do not know why she would lie to me. She said that whatever the Dragon Council discussed at your last meeting has been compromised."

Chapter Thirty:
NEW PLANS

Cobalt was stunned by the news. *The magic-users were spying on the meetings of the Dragon Council? That would explain much.* "I need to inform the other members of the Dragon Council immediately," he said to Emerald. "The attack on Middleberg is compromised. We need a new plan."

"Do you know how to find the Fire Dragons?" asked Jade. "Unfortunately not," replied Cobalt. "I know that their colony is somewhere in the Grey Mountains on the other side of the river, but nothing else." "Then how have you contacted them before?" asked Emerald.

"The last time, I contacted the Snow Dragons, who went to the Fire Dragons, who then sought out the Stone Dragon Clan. We do not have time for that now." "So, what will you do?" asked Jade.

"I suppose I will just fly in circles over the mountain range and hope a Fire Dragon sees me and comes to investigate," said Cobalt thoughtfully. "If that does not work, we will simply have to call off the attack once we assemble in the oasis west of Middleberg. We cannot attack if the magic-users are expecting us. How long have the humans been spying on us?" he asked Jade.

"I do not know. My informant simply told me that the last meeting of the Dragon Council was compromised. She did not say how long this had been going on," replied Jade.

"Why would a human give this information to a Dragon Changed One?" asked Cobalt suspiciously. Jade smiled, "She wrongly believes that the magic-users were responsible for the death of her daughter, who was killed by the Stone Dragon that infiltrated a mating ceremony inside the Wizards Academy. She does not know that her daughter was actually killed by a Stone Dragon."

"If her information is correct, it would explain a great deal," mused Cobalt. "The humans have been anticipating our actions and thwarting our efforts for some time now. If they had advanced knowledge of our plans…" "So, what use can we make of this information?" asked Emerald. "We can either deceive them at our next meeting by proposing something which we have no intention of doing, or we could seek out the interlopers and kill them," said Cobalt.

"Killing one or two magic-users is insignificant," opined Emerald. "We should use this information to greater effect." "I agree," said Jade. Cobalt noted Jade's youth and said, "Jade, I appreciate your traveling all this way to bring me this information, but this is a matter for the Dragon Council. You should return to Kingston in case your spy has additional information that would be of use to us. Just be aware of the danger to yourself. This human knows you, and where she can find you. She may betray you someday if she ever learns the truth about her daughter."

Jade was troubled by this thought, but he merely nodded and took flight, headed west, back to Kingston.

"Cobalt, the humans believe that we are about to attack Middleberg. What if we attack Grotton instead? We could catch them unaware!" said Emerald. "That is an interesting idea, but we will have to act quickly. It will all depend on how long it takes me to find the Fire and Stone Dragons. In any event, we should probably change the location of future Dragon Council meetings," said Cobalt.

As the HMS VALOR tied up at the pier in Sundock, Andrew noticed that Maria and a tall, older man were standing together by the gangplank. Andrew hefted his seabag onto his shoulder and headed for the pier. As he crossed the deck, the Bos'n blew a three-note tune on his pipe, "BATTLE MAGE ANDREW PERRUCCI, DEPARTING!" he bellowed.

It was then that Andrew noticed that the entire crew was on deck, saluting him as he left the HMS VALOR for the last time. "As you were, men. Thank you," he said, his voice choked with emotion. At the head of the gangplank stood Commodore Matthews.

"Goodbye, Andrew. I'll be sure to look you up the next time we're in port. You have served this ship and the Navy proudly. Admiral Cross has awarded you the Navy Star with

"V" device for valor. That is a rare honor. In almost thirty years at sea, I have only seen two others awarded. I know that mages do not wear medals, but you've earned this. The commodore handed Andrew a slim box with the medal in it and shook his hand vigorously.

As Andrew walked down the gangplank, the crew of the HMS VALOR gave a rousing cheer for their departing Battle Mage. When Andrew reached the dock, he gave Maria a hug, then shook hands with Mage Ben. "She's a fine ship and crew, Ben. Take care of her."

"I'll do my best," said Ben. As Andrew and Maria walked down the pier, headed for home, Andrew couldn't help but hear the Bos'n's pipe again: "BATTLE MAGE, ARRIVING!"

In the harbor, with just her eyes peeking above the wavetops, Emerald watched the ceremony. The Magic-user Andrew was no longer on the VALOR. It appeared that he would be remaining in Sundock with the woman who met him on the pier. *Who was she?* wondered Emerald. If she were Andrew's mate, the dragons might have another human to protect in the future.

Azure had departed for Grotton, leaving Gek behind with the children. He hoped that she would be OK. He was far from comfortable sending Azure into the place where he had been captured, paralyzed, and put in a coach for delivery to the Wizards Academy. If that happened to Azure, he would not be there to rescue her, as she had been for him.

He needed to do something to distract the children, who had sensed his discomfort with the situation. Gek looked at his rapidly growing daughter, Annalise, and decided on something. "Anna, would you like to learn how to breathe fire?"

Anna jumped with joy, "Yes! Yes! Yes!" she said excitedly. Richard looked on angrily. "Come along, Richard, this is something that you will be able to do someday too." Richard brightened at the news, and Anna lost some of her excitement.

"Now Anna, I want you to feel around on the inside of your mouth with your tongue. You should feel some 'lumps' on the roof of your mouth, one in the center, and lumps on each side. Do you feel them?"

"Yes!" said Anna. "Very good. These 'lumps' are really sacs of *inferno*, a flammable liquid. Each sac has a small slit on the front that allows the inferno to be propelled forward out of your mouth. You just open your mouth and push on the sac with your tongue. Dragons do not *breathe* fire, we spit inferno, which we ignite as it leaves our mouths. Do you understand?"

"I spit this goop out, and light it on fire as it comes out of my mouth?" she asked. "Correct. Now, the way to expel the inferno is to push on the sac hard with your tongue, while keeping your mouth open. Swallowing inferno will not hurt you, but I can tell you that it does not taste very good."

Anna nodded her understanding. "Come over here. I want you to spit inferno at that tree over there," said Gek, pointing at a palm tree twenty feet away. Anna worked her jaw back and forth, then spat a small amount of inferno. It went about three feet. Richard laughed, and Anna glared at him.

"This is not an easy thing to learn. When you run out of inferno in one sac, use one of the other two. The inferno comes out at a different angle, depending on which sac you are using. It took Ard weeks to teach me, and I have twice as much inferno as you do, Anna." "Why do you have more than me?" she asked. Because I am a Great Dragon, while you are a Great Sea Dragon. Your mother will teach you how to spit water forcefully enough to knock things over or cut them in half. *I* cannot spit water, only fire, so I have twice as many inferno sacs as you do." Anna nodded her understanding.

"I want you to keep practicing. Once you are able to hit that tree from here, we will move farther away. Once you can hit the tree from the beach, we will practice hitting the tree while you are running and flying. When you can hit the tree while flying, we will practice hitting a moving target." "It sounds hard," said Anna.

"It is *challenging*," said Gek. "But once you learn how, you will never forget. When you can hit a moving target while flying, we will move on to the next lesson." "What is that?" asked Anna. "How to ration your inferno. You see, you only have so much in your sacs. In a fight, you need to use as little as possible to do the job, otherwise, you might run out."

"How do I light it on fire?" she asked. "After you learn how to hit what you are aiming at, with as little inferno as possible. *Then* I will teach you how to light the inferno on fire. This will take time to learn. When you run out of inferno, the sacs will refill overnight, and you can try again tomorrow. Now, practice hitting that tree," said Gek.

Anna practiced until she was out of inferno, but never came close to hitting the tree. She walked back to the cave, exhausted and depressed. "Anna, it has only been one day! It took me three weeks to learn how to hit a tree! This is not something you can learn in one day."

"What am I supposed to do while Annalise practices spitting her goop?" asked Richard. "I'm bored!" Gek thought for a moment, then said, "Tomorrow, I will try to teach you some magic spells. You are young, but you already know the Sleep spell, so maybe you can learn some others." Richard smiled.

Azure landed in the field beside the Cannery and quickly transformed. She was happy that she had some well-fitting human clothes this time. Her first set of clothes had been *way* too tight, her second set was an old, discarded tarp with a hole cut out for her head, and her last set of clothes had become too small while she was pregnant.

She entered the Cannery and found Beau behind the counter, gutting fish. It smelled *wonderful.* "Hello, Beau," she said. Beau looked up, startled, "Azure! What are you doing here? Were you able to rescue Gek? We were curious when you never returned."

"Yes. I was able to rescue Gek, but he was injured when the carriage overturned. The stupid horses would not stop for me. Anyway, we made our escape and returned to Acropo, where I laid my egg. It was a girl. We named her Annalise."

"That is wonderful news," said Beau, "but why have you returned? It is not safe for you here. Where is Gek?" "Gek is on Perfo with our children," said Azure. "Children? I thought you said that you had a baby girl." "I did," said Azure, "but I was pregnant with twins. My human son, Richard, was born a month later. I did not even realize that I was still pregnant. I thought I was just fat from eating for two for so long."

"How have you raised two children of different species?" asked Beau. "It has not been easy. We had been staying with Bruce. He was very kind and helpful." "Was?" asked Beau. "Yes. Bruce died a few weeks ago. That is why we moved to a cave on Perfo."

"That is sad news about Bruce, but he was very old, and living as he did was not very healthy. I always wondered why he did not move back to Southport after Celeste died. Anyway, why have you come back?" asked Beau.

"I need your help," said Azure. "You should know that the Regional Mage and his Enforcers came by the Cannery a week after Gek was taken. He said that we were all too old to enter the Wizards Academy, so he placed a Binding spell on all of us to never use our magic to harm another, and never to counterfeit coins. Then he just let us go. He did not realize that we are Sea Dragon Changed Ones," said Beau.

"Then you can still help me," said Azure, relieved. "We are looking for a magic-user named Donovan and his mate, Rachel. We think they are in the city and we need to find them." "Why?" asked Beau. "Donovan is a descendant of Wizard Amanda. Ard placed a Binding spell on all of the members of the Dragon Council to protect any of Amanda's surviving offspring. The Fire and Stone Dragons are planning to attack Grotton soon, so we need to know if Donovan is here. We have also learned that his mate is pregnant, so we must now protect her too," explained Azure.

"Why not just ask Ard to cancel his Binding spell?" asked Beau. "Ard is dead. He passed away almost a year ago. He said that it was just his time; that he felt no pain, but no strength either. He was over three hundred years old after all," said Azure sadly.

"Is the Binding spell still active?" asked Beau. "Who would know? None of us is willing to take the chance. It could mean our death!" "Hmm, I guess you are right. That is a problem. So, you want us to find this Sorcerer Donovan and his wife if he is in the city?”

“Yes. I thought maybe your sons…” said Azure. “I will certainly enlist their help with the search, but with the Binding spell, Mage Charles no longer considers us a threat, so we will all look. Where will you be?” asked Beau.

“Is there someplace here that I can stay?” asked Azure, looking around. “Not at the Cannery,” replied Beau. “I have too many humans working here. One of them might find you. Let me see, I think Cyan and Cornflower have a spare bedroom where you can stay while we conduct the search. What will you do when we find him?”

“That is a good question,” said Azure. “I am hoping that they will be leaving soon. I believe that they are with a group of soldiers called the Royal Expeditionary Force.” “The Royal Expeditionary Force? Then I can tell you that they are certainly here in Grotton. The Expeditionary Force arrived in Grotton a few days ago,” said Beau.

“Tell me about the Royal Expeditionary Force,” said Azure. “They are the King’s Special Forces. They are all mounted and are said to be the best fighters in the kingdom. It was the Expeditionary Force that killed the Great Dragon near Farmdale a few years ago!”

Azure growled, “That was Gek’s mother! You say they are here now?” “Yes, but I do not know how long they will stay. The Expeditionary Force seldom remains in one place for very long,” said Beau. “Why would Donovan be with them?” wondered Azure.

"Most military units in Franconia have magic-users. It could be that Donovan and Rachel are assigned to the Expeditionary Force. I have never heard of a woman being in the Royal Expeditionary Force, though."

"Please see if you can find out whether Donovan is with them, and, if possible, when they are leaving. It would be best if they were gone before the Fire and Stone Dragons attack," said Azure.

"So, my love, are you ready to return to Kingston and prepare for our wedding?" asked the King. "Yes, Henry. I'm eager to return. This palace is spectacular, but I miss the familiarity of home," said Mage Celeste.

"Well, all of the wedding invitations are out, and I hope that my servants in Kingston have begun preparing the Cathedral. How is your dress coming?" "It's almost done, and I don't think there's room on it for one more pearl! It's lovely, but *heavy*." Henry laughed, "Well, you'll only have to wear it for a short time, darling. Just get through the ceremony, then we can throw it in the fire if you like."

"Never! I think I'll keep it for our daughter. If we have one, that is," said Celeste, blushing. "What a very wise and *frugal* thought," said the King. "I can see that you're not someone that I need to worry about bankrupting the treasury."

"No, my parents were not wealthy. In fact, they were overjoyed when both my sister and I were admitted to the Wizards Academy," said Celeste. "What did they do?" asked Henry. "You seldom mention them."

"My father was a stone mason, and my mother worked as a nurse in the Grotton Infirmary. They met when my father was injured on the job." "Are they still alive?" asked the King. "Sadly, no. They both drowned in a boating accident. Unfortunately, neither of them ever learned to swim." "How sad," said the King, "how old were you?" "We were eighteen when it happened," said Celeste sadly.

"I'm sorry for bringing up such a painful subject," said Henry. Celeste kissed him and said, "It's all right, dear. I should have told you about them sooner."

"So, how soon can you be packed and ready to leave for Kingston?" "How about *tomorrow*?" Henry laughed, "How about next Firstday? It will take at least that long to prepare the ship and load our luggage."

Cobalt flew low over the mountains, hoping to attract the Fire Dragon's attention. He had no idea exactly where the colony was in the Grey Mountains, so he had started in the middle and was slowly working his way north. He was flying as slowly as he could without crashing into the treetops below.

He had passed a large but shallow lake before reaching the mountains. *That must be the hole that the Fire and Stone Dragons mentioned. I guess it's filled with water,* thought Cobalt smugly. *That would certainly upset the humans.* The mountains were heavily forested, and mist rose from the trees, making it difficult to see into all of the narrow valleys and ravines, any one of which could be the entrance to the Fire Dragon colony.

As he turned back for another pass, a scarlet red Fire Dragon rose to meet him. "Are you trying to be seen, Cobalt?" asked Fern. "Actually, yes," replied Cobalt. "We need to talk. Immediately." "Follow me then," said Fern.

Cobalt followed the Fire Dragon down into a narrow glen that he had passed over twice already. There was a narrow slit between the rocks, which he had to turn sideways to navigate, before entering the cavern system of the Fire Dragon Clan. Once inside, he was met by Rose, the Clan Chief. "Cobalt! What brings you here?"

"We need to cancel our attack on Middleberg," said Cobalt without preamble. "Cancel it! Why?" "Because the human magic-users know we are coming." "How could they possibly know that?" asked Rose. "They have been spying on our Dragon Council meetings," whispered Cobalt.

Rose fell silent at this news. "How do you know this?" "A Sea Dragon Changed One in Kingston was approached by someone from the Chief Wizard's office. She overheard them discussing our plans," said Cobalt quietly.

"Why would she betray her kind?" asked Rose. "She mistakenly believes that a magic-user was responsible for her daughter's death, and wants revenge against them." "I find this story very hard to believe," said Rose.

"So did I. But the more I thought about it, the more sense it made. These magic-users have anticipated our every move! Right down to the Snow Dragon attack on their crab fleet! How could they know this? It would be easy if they knew our plans in advance!"

"But how would they know where and when the Dragon Council meets? Only members of the Council know that!" said Rose. "It could have been Victor, Lumen, or that Stone Dragon 'Queen,'" said Cobalt. "The humans may have used some kind of truth-spell on one of them before they died."

"I suppose it is possible," conceded Rose. "So, what should we do?" "Well, we certainly *do not* attack Middleberg on the day of the next full moon. It is undoubtedly a trap. The humans will have dozens of magic-users there, waiting for us," said Cobalt.

"Then what? We do nothing?" asked Rose. "We also discussed an attack on Grotton. If the humans think that we are going to strike Middleberg, they may not be prepared for an attack on Grotton," said Cobalt.

"We need to inform the Stone Dragons at once," said Fern. "Do you know where their colony is?" asked Cobalt. "I have only been there once before," said Rose, "but I think I can find it again. What is your plan, Cobalt?"

"We strike Grotton, two days *before* the full moon. We will attack before the humans expect it, and in a different place. This time will be different!" Where should we meet?" asked Rose. Cobalt thought. "There is a large swamp two hours' flight north of Grotton. It does not smell good, but no humans go there. You could assemble in secret and attack without warning," said Cobalt. Rose grinned wickedly, "For a dragon honor-bound not to attack humans, you have served us well, Cobalt. I will inform you of the results of our assault on Grotton."

Chapter Thirty-One:
BATTLE STATIONS!

"Welcome to Middleberg, Wizard Edward," said James. "Just Edward, please. I hope we have gone beyond the formalities of court." James smiled, "Edward then. Several of your sorcerers have arrived and have been working diligently, replicating everything from Stone Dragon scales to Healing Serum. I can't thank you enough."

"No thanks are necessary, James. We're all in this together. Is everything almost ready?" "The watch towers and civilian shelters have all been reinforced with Stone Dragon scales, and there are Guardbows in all of the towers and on most of the walls. My, I mean our— magicians are busy replicating crossbows and bolts. Is there anything else you think we should be doing?"

Edward smiled, "You seem to have things well in hand. Just don't tire the magicians out too much replicating crossbow bolts. We'll need them fresh and well-rested for the battle." "I understand," said James. "It helps to know exactly when the attack will occur. What are your plans?"

"I'm going to scout out the best location for Wizard Mira and apprentice Lisa to cast their Seemings, then return to Kingston to escort them here," said Edward. "You're going to use an apprentice to cast Seemings?" asked James, shocked.

Edward nodded sadly, "Yes. Lisa, though young, is the most adept student at the Academy when it comes to casting Seemings. Wizard Mira will be with her to shield her in case she is attacked." "Is there anything else you think we should be doing to prepare?" asked Elianna, as she walked up.

"Yes. All of your preparations have surely been noticed by any undetected Changed Ones in the city. I would like you to add a layer of deception to your work. You see, I happen to know that some of the members of the Dragon Council are under a Binding spell to spare any remaining offspring of Wizard Amanda's."

"Who is Wizard Amanda?" asked James. Edward explained about the end of the last war with the dragons and Wizard Amanda's role in healing the surviving dragons. "As far as we know, there are only two remaining members of Amanda's line, my son, Donovan, and Mage Andrew Perrucci," said Edward. "Somehow, the dragons have learned about Andrew and Donovan. Mage Andrew was posted on the HMS VALOR, and the Sea Dragons went to great lengths not to attack his ship. One dragon even sacrificed himself to save Andrew when another Sea Dragon accidentally attacked him."

"Incredible," said James. "But what use can we make of it?" "As you heard at the Wizard's Council, Mage Andrew was just reassigned to be the Regional Mage in Sundock. I want you to spread a rumor that he is here, in Middleberg," said Edward.

"Which may give the dragons pause," said Elianna. "What does Andrew look like?" Edward smiled, then cast a Seeming of Andrew. Elianna grinned and said, "Let me try." The Seeming cast by Elianna was close enough to *be* Andrew. "Very good," said Edward. If you cast that around the city and mention that Mage Andrew from Franconia is here to help you, I'm sure that information will make it to the dragons somehow. During the battle, I would suggest casting a Seeming of Andrew in several of the watch towers to keep them from being attacked."

James just shook his head, "That's extremely sneaky!"

"They are here," said Beau. "Both of them?" asked Azure. "Yes. Mage Donovan and Mage Rachel, along with the Royal Expeditionary Force, are in the city, and there is no indication that they will be leaving anytime soon. In fact, the whole city seems to be bracing for a dragon attack." It was late in the evening when Beau arrived at Cyan's house to give Azure the news.

"Why do you say that?" asked Azure. "The soldiers are fortifying positions along the city walls, and all of the building contractors in Grotton are installing these black shingles on the roofs of the buildings. Do you know what this is?" asked Beau, handing over a Stone Dragon scale.

"Yes," replied Azure, "This is a scale from a Stone Dragon. Why would the humans be putting them on their roofs?" "I heard that it was for fire protection. I expect these scales are fire-proof."

"I am sure that they are. They will also probably provide some protection from falling stones," said Azure. "I will need to inform Cobalt of this development. Are you sure that Donovan and Rachel are remaining in Grotton?"

"My son, Antwan, overheard two of the Expeditionary Force soldiers talking in a tavern. They were very glad to be staying in one place for a while. Apparently, they have been on the road for months. The soldiers were glad to be able to get a good meal in a tavern and flirt with the women."

"This is troubling. Do you know where Donovan and Rachel are in the city?" asked Azure. "Well, the Royal Expeditionary Force is staying in the garrison, which is on the east side of town, near the docks. I suppose, if you avoided attacking the fort, you would not have to worry about injuring Donovan or Rachel."

"That is a good idea! That is, unless they change into Great Dragons again," mused Azure. "Then just do not attack any Great Dragons," suggested Beau. "You have told me that this attack will be carried out by the Fire and Stone Dragons. The only Great Dragon in the attack will be Gek, right?"

Azure smiled. "You are a brilliant strategist, Beau. I will relay that suggestion to Cobalt." "When will the attack occur? I need to warn the other Changed Ones to take shelter," said Beau. "I believe that the Fire and Stone Dragons are going to attack the city of Middleberg, on the other side of the Amber River, before moving on to Grotton. I will try to get word to you. Now, I must return and speak to Cobalt. Thank you, Beau."

Azure left out the back door, disrobed, and transformed. She flew into the night sky, hoping that she could reach Acropo in time with her information.

"Mage Andrew is no longer on the VALOR," said Emerald. "It seems that he has been assigned as the Sundock Regional Mage." "Are you sure?" asked Cobalt. "Yes. I saw him depart the VALOR, and another magic-user, this one taller and older, arrive to take his place. There was some kind of ceremony as Andrew departed."

"How do you know he will be the Regional Mage?" "I transformed and went into the town. Everyone seemed very happy that a new mage had been assigned. Additionally, Andrew and his mate, Maria, have a dwelling on the outskirts of town, near the blacksmith shop," said Emerald.

"This is good news. As long as Andrew remains in Sundock, we need not fear any harm coming to him. I believe that there are also several Fire and Stone Dragon Changed Ones still in Sundock," said Cobalt. "I thought that the Fire and Stone Dragons were supposed to stay on the west side of the Amber River," protested Emerald.

"They were," said Cobalt, "but apparently, that agreement meant little to those Clans. It makes no difference now, since the Dragon Council decided to allow any dragon to live anywhere. It is probably a good thing. At least our dragon cousins can keep an eye on Mage Andrew."

"Unless he discovers them," said Emerald.

"What will you do now?" "I need to speak with Gek. The Fire and Stone Dragons will be assembling in the swamp north of Grotton for their attack in two days. He needs to be there," said Cobalt. "Who will watch over his children?" asked Emerald.

"I suppose that I will. Unless you are volunteering for the job?" Emerald shuddered at the thought, "No. Annalise is a good dragon, but I have no desire or knowledge of how to care for a human child." "Neither do I," said Cobalt. "I hope Azure returns soon."

"Is *now* soon enough?" asked Azure, landing beside them.

"Azure! What good timing you have! I was just telling Emerald..." "I heard you," said Azure, "and I have news. Both Donovan and his mate, Rachel, are in Grotton. Beau says that the town is preparing for a dragon attack. They are placing Stone Dragon scales on the roofs of their buildings to make them fireproof. Beau says that it is likely that Donovan and Rachel will fight from inside the fort on the east side of Grotton, and that if the Fire and Stone Dragons avoid the fort, there is little chance of injuring or killing them."

"What if they transform into Great Dragons?" asked Cobalt. "Beau had a solution to that problem as well: tell the Fire and Stone Dragons not to attack any Great Dragons they see. Gek and Ig should be the only Great Dragons on our side. Any other Great Dragons could be Donovan or Rachel."

Cobalt nodded his understanding. "Then we need to get to Perfo and inform Gek. He needs to leave immediately to meet up with the attacking force."

Donovan sat and fidgeted in the 5th Regiment's conference room. It was Firstday, only five days from the full moon on Endday, and Wizard Lake had called a meeting for all of the magicians in the city. "The 1st Squadron of 2nd Fleet will arrive tomorrow, adding their four ships to the city's defenses. The ships are all equipped with four Mark 1 Seabows, and each has a sorcerer, except the flagship, the HMS INVINCIBLE, which has a Battle Mage assigned. The squadron is under the command of Commodore Hunter, and he will be meeting with me once they arrive," said Wizard Lake.

"Battle Mage Donovan, will you repeat what you have seen about the attack on Grotton?" asked Wizard Lake.

"I saw dozens of dragons, mixed, Fire, Great, and Stone Dragons, swirling above the city, which appeared to be in flames. There were too many Great Dragons, so some of what I saw must be magicians, changed into Great Dragons. As far as we know, there is only one Great Dragon, Gek, who has been seen by anyone in Franconia. But Gek was present at the attack on Three Forks, and he caused considerable damage." The assembled magicians began whispering amongst themselves.

"Donovan, you recently fought a Stone Dragon. What can you tell us about the encounter?" "Stone Dragons are fireproof, so don't waste your inferno on them; their scales are incredibly tough. I was only able to kill the one I fought by biting into the leading edge of one of his wings, breaking the fore-bone, which caused him to fall into the ocean. Stone Dragons can't swim. The best way to kill a Stone Dragon is to enclose it in a protective shield and suffocate it; but they have to be on the ground for this technique to work."

"Didn't someone kill a Stone Dragon in Weaton a while back?" asked Sorceress Laura. "Yes," replied Donovan, "Sorcerer Justin fired a Blast spell into the dragon's forehead at point-blank range. He died from the power drain," said Donovan.

"What else do we know about Stone Dragons?" asked Mage Charles. "They are black or dark gray in color. They have less inferno than either Fire or Great Dragons, they are the slowest of the dragon breeds, both in the air and on the ground. Other dragons consider them slow-witted," said Donovan.

"And, what can you tell us about the Fire Dragons?" asked Wizard Lake. "Fire Dragons are red in color. They have the most inferno of any of the dragons. I killed a Fire Dragon by grabbing his back and carrying him high into the air as I shredded his wings with my hind feet. Then I dropped him. He did not survive the impact with the ground." The magicians murmured their approval.

"Donovan killed the other by spitting burning inferno into his mouth," said Rachel. "While dragons breathe fire, they can't *breathe* fire, if you get what I mean. If one of them opens its mouth too wide, you can spit a burning inferno into it to kill them. Fire Dragon scales are generally fire-proof as well."

"What do we know about Great Dragons?" asked Wizard Lake. "They are gold in color, and are the fastest fliers, other than the Snow Dragons. They are the biggest of the dragon breeds and are generally considered the smartest. Their scales are tough, but can be penetrated by crossbow bolts and Blast spells," said Donovan.

"As I understand it, we have a truce with both the Sea and Snow Dragons, so they should not be participating in this attack," said Wizard Lake. "We know that the dragons plan to attack the Baizian city of Middleberg this coming Endday, so we have some time before they will strike Grotton. If we can deal them a decisive blow in Baize, we may forestall any further attacks. Battle Mage Donovan will be leaving today for Middleberg. Good luck Donovan."

"Thank you, sir," replied Donovan. "The last thing that I would like to add is that, in my vision, much of the city was in flames, but I believe that some of those flames were Seemings. If we cast Seemings, the dragons may not waste their limited inferno on buildings that they believe are already on fire. I understand that Wizard Mira, the Seemings and Changes Instructor from the Wizards Academy, will be joining us here before the attack to assist us. That is, if she survives the attack on Middleberg."

"Another thing," said Wizard Lake, "recent dragon attacks on our fleet have involved dragons under Concealment shields, dropping heavy stones or other objects on our ships. This is a very difficult attack to counter, particularly at night. We've had some success deflecting these stones, but targeting a Concealed Dragon with a crossbow, Guardbow, or Seabow is nearly impossible. Unless the dragon is visible, or flying very low, it's better to just save the bolts."

"Over the next two days, Majors Adams and Gerald, Admiral Cross, and I will be assigning battle positions to every magician and soldier in the city. I understand there is currently an effort to install Stone Dragon scales on the roofs of our critical buildings, and that effort must continue night and day. Magicians, you need a sleep plan! You need to be at your best when the dragons attack," said Wizard Lake.

"Does anyone else have any suggestions?" Donovan raised his hand. "Yes, Mage Donovan?" "Sir, during my Sorcerer's Test, Wizard Daniel indicated that each city has a list of all of the 'rogue' magicians that were too old to enter the Wizards Academy when they were discovered by the Regional Mages. Do you think we should enlist their help as well?"

Wizard Lake looked at Mage Charles, who had a surprised and hopeful look on his face. "What a brilliant idea!" exclaimed Mage Charles. "Wizard Daniel is absolutely correct! I have a list of about sixty rogue magicians in Grotton! Some of them may have moved away since we identified them, but many should still be here!"

"What are their capabilities?" asked Wizard Lake. "They vary, of course, sir. Many of them were caught counterfeiting coins, which means they know the Replicate spell. We could put those to use making crossbow bolts. But most of them should be able to conjure Seemings!"

"Please begin contacting these rogue magicians immediately after this meeting and determining their capabilities," said Wizard Lake. "You are dismissed." Mage Charles and his three sorcerers left quickly, and the other magicians began filing out of the conference room. Wizard Lake came over to Donovan. "You may have just saved the city with that last suggestion, Donovan. Sixty magicians! I had completely forgotten about them. Well done!"

Donovan blushed, "Thank you, sir. I'm still not convinced that the dragons will attack Middleberg first." "But, didn't Wizard Edward listen in on the last meeting of the Dragon Council?" "Yes, sir. He did. I'm just not buying it. The dragons may have changed their minds, or it may have been a trick, if they somehow knew we were spying on them," said Donovan.

Wizard Lake looked troubled by this idea, but he said, "Nevertheless, orders are orders. Besides, with your idea about the rogue magicians, we should have an overwhelming magical force to face the dragons with. You've proven yourself as a fierce fighter, but one more Battle Mage really shouldn't make that much of a difference," said Wizard Lake.

Donovan nodded, "Sir, there's one other thing I just thought of. We're going to need a way to distinguish dragons from changed magicians, so our forces on the ground don't attack friendlies." "You're right. I should have thought of that. What do you suggest?" Donovan thought for a moment, "Well, it would have to be something that can be seen from above and below. We don't want magicians attacking each other. How about something painted on their wings?"

"Like what?" "How about 'RAF' for Royal Air Force?"

"I hit it!" screamed Annalise. "Daddy, did you see? I hit the tree!" "I saw," said Gek. "Good job! Now back up another twenty paces and try again." This time, the unlit inferno fell short of the tree.

"Damn it!" said Anna. "You need to push *harder* on the sac to get more range, Anna. Do not get discouraged. I told you, it takes a lot of practice," said Gek.

"Now, while you work on that, I am going to try and teach your brother the Dig spell." "Will you teach me too?" "Yes. Once you are out of the inferno. We will be over there," said Gek, pointing to a nearby sand dune.

Anna pouted briefly, then resumed her inferno-spitting practice, while Gek and Richard moved off a short way. "Now, Richard, all magic spells involve a word and a gesture. Some gestures are impossible for dragons to make, so we cannot perform all of the magic spells that humans can. Do you understand?"

"Yes," said Richard. "What is the Dig spell for?" "Using the Dig spell, you can dig holes in the ground," explained Gek. "Why would I want to dig a hole in the ground?" asked Richard. Gek sighed.

"Consider our new home; a dragon probably used the Dig spell to make some of the caverns and sleeping chambers. If you are outside and it starts to rain, you can dig a hole in a cliff and go inside to get out of the rain or snow."

"OK. How do I conjure the spell?" asked Richard. "The word is *'ENTRENCHO,'* said Gek. "Say it, please."

"ENTRENCH," said Richard. "No," said Gek, "the word is *'ENTRENCHO,'* you forgot the 'O'. The spell will not work unless you say the word precisely. Try again."

"ENTRENCHO," said Richard. "Correct," said Gek. "Now, the motion is to make a scooping gesture with your right hand. If you try it using your left hand, it will not work. Show me the gesture without the incantation." Richard demonstrated a scooping gesture several times before Gek was satisfied.

"When you say the word and perform the gesture, a hole will appear in the ground," said Gek. "How deep will the hole be?" asked Richard. "As deep as you think about making it," replied Gek. "Are you ready to try the spell?" Richard nodded eagerly.

"ENTRENCHO," said Richard, making the scooping gesture. A three-foot deep hole in the sand appeared, and Richard collapsed on the ground. "Richard!" said Gek. In the distance, Anna laughed.

Richard sat up groggily, shaking his head. "Why am I so tired?" he asked. "I forgot to tell you that performing magic spells drains power from the conjurer. I am sorry, I learned this spell as a dragon. I forgot that humans are weaker than dragons. You will get stronger, the more you practice. Rest here for a while, then we will try again."

Gek moved back to Anna, who was growing frustrated at being unable to hit the tree again. "Do not be discouraged, Anna. This takes time to learn."

"You are starting them young, I see," said Cobalt, as he and Azure landed in the sand beside Gek.

"Azure! Cobalt! Welcome home! Am I ever glad to see you!" said Gek. "I imagine so," said Azure. "Especially since you need to leave tomorrow to get to the swamp."

"The swamp? Why in the world would I ever go there again?" asked Gek.

"The humans have been spying on our Dragon Council meetings," said Cobalt quietly. "They know that we planned to attack Middleberg on the night of the full moon. So, we are going to strike Grotton two days before the full moon to surprise them! The Fire and Stone Dragons will congregate in the swamp prior to the attack in three days. You need to meet them there."

WIZARD MIRA

Chapter Thirty-Two:
DISOBEYING ORDERS

Donovan paced about the room in a state of agitation. "What's wrong?" asked Rachel. "I can't go to Middleberg! I just know that the dragons are going to attack here, and soon!" "Another vision?" asked Rachel.

"No. I have tried casting the spell of Foresight several times, and it always shows me the same thing! It's maddening! What good is this damn spell if it won't tell me *when* something will happen?" said Donovan.

"The spell has never failed you," said Rachel. "What are you going to do?" "I'm going to leave tomorrow morning, but I plan to land a short distance north of the city and wait," said Donovan. "Wait for what?"

"Wait for the dragons to attack." "What if you're wrong?" asked Rachel. "If you don't get to Middleberg, and they are attacked, your father might bust you right back down to sorcerer and assign us to Frostberg!" "I know," said Donovan softly. "I don't know what to do."

Rachel sat beside him on the sofa. "Are you sure that the dragons are going to attack here first?" "I am. More than that, I think that if I'm not here, you're going to be injured. I told you before, *I will risk no harm to you*," said Donovan emotionally.

Rachel smiled at the memory of the scavenger hunt that Donovan had led her on on the day he proposed. "Then you must follow your heart and stay," she said. "Even if we get sent to Frostberg?" he asked. "If we get sent to Frostberg, at least I will have you to keep me warm."

Edward landed back at the Wizards Academy boat dock just after dawn on Twoday. He transformed quickly, opened the portal, and walked to Wizard Noland's cottage. The door opened before he knocked. "Come on in, Edward," said Wizard Noland. "I'll be right with you."

Edward took a seat in the parlor, exhausted from the flight from Middleberg and all of the traveling from place to place in dragon form that he had been doing lately. "You look weary, my friend," said Noland, handing him a cup of tea.

"I *am* weary, Michael. All of this jumping about is tiring. Thank goodness you determined that we could use the Change spell to transform into dragons. Messenger Hawks would be much too slow for this crisis," said Edward.

"So, how are the preparations going in Middleberg?" asked Noland. "I think they're as ready as they can be. There are three Baizian wizards and a dozen mages and sorcerers, plus the six sorcerers I sent them. Once Mira and

I arrive, there will be five wizards in the city." "Don't forget about Donovan and Level Two Lisa," said Noland.

"I haven't forgotten them," said Edward. "I just hope Donovan leaves Grotton soon enough so that he has some time to rest before the dragons attack. I know he doesn't like the idea of leaving Rachel behind. But she couldn't make the trip in her condition."

"How is she doing? Asked Noland. "According to Donovan, she is grouchy, beautiful, and sick all of the time. She had a craving for water chestnuts the last time he was here," said Edward.

"How far along is she?" "I'm not sure, Donovan first noticed her condition after he healed her after a Sea Dragon attacked their ship on the way from Sundock to Eastport. The dragon tried to knock Rachel into the sea with a blast of water. Donovan tethered her to stop her slide, then adhered her to the deck to keep her from going overboard."

"Wait, Donovan glued her to the deck?" Edward nodded, and both wizards laughed at the thought. "Anyway, after Donovan killed the dragon with a well-placed shot from a Seabow, he took Rachel below deck to heal her. He didn't realize that she was pregnant and passed out again. Healing a mother and child takes more than twice the power," said Edward.

"Anyway, I'm going to stop by my office and check on Kathy, then go home and get some sleep. Please have Mira and Lisa ready to depart at first light tomorrow. It's a two-day flight to Middleberg, and I've never tried flying with someone on my back. Have you worked out some sort of harness for Lisa?" asked Edward.

"Yes. It's just some leather straps, but it should work. Actually, Lisa is very excited to go flying on a dragon," said Noland.

Edward rose unsteadily, and Wizard Noland held out his hand to steady him. "Would you like some Stamina Serum?" he asked. Edward shook his head, "My water bottle is full of the stuff. It's all that's been keeping me on my feet lately, and I need to stop drinking it."

"I understand," said Wizard Noland, "just make sure you arrive in Middleberg in time to get some rest before the attack." "It's still Twoday, right?" asked Edward wearily. Noland nodded. "Then if we leave tomorrow, I'll be able to sleep on Foursday night before the dragons attack on Endday."

Edward left the Academy and walked swiftly to his office. Despite the early hour, he found Harriet at her desk and Kathy in the office. "Edward! Welcome back! You look terrible!" said Kathy.

Edward smiled, "That's not exactly what a husband wants to hear after he returns from a long absence." Kathy crossed the room and gave him a passionate kiss. "Better?" she asked, playfully. "Much better," replied Edward. He sank down onto the sofa with a sigh. "You really do look weary," said Kathy with concern in her voice.

"I *am* weary. Flying around from here to Grotton, to Southport, then Middleberg and back is tiring," said Edward. "Would some Stamina Serum help?" asked Kathy. Edward shook his head, "No. I've had too much already. I just came by to check on you, then I'm going home to get some sleep. I have to leave with Wizard Mira and Level Two Lisa for Middleberg at dawn tomorrow."

"Are you sure you don't want me to come with you?" "Positive," said Edward. "I can't begin to imagine how taxing it would be to conjure killing spells while pregnant. Besides, you need to fill in for Wizard Mira at the Academy while she's gone. How long has it been since you taught a Seemings class?"

Kathy smiled, "It's been *ages,* thank you for reminding me. I'm sure I'll do fine. There is one thing that we need to do before you go." "What's that?" asked Edward.

"We need to talk to Harriet. We've put it off for too long already," said Kathy. Edward groaned, "You're right. It's just not a conversation I'm looking forward to."

Kathy rose from the sofa and went to the door. "Harriet, can you make three cups of tea and join us? There's something we need to talk to you about before Edward leaves again."

Harriet felt a moment of panic, thinking that her betrayal had been discovered. Then she realized that Edward had not even been in the city for the last three weeks, so there was no way that he could have learned of her meeting with the

Sea Dragon Changed One. She made tea quickly and entered the office with a smile.

"Here you go. Wizard Edward, you poor man, you look absolutely dreadful!" "So I've been told," said Edward with a smile. "Thank you for your concern. I plan to go home and get some rest soon, but there's something that we've been meaning to discuss with you."

"Harriet, this concerns how your daughter, Doris, died," said Edward gently. "Wizard Noland told me that one of her heating elements exploded and killed her," said Harriet. "I know, and I'm sorry that we had to keep the truth from you. The fact is that one of the subcontractors that Doris hired for the event was a Stone Dragon Changed One. During the reception, my son, Donovan, detected the scent of a dragon and shouted a warning. The Changed One transformed into a dragon and began spewing fire at everyone. Doris was closest to him, and Wizard Noland was not able to get a protective shield around her in time to save her. I'm so sorry."

"Wait, you mean that it was a dragon that killed my little girl? Why didn't you tell me?" she asked. "Because if news of a dragon attack got out, there would have been panic in Kingston. We had to cast a Secrecy spell on all of the attendees to keep the news from spreading. The exploding heating element was the best explanation we could come up with to account for the burns on your daughter's body. Again, I'm so sorry."

Harriet put her head in her hands and sobbed, "What have I done?" "I don't understand," said Edward.

"I never believed the 'exploding heating element' explanation," said Harriet through her tears. "I always figured that it was some magician's spell gone awry. I blamed Wizard Noland for her death! I figured that was why he was giving me money to pay my rent, out of a sense of guilt." "No. It's true that Michael felt sorry for your loss, and tried to help you, but he bore no guilt for her murder by the dragon," said Edward.

"Then I've done a terrible thing," said Harriet. "What are you talking about?" asked Kathy. "I overheard you talking about spying on the Dragon Council meeting…. So I, I— told a Sea Dragon Changed One about it."

Edward was shocked by this admission, "Why would you do such a thing?" he yelled. "Because I wanted to hurt you all! I believed that you killed my baby!" said Harriet.

Edward's head was spinning. *The dragons knew that their meeting had been compromised. What would they do?* "I've got to leave immediately. Donovan was right, the dragons are going to attack Grotton, not Middleberg. I've got to find Wizard Mira and Lisa and get to Grotton before it's too late!"

"What about Harriet?" asked Kathy. Edward thought quickly, then cast a Silence spell around them, "Put some Truth Serum in her tea and find out about this Sea Dragon Changed One. She has betrayed us, no matter what her reasoning. She can't work here anymore. Perhaps Wizard

Noland can find her a place on the Academy staff where she can do no more harm. I don't have time to think about that right now. I've got to go." He gave Kathy a quick kiss, then bolted for the door.

Gek landed in the Jade Swamp on Twoday afternoon. The swamp still smelled bad. It had only taken a few passes over the swamp to locate the Fire and Stone Dragons, who were congregated on a small island in the center of the immense swamp. There were ten Fire Dragons and Six Stone Dragons. Ig was nowhere to be found.

"Rose! Is everyone ready?" "Well met, Gek. Yes, my Clan is ready, as are the Stone Dragons. Unfortunately, we were unable to find Ig in time. He is probably waiting in the oasis west of Middleberg, wondering what is keeping us."

"No matter. Our surprise should be complete. When do we attack? How about right after moonset tonight, during the darkest time of the night? We will begin by dropping stones while concealed, then follow up by burning the entire city to the ground, as well as any ships that are in the port."

"There is a problem with that plan," said Gek. "What is that?" asked Rose. "Sorcerer Donovan and his mate, Rachel, are in Grotton." Rose cursed, "How can we avoid them?" she asked.

"We have a Sea Dragon Changed One in the city who told Azure that Donovan and Rachel are in the army fort on the east side of the city. As long as we avoid that section of the town, we should be safe," said Gek. "What if they change into Great Dragons?" "Then *I* will deal with them, without killing either of them," said Gek. Just tell your Clan not to attack any Great Dragons they see," said Gek.

"I like it. I will inform the Stone Dragons. I just hope they can remember such a simple instruction: 'Kill the humans. Leave the Great Dragons alone.'"

Edward entered the Wizards Academy in a rush, calling for Noland, Mira, and Lisa. Noland appeared quickly. "Edward, what's wrong?" "We have been betrayed. Harriet, Doris's mother, whom I hired as my receptionist, informed an unbound Sea Dragon Changed One about our eavesdropping on the Dragon Council meetings," said Edward.

"Why would she do that?" asked Noland. "She blamed us for her daughter's death and wanted revenge. When I got to my office a few minutes ago, Kathy and I told her what really happened to Doris, and Harriet confessed her betrayal." "Where is she now?" asked Noland angrily. "Kathy is plying her with Truth Serum to get information about the Sea Dragon Changed One we missed. I told her to bring Harriet here later, and that you might find her a position on the staff where she can't betray us again."

Noland nodded, "I'll have her mucking the stalls in the stable for the rest of her life," he said. "What are your plans?"

"I think Donovan was right. The dragons think they've tricked us into believing that they're going to attack Middleberg in three days, but I think they're actually going to attack Grotton instead! Mira, Lisa, and I need to leave immediately!"

As Edward was explaining, Wizard Mira and Level Two Lisa approached. "Mira, Lisa, we need to leave immediately. I think the dragons are going to attack Grotton instead of Middleberg. Gather whatever you need and meet me at the marina. Hurry!" The two women raced for their respective quarters.

Edward and Noland walked briskly to the boat dock and waited for Mira and Lisa. Edward took a deep drink from his water bottle, and Noland waved a cautionary finger at him. "I know, Michael. Hopefully, I will have time to rest once I get to Grotton. It's still three days until the full moon, if the dragons keep to their original schedule."

Before Lisa and Mira arrived, Edward disrobed and changed into a Great Dragon. Once the women arrived, Noland and Mira affixed the leather straps and helped Lisa climb onto Edward's back, then Mira changed into a Great Dragon. "Hang on tight, Lisa," said Edward. "Michael, send a Messenger Hawk to King Donald, informing him of our plans. I hope I am right about this." Edward grinned, "Donovan was right, dragons cannot use contractions."

With that, Edward leapt into the sky, followed by Mira, with Lisa screaming with delight.

Chapter Thirty-Three:
GROTTON

Donovan landed in a field just north of Grotton. He was taking a huge risk, and he hoped he was right about this. If he were wrong, he'd have a lot of explaining to do to his father and the other magicians. He changed back into human form, wrapped himself up in his Concealment cloak, and settled down to wait.

He was unsure about what he was waiting for. There was no way, even with a Hearing Enhancement, that he would be able to hear an attack on Grotton from so far away. He laid back on the ground, resting. The last few days had been exhausting, both physically and emotionally. He had spent a great deal of time replicating iron crossbow bolts for the soldiers of the Royal Expeditionary Force. Many of them were uncomfortable with the idea of their Battle Mage leaving them with a dragon attack on the horizon. Donovan had done his best to reassure them that he would be back before the attack, but they could see his doubts.

He drifted off to sleep briefly, coming awake when he heard the sound of beating wings. Looking up, he saw a Great Dragon, circling over the Jade Swamp. *That must be the dragon that pushed the treasury building over on us,* he thought. He watched as the dragon descended, landing somewhere in the swamp. *Why would a dragon land in the swamp?* he wondered.

He briefly considered entering the swamp to see what the dragon was up to, before deciding against it. Even with his Concealment cloak, splashing through that mire would alert the dragon long before Donovan got close enough to see what was going on.

So why would a dragon land in the swamp? Food? There was probably something in there that a dragon could eat, but the swamp didn't seem like a likely hunting ground for dragons. *It was certainly a good place to hide,* thought Donovan. No human would enter the swamp willingly. At least not since the abortive attempt by the king to build a road through it all those years ago. Some idiot engineer had convinced the King that it would be a good idea to have a road between Smithville and Kingston, right through the Jade Swamp.

Donovan remembered his father saying that the Road Crews had spent a year trying to carve a path through the swamp, but had only succeeded in building a few small islands in it. The plan to build bridges between the islands proved impossible. The swamp was too deep. When the expensive project failed, the engineer ended up serving on a Road Crew himself.

A place to hide. That had to be it. Dragons were hiding in the swamp in preparation for an attack on Grotton! Donovan's mind raced, *should he rush back to Grotton to warn them? How long would the dragons stay in the swamp? Probably not long,* he thought. *They were supposed to attack on the night of the full moon. So why was the Great Dragon here now?* If it were up to him, he wouldn't spend any more time than necessary in that stinking swamp.

Donovan lay there, pondering the situation, until, unpredictably, he fell asleep.

An exhausted Edward landed in Grotton late on Twoday afternoon. Lisa had thoroughly enjoyed her dragon ride, but was much more stoic now. Edward found Wizard Lake in the garrison, giving instructions to the magicians that had just arrived with 1st Squadron. "Edward! What brings you to Grotton? I expected you to be preparing for the attack on Middleberg. Hello, Mira, always good to see you," said Wizard Lake.

"Hello, Bill. I've got bad news, the dragons know that we eavesdropped on their last Dragon Council meeting, and I believe that they've changed their plan and are going to attack Grotton soon." This news was startling, but Wizard Lake took it in stride. "So, Donovan was right." Edward nodded, "He was. Where is he?" "Donovan? He left Grotton this morning for Middleberg. He argued, but I told him that 'orders are orders.' He wasn't very happy when he left."

"Damn!" said Edward. "Well, how are the preparations for the attack coming?" "We're ready. Especially after

Donovan's brilliant idea." "What idea was that?" asked Edward.

"Why, to enlist the help of all of the rogue magicians in the city. Mage Charles is out rounding up the last few right now," said Wizard Lake. "The rogue magicians? I completely forgot about them! How many of them are there in Grotton?" asked Edward.

"Mage Charles says there are about sixty on the rolls. We've been using most of them to replicate crossbow bolts, but we've also taught a fair few how to conjure Seemings, shields, and Blast spells. They're all working hard." Edward smiled. "You're right, that was a brilliant idea. I should have thought of it myself."

"So, now that you're here, what would you like to do?" asked Bill. "I need to find a good vantage point for Wizard Mira and Level Two Lisa to cast Seemings from. Then I need some sleep. Stamina Serum is the only thing keeping me on my feet right now, and I don't want to be worn out when the dragons come."

Wizard Lake thought, then said, "I've got just the spot. There's a high, flat rooftop that overlooks the harbor. You can see most of the city from there, in addition to the 1st Squadron ships along the pier." "That sounds perfect," said Edward with a yawn. "Can you take Mira and Lisa there? I'm afraid that I just can't keep my eyes open any longer."

"Of course, Edward. There's an empty office with a cot, just through there. Why don't you get some sleep? I'll escort Mira and Lisa to their posts." Edward nodded and headed into the empty office. He was asleep almost as soon as his head hit the pillow.

Mage Charles and Sorceress Laura entered the Cannery together, looking for the old, rogue magicians that Mage Charles had placed under a Binding spell a couple of years ago. He had saved them for last because of their age. He really didn't expect that they'd be much help against the dragons.

"Where is the owner?" Mage Charles asked. The floor supervisor shrugged, "I'm sorry, sir, but I haven't seen Beau for a couple of days. He may be ailing. He's no spring chicken, you know." Mage Charles grumbled his concurrence. "The last time I was here, Beau had several friends with him, but we can't seem to locate any of them. Do you know where they might be?"

"I'm sorry, sir, but no. I know who you're talking about, but I haven't seen any of Beau's friends around lately. They're all too old to work here, you know."

Mage Charles and Laura left the Cannery. He wasn't really expecting much from the six-aged rogue magicians, but he did find it odd that, of all the rogue magicians in the city, only these six were missing.

Donovan woke with a start at the sound of flapping wings. A *lot* of flapping wings. He looked up at the dark night sky and could just barely detect the distortion caused by Concealed Dragons. He lost count after about ten, and he wasn't sure how many flew over his head while he slept.

Fool! he thought. *How could he let himself fall asleep? He must have been more tired than he thought.* Once the last of the distortions flew overhead, Donovan counted to ten, slowly, then changed into a Great Dragon, remembering to picture the letters 'RAF' on the top and bottom of his wings in black print. After the change, he examined his wings. The letters were upside-down. *Close enough,* he thought. He cast a Concealment shield over himself, and took off, following the dragons towards Grotton.

It was much harder flying with a Concealment shield. The power drain was significant. *And I'm not even carrying a stone,* thought Donovan. He flapped harder, wanting to gain altitude and get above the Concealed Dragons. It was much easier to see the distortions against the backdrop of the ground than the moonless night sky.

From above, it was easy to see the distortions caused by the Concealed Dragons and pick out the slower-moving Stone Dragons from the faster Fire and Great Dragons. *At this pace, the attack would come in two waves. The Fire and*

Great Dragons would reach Grotton first, then the slower Stone Dragons a few minutes later.

The dragons were attacking earlier than anticipated, and Donovan hoped that someone in the city was standing watch. He realized that the first wave would undoubtedly be able to drop their load of stones before the defenses were ready. Those stones could kill and injure many of the defenders. Donovan decided that he had to warn the people of Grotton before the dragons attacked. He flapped harder, overtaking the Stone, and then the Fire Dragons. *I have to get to the city first,* he thought.

The dragons had no trouble finding stones to drop on the unsuspecting city. The island was made almost entirely of large stones. The dragons did not understand why there were big rocks in the swamp, but they were grateful that there were. "Remember to focus your attacks on the merchant ships and warehouses," Gek reminded the dragons. "The navy ships have spear-throwers that are deadly to dragons. The ships and buildings should burn easily, since they are made of wood."

"Our goal is to strike quickly and depart," Rose reminded them. "If there is little or no resistance, burn the entire city, but Grotton has quite a few magic-users, so guard yourselves. I expect to take them by surprise. Meet back in the swamp after the attack. We may re-arm and strike them again."

Each dragon selected a large stone, the heaviest that they could carry. The extra weight would make their flight speed slower, but since the humans were not expecting them, it should not matter. Once all of the dragons had chosen a projectile, Rose nodded, and the dragons took flight, casting their Concealment shields once they were airborne.

They flew directly south, knowing that the lights of the city would be visible as they got closer. This was going to be *epic!*

As Donovan raced past the lead dragon, he dropped his Concealment shield and increased speed. Without the power drain from the shield, he was able to increase his speed, ensuring that he would reach the sleeping city before the dragons.

As he reached the outskirts of Grotton, he conjured a Voice Enhancement spell and began shouting, "DRAGON ATTACK! TO ARMS! MAN YOUR POSTS! THE DRAGONS ARE COMING! DRAGON ATTACK!" Donovan repeated the warning as he flew over the city, sweeping over the garrison and the Navy ships. He was gratified to see several protective shields spring up over the 1st Squadron's ships. *At least someone was awake and alert.*

Edward was asleep on the cot in the Supply Sergeant's office when he heard Donovan's voice. He sprang from the bed and ran for the tower, shouting for the soldiers to wake up, gather their crossbows, and get to their stations on the battlements. He ran to the rooftop where Wizard Mira and Level Two Lisa were awake, but bleary-eyed.

"The dragons are coming," he said. "I don't know why they're early, but we have time. You must wait until they begin flaming the town before casting your Seemings, or it won't fool them. Mira nodded her understanding, but Lisa was shaking with fear. Edward put a comforting hand on Lisa's shoulder. "This is what it means to be a Sorceress. It is all alright to be afraid, as long as you do what is expected of you. We are all afraid," said Edward quietly. Lisa nodded.

"Protect her," Edward whispered to Mira as he left the rooftop. Mira nodded grimly. Edward ran down to the courtyard, taking another swig of Stamina Serum from his water bottle, then emptying it and refilling the bottle with Healing Serum, and taking a healthy swallow of that as well.

He found Wizard Lake in the courtyard, giving orders to the magicians who were tasked with changing into Great Dragons and fighting in the air. "Remember to think of having the letters 'RAF' on both sides of your wings, so we can tell friend from foe," he reminded them. "Good luck."

When Edward approached, Wizard Lake asked, "Is that Donovan up there?" Edward smiled, "Yes. That boy never did listen to me." Wizard Lake laughed. "I'm glad he didn't this time. We would have been caught off guard without his warning."

The Concealed Dragons swept in, surprised that their approach had been detected, but determined to inflict as much damage as possible, regardless of the humans' defenses. They began dropping their stones on the few merchant ships in the harbor, sinking several and damaging others. Several stones also fell on the warehouses that lined the waterfront, but eleven stones could only do so much damage.

Once the dragons were free of the weight of their payloads, they dropped their Concealment shields and began flaming the city. As the flames began, a dozen Great Dragons rose from the garrison courtyard and began attacking the Fire Dragons. Seemings of fire erupted from several places in the city, confusing the dragons. Crossbow bolts filled the air, hitting several dragons. From high above the fray, Donovan saw his vision come to life.

The red Fire Dragons were easy to target, and they were confused. They had been ordered *not* to attack the Great Dragons, but the air was suddenly full of them. Eventually, they decided to disregard their orders and began flaming and biting any Great Dragon that came within range.

One Fire Dragon shot a burning inferno at Gek, who dodged the blast and screamed. "NOT ME, YOU IDIOT! I AM ON YOUR SIDE!" Donovan heard the exchange and began repeating the cry, "NOT ME, YOU IDIOT! I AM ON

YOUR SIDE!" Soon, all of the changed magicians were yelling the same thing, further confusing the bewildered Fire Dragons. Gek cursed.

Despite the defender's best efforts, several warehouses and merchant ships were on fire. Magicians conjured Water spells to extinguish the flames, but inferno was hard to put out completely. Just as the defenders were beginning to get control of the situation, the Stone Dragons arrived.

Wizard Mira and Lisa were still casting Seemings of fire, which repeatedly vanished in flashes of light as stones and/or dragons touched them (as Seemings do). They were so focused on their task that they didn't see the Stone Dragon above them, who dropped a large stone towards Wizard Mira. At the last second, Lisa saw the stone, and yelled a warning. She hastily cast a protective shield over Mira, but the stone was only deflected slightly, and it struck Mira on the shoulder, driving her to the ground.

The arrival of the Stone Dragons was a problem for the defenders. The changed magicians were unable to claw or flame the heavily armored Stone Dragons. Donovan raced around in front of one of them and shot flaming inferno into its gaping mouth. The Stone Dragon gagged and thrashed, then fell to the ground, landing on a soldier who was aiming a crossbow at it.

The five remaining Stone Dragons continued flaming the city until, mercifully, one by one, they ran out of inferno. Two of them unwisely landed in the city square and began smashing everything in sight. Before they had gotten very far, Wizards Edward and Lake enclosed them both in protective shields and suffocated them.

Rose saw that the attack was failing. Five of her Fire Dragons were dead, and three of the Stone Dragons had perished. She couldn't find Gek in the melee of Great Dragons. As she considered whether to withdraw, one of the remaining Stone Dragons took a Seabow bolt through the chest and fell to the ground. "RETREAT!" she shouted, "BACK TO THE SWAMP! HURRY!"

The remaining Fire and Stone Dragons quickly disengaged and headed north, crossbow and Guardbow bolts chasing after them. Gek heard Rose's order, but he was busy killing one of the magic-user Great Dragons. He had taken a lesson from the fight in Three Forks and seized the other dragon, shredded its wings, and was looking for a good place to drop him.

He spied a human magic-user on the battlements and dropped the screaming Great Dragon imposter directly towards her, not realizing that the magician on the battlements was Rachel.

Fortunately, Donovan saw the threat. He raced down and grabbed the falling sorcerer/dragon, just before it landed on Rachel, who was cowering under a protective shield. After he landed, he looked up to see a Great Dragon quickly circling the garrison and heading north. As he watched, the dragon cast a Concealment shield and vanished from sight.

Donovan transformed and said to Rachel, "I told you I needed to be here."

As the dawn broke, the soldiers, sailors, and magicians of Grotton began assessing the damage and tending to the wounded. Donovan and Rachel addressed the injured Great Dragon/magician that Donovan had grabbed as he fell. "I need you to change back into a human, so I can heal you," said Donovan. The injured dragon nodded and, surprisingly, it was Mage Charles. Both of his arms were torn and bleeding. A quick Healing spell stopped the bleeding, but Charles was still in shock, and his arms were misshapen.

"Do you have any Healing Serum?" Donovan asked Rachel. She quickly handed over her water bottle. "You're sure this isn't orange juice?" asked Donovan wryly. Rachel laughed, "It may be orange-flavored, but it's Healing Serum." Mage Charles drank some eagerly and said, "You know, the orange flavor actually improves the taste."

Donovan laughed, "We'll have to tell Wizard Toffin when we get back to Kingston." The Healing Serum restored Charles's color, and his arms straightened (slightly). "I'm not sure we're going to be able to restore full mobility to both your arms," said Donovan. "Gek sure did a number on them." "That was Gek?" asked Mage Charles.

"I believe so. At least he was the only Great Dragon in the attacking force," said Donovan. "I thought he was one of us," said Charles bitterly. 'I should have been more careful."

"It's understandable, given all of the confusion up there," said Donovan.

"So, how did we do?" asked Rachel. "I think we killed five of the Fire Dragons and four of the Stone. Some of the others undoubtedly have crossbow bolts in them. I got hit with one myself," said Donovan, displaying a large bruise on his left bicep.

"If you three are done lounging around, there are others that need healing down in the city," said Edward as he walked up. "Mage Charles needs to go to the Infirmary, but we can certainly help," said Donovan, giving his father a hug.

"I'm sorry I disobeyed your orders, it's just…" "All is forgiven, son. *Just don't do it again.*" Donovan and Rachel laughed.

Despite the victory, the city was a mess. Several warehouses had fire damage, and one burned to the ground despite the magician's best efforts to save it. Five merchant ships were sunk, and three more were damaged. None of the Navy ships had been targeted. "You were right, the dragons were targeting our commercial assets. I didn't expect them to attack warehouses and merchant ships," said Donovan.

"The commercial ships were 'soft' targets, since they had neither magicians nor Seabows to protect themselves with. If these types of attacks continue, we may need to rectify that. Where did the dragons come from?" asked Edward, "And how on earth did you arrive ahead of them with the warning?"

Donovan grinned, "Well, after Wizard Lake insisted, I left Grotton yesterday morning and flew north for about an hour. Then I landed in a field and transformed. I wrapped myself in my Concealment cloak and got some sleep. I woke up when a Great Dragon flew over me and landed in the Jade Swamp. I thought about going in after him, but decided that was a really bad idea." Edward grunted his agreement.

"Anyway, while I was laying in the field, wondering what the dragon could possibly be doing in the swamp, I fell asleep again. I woke up when I heard all of the Concealed Dragons flying overhead. After they passed, I changed, cast a Concealment shield, and followed them from above. I realized that I had to warn the city before they got here, so I raced ahead of them. It's lucky that they were carrying heavy stones. That's what slowed them down so I could get ahead of them," said Donovan.

"You did well, son. I'm proud of you. Now, let's get to town and see what we can do to help." Mage Charles said that he knew the way to the Infirmary and he would see them later, so the three magicians headed into the city. "Where's Wizard Mira?" asked Rachel. Edward stopped suddenly and said, "She and Lisa were on the roof. We'd better go check on them."

When they arrived, Mira was sitting up, nursing a bruised shoulder and a broken left arm, while Lisa was unconscious beside her. "Are you OK?" asked Edward. "My arm is broken. Lisa tried to heal me, but the power drain was too much for her. A Stone Dragon dropped a rock on me. If Lisa hadn't seen it and cast a shield over me, I'd likely be dead." Rachel handed Mira her water bottle, "Here. It's Healing Serum." Mira nodded her thanks, and drained the rest of the liquid in the flask. "That doesn't taste like Healing Serum," she said, "but it works."

Rachel blushed, "I had orange juice in the bottle before I added the Healing Serum. I guess there was still some left in there." "It tastes much better. We should start adding orange juice to all our Healing Serums," said Mira with a smile.

Her injuries healed, Mira carried Lisa down to the Infirmary and instructed the staff on what to do for her. "She will likely sleep for some time, maybe even days. She will need water and food when she wakes. Please let me know immediately when she regains consciousness." "Of course, Wizard Mira," said the nurse.

"Dad, the dragons may still be in the swamp. Should we go after them?" Edward considered the question, "No, son. I think we just call this a victory and let them return to their respective colonies. I'm hoping that they'll be amenable to Peace talks after this."

"How did you know that they were going to attack Grotton, instead of Middleberg?" asked Donovan. "You remember my receptionist, Harriet? Well, yesterday she confessed to telling a Sea Dragon Changed One in Kingston that I had listened in on the last Dragon Council meeting."

"Why would she do that?" asked Rachel. "She blamed Wizard Noland for her daughter's death. We should have told her the truth sooner. That's my fault. I just wasn't looking forward to that conversation," said Edward.

"So, once the dragons knew that we knew their plan, they changed it," said Donovan. "Exactly right." "What happens to Harriet now? She betrayed us!" said Donovan. "I know," replied Edward. "Wizard Noland is going to make her a member of the Academy staff, where she won't have another opportunity to contact any Changed Ones."

"That seems awfully generous," said Donovan. Edward smiled, "Not really, I think Michael said something about her mucking out horse stalls for the rest of her life." Rachel laughed.

Gek landed in the swamp and found several angry and confused dragons. "How could this have happened?" one of the Fire Dragons asked Rose. "I thought this was going to be a surprise attack! Where did that Great Dragon come from?" "I have no idea," replied Rose.

"Somehow, the humans anticipated our attack," said Gek. "I guess they knew that we were planning to attack Grotton eventually and were preparing. Nevertheless, we did succeed in sinking several of their merchant ships and damaging their warehouses. This was not a total failure." "How can you say that?" shouted Jasper, the Stone Dragon Clan Chief. "Four more of my clan are dead, five of the ten Fire Dragons perished, and several more are wounded!"

"I can heal any wounded dragons," said Gek. "I did not say this was a victory, but it could have been worse." "We are withdrawing," said Jasper, "and I am not sure that we will attack the humans again. At least not without a better plan. We will discuss this next month at the next meeting of the Dragon Council."

"Where will we meet?" asked Gek. "We know that the humans know about the rock quarry." "Maybe we should use that to our advantage," said Rose. "How?" "Perhaps we should capture the spies next time, and hold them hostage."

WIZARD TOFFIN

Chapter Thirty-Four:
A ROYAL WEDDING

King Henry and his entourage arrived back in Kingston without fanfare. With the dragon threat, Celeste had prevailed upon Henry to forego the normal parade through the city. Once they had settled into the palace, Celeste headed over to the Wizards Academy to confer with Wizard Noland.

"Wizard Noland, what is the latest news?" asked Celeste. "There is a lot to tell," said Noland, "first, the dragons attacked Grotton a few days ago. We repelled the attack and killed several Fire and Stone Dragons, but we lost a few merchant ships, and one warehouse full of cotton bales burned to the ground."

"What were our casualties?" asked Celeste, "We had five magicians killed and several wounded, including Wizard Mira and Level Two Lisa, who are still in Grotton recovering. Additionally, thirty-seven soldiers and civilians were killed, and over fifty were injured. The injured have been healed, and the repairs to the city are underway."

"Why would the dragons attack merchant ships?" asked Celeste. "It is as I told you and the King earlier, the dragons have seemingly decided to focus on our commercial assets, which are softer targets than our military," said Noland.

"So, what's happening now?" "Wizard Edward is working to replace the magicians that were killed. Our magical support has been depleted recently, so some Regiments may be short on sorcerers in the near term. On the plus side, the Sea and Snow Dragons have apparently withdrawn from the conflict, leaving only the Fire and Stone Dragons to contend with." "And the Great Dragons," said Celeste.

"Other than Gek, there is only one other Great Dragon that we are aware of, and he was not present during the attack on Grotton. His whereabouts are unknown." "I see," said Celeste. "Is there anything else I should know?"

"Please calm the King when he learns about the damage to Grotton. I know that the Merchant Council is upset at the loss of the ships and some of the goods, but it could have been worse. We are also considering selling Seabows to the merchants to arm their ships with. That could be a profitable venture for the crown, but it comes with risks."

"Such as?" "Traders attacking each other's ships to gain a commercial advantage, piracy, and rebellion, to name a few. Admiral Cross is uneasy with the idea." "I understand," said Celeste. "What is your position?" "I am generally opposed to arming civilians, especially since we have a non-aggression agreement with the Sea Dragons. I worry that a trigger-happy merchant seaman could rekindle the conflict by killing an innocent Sea Dragon."

"I understand, and I will present your arguments to Henry when the matter comes up. Thank you," said Celeste. "So, how are the wedding plans progressing? Thank you for taking our security concerns into account," said Noland.

Celeste nodded. "The plans are complete. It seems incredible that in four short weeks, I will marry Henry and become the Queen of Franconia." Noland smiled, "I wish you and Henry all the best, Celeste. Rulers have a lot of stress in their lives, most of it not of their choosing. I am always here if you need advice or counsel, especially concerning magical matters."

Gek landed on Perfo a day after the attack on Grotton. He was disappointed with the results of the attack and the reluctance of the Stone Dragons to try again. It seemed hopeless. "Daddy! You are home!" said Richard as he ran out of the cave to greet him. "Yes, son, I am home. I promised you that I would return."

"Richard, leave your father alone. I am sure he is tired from his long trip and needs to rest," said Azure. Gek nodded wearily. "How did it go?" asked Azure softly. "It could have been better," said Gek. "We managed to sink a few merchant ships, damage some warehouses, and kill some humans, but we lost five Fire Dragons and four Stone Dragons," said Gek.

"So many? How did that happen?" asked Azure. "I guess the humans had prepared for an attack. It certainly did not seem like we surprised them very much. Plus, several of their magic-users changed into Great Dragons and flew among us," said Gek. "So?"

"So, we told the Fire and Stone Dragons *not* to attack any Great Dragons, believing that Donovan and I would be the only two! That was a mistake," said Gek.

"What happened after the attack?" asked Azure. "We flew back to the swamp to discuss what had happened. Jasper, the Stone Dragon Clan Chief, said that he was unsure whether the Stone Dragons would continue in the conflict. They have lost many of their best fighters, and their clan was never very big. He said we would discuss it at the next Dragon Council meeting."

"Are you going to meet in the same place? I thought that the humans knew where we met!" "Yes, and Rose thinks we should meet in the same place, only this time, capture the spying magic-users and hold them hostage. I am not sure to what end," said Gek. "I need some sleep. It has been an exhausting couple of days."

"Of course. Go in and rest. I will take care of the children and ensure they do not disturb you," said Azure. Gek nodded, then headed toward the cave.

Just then, Anna came running up, "Mom, Dad, I DID IT! I HIT THE TREE!" "That is good, Anna, now back up another twenty paces and do it again," said Gek. "If I back up that far, I will be in the water," said Anna.

"You hit the tree from the beach? Well done!" said Gek. "Now will you teach me how to light the inferno on fire?"

asked Anna. "Not yet. First, I want you to practice hitting the tree while you are running, then flying. Once you can hit the tree while flying, we will practice hitting moving targets. Once you can hit a moving target, while flying, I will teach you how to light the inferno," promised Gek.

"That will take forever!" said Anna, pouting. "Not really. Now that you can hit the tree from far away, you will pick up the other tasks faster," said Gek. "She has been practicing every day," said Azure proudly. "That is good," said Gek. "What has Richard been doing?"

"He has been busy digging holes. Which spell should we teach him next?" "How about the Fire spell? It is easy and useful. Has Anna learned the Dig spell also?" "Yes," said Azure. "They are both eager to learn magic."

"Once they learn the Fire spell, we can teach them the Concealment spell and they can play hide-and-seek with each other. That should keep them busy for a while," said Gek.

"You realize that once they learn that one, all that remains are the Healing and *Change* spells," said Azure. "They are too young to learn the Change spell," said Gek. "Anna is only two, and Richard is like a six-year-old human!" "Yes, but didn't you learn the Change spell at age two?" Gek grumbled that Azure was making his head hurt, and they would have to talk about this later. He retired to the cave and was asleep in minutes.

Lisa woke up slowly. She was in an unfamiliar place. "Where am I?" she asked. "You're in the Grotton Infirmary," said the nurse. "I'll send for Wizard Mira immediately." "Is she OK?" asked Lisa. "Yes, she's fine. Mage Rachel gave her some Healing Serum, which fixed her arm. She's been sitting with you for the last two days while you slept. She'll be here soon. Would you like some water?"

Lisa nodded, and the nurse held a cup of cool water to her lips. She drank deeply and felt better. "I'm hungry," she said. "Of course, what would you like to eat?" asked the nurse. "Just some bread and cheese will be fine for now," said Lisa. "Right away."

The nurse left to find Mira and get some food for Lisa. While she was waiting, Lisa drifted back off to sleep. When she awoke, Wizard Mira was sitting next to her. "I'm sorry, I didn't see you come," said Lisa. Mira laughed softly. "I sat down here two hours ago! I would have let you sleep longer, but the nurse said that it would not be good for you. You need to eat and drink something, then get up. The longer you lay in bed, the harder it will be to get back up."

As Wizard Mira was speaking, the nurse came up with some bread, cheese, and soup. "You need to sit up and eat something," said the nurse. "If you feel strong enough, you should get up and walk around after you eat, then sleep tonight. Tomorrow you will have to return to duty. We need the bed for those more seriously injured than you."

The nurse winked at Mira as she left. "I have to thank you, Lisa. Without your shield, I might have been killed. I was too focused on my Seemings and I didn't see the dragon or the falling stone." Lisa smiled happily, "I only saw it because I turned to ask you something, and I saw the rock falling toward you. Are you all right?" asked Lisa.

"Yes. Mage Rachel had some Healing Serum in her water bottle." "I bet it tasted yucky," said Lisa. Mira smiled, "Actually, Rachel had some orange juice in her bottle before she added the Healing Serum, and it tasted much better than it usually does. We will have to tell Wizard Toffin about that when we return to the Academy."

"When can we go back?" asked Lisa. "Maybe tomorrow. Wizard Edward has already left, so you will have to ride on my back on the way home," said Mira. Lisa smiled. "If you are finished with that soup, we could walk around a bit. There is someone who wants to see you." Lisa brightened, "Yes, I'm done. Let's go."

They left the Infirmary and proceeded out into the courtyard. The bright sunlight was welcoming after the gloomy interior of the Infirmary. "Where are we going?" asked Lisa. "You'll see," said Mira with a smile.

They walked into the garrison stable and found Rachel and Donovan loading their wagon. "Lisa!" said Donovan. "It's good to see you up and about. How do you feel?" "I'm tired," said Lisa. Donovan smiled, "I know *exactly* how you feel," he said. "He should," said Rachel, "he's fallen unconscious from using too much power, what is it, three times now?"

Donovan laughed, "Yes, only three times so far, but pushing your limits is supposed to make you stronger." "Then you may end up being the strongest magician in Franconia someday," said Rachel.

Donovan looked at Lisa and said, "I hear you did good work during the attack. I know it was scary. I'm proud of you." Lisa beamed. "Are you going somewhere?" Lisa asked. "Yes," said Rachel, "the Royal Expeditionary Force has to get back to Kingston and report to the King about our tour of the kingdom. Unfortunately, the merchant ship we were going to go home on was sunk by the dragons, so we'll have to take the long way home."

As they spoke, Major Gerald walked up, "Are you about ready to head out?" he asked. "Yes, sir. We're all loaded up. Major Gerald, may I present Wizard Mira, the Seemings and Changes instructor at the Wizards Academy, and Level Two magician Lisa? Wizard Mira and Lisa helped cast Seemings during the dragon attack."

"I'm honored to meet you both," said Major Gerald. "Thank you for your help. I'm sure your efforts saved the lives of many of my men." Major Gerald bowed, then moved off to saddle his horse. "How many men in the Expeditionary Force were killed?" asked Mira softly. "Only one," said Donovan, "and that was partly my fault. The Stone Dragon I killed fell on Corporal Storch and killed him."

"You didn't know he was below you," protested Rachel. "No, and I didn't have time to look either. I can still feel bad about it, though," said Donovan. "Well, we need to be going. I'm sure you two will beat us back to Kingston. Fly safe, and don't talk to any strange dragons on your way," Lisa giggled and waved 'goodbye' as the Royal Expeditionary Force filed out of the garrison compound and got on the road to Kingston.

Edward landed in Middleberg, transformed, and headed over to the Garrison Headquarters building. He ran into Wizard James on the way. "Edward! What happened? We were expecting you back days ago! The dragons didn't attack as you predicted!"

"I know, James. I had Wizard Noland send a Messenger Hawk to King Donald, but I guess the word hasn't reached you yet. I'm sorry. The dragons decided to trick us and attack Grotton instead of Middleberg. I had to rush to Grotton to help defend the city," said Edward.

"Why would the dragons change their plan?" asked James. Edward spoke quietly, explaining about Harriet and her betrayal. "I deduced that the dragons would attack Grotton, thinking we would concentrate our magical forces here in Middleberg. I'm glad I was right."

"So, when can we expect them to attack here?" asked James. "Hopefully never. We gave them quite a beating in Grotton. I'm not sure they'll have the stomach for another big attack any time soon," said Edward. James smiled, "That's good to hear. Tell me about Grotton."

Edward explained about the dragon attack on Grotton and how the dragons focused their efforts against the Franconian merchant fleet and warehouses. "I wish we could have done more to defend the traders," said Edward. "The loss of five merchant ships is going to put a dent in our shipping this year."

"Perhaps the ships can be re-floated and repaired. We've had some success doing that. I'd be happy to send some of our recovery and repair craftsmen to help you." "That would be much appreciated," said Edward. "Thank you." "It's the least we can do after your assistance here. So, what are your plans for the dragons?"

"We need a way to open a line of communications with them, to see if we can come to some sort of agreement. This conflict is not doing either side any good. We almost lost Wizard Mira during the attack on Grotton, and if Donovan hadn't disobeyed my orders, and had come to Middleberg, we would have had no warning."

"Mage Donovan was coming here?" asked James. "Those were his orders, but he was convinced that the dragons would attack Grotton, so he stayed close to the city. When he saw the dragons fly over him, he raced ahead of them to warn the city." James whistled.

"That kind of insubordination seldom works out for the best," observed James. "Donovan can cast the spell of Foresight," said Edward, shocking Wizard James. "He was convinced he was right, and that coming to Middleberg would be a mistake. I should have listened to him," said Edward. "Still…" said James.

Edward laughed, "If you ever have children, James, you'll understand." As they spoke, a Messenger Hawk flew overhead and landed in the Middleberg Message Center. "That should be your message from King Donald. Better late than never, I suppose," said Edward.

The two Wizards walked into the Message Center and, as expected, the message was from King Donald, informing James that Wizard Edward would be remaining in Grotton, that the attack on Middleberg was unlikely to happen, and that the King was boarding a ship bound for Kingston, and King Henry's wedding.

As Edward prepared to depart, he asked James to send his magicians back to their posts in Franconia, but to stay on guard against a small dragon attack. "You never know what these dragons will do," said Edward. "Except when you do," replied James with a smile.

The Royal Wedding was spectacular. Since Celeste's parents were deceased, King Donald of Baize gave the bride away. All of the ministers wore their finest outfits, and the Royal Expeditionary Force served as the royal couple's honor guard. Queen Celeste looked lovely. Mercifully, there were no dragons in attendance. After the King and Queen departed for the Winter Palace in Southport for their honeymoon, Wizards Edward, Kathy, and Noland, along with Donovan and Rachel, sat down at a table in the King's Table Tavern for a celebratory meal.

The food was excellent as always. After the meal, Donovan said, "That was so good! I wish I could replicate it and eat it again tomorrow."

"THAT'S IT!" exclaimed Edward.

Chapter Thirty-Five:
AN IMPERFECT PEACE

Edward landed in Sundock, transformed, and walked to the Regional Mage's Office, where he found Mage Andrew. "Wizard Edward! Welcome to Sundock! What brings you here?" asked Andrew. "Andrew, it's good to see you. How is Maria?"

"She's fine," said Andrew. "We've purchased the blacksmith shop and some extra land around it in order to open a branch of Prestige Arms. We've already got orders for over a hundred Compound Seabows and Guardbows from garrisons all around Franconia and Baize. I understand selling them to Baize was approved by the King?"

"Yes. I was able to convince King Henry that Baize is a worthy ally, and that he would receive significant tax revenues from the sale of Seabows and Guardbows to them. He was overjoyed," said Edward.

"That's good. So, what brings you to Sundock?" repeated Andrew. "I need you to meet me in Colton in three weeks' time," said Edward. "Colton? Why?" asked Andrew. "I want you, Anne, and Donovan to attend the next meeting of the Dragon Council," said Edward.

Andrew paled, "You can't be serious." "I am. You and Donovan are protected by the Binding spell, and Anne is a Dragon-friend. I need the three of you to convey a peace proposal to the dragons," said Edward.

"Why would they even consider such a thing?" asked Andrew. "The Fire and Stone Dragons suffered serious losses during their recent attack on Grotton. I think they may be amenable to a reasonable agreement. At least, I think it's worth a try," said Edward. "Don't worry, Wizard Noland, myself, and several other magicians will be close by if the dragons become unreasonable."

The palm tree was slathered with burning inferno. "Well done, Anna!" said Gek, "I think you have got it!" Annalise had just flown around the island and finished the flight by flaming the palm tree that she had been practicing on for several weeks. Anna landed happily and said, "Mommy said that she would teach me how to spit water next week!"

Gek smiled, "When that happens, you will be the only dragon in the world that can both breathe fire and spit water."

Nearby, Richard was practicing making Concealment shields. He was playing hide-and-seek with Azure. It was a spirited game, which neither of them liked to lose. The last few weeks had been peaceful, and Gek was enjoying spending time with his family without the worries about the war with the humans.

Azure landed by his side, dropped her Concealment shield and said, "The Dragon Council is this week. Are you still set on meeting in the same place?"

"Yes. I spoke to Cobalt last week, and that is still the plan," said Gek. "Is that wise?" asked Azure. "I am not sure. Rose's plan to capture the magic-users who have been spying on us is dangerous. But with ten dragons, we should be able to handle a few magic-users if they become violent," said Gek.

"Please be careful," said Azure. "I will. Have you given any more thought to what we should do about Richard?" Richard was not happy on Perfo. He disliked living in a damp, cold cave with little human companionship other than his parents. While Anna had been free to return to Acropo and play with the young dragons of her clan, Richard had no such outlet.

"No. I am not sure what to do. I now wish that Alice had not returned to the Sea Dragon Clan. Richard could have stayed with her for a while," said Azure. "What about Beau?" asked Gek. "No. Beau and his friends are too old to care for a child. Perhaps one of us should return to the mainland and search for other, younger Changed Ones who might be willing to foster him for a time," said Azure.

"I will consider it once I return from the Dragon Council," said Gek.

Two days later, as Gek and Cobalt were preparing to depart for the Dragon Council, Azure said, "Gek, on your way home, can you pick me up a Sea Urchin sandwich?"

Anne, Andrew, and Donovan stood alone in the center of the rock quarry above Colton. None of them was confident in Edward's plan, but they knew that Edward, Noland, and six additional sorcerers were concealed in the rocks surrounding the quarry, should the dragons turn hostile.

Cobalt, Emerald, and Gek were the first dragons to arrive, and they were shocked by the three magicians who stood boldly in a place they should not be. "Anne, why are you here?" asked Cobalt, "and why is Andrew and this other magic-user with you?"

"Cobalt, Gek, it is good to see you again. Andrew and Donovan are here with me to present a peace proposal to the Dragon Council." "So, this is Donovan," said Gek, "if it were not for Ard's Binding spell, I would have killed you years ago for murdering my mother!"

Donovan looked at Gek and said calmly, "*I* did not kill your mother, Gek, but your mother nearly succeeded in killing my father. You almost killed me and my wife in Three Forks. Your friend, Victor, killed *my* mother. I guess that makes us even."

"Victor was no friend of mine!" shouted Gek. "Peace!" said Cobalt. "This argument gets us nowhere. What is your proposal, Anne?" "We should wait for the other members of the Dragon Council," said Anne. "Since this concerns you all."

They waited many long minutes, each sizing the other side up. Gek was frustrated. He hated Donovan, but knew that if he, or any member of the Dragon Council, killed Donovan or Andrew, he, his father, and Azure might die as a result of Ard's Binding spell.

As the other members of the Dragon Council arrived, they all had angry questions about what the humans were doing there. Cobalt explained the situation, and who the three humans were. Eventually, the Dragon Council members agreed to at least hear them out.

"What is it that you would say to us, human?" asked Rose.

Anne stepped forward and said, "Two hundred years ago, dragons and humans agreed to a Peace Treaty. We would provide 20,000 head of cattle to you every two years, and you would not eat humans. We all know what happened. We are proposing a second chance. We regret the actions of our forebearers, but we cannot change it. We also suspect that 10,000 cattle each year, divided between all of the dragon clans, would not have been enough food to sustain you."

The dragons murmured amongst themselves. Finally, Cobalt said, "Agreed. What is your new proposal?" "First, since the conflict was over *food*, and we recognize your need for such, we will teach you the spell of Replication. With this spell, you can make all of the food you ever desire. You will never be hungry again. Second, we will cease our search for your Changed Ones. If a dragon suffers from hunger, they may change into a human and sate their hunger that way," said Andrew.

Now the dragons were thoughtful. The idea of making food of their choice was appealing. This proposal also provided safety for their Changed Ones. Jasper asked, "And what do you require in exchange?"

"Simply that you cease your attacks on humans, our crops, and our livestock," replied Donovan. "It is time for this conflict to end."

The dragons moved off to the far side of the quarry and discussed the proposal. The Sea and Snow Dragons were quick to agree, the Stone Dragons saw no downside, and the Fire Dragons eventually conceded. Gek was the only holdout.

"I have one additional condition," said Gek. "What is that?" asked Anne.

"I want my son, Richard, admitted to the Wizards Academy."

THE END of Book V

Watch for Book VI, *The Resumption of Hostilities*